Angels in the Architecture

Sue Fitzmaurice

For Ruby & Madison

Without whom I fear my life may have been most shallow

Note to Readers

Some of the dates provided in quotes at the beginning of chapters, and during events through 1981, hold clues to the story.

I use a phonetic language for several characters in the Middle Ages; opinion varies as to the necessity for this in modern fiction, however it seemed an appropriate and interesting challenge at the time.

This is a second publishing of this book. I was not happy with the editing by the previous publisher, nor was I content with some minor story gaps I felt a need to fill. Neither makes any particular difference to the overall story.

Principal Characters

1185

* *Bishop Hugh* – the Bishop of Lincoln, (c. 1135-1200)
Father Taylor – a parish priest
Alice Warriner – a peasant woman
Gamel Warriner – her husband
Geoffrey (Gree), Denholm (Dem) & Thurstan Warriner – their eldest sons
Thomas – their youngest son, an idiot
Bennet Williams – a physician
Berta Draper – thought to be a witch
Fulk – a forest-dweller
* *'Iṣmat ad-Dīn Khātūn (Asimat) & Eleanor oj Aquitaine* – two Queens
* *Saladin & Richard Lionheart* – two Kings

1981

Pete Watson – a father and a journalist
Dr Alicia Watson – his wife and a physicist
Tim – their son, an autist
Jillie – their daughter
Rose Draper – a deaconess
Loraine – her friend, also a deaconess
Maitland – a local gentleman
* *Khalid Islambouli* – an Egyptian army officer (1955-1982)

* real historical figures

On His right hand flow the living waters of grace,
and on His left the choice Wine of justice,
whilst before Him march the angels of Paradise,
bearing the banners of His signs.
Beware lest any name debar thee from God,
the Creator of earth and heaven.
Leave thou the world behind thee,
and turn towards thy Lord,
through Whom the whole earth hath been illumined.

Surih of the Temple

Women find peace in the evening. Even the Earth heaves a sigh at the twilight, as though on their behalf. Particles of energy slow their elliptical orbits and thoughts stop thinking. In the quiet, after nightfall, woman's heart once more registers the rightness of her task. And because of that she knows that the circle of Matter, that is her home and her family, will make its correct orbits again tomorrow.

Time is not linear. It goes around, and meets at its beginnings and its ends.

1

Skinning ferrets would have been one of Alice Warriner's least favourite jobs had she stopped to consider it, but her life did not afford the privilege of such judgement. Her sons had brought a catch home from the woods at dusk, and she completed the bloody task then since it would be one less thing the next day.

All the days were taken up from before dawn till after dusk with the endless tests and tasks of land and lords. A peaceful work, like the one Alice undertook now, alone in the quiet, came as a rare indulgence and occasional reward. It was a valued time in the day now for all wives and mothers, when the sound was motionless and hardly seen, and the time was no longer light, but not dark. It was perfect, and there was no woman who did not relish it.

Alice sat at a low bench seat at the door of her home which was a low stone hut, round and thatched. It wasn't a place to stand up in, nor to move about too much.

From this outside vantage point, she had her main view of the world and of each day. It was here that the work that produced the detritus of her life folded into her fingernails – flour and peelings and blood and sinew. The blood that had spattered up her arms was mixed with fragments of flesh clinging to her skirt but was barely noticeable to her in the context of the dross of her life.

Alice found she needed little by way of implement to assist her task, preferring instead to feel her way through the pulling and tearing of the pelt with her fingers alone. She had long grown used to the grisliness of this method and was so deft at it that she could allow her mind to attend to other thoughts even while her hands went about their business, producing only the rhythmic suck and slurp that accompanied their motion.

There was not so much to think on though. Aside from endless drudgery, Alice's daily experience was of large man bodies, her husband and her sons; their strength of labour, the jostling for their share, grunting messages to one another, always moving, yelling, arguing, hitting, or kicking. Voices were raised sometimes in cheer, frequently in rage, often in pleading, excuse or defence. There was little of prayer and nothing of sweetness except that she created herself. Men all around seemed in no need of such things, and a woman who wanted too much for softness would be disappointed, not to mention that such desires could not feed families or bring even any meagre fortune. Alice noted only in a sort of passing, but by no means for the first time that hers was a life of men and maleness, but that at least brought strength to her existence and some kind of sanctuary of its own. So to ponder and allow her mind and senses to go where they will was her main activity this evening, aside from the work of her fingers.

Alice now had several carcasses in a large metal pot, their furs draped over a frame for the purpose. One boy or another would stretch and fasten them in the morning; they would not shrink or harden in the cool night before then.

Her job done, and some kind of cleaning up afforded, Alice heaved the pot and went inside. Deftly tying a twine and hook to each pair of forelegs, she hung the small beasts from a low railing over the central fireplace to smoke. She picked up a small metal prong and picked at the gunge in her nails, dipping her hands then into a bucket of water and swirling them about to release some of the day's grime. She sat a moment and whispered a verse she'd learnt long ago. A set of black wooden beads, smoothed these years now almost to the like of stones, counted themselves across her fingers, quiet and light. Alice closed her eyes and instinctively raised her face to the heavens. She smiled, and a fissure came to split in the dirt and grime about her, and she could feel the silky shine of the spirit that came from the prayer as it entered her soul. This was Alice's softness, and it nourished her enough each day, in this brief stay in time, such that she would feed and strengthen those who depended on her for another day. If it were possible, she would choose to sit in this communion forever, but it was certainly not Alice's life to do so, nor would she even think about it.

It was quiet in the small dwelling, and she could feel the darkness around her, punctured by the light of the single candle and its occasional flicker from the draught beneath the sack door. The peace was rare, and she craved these evening moments after her family had finally given up its relentless activity to rest.

Lord, bestow on me your grace that I may accept my distance from thee. Preserve me from complaining. Keep my sons from fighting and keep Thomas safe.

Alice's peacefulness was succumbing to mounting tiredness, and she forced open her eyes to look around the small, mostly unfurnished room. The fire was dying in the hearth. She hadn't noticed it before.

A log is needed. Why is there none waiting? Didn't I ask ...

She placed her beads in their small, lightly carved case, latched the tiny lid, and slid it back beneath a mat, the precious case the only thing of any beauty around about, but of value only to its devoted owner. Nearby on the floor, several crudely hewn wooden animals nestled, each a finger high, the beginnings of one boy's talent for the crafting of wood and stone. She thought of her boys, all asleep, and pictured each of them having played with the small collection, Thomas lining them up in a perfect row. She brushed a strand of long brown hair from her face and pushed herself up with both arms, stiffness slowing her a little.

How long did I ache through so much of me. The Lord tests me.

She straightened, trying to imagine her body young and strong again. Her determined steps to the door belied her real bones.

Alice understood some sense of the physical illusion that is life. And that God's expectation was for her to strive each moment to find unity with His will. She only *just* knew this. She only just knew that she grasped this different reality. She did know for sure that she could see the flow of spirit in things, in a way that she had long realised others could not. She'd always understood this to be a normal thing, although she never mentioned it to anyone. Since, as a child, no one else spoke of it, Alice thought she ought not to either. It must have been a sacred thing, she'd thought, that it was never mentioned, and far be it for her to be so disrespectful as to comment on the pools of light she saw around some people and things, but not others. Once when she was a girl, a brother had blamed another for a theft of some trivial thing. It was nothing, but his lie was so convincing that the innocent brother was punished. When the two boys had stood before their mother, the thief had the merest dark ring about him while the other shone a pale blue that reflected the sky the boys had played under that day. Alice knew straight away who the guilty one was and was surprised when her mother believed the thief. She protested briefly but had no proof of her assertion other than that which she thought at the time to be self-evident, but which she knew in herself she should not speak of. From then on there were other incidents that made her realise that other people did not see what she saw. For a while she became afraid of it. Others may find this out about her, and she continued to feel intuitively it would not be a good thing to reveal. Worse, perhaps it was devil's work. She came to believe it was not an evil doing when one joyous harvest festival, the wooden Virgin that would be brought into the fields from the small parish church near her parents' home, shone a golden halo all around. Even some of her mother's friends said they felt sure the Virgin was smiling, as they all danced and laughed on a rare occasion of fun and particular prosperity. No one mentioned the light Alice could see, but she began to wonder herself whether it was instead a particular gift God had given her, and she became grateful, and because it was her view of the world to do so, she was also humbled. She did not think much further on this phenomenon through her life, just that it was for certain of God, or at least of the Angels..

I give thee thanks Lord. How may I serve you? Speak me your will that I may obey.

Alice moved aside the sacking curtain covering the entrance and greeted the cool evening air another time.

Alice now viewed her real weakness, the real devil in her, to be the slowness and tiredness that stood more and more between her and her endeavours.

I will wrestle these demons from God's creation.

She smiled across the mud before her, and beyond, looking to the fields for all the world as though they grew gold, and the shack on whose threshold she stood a palace. Her thankfulness was real.

My heart is open Lord. Thy will be done.

Alice lingered, closed her eyes, and took in the night noises: an owl calling its night sound, a tiny scurry-scurry of rats, trees shushing themselves, a horse snorting, and snoring from a boy or man – each one a silvery mass of light and each a mystery of God's unseen grace.

Nearby, several already dried ferret pelts lay nailed to crude boards, leant up against a low stone wall surrounding. They would be taken to market tomorrow, along with a small excess of turnips and hay. There they'd be traded, or the meagre earnings would be used for the purchase of some ground wheat and a small weight of rye – the small dealings of small landholders that could make a family's table more or less redolent for the week. The business was undertaken with due seriousness by all transactors, bargaining almost to the last grain, with generally none feeling wronged or cheated, for there was rarely such intent. And it was an adventure and learning for youngsters to see the village business and its ways, and observe their fathers' doings. It was most sons who were in awe of their fathers, all solid men of fighting and moral substance that did what they did as they'd learnt from their own fathers.

Alice breathed deeply and felt the air cool her forehead, around her nose as the breath passed the space above her mouth, her eyelids, and her open eyes.

She turned to a pile of logs by the door. Selecting two sizeable blocks, she tucked them into an arm, stepping back inside. The musty warmth stayed in. The fire was low in the hearth now, but she knew the logs would take, and her family would stay warm through the coolest hours of the night, although the early morning would bite at them.

Lord protect us.

The air inside was thick with smells of cooking, of animals, mud, sweat, and smoke. The colours of Alice's life were all around her: grey, black, dirty yellow, brown, and blood-red on filthy cotton. Alice wasn't even sure what was colour and what was smell – grass stains on worn leather, wrinkled and old, always old, old before you want to be, and old as everything here was old. Even the newborn seemed old, which is to say if they lived at all.

Alice had lost five. The first came dead and too soon. Two might as well have, for they lasted one an hour, one a day. A little girl passed in the winter, a tiny sweet thing. And Thomas's twin, a strong boy, as chattering as Thomas was dumb, his leg crushed beneath a cartwheel and unfathomable, unjust pain and fever overtook him after a week. His little eyes wept and screamed and stopped shining back the sun. But no one who saw him or heard him in those days really remembered him anymore, except his mother, and Thomas who was curled up now with his brother's tunic. And these were Alice's babes with the Lord's Mother. But seven lived, and Thomas, he was the seventh, and a nine-year-old baby. Alice prayed for all their souls, because she knew she must. She felt certain that Thomas at least received some blessing and special care from Heaven.

Alice was sure Thomas saw things as she did, although he could not say so. She saw him look at nothing; although Alice may see a swirl of energy in his sight sometimes, it seemed often to tease him and be playful. Alice knew this was the existence of Angels, as surely as she knew the existence of her own sons. There was a mystery to this that she couldn't put words to, because she had no such education, but she had more than a sense of it. Alice knew that her Thomas and others such as him were as invisible to most ordinary people as the Angels were, but she did not blame them for that.

Alice kissed her boys and lowered herself to the mat by her husband, cradling her Thomas, his mouth open a little, catching the stifled air. How was it that these great boys, almost men, looked so sweet and young when they slept, and there was Thomas who looked almost an infant? Alice thought it must be such that their mothers will keep to loving and protecting them, as their sleepy sweetness sang straight to a mother's heart and pulled on its fibre.

Thomas nuzzled into his mother's shoulder and hair.

Thy will be done, Lord.

Alice held her son close and slept.

The sound of running water turned Thomas around, smiling and giddy with joy. Light bounced around and ricocheted between objects; it was both still and moving, and alive and inanimate, all at the same time.

Water had the most special light. It told Thomas stories that delighted and excited him. The stories made him jig and shake about, smiling, laughing, and singing in his way. They were full of silliness, caught him up and made him part of their telling. He didn't know the light told him more than just stories. He knew only to be joyful from it, and that dancing was a response that also spoke of respect and love for the light.

Don't run, Thomas. Go calmly. Listen.

The light on the water bounced up to Thomas's face and spoke to him directly. This happened often, and Thomas struggled sometimes to hear, to listen, and to take heed, although he knew he was being compelled to do just that. It was finding what response to give; to come to this was a struggle for his brain such were the obstacles of his senses, so he kept on dancing and spinning and laughing.

'Thomas, ya' git, sturp ya' drubble ya' weed!'

There was laughter amid heavy work. Things were being lifted to the cart for taking to the village; sacks, baskets, wooden this-and-that, some pots of food, pelts, some wool, and a few vegetables were stacked to keep stable along a potholed journey; every item precious and worth food and strength for its owners. Nothing could be lost or broken, or else some boy would pay and none wanted such, nor to go hungry either.

Thump. And again Thomas felt the pain, but only fleetingly. These blows came often to him, but he didn't know that pain could last and so it didn't. There was no sense of wrong, just less that was right.

You're happy today, Thomas. We'll start soon. Are you ready?

Thomas smiled at the words and the something of a sound behind them. He liked these voices more than any other.

'Wha' ya' starin' at ya', moron? Look at 'im, Gree, look a' the empty-headed stink. Wozee grinnin' a'?'

'Aye, the turd. Ger'out, Thom, yer sprayin' water all over. Ya' lame pigeon. Ger' off!'

'Ay, Thomas, look over 'ere, look over 'ere!'

Splot! Mud and tunic meet. Wet and sticky neck! Laughter! Others' laughter.

But Thomas laughed with them. He liked the laughter as long as it wasn't too loud. He sensed when the laughing was callous and when it was just the usual roughness of his brothers.

Thomas hasn't heard the message yet. It's difficult to find a way to both his soul and his mind at the same time. They don't connect.

He will find some Faith along the way. We'll continue until we're understood. There are few who can achieve what he can, if he tries.

Thomas felt lights glowing above and around him. It came often now. He liked the lights coming, and he had learnt how to glide with them. They rested on the air. They moved and they stayed still. If you tried to look at one, it wasn't there. You could catch it only if you moved with it, as if the only way to catch a fish was to swim with it through the water, which is to say it could not be caught at all. You could just *be* with it for a time, thinking you'd caught it but then having to let it go, unless you wished to drown and lose every sense of the world and that was a frightening thing to do and only for the very skilled. Thomas nestled in its safety and knew the lights were his and that he was one of them. He smiled at the light. The light smiled back, so he smiled even more. He forgot the heavy part of him that had ground to walk on, and unlovely noises to hear, and hard blows on the walls of his Self. But still those things tore at him often, tore him away from the light. And when he couldn't always keep with the light, he felt this tearing as a real pain, a pain that lasted as a bitter parting.

Perhaps today he will learn something. A connection.

The sun had long risen in the Warriners' tiny hamlet, and farmers, the Warriners included, were readying their tradable goods to take to town. The elder Warriner boys were loading their family's cart for the market.

There had already been several hours of work and activity, as there would have been in all the peasant households. The Warriners were lucky to have so many sons to tend their land; it gave them time to create some other industry, such as the pelts they dried, some furniture made to be sold or traded, walls mended for themselves, and others. But then it also gave them more hungry mouths to feed. Mostly the boys would have said they were hungry most of the time, mostly their whole lives. It was a long-reaching memory of their childhood and youth.

'Get tha' mute on the cart, Dem.'

'God what's he lookin' at, idjit. Some pretty picture in eez noggin, eh.'

'Mus' be 'e's dreamin' of tha' Elspeth Draper showin' 'im 'er ankle in the back pew, loik she did you, Dem.'

Laughter! Elbows! Thumping!

'Ow, ya,'

'Tha's enough! Ger' away ta ye Ma, ya pickle!' The biggest voice.

Laughter again.

'Yay, ye pickle!' Teasing.

Some boys jumped on to the cart and some jumped off. Each knew where it was supposed to be.

'Pickle, pickle, pic-kle,' singing.

'Hyup!' A whip and a horse gee'd up.

The cart's wheels winced and groaned and the bodies aboard it jostled, their sweaty stink wafting; the day was hot early. Thomas grinned at the faces left behind on the dirt road – Alard and David and Michael, their names – but they didn't hold much light, and he looked away. Thomas knew these hulking moving beasts sitting about him. They didn't move with the light like he did, but they were like a row of simple houses neighboured together, and knowing them was some sort of protection, even if neighbourliness was not a much known about thing among them..

Light flowed through the corridors, gateways, and river beds of his body. His body became not a body at all but a part of the bodies next to him and a part of their smells. He became the air that he breathed in through his own nostrils, and he was the spark and the crack of the whip, and the flow of it all was warm. The light rewarded his stream of happiness and sent more light, and then he could easily melt completely – first into the space between the planks of the cart and then even into the wood itself and the hard metal nail. And he understood from this the nail's task, and that it had to stay together with the wood. Some part of Thomas knew this is the way things were, that things had a reason. And then he flew way over the cart and was high, high above it, but a bump in the road carried him back to the space between the others and the light moved out of him. He looked to the very corner of his eye and stayed looking to the furthermost corner of his eye because that's where the light sometimes came back, and he waited like that. It didn't hurt his eyes to look like this. He knew just to wait.

Thomas, a calm, gentle voice coming from the light, *the joy is just one part, Thomas. You can't just be in the light. There is a message too. Listen for the message, Thomas. What is the light telling you?*

'Ah, look, 'e's doin' 'eez madman look again.'

'Don' i' hur' eez oiz doin' tha'?'

'Aye, look, Oi couldn' do tha' for long.' The third boy turned his eyeballs to the corner of head and demonstrated. 'Ugh.'

'Stop it, Thom, ya freak. Ye'll 'ave all 'em ladies in the tarn crossin' t'other soid of road. Ey, kick 'em, Geoffrey, make 'im stop it, willya?'

'Ugh.' Sharp, from one side.

'Oi, Tommy, look 'ere! O'er this way! Tha's be'er.'

'Leave 'im be!' The big voice, deep and loudest. Always loud. Only loud. No light. No quiet spaces between the sounds, where the light comes in. But no pain ever came to Thomas from this voice.

The voice occupied the hulking figure of Gamel Warriner; rough, strong and simple, as straightforward and uncomplicated are simple. He was a man who knew how to work hard, how to grow things and fix things. And he knew what was right and he did it. He was as respected as any other who went about his own business and got things done and provided enough for his family. That his wife was a good woman and a pious one was a further asset to Gamel's reputation. That he produced so many sons was an indicator of his masculinity, which although of no consequence to Gamel himself, and certainly not his wife, confirmed his power as a man and a citizen and caused other men and women to regard him with favour.

There were four of Gamel Warriner's seven sons in the cart that day. Geoffrey, called Gree; Denholm, called Dem; and Thurstan, were the oldest Warriner boys; and Thomas was their mute, idiot last brother. They didn't mind Thomas, but he wasn't good for anything and life was to work. It left their mother some sweetness though to have this empty-headed son, and this was better for her since she had no girl.

There was little exchanged between Father and sons at any time, and a ride in the cart was when many simply gazed and felt the unusual but special gain of just sitting, with no effort and nothing to have to say or teach. There were waves to others passed by, every one of them known to each other; brief exchanges of economy or weather, fundamentals to existence, but directed with practised casualness, for a man or a boy should know what to say or keep himself quiet.

Gamel Warriner's cart rolled into Torksey, with others from along the way, all dusty and dozed, all with their hopes of some small wealth, or of procuring some pretty thing to appeal to a girl or a woman, all anticipating the sociality of the market and its affairs. Gamel rode slowly so the dust didn't coil up around them all and their load. It would be a long enough journey without having skin and breath full of dry dirt.

The ancient town stood at the commercial centre of the Warriners' world and was a hub of the walled cathedral city of Lincoln, several miles away. People came by cart and on foot; by road from all around, with their vegetables and hides; and by canal boat with wool on the Foss Dyke from Lincoln. The canal was older than anyone knew and every family had stories to tell of it. Gamel Warriner heeded its integral role in the expanding market life of his small world. His sons thought little or nothing of either the dyke or the river Trent with which it connected, although Dem had once ridden a canal boat along the Foss to Lincoln with a kindly trader who'd bought some of the Warriners' pelts, as an adventure for the boy. Alice had been troubled to find her husband come home that day having put their eldest child aboard a stranger's boat, but a week later the boy was back, with a glow about him and many stories to tell. Such were the grand adventures of a Lincolnshire lad, rare but exotic, and there were few full-grown men had more than one or two such journeys in a life.

For Thomas, the canal held a different mystery; it was an opiate of light, bouncing off the silky surface, glistening to his spirit.

Thomas, can you hear the message in the light on the water. Thomas. Try to see what it's telling you, Thomas. Can you feel it?

The cart rolled past the edges of the town, and the boys recognised friends they waved to and strangers whose eyes they avoided. The unknown was feared or at least suspected, although it would be just a word or two made kindred of most strangers anyway. Travelling workmen and traders came through looking for a small sale or a day's work. Most would try to stay in a town if they could, if someone would hire their labour or skill. They were generally poorer, hoping for enough to eat and to buy materials to sell more. Generally they would move on. Townsfolk and those around about, were friendly enough but poor themselves, and everyone understood that extra labour could only usually be afforded in prosperous times, and prosperous times came usually for all or no one. It would be rare a single peasant or trader stood out as more successful than others, and such an ambition would not be harboured at any rate.

The Warriners' cart rattled and bounced on. The town, such as it was, was no more than a single street along the canal, sitting in the elbow of the canal with the river Trent. As they approached the centre of the small town, where the market was held, Gamel Warriner could see a crowd gathered ahead. There was shouting and some shoving going on, and a group of craning necks and peering heads jostling to see a thing happening amid the grouping. Gamel thought he noticed a glance of fear upon one or two as he came alongside the hubbub. Some standing there turned to see who it was they might whisper to now.

'Hamond,' Gamel called out to a villager emerging from the crowd. 'What's hapnin' there?'

A big man as broad as Gamel strode towards him; a few others were standing aside in deference to size and respect.

'Aye, Gamel, it be a good thing yer 'ere with yer cart.' He turned away. 'Bennet!' Hamond Archer called to someone unseen behind a wall of villagers. 'Bennet! Gamel has 'is cart here. We can load the poor creature on it and take 'er to Priory.' The talkative crowd quietened as someone to be trusted was taking control of the situation.

'Wha' creature, Amond? Wha' 'n God's name?' Gamel still sat upon his cart seat, his sons waiting out the exchange as they knew it was nothing for them to interfere with men about some unclear business, although they were curious just the same.

'It's a Swan, Gamel. Someone's killed a Swan.' Hammond was booming and final in his statement of a fact, behind which lay a deep reservation.

In one quick movement, Gamel Warriner's three oldest sons, hitherto less interested in the crowd and its goings-on, now jumped from the cart and began to push through the outer layer of hushed onlookers, some of whom were backing away, just as others were unable to move at all, transfixed by what they saw.

At the centre, Bennet Williams, the town's physician, knelt over an enormous mass of white feathers. Young Geoffrey Warriner had first seen the great birds on the Brayford Pool at the heart of the Lincoln market. For one so immune to the wonders of the world, the birds had seemed to him a wondrous sight, and he'd understood then the many tales from his childhood of magic white creatures that had saved a knight's life, wrestled a dragon, and saved fair maidens hither and yon. The birds were called Mute Swans, for their call was so mild and the birds so gentle. Custom made all swans the property of the King. So admired were they that to kill one was not just a poaching offence but an offence also against Nature, certainly against the King and therefore treason as well, and in some people's minds an offence even against God. The excitement of such a mystery had brought Gamel's sons out of their reverie.

And now one of the magnificent creatures lay in the dust surrounded by hanging heads and solemn faces. Gree recalled the hugeness of the birds as they floated on the Brayford Lake, but what he saw now, complete and up close, took his breath away. The dead bird was enormous, larger than a small calf; its wings collapsed and spread out in the dust, the width of them as long as his father's cart. With the sight of it he felt as though his innards would wrench from his body. It was an unholy and frightening spectacle.

Geoffrey's brothers broke through the crowd behind him.

'Jesus, Lord,' exclaimed Thurston.

'Wha' 'appened? Is i' dead?' Denholm asked.

'Arya sure it's dead, Mr Williams?'

'Aye, boy, it's dead all right. 'S'neck's broke. See?'

The boys saw the creature's long, once-elegant neck askew on the ground.

''Ow tho'? 'Ow'd its neck get broke?'

'Dunno, lad.'

'It'd take a moighty strong arm to wrestle one a dem t'ground.'

A squawk came up from a fat old woman at the scene. 'Someone's killed it though,' croaked the bent crone. 'All the same. An' there'll be trouble now. Someone means 'arm to us. It'll be trouble. An' who'll tell Thane? Who'll pay 'is penance for 'im?'

Berta Draper was one of the village's oldest inhabitants and unofficial custodian of the laws of nature, the intentions of God and all superstition. Many tried to ignore her, although this was difficult, and despite intentions to the contrary, most were mindful of her voice.

'You don't know any o'that old woman?'

'Mark my words tho' leech-man. It'll bring trouble. Migh' be Thane, migh' be God, but ther'll be 'n account t' be had sum tarm. 'N i' won't be far off neither.' Berta stated all this as simple fact and without fear or threat in her voice, although her croaky rattle of a voice bade most listen and take heed, and indeed they did, as nodding worried faces attested.

'Ere, Gree, Dem, 'elp us lift 'er ont' ya' Da's wagon. Best we get'er to Priory. Le' Father Taylor deal wi' Thane.'

Geoffrey and Denholm stared agog at Bennet Williams. Were they to touch the beast? Carry it forlorn and murdered? Momentarily this seemed a danger before they responded to Bennet's command and shuffled anxiously about the dead bird.

'Thurstan, ge' baskets offa cart an' make room for it.' Gree instructed his younger brother.

'Wha'?' Bewildered.

'Baskets, ya' rock head, go on!'

Thurstan jumped from his own daze and pushed back through the crowd. Gree and Dem crouched around the great torso, sliding their hands across the soft, dusty earth and placing their big arms deftly beneath it.

'Hellfire.' Bennet Williams leapt to rescue the bird's long neck and head as it slumped straight down.

The onlookers parted and the cortège limped its way to the Warriner cart. They made a grim procession as all eyes followed the bird's slow progress. Gamel Warriner had remained at the seat of his cart and turned now to see the bird brought over. Thomas sat behind him and had noticed none of these events. Thurstan offloaded the last of the cart's contents, and Bennet Williams climbed the rear of the cart with great deference to his part of the load, the boys manoeuvring the heap of white feathers carefully onboard, a surprisingly gentle grace to their expected roughness. The jostling and exchanges of the crowd had stopped now, folk feeling an onus of tragedy and prediction.

The boys stepped back from the cart.

'You boys go on an' get them baskets o'er market,' Gamel instructed his sons, turning back around to his nag. 'Me an' Mr Williams'll take this load up t' Priory,' he called over his shoulder.

'Aye,' they said as one, still dazed, staring as the cart jerked forward and the odd band departed slowly from the still gawping crowd. The bird was clear to all, taking up the cart as it did, resting a little on a mute boy's lap, who himself did not care to notice..

It was some moments before someone moved away from the group, signalling the same to the rest of the crowd. Berta Draper remained where she'd been, hands on her broad hips, looking at the ground and moving her head around about. She bent down to touch something and then stood again, brushing the dust from her hands and her skirts, shaking her head. Some looked back at her, and their looks suggested that she frightened them still. It wouldn't have surprised any of them to see her dance on the spot and mumble an incantation, but in this at least she disappointed. The boys turned sombrely to their collection of baskets and pots. Hamond Archer drafted a handful of nearby youth to help the Warriner boys convey their baskets the short distance to the market square, which they did with still great silence and a lack of assuredness as to what their response should be to this happening, not to mention the occasional glance back to Berta.

'Stop look'n' at 'er, ya' thick 'eads. She don' need no encouragin' from likes a' you boys,' Hamond warned them, heading back apparently to have a word with the old woman.

'Was an 'eavy beast weren' i'?'

'Aye.'

'Were weak in i's neck tho'.'

'Only seemed tha' way as t'was dead. I seen them birds o'er Lincoln fight'n' each other w' them necks. They's as strong as you can 'magine. Wid knock a gro'n man o'er lark a wee pup I reck'n. Would'n a' bin a simple thing a' kill a beast lark tha'.'

'Maybe it's got trapped, y'knaw in one them traps lark porchers use?'

'Nah, is naw hurt i's legs o' feet. Woulda bin marks a' trap. Naw, i's had i's neck broke, bu' can't see 'ow as any man could do tha' though. Bird more likely woulda killed a' man.'

'Bu' wa's fer kill'n' i'? Didn' eat i'. Didn' take skin or feather. Woi'd ya bovver then?'

'Maybe i's got startled by Thane's men 'n' run orf. Oo knows.'

'Maybe.'

'Maybe's no' man killed i'. Maybe's some monster, or is devil's work.'

'Stop tha' story-tellin', y' idjit. Is no such thing and you jus' let'n' tha' old woman ge' in yer 'ead, jus' lark she wants. She's a fool an' is no reason t' listen anythin' she 'as t' say. Is a man, or some animal we kno', 'nother swan maybe. I says I saw 'em foightin' each other a' Lincoln. Maybe's wha' 'appened. Jus' forge' i' now, we go' work t' be doin'. So ge' on.'

It was a short distance to the Priory, although to Gamel Warriner drawing his precious cargo slowly along, it seemed a while to get beyond the town and up the river road to the lord's manor. They saw no one, since anyone who would be on the road was already in the village for the market, or they were in their fields working. There was a daily rhythm to peasants' lives that would have caused Bennet and Gamel to wonder at the presence of any person on the road at this time had they seen any. Apart, of course, from the lord himself or his men, no one ever wanted to come across them if they could avoid it, most especially not as now as they were carrying a dead beast, property of the King, effectively therefore owned by the local Lord. Bennet and Gamel may be leading men among the peasants but to the lord or his men, they were the same human dross available for their pleasure, sport or waste as any other.

'Wha' ya' thinkin' then, Benne'? Who'd d'a thin' lark this?'

Gamel was not a suspicious man. It wasn't that he didn't abide Berta Draper or her like, but he certainly did not regard them. A realistic man though, he saw the seriousness with which the swan's death captured the village and its thoughts.

'Aye, aye', Bennet Williams just shook his head, distraught. He'd seen more than his share of sickening, appalling scenes. His medicine was largely herbal, and some of it still reliant also on superstition, even though he would put himself about as a man of science; in fact, he was as likely as any other to be stirred by this death of a Swan, and he felt an uncertainty around him and in his small world. This was the sense of both men, and neither had any other words for it.

Thomas though was neither distraught nor anxious nor in any way frightened. As the swan had been placed at his feet, he'd been drawn to the bird's hard leathery beak and its open red-brown eyes. While those about him knew the creature to be dead, Thomas could see the light that still remained in it. A pure light, holy and gentle and sweet. The light reached out to touch Thomas, and he toyed with it a few moments, enjoying it for what it was. It beseeched him and longed for connection with the boy's own light, some energy to nurture it a small enough amount. The light of the bird did not play with Thomas though, as Thomas wanted it to, and Thomas did not hear the bird's prayer either and so left its message hanging in the ether between them. And then the light faded from the dark red eyes and was gone, and the bird's eyes closed slowly on the world. Thomas cocked his head to one side and measured their closing and some distant remembered pain circled briefly around him, so he looked away to the corner of his eye hoping for the goodness he liked, that he loved, and that warmed him.

The two men and the boy delivered the sad load to a shocked Father Taylor at the Priory, promising to send some men back to bury the bird should the Father need it, for they themselves had to return to their tasks at the town.

'Where was the bird found?'

'At edge of Thane's land, Father. Between there and town,' Bennet replied.

'And who is responsible then? His Lordship will want recompense.'

'There's no knowing at all, Father. No knowing. I'm not so clear as how any man could kill such a great beast as this. And broke i's neck indeed. A mighty strength is what it would've took. Maybe no' a man 't'all.'

'Of course it was a man. A poacher, no doubt. We cannot tolerate this lawlessness. The Thane will surely bring in more of his thugs, and heaven knows they only add to the lawlessness, bullying as they do. It's more than we need. It's more than *I* need!'

'Aye, Father.'

Father Taylor sternly bade them keep about their business and he would report the loss to the King's Thane, for which the men were more than a little relieved. Poachers were treated swiftly and violently and neither man wished to be mistaken for such, despite their honest paths and obvious standing in the town, albeit the physician's was much lower than a churchman, and the peasant's much lower still. A man's reputation was something better than nothing.

Neither man was ever encouraged by the disposition of the local priest, who took a too serious and dark view of the World and its peasants. But to deliver the consequences of this monstrous deed to a Man of God seemed far and away less formidable than to venture anywhere near the Thane's manor. Better leave that mission to the Father. And so they turned back to the village in silence to resume the tasks they'd set upon that day, Gamel back to his sons at the market square and the dispatching of their goods. He was keen to leave behind the experience of the morning and distance the superstition and fear from his thoughts. It had no place with him and no good could come of it.

A whispering lingered about the villagers and none took their commerce too seriously the rest of that morning. By the afternoon, Gamel was annoyed not with the ruckus of the morning so much as with its impact on people's pockets, and he was more than usually brusque in setting his sons to reloading their cart and turning their thoughts to their return journey. All thought of superstition was gone from Gamel but apparently it clung elsewhere. Berta Draper's reputation for prescience was simple enough – a death predicted here and a birth there, some of course unexpectedly as there'd be no such reputation otherwise; folk weren't so foolish as all that. So her predictions of impending threat hung in people's minds, and they were hard-pushed to ignore them; indeed they could not.

It was the social nature of the market that aided its business. People wanted to meet up with friends and family from around the parish, to hear each other's news and pass on wishes. There was no other means by which they connected. So they wandered stall to stall to talk, and along the way bought a bit of this and that, or exchanged one thing for another. Events of the morning, followed by Berta's outburst, had stifled all notions of small talk and camaraderie, and many left the market early. If there was to be trouble, best be behind their own closed doors when it came.

And so the Warriner men and boys, rattled and begrudging, set themselves back in their cart with less traded than they ought, and each boy knowing the hunger of a poor trade, and the father knowing the guilt of it. Not a man to wonder why though, but consider instead the means by which his fortunes may be reinvigorated, Gamel wandered through a list of possibilities in his head. The effects of the day would pass before the next market so this hardship would be short-lived. Gamel had no particular fear of the old woman's warnings. It was possible of course that some other minor calamity would ensue and then folk would point to

Berta's prescience and they'd feel safe the worst had passed, and then of course it all would.

Gamel was as simple as any other such man in that his life and the laws of it were simple and clear-cut, and that he was no man of learning. But he held a strength of insight that went beyond the superstitions of his day and for that he was unusual. He did not tolerate much small talk, could not abide gossip, and he knew of little that was not of this world that he ought to give much attention to, other than that it was wise to give heed to Church teachings and whatnot, for appearances mattered in some things..

Thomas noticed, in part, the feelings of those around him. They came as a dulling of the normal light, and he instinctively knew to remain more still and quiet.

Later that day, the water of the Dyke went unusually calm. Riding along its side and atop their wagon Thomas eyed its shining surface and his soul knew that it foretold a warning. Thomas felt the same pang of darkness that he felt briefly with the swan in the cart earlier in the day, although he'd forgotten that now. He was used to seeing the lights play on the water of the dyke, but the way the light played out now did not make him want to look, and he looked at his father's back instead.

When a great rumbling began to be heard, which was not the noise of a hundred cartwheels turning, Thomas was the only one not to wonder what this was and not to feel so uneasy.

Because Thomas saw light that others didn't, he knew also when his brothers began to be scared. He saw the light go dark in their stomachs first, and then in their hands and finally their eyes. He couldn't see his father's hands or his eyes as he drove their cart home, but he felt his father's stomach greyed just like the others. They didn't draw light into their mouths, and even though no one breathed many still screamed. Because they screamed without taking breath, they were swallowed into a dark fear very quickly, and Thomas couldn't see them anymore.

Gamel Warriner halted his nag and fought to control the horse's uppitiness, as the earth shook and swayed beneath wheels and hooves. The boys weren't sure to jump from the cart or hold on for dear life, as it jostled as much from the horses' rearing as the ground's uproar. Pots and baskets fell about, and some of their unsold produce leapt into the dust, spoiling now for its further trade, although no one cared nor even really noticed. A split fissured from the side of the dyke ahead of them and water spilled into it, a small rivulet crossing the cart's path.

'Wha's i', Pa?' screamed one of the boys. 'Wha's i'?'

Gamel struggled with his horse and did not answer the boy as the shaking went on and on. As with any event causing great fear, time slowed down and the agonising over life or death in such uncertainty was an interminable suffering for almost everyone in the County, but especially the ignorant, which was still most people.

For Thomas there was some more message reaching out to him in-between things, and some part of him tried to distinguish a new light from an old one. And it seemed like a reflection of himself in the far distance and he thought perhaps he might respond to this mirror image in some way, as indeed it seemed to want to connect with him also.

History would record that day the almost complete collapse of the cathedral at Lincoln and the multiple ruptures in the Foss Dyke. The practices of God and Commerce were equally disrupted. The rational called for repairs, the ignorant called for heads, and it was never a simple matter to predict from whence the powerful holders of such divergent views would emerge.

The social fissures exceeded the earthen ones, and their tremors ran for weeks, months, and even years. Some women and children whose husbands and fathers were lost to the earthquake, or called to the mason's lodge at Lincoln for work, were taken in to some of the kinder homes of Lincolnshire, although it was a struggle to feed more bellies. Others were less fortunate and were forced to a wandering life, lucky on occasion to find company with some younger roving labourer, less lucky to find an older one, having only themselves to give alongside their own pair of working hands and those of their children.

Families were rent, and new embitterments would be sure to keep them divided for a generation's memory and more. God Himself became a particular victim of rancour among those less inclined to fear Him, and even among those who did.

There was no logic to the varying physical effects of the earthquake. Some things fell and some things stood. In a single street in Lincoln, among an entire row of houses all exactly the same, one house fell completely and not another. In another street, almost the opposite: all fell but two or three. When the news was heard of the cathedral though, there was not an inconsiderable fear and superstition as to why God would allow such a thing to occur, and ordinary folk wondered what they or someone else had done to offend the holy order of things and whether enough retribution had been exacted by the earthquake or whether there may be more of such to come.

Gamel Warriner had no care for this superstition any more than he did for dead swans or the like. He sought simply to get his boys, his horse, and his cart home again to their small holding, along roads whose obstacles were previously only well-trodden ruts in the clay, but which now offered up no-longer-bridged streams, and bottomless clefts in their once familiar and worn track now filling with silt and water from countless creeks and streams whose courses had already shifted. Gamel offered no peace of mind to his children; he had little himself, and he used a great strength to maintain the sort of composure suited to a man before his sons, despite his own unnerving. Besides which, life held fear aplenty, and the sooner boys became men the better for them. Best they learn that to carry on with a view to protecting one's own and putting one's fear aside was the best course.

Still, the shaken earth rendered up shaken hearts and minds and bodies, and each fresh rumbling heard from the distance set the guts of Lincoln and Torksey and their surrounds to shiver anew.

At the ruins of the cathedral in Lincoln, all that remained was a part of the limestone west end of the great Church. It had been consecrated nearly a hundred years before by Remigius, a Benedictine monk and a supporter of William the Conqueror.

The new Bishop, Hugh of Avalon, a Frenchman, away at his palace at Stowe, forsook any thought of prayer for the ruins he was soon told of and prayed instead for the souls of Lincolnshire. Walking from his manse to the Minster Church of St Mary – or Stowe Minster as it was generally referred – he was frustrated by the fawning of young monks from the Abbey, offering their assistance to him. He would soon return them all from whence they came in Oxfordshire and be rid of the daily reminder of the multitudes of useless clergy who had no sense for the aid they may provide the community they supposedly served. He glared and muttered past them all.

At the little church in Torksey, Father Taylor held a less charitable view of things. He had not yet been to the Thane's manor and felt some relief that this new turn of events would, if briefly, overshadow the finding of the dead swan and thus his task of bringing such tidings. He was angered at what he knew would be the response of characters such as the old Draper woman, who would make much of the connection and create a renewed superstition that he himself sought always to undermine to only meagre avail. He despised the small-mindedness about him, and sympathy or sensitivity deserted him as usual, as he knew it would. And he disliked his own heart, for he wished above all to be more charitable, but could not find it in himself.

At the village of Nocton Fen, several miles directly the other side of Lincoln from Torksey, young Timothy Watson made his first really noticeable acquaintance with an Angel.

Hello, Timmy. We'll start soon. Are you ready?

Timmy looked at the light. He liked the light. It made him laugh. So he started looking for it as often as he could. It was very playful with him, hiding and then coming back out again.

He'd seen the light before – often in fact – but today it was brighter than usual, and he eyed a reflection of himself in the angles the light struck, and along which he liked to stare. Tim wondered how he might get that particular light to play with him; it didn't seem too hard because after a while he could tell that it very much wanted to.

Not that he knew it, but with this exchange Timmy had just taken part in the most important scientific discovery of the twentieth century.

2

Don't be afraid to see what you see.
Ronald Reagan, fortieth US president (1911–2004)

If Faith was the essential element of religion, so it was also with science.

Dr Alicia Watson lived on what she liked to refer to as the dark side of physics. Her bright office walls were a testament to it. Two vivid blue walls, two crisp white ones, with low bookcases all around, all evidenced a desire to clear the rubble of the true theoretician in favour of newness and clarity – a blank slate.

Alicia felt any inspiration that came to her in her work came from a universal ether of scientific truth, not from within her own head. She disliked the terminology of discovery. She knew all science already existed; hers was only to come to know it herself. That knowing came in part from experimentation, but more from her thoughtfulness about information known and consideration of other information that may be lying just beyond the known. She thus claimed her work not entirely as her own, although this was not a view she shared with those other devotees about her. She would never have said she had any belief in a god, but her own studies and research indicated the reality of a universal energy underpinning all things, that had will of its own and existed outside the minds of men. Some may have called this God, but Alicia was never so foolish as to cross over entirely from the dark side and into sheer quackery. She believed in what she saw, and what she saw was more than just particles and more than just light, and it did not conform to most of recent known science. She wondered at times that it had more to do with the ancients of Aristotle and Plato and Pythagoras whose science at least connected them with the universe instead of putting them apart from it, and whose search was one of heart and soul as well as mind. That they were philosophers as well as scientists – and philosophers first, and that these two departments were separated by most of the rest of the university – was an irony of history not lost on Alicia.

Alicia's science required an open-mindedness that would surely have been a prerequisite for any self-respecting scientist, except that in Alicia's view this was shamefully not always the case. She tried to encourage that openness among her students, along with a sense of fun and adventure also not common among her profession. She fancied her office a breeding ground for young talent, with an odd kaleidoscope of thick felt-tip penned equations covering one white wall, a reward to creativity in students. Not just any old brilliance, but daring and imagination were the criteria for this privilege.

'Write your favourite equation up – one that's meaningful to you,' she'd say.

And if the offer baffled, clearly they were not, at least yet, of the chosen. Some needed encouragement not to write shyly, but in large and bold characters, and this was her spur to those she felt may benefit from such a declaration. Many were even given repeated opportunities. Similarly, there was evidence of the mass of fondness for the same equations. $E = mc^2$ was written several times over, in different colours and scripts. As was also $E_8 \times E_8$ – string theory, and $\Delta x \, \Delta p \geq h/2$ – the uncertainty principle. Indeed, Einstein's oft-quoted formula had rather poetically found itself in one instance at the centre of the wall scrawled largest of all in multiple colours, a spectrum of imagination and potential she sought to foster, mirroring the brightest of young students of her science.

Among the plethora of wan, consumptive scientists occupying the floor that was the physics department, Alicia lived a relative aloneness she relished. The irony of her criticism of science was that her inner rebel dictated others would never meet her standard anyway. Far from wan herself, Alicia boasted a style reminiscent of the philosophy or religious studies departments with a head of wildly curling red hair and a fashion sense of gypsy proportions. Despite the staid environment of the university, it was as any other in the Western world a place of diversity, as indeed universities had always been; the oddest mixture of conservative and liberal. Anything goes.

'You know, that's not at all sound theory. Just guess work at this point, I really feel.'

Dryden Cooper leant in the door of Alicia's office. He was Head of Programmes in the physics department and had come to respect Alicia's teaching ability. He was one of the few scientists on the floor who was friendly with her, one other even refusing to enter the lift at the same time as her and preferring to wait for another. *Bollocks to you,* she would say to herself, even as she would voice a determined and polite greeting, and always making *them* be the one that had to wait for the next lift. *Not my bloody issue.*

'Oh and you would know. Don't be so arrogant! You should be looking to every new development from such auspicious sources as Alain Aspect and his team. They're not beneath any of us. See what happens, I say. And see what the international commentary is. You might be surprised. He's not without respect and esteem among the World's best.'

'I'm not being arrogant. You're making huge leaps of faith. No one in their right mind will think Bell's theorem has gone west yet. The Paris trials are only one set of experiments. And anyway they're French – can't trust 'em. And someone's got to live in the real world, Alicia – we can't all be travelling through time like a Tardis now, can we?'

They both grinned and Alicia pulled a face. She was used to Dryden's teasing.

'It's not about *travelling* through time. It's about communication; influence, synchronicity, and even those words don't describe it. Look, it's an equation okay, like any other hitherto unfathomable piece of physics we now take for granted, just some simple – well, no it's not simple – but anyway it's just maths, numbers on a page. And those numbers deserve our consideration, our response, whether respectful or not.'

'You don't believe that for a second. You don't care about the figures. You're a traitor to your profession, Alicia. You're looking for God in those numbers, and I'm telling you, you won't find Him. So there, write your response. I'll be happy to review it for you, but it's not a focus of this department to consider the quantum, as you know. This is popular science, undeserving of serious attention. Let some other scientists risk their reputations on it. We can't afford to be blasé.'

'Now that's just too extreme and you know it. The quantum underlies all else.'

'You know what I mean.'

'Oh, c'mon, Dryden, it's at least interesting, which is more than can be said for a lot else that goes on around here.'

'And what makes it interesting, my dear? I'll tell you what. You want your profession to give meaning to your life. And you'll find that in a Church or some such, not here. This is a job and you have a good head for it, but it's not about your heart and soul. You need to leave them at the door.'

'So you're saying you have no passion for what you do here then?'

'That's not what I said.'

'That's exactly what you said actually. You've got no desire at all to find something new. You don't revel in the dream that some discovery one day is going to sweep everything you've always believed in aside. You don't harbour any possibility of finding the answer to everything.'

Laughing. 'Of course! I want international renown for being the best at being the same as everyone else!'

They both laughed.

'Oh, Dryden, now you're the one that's joking. We're not so different, you and I.'

'I've always been afraid of that!'

Alicia's sparring with Dryden allowed her at least some sense that she belonged in the field. Despite his show of cynicism, she knew Dryden meant in fact to demonstrate his support and that by this exchange he meant only to test her own conviction. It was worthy of him, and of her.

'But seriously, it is time travel, isn't it?'

'Well, yes, sort of, but not in some popularist *Doctor Who* sense. It's particle influence across space, but the particles have to have been in the same locale at some point.'

'And a million miles away implies the possibility of bending time.'

'Well, light theory is undermined by their results, yes.'

'Theoretically.'

'Theoretically.'

'So you're going to shout this from the belfry tomorrow?' Dryden smiled.

'Well I shall try and find a way to do so within the narrow confines of my profession as you've so clearly defined it, if that's what you mean. Anyway while I'm up there – in the Belfry that is – I'll try and get a book deal going with a few Angels shall I?' They laughed again. 'After all, our science still depends on the whim of the wider community and those that fund us. Ordinary people are interested in this stuff. We have to be able to communicate it in ordinary terms to them.'

'This *stuff*! *Stuff*! We don't do *stuff*, Alicia. We're scientists. *Stuff* is for the management department and other woolly-headed so-called academics, trying to prove their righteousness to the economists. We're above that sort of thing. Science is not dependent on ordinary people and their small-mindedness. We don't subscribe to *Scientific American* around here. We're publishers of serious, internationally reviewed and reputable work.'

'Now you're definitely being arrogant!' She smiled as she said it.

'Well, my sweet, you have a good day and I hope you're still in this quadrant tomorrow,' Dryden said, backing out of the doorway with a grin.

'Oh ha ha!' Alicia turned back to her computer and her thoughts.

She wanted to be part of this exciting new world of science, and while Lincoln had been good to her, aside from Dryden's easy banter, she lacked the day-to-day conversation with others for whom the new science was stimulating. She was at risk of becoming bored, and she knew from experience that was not a good thing. She had to be engaged. It made her feel alive, and god knew everyone around her was a lot happier if she was.

In a sprawling cottage on the edge of Nocton Fen, Pete Watson had emerged from his garage workshop, the BBC blaring from an old radio-tape player on a shelf in the corner. He was seeing off one of his son's team of therapists after their morning play session.

'Thanks, Kaye. How was our wee sunshine today?'

'He said *swan*.'

'*Swan*? What'd 'e say *swan* for? Why can't he say *Daddy* or *Shakespeare* or *steak 'n' chips*? How'd he get *swan*?'

'Don't know. Some picture he liked I guess. Boy, he's into those chocolate chip biscuits, isn't he? I had to hide them. He was just about livid with me. It took all my effort to distract him.'

Pete was wiping grease from his hands on to what was possibly an even greasier old cloth. He wore once-white overalls with the sleeves cut off at the elbows, and bare feet. Two-day-old stubble covered his rugged friendly face. At some point in the morning, he'd wiped sweat from his forehead or rubbed an eye since a sizeable oil mark ran solidly across one brow.

'How was your morning?' Kaye asked. 'Have you got that old crate running yet?'

Kaye was the chattiest of Tim's therapists, and Pete enjoyed her company. He was sure her garrulous humour was an enormous boon to Tim's day as well as his.

'How dare you call my baby a crate? The least you could come up with is jalopy or fender bender or something. After all, this is a work of art you know, a veritable *Mona Lisa* of mustangs, a...'

'Yeah, yeah, yeah. I get the picture,' Kaye interrupted. 'I'd just like to see the bloody thing get its rubber to the road sometime.'

'Ah, but this is not necessarily the goal of course. Should it ever become roadworthy I may have to come forth from my sanctuary and speak to people, and my wife and I may not know what to say to each other after such a long period of man-shed hibernation.'

'You sure she's not hanging out for you to finish it so she *can* talk to you?' Kaye asked.

'Hmm, there's a thought. But on the other hand, perhaps she prefers it this way. Hard to know.'

'Uh-huh.' said Kaye.

'Anyway, how's Tim coming along do you think? Are we winning?'

'You know. It's one step at a time. One day at a time. I haven't felt much change lately.'

'No,' agreed Pete.

'Sometimes I think he's actually just so smart that he's really bored witless with this training we do with him and he's waiting for the good stuff to start, whatever that is. I don't know. What about more socialising, more outings, and more experience with people and the wider world?'

'I've wondered that. Maybe I'll take him up to Lincoln on the weekend. Perhaps we could see the swans at the Pool, since he's got a new thing for them.'

'Good idea. Let me know what he makes of it,' said Kaye. 'There's no doubt he's not in any way severely autistic. He's never been a headbanger, he's got great eye contact, all kinds of things that take him away from that extreme end of the spectrum. We've got to remind ourselves of that.'

'Yeah, he just runs in circles, shakes his arms around, blabbers on about nothing, and laughs at empty space.'

'I know, I know. But honestly it could be worse. You should see some of the kids I work with. Really, I do have high hopes for him. You'll see. He's only four. There's plenty of time. Really.'

'Thanks, Kaye. I really do appreciate all you do for him. Sometimes it just doesn't seem to be having any effect. And then other times he's off in leaps and bounds. Not much different from most kids I s'pose.'

'Well like I say, step by step.'

'Yeah.'

'Okay, well, I'm off. See you Monday.'

'Thanks, see you then.'

'Bye, Timmy,' Kaye called to the small boy at the front door.

Timmy did not respond. He was concentrating on the vertical line of the door frame, which he did by standing right up against it, with his nose touching and his head angled to one side. His eyes did a slow dance between the point at his eye level and the top of the door frame, and back again.

'Tired him out for you sorry, but he's kinda relaxed too I think.'

'Oh, he'll be fine, won't you, Tim-Tim?'

Tim's eyes stayed locked in his up and down investigation of the door frame.

'Sweetie-pie. Okay, seeya.' Kaye turned down the path with a wave.

'Bye.'

Pete waited another moment as Tim studied the door frame. It was apparent that there was something to do with vertical and horizontal lines that drew his attention, regardless of where they were. When it seemed he was likely to be in this position for some time, Pete wandered past him, not resisting the suggestion of a hair tousle, and headed towards lunch-making duties, his couple of hours of freedom over for the day. Not that he minded.

Pete told himself he was blissfully happy. He'd gone from student to almost professional protestor, to political reporter and then to his version of house husbandry, as childminder, occasional writer and long-time car and engine tinkerer. Parenting Tim proved the most challenging and most rewarding of his roles. He considered himself lucky to have such a child, a gift of sorts.

'Still talking to the Angels,' the lead therapist had said one day, not quite mirroring Pete's thoughts as Tim would smile up at something not there, or laugh out loud. At what?

'Hey, mate, ready for some fuel?' Pete peered round the kitchen door a few minutes later to see Tim still glued by his nose to the door. He took a slight tumble backwards and recovered. He turned towards his father, although did not apparently notice him. Instead, his attention to the door broken, he set off past Pete on some new mission – probably an attempt on the pantry.

'Biscuit?' would be the inevitable next thing.

Right then, Pete said to himself, reviewing his list of possible diversions from biscuits.

The phone rang.

This might work.

'Hello,' he said into the phone, and then covering it, 'look, Tim, the phone. Who is it?' Back into the phone, 'oh, hi hun; how's your day? Tim, Tim; it's mummy, come and listen.'

Pete reached the phone out to Tim who stood with his ear to it. Pete could hear his wife's chit-chat through the earpiece. Alicia took the view, much as Pete did, that it didn't matter what they said to Tim as long as they said a lot. Alicia would lecture him on quantum physics, since she could talk on the topic endlessly and it fitted with the idea of simply saying a lot. She would practise actual lectures and speeches to him in the bath, on the sofa, wherever and whenever. Pete noticed that in this way she sometimes even clarified her own thinking on things.

'Biscuit.' Tim had had enough of the phone.

'Well, that didn't work for long. Hi, love. What's up?' Pete spoke back into the phone and reached for the biscuit tin..

'Oh, we're good. Just the usual sort of morning. You sound restless.' Alicia's phone calls to home were often a way of grounding herself or as a distraction from boredom.

'Interesting. Well, I'll look forward to hearing about it later. Yes, the washing's in. Enjoy the rest of your day, hun.'

'Biscuit.'

'No, Timmy. Like this.'

A pair of small and gentle hands guided even smaller loose fingers across brightly coloured wooden puzzle pieces, placing them correctly in the different shaped holes.

'See?'

But the little boy did not see and picked up the wooden box containing the pieces and shook it, enjoying the sound of it more. He laughed. At the sound? Who knew what.

The two children were fair-haired with happy round faces. Toys were strewn about them, and there was a long row of different size cars and trucks lined up end to end across the room. The children's play was relaxed. If there were rules of any kind, none impacted the enchantment of this scene. They weren't hurried or trapped by a time that said they had to be here or there. Nothing bound them in any way except they were with each other and doing as they wished, the one helping the other to learn, the little student happy with this sweet friend who had always been with him.

'It's funny, isn't it, Tim? Do you want to try again?' Jillie Watson, with a devotion and patience beyond her seven years, gently took the box from her younger brother and emptied the shapes on to the floor where they sat. If anyone else had taken the box from him, he would have screamed. But Jillie usually had Tim's complete cooperation. She never became bored or frustrated with him although the children's parents were willing to concede she one day might. For now they took pleasure in her custodial attitude.

'See. This one goes in here. This one here. Where does this one go, Tim?'

Jillie passed a red wooden circle to Tim, and he took hold with his thumb and forefinger, letting it drop into his lap and turning it over with his hand.

'You put it in here. C'mon, put it in here.' Jillie held the circle side of the box out to Tim.

Putting it down again, she picked up the red piece in Tim's lap, put it into his hand and guided his hand to the circular opening in the box, manoeuvring the piece through the hole.

'Yay, you did it! Let's do that again, shall we?' Jillie began the process over. She'd watched Tim's therapists many times and knew that repetition would eventually pay off.

Timmy smiled at something. A huge smile that went on and on, and he laughed.

'You don't want to do that? Okay, what do you want to do, Tim?'

Jillie waited, looking as Tim continued his smile and giggle and stare. He rolled backwards on to the floor, giggling still, as though he were being tickled. Jillie rolled back with him, not sure of the game, until it seemed just as suddenly to be over and Tim sat up.

'Shall we go outside and kick the ball?'

'Ball.'

'C'mon then.' Jillie held out her hand and took her brother's small chubby one.

Tim got up from the floor, still smiling. Whatever amused him had gone by the time they got to the back door. Jillie took the steps carefully, watching her brother's footing and then running together into the yard. Jillie retrieved a rubber ball from under some bushes and launched it carefully towards her brother. Tim jumped up and down, feet together in one spot on the lawn.

A while later their mother's voice called them inside to get ready for a Sunday drive.

3

It is not known precisely where angels dwell. It has not
been God's pleasure that we should be informed of their abode.

Voltaire (1694–1778)

Giles Johnson was a barman at the *Magna Carta*. He was a
big northerner with a generous ear and a solid word of advice for
most. He was also large enough and fearsome enough that a look
from him across the pub would still almost any kind of fracas about
to happen.

Giles stood behind the bar, sleeves rolled up and tea towel
scrunched and twisted round the inside of a pint glass. It was quiet
yet, apart from the two fellows in the corner, one old and one
younger, with a chessboard and a very slow pint each. They were
often in, always just the two of them, always the chessboard. The
pair of them always looked like they'd seen better days – a bit
scruffy, worn collars and cuffs, and shoes that might do with a
polish. They were an odd couple. He'd been surprised the first time
he'd gone by them and heard their conversation – well spoken and
gracious in an unexpected way. He could imagine the old boy was
retired from something, a university perhaps, but never quite
fathomed the younger one. Giles figured he was an oddball, just
too unusual for anyone to employ. Or just maybe the old guy was
an eccentric millionaire and this was his nephew – no need to work,
could just do as they liked.

Giles had begun to look forward to seeing them. They
usually came in at fairly quiet times – early to mid-afternoon – and
their presence became like that of other regulars, like a visit from a
favourite old uncle or cousin. They made the place their home, and
that made it a home-away for others just with the feel of it.

Giles watched them chatting away. He thought he might offer them an extra pint later on – on the house. Why would you not? He liked their chit-chat, and they were always kind and friendly with anyone coming within their small tableau, and they enjoyed a joke as much as any, never taking offence at even the most raucous of the typical displays of an English pub.

The mother doesn't quite understand what it is that she can see.

No, but she doesn't need to especially. Words aren't everything. She's very connected, most devout.

But surely understanding...

Yes, of course it helps. Your move. Focus on one thing at a time.

The younger moved his bishop from harm's way.

There. Well the Earth keeps turning just the same.

Aye. And so do the Angels look still for those who would speak with them.

And what do they find indeed?

Mostly just those newly arrived, who stare past their mothers' eyes and over their shoulders, attracted by the beauty lingering above, which waits to provide its special protection. But after a while, these little ones usually forgot how to see Angels.

...which I find so disappointing, don't you? As I feel sorry for God when I hear someone say they don't believe in Him.

Infants hear more and more the voices of the World, and although these are not so soft as Angels' voices, they listen anyway because there is magic in the World as well, and it lures and it captivates and it steals souls.

The older man responded with a more aggressive move towards his friend's queen.

And so all through a single life there is nothing but this moving away? Such a waste.

So many temptations exist to tantalise the eyes of the heart instead of the window of the soul.

Others find their way back.

The older man raised his head to eye his companion and see what nervousness might exist in his face, but he could see that the younger man did not recognise his plan for the board that lay between them.

Some think they have avoided or escaped the clutches of worldly traps, but sadly most of them are deluded.

I have seen many pretend, for their own purposes, that they commune with Angels, but of these I have never known a one that has heard, seen, or even felt me such that they answered in kind.

Your energy is not strong. There are a small few who do see. As with the boys, they don't know that this is not the conventional way of the World. These souls are the most blessed, for they understand the meanings of things and the intentions of God and the power of the Word. But they are not people to take or make any advantage of this sight, and many are as empty of the world as one of these boys.

To ordinary folk, a Thomas is as hidden to them as God and the Concourse on high.

If they had any thought to such folk, it is mostly that they are strange, and perhaps even dangerous, and certainly not understood. Play.

You make your light brighter than me. How do you do that?

I have less thought. And I trust more. You know this.

Instinct.

No, not instinct. But natural.

I sometimes find I have to force *the natural.*

A contradiction.

Yes.

We are not speaking of the light of the Sun, although even that you may bend to your will. That light comes from gas spat out into the Universe and takes just minutes to reach Earth. The light the boys wait for is the light that is the space between all things, and the substance of most things, that carries the messages of the Universe, and gives the World unseen instructions. It doesn't have to travel anywhere; it's all around all the time. Don't force. Check.

Drat! I should have seen that. When I don't concentrate, I'm duller.

Then let it be so. It will come brighter in time. Let go. It's what we are encouraging in them, expecting in them, except for your game: that you need to focus on more.

They have no training.

It's better that way. Their approach is wholly natural.

But they can't connect with the world.

They don't need to, at least not as you'd think. Which is to say again, don't think. Feel. Sense.

It just amuses them. Your contact. They laugh at it.

It is happiness that will help them find their way — Joy. It's love in movement.

It seems indulgence only.

When was love indulgence?

Then love is light; light is love.

Every object visible to man emits a stream of particles that meet the eye. Pythagoras put this idea into words first; that light consists of rays, which act like feelers, travelling in straight lines from eye to object. People see a thing when those rays touch it. Not many people know that they can also touch light; nor do they know the finer points of light lines, as they impart their true essence, which is love. Pythagoras was a mathematician, but our young companions would find in him not only a friend of the light but also someone who understands that earthly domains are a mirage for the undiscerning..

He's very sweet, the younger one.

And he wants to talk with us. He knows.

How can you tell?

He has more joy than the other.

Such a burden for them to have to live in two worlds — the one their parents are in, and their own one, inside their own heads. You think we can reach this one?

He can certainly avert great disaster. Perhaps even that of his brother in time.

No one would believe so.

Oh, some would. Some would like to. Checkmate.

'Och, I see I've come at the right time, then!' Giles set a pint in front of each man.

'Giles, you shall be a Saint. I shall make sure of it personally.'

'No need, sir. Just doin' my job. That's on the house 'n' all.'

The two men grinned and raised their glasses to their host.

'Cheers!' they beamed at him and the light coming in through the windows at the front of the pub seemed to shine brighter.

4

Our deepest fear is not that we are inadequate; our deepest
fear is that we are powerful beyond measure.

Marianne Williamson (1952–)

Signs along the Brayford Wharf warn tourists and
picnickers of the dangers inflicted on *Cygnus olor* from a diet of
chips and stale bread.

Timmy walked between his parents, occasionally holding
one of their hands and then the other as the Watson family walked
along the path at the edge of the lake, the stunning new glass-
fronted main block of Lincoln University on the very edge of the
pool opposite..

It was early spring and it was cold, but since there was
sunshine and this was England, a great many people were out
inspecting cafes, houseboats along the canal, or just strolling.

What Alicia wanted more though was to be in her office
across the lake. She craved the isolation it offered. Ironically, when
it came, it was also often unwelcome. She would find she had less
to do than she thought and her life would sometimes seem
singularly uncreative. She'd long for the company of her husband
and children even though she knew she'd feel immediately irritated
again the second she walked through the door of her home..

Now at least they were outside and she had bargained with
Pete for work time after the trip to the pond, despite the weekend.

Timmy stared this way and that at nothing in particular.
Occasionally he looked into the corner of his eyes, so far that it
would hurt most people to do it for long. But Timmy could hold
this look for several minutes.

'Mummy, there they are. Look.'

Jillie had seen the enormous white swans. Some swam on the Pool. Some sat or stood on the bank.

'Don't run, darling. You might scare them away. Just go slowly. And don't get too close.'

'Look, Timmy, look! The swans! Look!' Jillie put her hand to Tim's shoulder and pointed with her other.

Timmy's eyes followed her line to the large birds several metres off the path. His parents stopped walking and watched his face waiting for some response. His eyes stayed fixed on the birds. For a while they all stood still: Tim looking at the Swans and his parents and sister looking at him. Tim pulled his hands away from his parents, took a few steps forward and jumped a couple of times on the spot, still looking at the birds. He shook his head from side to side and waved both hands vigorously, his elbows bent at his sides. He turned his head away and looked at the swans from the very corner of his eye. After a moment he looked back at them, lifted one hand and a pointed finger up a little, and blew a 'wi' sound several times.

He kept his attention on the birds and his parents kept their attention on him, unconsciously linking hands with each other.

Tim smiled at Alicia. 'What do you think?'

'Dunno,' Alicia wondered, her eyes squinting just a little as she studied her son.

'Wa',' Timmy said.

He moved a few more steps towards the birds..

'Do you think that means *swan*?' Pete hoped aloud.

'Might be wishful thinking, darling.' Alicia leant towards Pete and whispered, 'I don't want him to get too close.'

'He's fine, he's fine. Just... wait...' Pete whispered, curious at what he hoped may be some recognition.

'What's he doing?' Jillie picked up on her father's tone.

'I don't know, sweetie. Let's be very quiet and see what happens.'

Tim smiled, looking at two large birds several metres away which seemed to be watching this small group of people watching them. He walked and half skipped towards them.

'Okay, that's close enough,' said Alicia.

'No, wait.' Pete grabbed Alicia's arm to hold her back. 'Look, he's not scared. This is amazing. He's always scared of animals.'

'Jesus, Pete. Look at the size of those beaks. What if they peck him?'

'Actually, they're more likely to break his back with one of their wings.'

'Okay, that's it.' Alicia pulled away.

Pete grabbed her again. 'Look, just trust me. He's fine. They're not going to hurt him. He's no threat to them.'

'I was more thinking about their threat to him actually.'

'Shh! watch.' Pete was mesmerised by his son's approach to the swans.

'He's fine, Mummy. Look, he's gonna make friends with them.'

Alicia did a half eye roll.

Timmy skipped up to one of the swans, which raised itself on to its feet. The little boy looked to the bird's dark red-brown eyes as it turned towards him and eyed him closely. Only a few inches from the bird, Tim giggled and the bird cocked its head very slightly. Tim's head angled a little too, but he couldn't find the straight lines he liked most, and he straightened his neck again. The bird's long neck curled down very slowly, and an orange beak touched Tim's chest in an almost imperceptible pecking motion. Tim's eyes followed the bird's head – a little giggle, another small peck. The long white neck curled back up again and the two eyed each other a while longer. Then the giant bird turned its head to the lake and sat down, seemingly satisfied that no threat arose here.

Jillie Watson saw the air around her brother and the bird turn pale white. It didn't seem like anything you'd mention so she didn't, and besides she'd seen it many times before about her brother. It was one of the special things she liked about him.

'Look, darling,' said Pete, 'doesn't it look like he's just found a new friend?'

Alicia's look at her husband suggested recognition of the Missing Link. 'No?'

Tim plonked himself on his bottom immediately beside the great bird, the animal's head nearly a metre above his own. He blinked up at it, the light from the sun almost directly in his eyes.

His parents heard him laugh quietly again and saw him smile.

'I'm enjoying this. This is amazing,' said Pete.

Alicia was less enthralled. 'This is a dumb idea.'

'He's perfectly content. What a sight.'

'I've never seen him do this before.' She was resigned.

The bird lowered its beak for another quiet peck, this time at Tim's head. The little boy raised his hand and laughed anew. Then the giant Swan came up on to its feet again, waddled gently to the water's edge, and took a graceful stepping launch into the water, gliding quietly away. Tim watched.

Jillie wandered over to her brother, sat down beside him, and shared his pleasure at the sight of the gliding bird. She briefly checked out the top of his head, but apparently found nothing. Tim grabbed at her hand and laughed again. Their parents joined them and sat down, quietly examining their child in the light of an apparent minor miracle.

'Swa',' Timmy said, raising a finger in the direction of the just-departed bird.

'Can't mistake that,' Pete said to no one in particular.

'All right, you've convinced me, although I'm not sure of what. What is it about the Swans, do you think?'

'What is it about Timmy, you might ask?'

'Well, yes, I guess so.'

'What d'ya think the Swan said to Timmy, Daddy?'

'Well, I don't think it said anything exactly, darling, but it did seem to like him, didn't it? Actually these swans don't talk – I mean they don't talk swan talk. They're Mute Swans. They don't make normal swan sounds.'

'That's a bit like Timmy, isn't it? He doesn't make normal sounds either. Maybe that's why they were talking.'

'Maybe.'

Tim smiled a big dimply smile and looked sharply to the corner of his eye.

'I'd like to have a nosy up at the cathedral, so how about you pick us up from there in an hour or so?'

'Yay!' Jillie interrupted. 'Can I come? I like it there.'

'Okay, that'll work,' said Alicia.

The Watsons packed picnic remains into their car. Timmy continued to utter the odd *Wa'* or *Swa'* to general amazement and all-round delight.

Alicia took Orchard Street past the City of Lincoln Council, behind the wharf and the narrow winding streets to Drury Lane and the castle and cathedral on the hill. The cathedral presented one of the finest sights in England, sitting atop the hill and old town of Lincoln, and could be seen for miles around. It had an extraordinary architectural history being built and rebuilt, in part or in whole, several times.

Turning past the tourist centre into Castle Square, a short way from the Cathedral, Alicia pulled over by *The Magna Carta* pub.

'And don't even think about getting stuck in there!' Alicia smiled at her husband.

'I wouldn't dream of it.' Pete leant over and kissed his wife. 'See you back here at three?'

'Sure. Have fun.'

'Okay, you two, let's pile out then.' Pete climbed out and opened the back door for his children. 'Timmy, did you undo your seat belt?'

'It's all right, Dad, he just undid it just then.'

'Okay, good. C'mon then. Bye, hun.' Pete and Jillie waved to Alicia as she turned back around to go back down the way she'd come.

'Can we go down the steep street, Daddy?' Jillie pointed down Steep Hill, the cobbled, handrailed lane leading down the hill.

'Maybe later, sweetie. It's pretty hard work getting up again.'

'You won't have to carry me.'

'I think I heard you say that last time, and I think I did carry you some of the way, and Timmy. Let's go see the Cathedral and we'll see about it after, shall we?'

'Okay, let's go.' Jillie took her father's hand as they turned right at the corner of the pub and under the medieval archway of the cathedral's Exchequer Gate.

Pete never ceased to be in awe of the incredible facades of the Cathedral, no matter from which angle he approached it. The extent of the stonework was something to marvel, in the sheer size of single stones, but mostly in the height of the whole structure. The cathedral had been the tallest building in the world until the sixteenth century when its spires collapsed. Up close, both inside and out, the stones told a story to the touch – warm or cold, some more smooth, some older, some newer – and in their detailed work. There were thousands of stories within and without he knew. Each stone told a tale.

Pete headed to the South Door in the West Front of the cathedral, a child holding each hand. The stone threshold was worn into a smooth concave. Jillie skipped inside the small foyer, and they turned left into the main cathedral.

'See this bit of wall, Jillie?' Pete indicated the outside wall. 'It's nearly a thousand years old. It's a part of the original cathedral.

There was a big earthquake hundreds of years ago and most of it fell down.'

'Is it going to fall down now?'

'No, darling, it's not.'

'How do you know?'

'Well, it's a lot stronger now than it was then.'

'What if there's another earthquake?'

Pete regretted this particular attempt at a history lesson. 'I'm sure it won't happen today, sweetie. See this?' He indicated a clear change in the stonework, where two different types of stone met, one a little darker in colour than the other. 'See, this is where new stones were put on top of old ones when they were rebuilding the cathedral.' The story the diagonal change told never ceased to overwhelm Pete, as he imagined stonemasons smoothing the old to make way for a well-fitting new. The craftsmanship he knew was little known now, and that medieval understanding of the weights and balances and engineering could rival much of contemporary expertise.

He walked over to the large square black font. It resembled marble but Pete knew, from his reading of the Cathedral's history, that it was polished and waxed limestone brought from France in the mid-twelfth century. 'This is a font. Do you know what it's for?'

'To wash your hands?'

'No, it's for baptising new babies. The priest puts water over their head and...'

'What's baptising?'

'Well, it's a thing parents do to say we want our baby to believe in God and we're going to teach her about God as she grows up.'

'Did you do that about me?'

'Let's look around, shall we? Oh, look at this...'

'Okay.'

Pete turned towards the Nave, still holding his children's hands. They were relaxed and in no hurry. Pete revelled in this element of his children and parenting more than any other. There was no hurry, no deadlines, no copy to get to the editor, no coffee date appointment to meet, no traffic to battle, and no dinner to cook by a certain time. It was the weekend, and for Pete, even weekdays now afforded much of that peacefulness. He appreciated the opportunity to guide his children through the beauty of this place, not because he needed them to understand God – he wasn't so sure about God himself – but to show them the power of a people and a history, and even an empire for all its strengths and weaknesses, and how the Church and its buildings fostered a nation. Not a religious education, but an education just the same. Not a celebration of the power of a state, but an observation of the labours and devotions of hundreds of thousands of people across hundreds of years. That was Lincoln Cathedral to Pete, and he immersed himself in it.

The Cathedral was enormous, not dark but not light, afternoon sun pouring in just the same, through the high northern windows and stained glasses. The effect was appropriately celestial. The size of the space he was in, up, across and looking the long distance towards the eastern end, still staggered him.

The high, lengthy Nave was neatly laid out with moveable seating, and several people were dotted about – some obviously locals and in prayer, others tourists quietly taking in their surrounds. A large pulpit with a spiralling staircase stood empty. A few obvious church officials were about – some busying themselves with administrative tasks; another middle-aged woman in cassock speaking with a visitor or parishioner.

Jillie was happy to walk slowly beside her father. Holding hands had been openly agreed as their favourite thing. Pete observed the relative quiet of the enormous building, oddly without much echo. Jillie had a sense of the place and had made an assumption that it was a place of whispers. Tim was compliant, for now. Had he thought it in so many words, he would also recognise that holding his father's hand was one of his favourite things.

They walked along the south wall, stopping at each giant window, in part looking at what each tableau contained, in part simply taking in the beauty of the colours and light plays of each. This particular craftsmanship was never lost on Pete either and his appreciation never became saturated. Jillie could not seem to get enough either and had remarked once 'it's so beautiful, Daddy – can we come and live here in the Church', to the bemusement of bystanders.

They passed the cassocked woman chatting to another visitor. Pete saw that her name tag read 'Duty Chaplain', as she introduced herself to the person she was with as 'Jane'. She spoke softly and kindly in a well educated accent, and Pete wondered about a lifetime of devotion to the Church.

He said quietly to Jillie, 'Is there anything you'd particularly like to see, sweetie? Mummy'll be a wee while.'

'No, I like all the parts. Look, there's a picture of a swan in that glass up there.'

'It is too. Do you think that's the swan we saw today?'

'Don't be silly, Daddy.'

'But it could be the great-great grandfather of the one that talked to Timmy. Probably ten times that number of *greats*. Probably infinity *greats*.'

'Wow!' Jillie continued to stare up at the window.

Pete wallowed a moment in her delight.

At the other end of the nave, across the West Transept, the Choir screen marked the midpoint of the Cathedral.

Pete turned and looked back down the Nave with its twin lines of great columns. There was surprisingly little noise, even with people milling about. To his left now, the afternoon sun poured down into the southern end of the transept through an enormous round stained glass window, the *Bishop's Eye*, set high in the wall.

Tim was standing, head back, blinking up through the central tower rising directly above them. The perfect symmetry of the many vaulted and arched lines in this view was like one section through a kaleidoscope. Tim was mesmerised, until Jillie stood right in front of him, looking up too, and his attention was broken and he giggled at his sister.

They wandered along the southern choir aisle, and Tim pulled away towards a black stone resembling a seat built into the surrounding internal Cathedral wall. He meandered over, moving his head left and right as he walked, keeping his eyes though on the seat. He stopped in front of it and stood, a little tentatively, the fingers of one hand lightly brushing the edge of the structure. Then he sat down on the floor, rested his head, and stared along the edge of the metre-long seat.

Tired, thought Pete.

A shuffle to one side drew Pete's attention to a stout red-haired cassocked woman emerging around the Choir Screen with a small stack of books. She walked towards them and, as she got close, slowed to consider the view of the boy perched on the stone floor.

'Sorry,' said Pete. 'He's just plopped himself down there. A bit tired, I think.'

'Oh no, not at all. He looks very sweet. Quite at home,' said the woman, smiling.

Tim leant further on to the seat and put his hand on it, as though listening for something inside the box.

The woman also cocked her head to one side, studying Tim. 'Do you know what's in there?'

'Ah, no. I don't. What is in there?'

The woman was clearly pleased with the small spectacle. She turned to Pete. 'Actually, it's a shrine.'

Pete's eyebrows rose.

'It used to be a lot bigger and more ornate but was destroyed during a war once. It's known as the Shrine of Little Hugh.' She looked back to Tim. 'A young boy from the Middle Ages. Quite a horrendous story. Supposedly he was crucified and then tossed down a well. His death was blamed on the Jews, although undoubtedly that wasn't the case. Some were executed though for the crime. The boy was considered a martyr and was interred here. No one knows now, of course, who he really was or what really happened.' She stared still at Tim and then turned back to Pete. 'But perhaps your wee boy does.'

Pete stared at her.

'But never mind me, I like to imagine these things.' She laughed a little, at herself it seemed.

Pete looked to Tim and back. She was rather jolly, this woman, and open, as she smiled at them all. 'Tim ... he knows ... some things we don't know, for sure.'

'Well, I find most small children do have some wisdom about them, I have to say.'

'Tim's autistic,' Pete explained.

'Oh,' she said. 'Oh. Well.' She looked intriguingly at Tim. 'I'm Rose Draper. I'm a deaconess here.' She turned back to Pete and extended her hand.

'Pete Watson.' Pete shook her hand. 'This is Jillie. We live at Nocton Fen. Jillie and I've been a few times to the Cathedral, haven't we?'

'Yes, I like it.' Jillie stepped forward.

'Well, I'm glad.' She seemed genuinely delighted.

'Mmm,' Jillie responded shyly.

'Well, it's a curious attachment your Tim has to our Little Hugh.'

'Oh, you know, he's just tired really. We've had quite a day. And he does this thing looking along vertical and horizontal lines like this, especially when he's tired. It's called local coherence – when things are getting a bit much, if there's too much going on – autistic kids will activate some little habitual behaviour they have, and it keeps anxieties and uncertainties about their environment at bay. So that's one of the things he does.' Pete looked at his son. 'Looks like he's on to something else though now,' he said.

Tim was smiling, wide-mouthed and wide-eyed.

Jillie was holding her father's hand again and also watching her brother. She could see the light again, that had come before when Tim talked to the Swan.

'You know, he smiles like this – at nothing seemingly – all the time. Sometimes I swear it's to the same vacant spot in mid-air, completely as though there's something there that no one else can see. We've just been down to the lake, and he's been having the most unbelievable little chat with one enormous swan. My wife was just about beside herself. He practically walked off with it.'

'It was talking to him, Daddy. I could see it.'

'Yes, well, it did rather look like it, that's for sure.'

'You know that the real St Hugh – Bishop Hugh – who rebuilt the cathedral in the Middle Ages, is the Patron Saint of swans and sick children.'

'Really?' Pete said.

'So that makes for a nice little story, doesn't it? Your wee man here chatting with swans just like a real saint.'

'Oh, well ... '

'You know, I really do think some children can connect into something we can't – as though we've lost it – and they haven't yet. And there are children like Tim – I've seen this before – you're right, they see things we don't. And I do wonder about that, I really do. It gives me enormous pause to consider the ways we conceive of God, that I wonder may be quite ... well, not so useful. I don't know. Anyway, you're quite blessed I'm sure, Pete, to have Tim.'

'Thank you. Not many people would think that. It's nice of you to notice.'

'Well, I must away. Things to do – song sheets to prepare, etcetera. Lovely to meet you.' Rose extended her hand again and Pete took it.

'Yes, you too.'

'I hope I'll see you again some time. Goodbye, Jillie. Enjoy your afternoon with your dad.'

'Bye.'

Rose walked off and then turned back after a few paces.

'Forgive me if I'm being rather bold, Pete. It's just that I'm about to pin this up to the noticeboard. We run several adult classes – discussion groups really – where we explore questions about what do we know and how do we know it, God and so on. Maybe you'd be interested. There's one at my cottage on Thursday evenings. There are nine or ten of us, I suppose. We start at seven thirty. Here ...' Rose handed over a leaflet from the pile of things in her arm. She scribbled on the corner and handed it to Pete. 'It's just along from the Cathedral, easy to find. You don't need to bring anything, although a bottle's always welcome.' She grinned. 'Right, well, must away. Cheerio!'

Pete's views on the eccentricities of the Church and priesthood felt both confirmed and dismantled all at once.

'Thank you.' Pete didn't know what else to say. *That was a bit odd. Cheerful sort though. And she had Tim's number all right.*

Tim walked along with his head hanging back almost as far as it could go, holding his father's hand for balance and staring up at the vaulting far above. They'd walked to the eastern end of the Cathedral, past St Hugh's shrine, an enormous affair, and back down the northern choir aisle. Pete noticed the vaulting here was irregular and asymmetrical as though two different halves of two quite different cathedrals had been joined together by accident, but cleverly just the same.

How odd, thought Pete. *Bet that disturbs Tim's linear aesthetic.*

The bright light in the rafters reminded Tim of the reflection he'd seen earlier, and he knew then that he would see it again, and often, because 'it' was a special friend who saw the world just as he did.

'Thank God!' Alicia fell into bed next to Pete.

'That was a bit of a mission sorry. He's in that super-stimulated but super-tired state.'

'Isn't he always in that state? Honestly, if there's a balance between giving him plenty of stimulation to get those cogs going, and not giving him too much so he goes completely mental, I don't know what it is.'

'Yip.'

Alicia grabbed the top book from a pile by her bed. Tim, bespectacled, had *The Times* in his hands.

'Isn't that yesterday's?'

'Yeah, I didn't get to it. Tim. You know.'

'I do know.'

Neither Pete nor Alicia found much benefit in complaining about the trials of parenting an autistic child, but both offered a silent support and a quiet knowing to each other's quite separate battle with this reality.

'How was the cathedral?' Alicia had collected her family that afternoon as planned and the evening was then taken over with the usual dinner-bath-story-bed ritual, albeit that this particular evening's ritual was vastly extended by Tim's considerable and chaotic energy.

'It was lovely. I really do like it there, so much history and fabulous stories. In fact, I heard a new one from a priest-woman while we were there.'

'A priest-woman? What's that ya' dork? There's no such ...'

'I think she was a deacon – a deaconess, yeah, she was a deaconess.'

'What's a priest-woman?! Ya' nong!'

'Well, she *was* a deaconess, I remember now. Anyway, what I was saying ...'

'Carry on.'

'There was this box Timmy sort of sat on ... leant on. Well, it turned out it was a shrine – just a wee thing, stuck out of the wall.

Didn't look like anything unusual, kind of a seat really, a black stone box. Turns out it's the body of a child, thrown down a well in the Middle Ages, and it got put there. No one knows who it is, but he's referred to as *Little St Hugh*, after the real St Hugh, who was bishop at the time.'

'How'd you know all this?'

'The *deaconess!*'

'Right. Name of ... ?'

'Ah. R ... r ... Rose!'

'R-r-rose!'

'I was just trying to remember it. I knew it was R-something. You're being very cheeky tonight, y'know.'

'Sorry. Feel like taking the piss. The alternative may be that I yell at someone.'

'Really? Why's that, love? Those quantums getting you down again?'

'Oh, I'm just not sure about what I'm doing, and where I'm doing it. Bit bored, I suppose. Would rather be in the thick of it somewhere and instead I'm sat here in Lincoln with a bunch of dreary odd-bods who're not at all interested in anything new – anyway, whatever. Don't get me started.'

'I know the perfect recipe for boredom.' Pete put his book down and rolled towards his wife.

'Nuh. Don't even think about it.'

'You're kidding.'

'No. Not interested. Sorry.'

'Oh my, things are bad.'

'Don't joke. It's not funny.'

'Right then.' Pete went back to his book.

Alice put her book aside, turned out her light, and slid under the covers, away from Pete.

'Nice chatting,' said Pete.

'Careful. Honestly.'

''kay. Sorry.' Pete put his book down, turned a light out, and cuddled in behind his wife. 'It'll work out, hun.'

'Yuh. Thanks.' And an afterthought, 'Love you.'

'Love you too.'

That night, Loraine Warren, who was staying with her sister in Torksey, walked to the gate to put the milk bottles out. She looked up at the night sky and happened to see a falling star.

'Hmm.'

She was observing the interconnectedness of all things, knowing that the light from the stars had taken an infinite time to reach her eyes. Also she knew that a 'falling star' was really just a meteorite burning up as it traversed the atmosphere, acknowledging, nonetheless, the portent of an event yet to come.

Loraine, unapologetically fat and unapologetically not fit, puffed back up the front steps and into the living room where her brother-in-law, Arthur, sat bespectacled and reclined with his feet up, a *Scientific American* in his hands.

'A world leader's going to be shot tomorrow,' she announced, 'but he won't be killed.'

Arthur looked up, realising, after a few seconds staring into Loraine's face that this would probably be the case.

'Right,' he said, as if that was that.

Loraine nodded a little nod, as if that was also that. 'Well, goodnight then.'

'Goodnight.'

His eyes followed her out. He glanced down at his magazine, and then back to where she'd been standing.

Right.

It was 29 March 1981.

5

The day science begins to study non-physical phenomena; it will make more progress than all the previous centuries of existence.
Nikola Tesla (1856–1943)

Going about his own business and little more was what made up the foundations and pillars of Gamel Warriner's life. Anything that threatened to disrupt his easy rhythms and habits, he either didn't notice or he closed his mind to. He was not a cruel man, but he was insensitive, through simplicity of life and habit. He cared little and felt less. He was just like that. A day in his blinkered life was preferably never an exception to any other. Every moment followed the previous one through however many hours the day sent, through weeks and seasons, moons and harvests, each year bringing him nearer his mortal limit. It was the way of things, and he conformed to this without even considering his conformity a deliberate act. It was the way of things and that was as sure a thing as there could be.

There were two things though that daily threatened Gamel's footing – his wife, and his youngest son. To Gamel, most people were more or less the same as each other. He preferred it that way. Trees and the like, which he knew and understood well, they were different. They had variations in the qualities of their wood and thus the uses to which they could be put. Rock and stone were likewise. Seasons were different, and parts of seasons, and these ruled Gamel's life more than most things. But not people. People were the same, they were predictable, and mostly they went about their business the same as he, each one knowing his part and path. For his own part, Gamel knew people expected certain things of him; they knew him to be law-abiding and hard-working, and they knew if they passed him by on the road, he would tip his hat and nod a *Mornin'*, not so much as a courtesy, but not just as a thing that must be done either. If some neighbour needed help to haul a log, or shift some beast dropped from lameness or disease, then they knew, and Gamel knew, that he could be relied on for aid, with no expectation of favour or such recompense of the small kind as may be afforded or occasionally offered. Daily life required attention to cooperative engagement with those living near. This was not an act of affection or friendship on Gamel's part. Nor though was he unfriendly or cold. Survival relied on the flexible and committed operation and unfolding of this kind of mutual dependency. It was natural.

There had been a time when his exchange with others was less perfunctory. As a youth, he had the same boisterous vitality of his sons; and although brief, his courtship of the young girl Alice provided an excitement, an impulse to dream and a thirst for something more; accepting all along that such an attitude was not to be entertained for long.

Gamel's view was not black and white. On the contrary, it was full of colour, natural colour. Alice and Thomas were not natural though. They did not fit comfortably into the spectacle of Gamel's world. They demanded nothing of him, but their presence was ill-fitting in his otherwise predictable, unvarying existence, and it tugged on some part of him, in a way he could not fathom. Of course he loved them, after a fashion, as he imagined all men did their wives and children – which is to say, it was assumed and unspoken. It did not require imagination or consideration. Largely it carried just the daily responsibility to feed and shelter those in one's care.

Gamel knew his wife to be deeply religious. He himself understood and accepted with little thought the structure of the Church's rule and laws in his life, as did most people. But this invoked no more sensibility in him than some vague foreboding. His obligations in this regard inhabited the conventional framework of his existence, where God and the elements were due equal attention in the matter of living and in the business of husbanding animals and crops. More than the extent of her piety though, which alone seemed more elevated than he could comprehend, Gamel's wife displayed a grace and dignity that seemed all but to raise her to the plane of the Virgin, and far from engendering pride, it created a fear in her husband, a disquiet that this was an unholy contrivance, perilously disagreeable to the Church. As well, a cowardly misgiving tormented Gamel, and provoked an awareness of his own oafishness, next to the finer person of his wife, that he would sooner not scrutinise. The idea of intellect or scholarliness was nowhere near Gamel's thoughts, neither was his own lack of such, nor even of any education at all, since no one of their class had any such thing. Nor was he an idiot such as his son, nor unenlightened in his awareness of the elements and their role in his life, and his role in theirs. But he was uncivilised and his view of the world did not go deep.

Gamel would not have said he was embarrassed by the ubiquitous presence of the idiot boy, not as he knew some men might be who felt their maleness established in the world by the birth of only strong sons. Nor was he so blighted by any oppressive manipulation of Godly intent as to think the boy represented a chastisement for unknown wickedness. If he thought about it at all, which he did not, then he may consider the boy a challenge from God to rise to some height of communion with Him. But the possibility of any such consideration lay, if it existed at all, buried in some dank cellar of his being at the bottom of steep dark steps at the end of a passageway his mind never negotiated.

The pressure this woman and boy unwittingly and unintentionally applied to his being caused Gamel to resent them. Whereas he knew somehow that he should exert a greater regard for them, and because this task was instead so mountainous as to seem beyond him and so out of the usual as to be unrealisable, instead he daily pushed them from his thoughts and from the agenda of his obligations. Because of the increasing force with which he barred thought of them from the closed door of his mind, over many years, he felt the crushing insistence of their knocking as a fearful darkening of the corridors of his mind and soul, through which the ordinary meaning and clarity of life's purpose had hitherto flowed. His consciousness responded though with an even greater reliance on structure and defined boundaries.

Gamel's one concession to his seventh son was to roughly but silently protect him – to the extent he could – from danger, and from the cruelty of others. If the boy needed more kindness than this protection, Gamel knew that sufficient of this came from the child's mother, and he left it at that.

Gamel's natural inclination was towards a monofocus, a blinkered view. So when the earthquake struck Torksey and Lincoln and their surrounds the picture immediately before Gamel held just the faces of his wife and sons and he single-mindedly pursued that vision to secure his family whole.

Halting his cart that day outside the rock wall that partly enclosed his tiny stone and thatched hut, his wide shoulders had sunk perceptibly in relief as the sight of the unfallen structure presented itself exactly as it had when he'd left it a few hours before. He'd known already that the fearsome spectacle his sons had witnessed was receding, and relief likewise registered on their faces.

Alice had heard the wooden wheels of the cart coming near that afternoon, had let out a small cry of gratitude, and crossed herself as she'd gone to greet this other half of her family; little passed between husband and wife. Alice had asked of the state of the village, to which her husband had simply responded, ''Tis hard t'know, Mistress, 'tis hard to know', thinking himself of the spectacle of the swan, now much more distant in his memory than just the morning ago. Alice knew she would hear little more. She'd lifted her youngest from the cart, half cradling him, although knowing he was the least affected, if at all, by this unnerving episode. She'd seen instantly the terror that had passed through the boys that day and knew the task to soothe and placate them was hers.

In the late evening quiet she sat beside each of them as they slept and prayed for the darkness to pass from them. She placed a hand on each in turn – on a shoulder or chest or head – and closing her eyes, appealed to the Spirit that lighted all things to fill them with His tender grace. She made herself a willing conduit for the spirit-light to melt into her and then through her into these young men and boys.

She had no mind to hurry. Things took time as warranted. She may have sat a minute or an hour with each lad and not known either way the time past. This was her time where she was alone with God, able to fulfil her part to bring these souls to God and ensure their strength, and their safety in Heaven.

She did not view her ability to transmit the Light as an art or skill on her part, more as a consequence and reward for her own piety and diligence in keeping faith in every moment, for it was in *every* moment she had long since understood she must dwell with the Power, and she felt a favour assist her to do so. Alice knew that Light dwelt in all things, some things more and some things less.

It was not a magic or an illusion or a madness that Alice could see it, but it was as though a secret, and it would have been ill-wise to speak or share it, as the Church held more superstition than the ancient fire-stories of elv'ish doings and fairy folk.

When she came to her husband though, asleep as he was, meaning to take some of the darkness from him likewise, she found she could not touch him, and she felt his darkness push aside the promise of the Light, like a repelling magnet, and she had no power herself to contend with this.

So it was that Alice's boys grew lighter from this outpouring of Energy, but Gamel Warriner was left with his darkness and with no escape from it.

Two days had passed since Gamel had returned to his home from Torksey, and there being no apparent reason to do otherwise, the family had continued their customary daily toil. Nothing was said of the terrifying quake and little was heard of it either, save snippets of prattle and idle talk, the beginnings perhaps of malice to come.

The weather was unseasonably warm and still and hinted at more stirrings from the ground, although no more came by then.

On that Wednesday morning, as the Warriners tended their holding, a galloping rider drew up near where Gamel worked with some of his boys, and leapt from his mount. Gamel emerged through scrub, a hefty log balanced comfortably on his shoulder. Seeing the rider, he let the front end of the log slide gently forward and down, to make a quiet thud on the hardened mud. Thomas, sitting on the ground nearby, blinked. The rider was Gerard Archer, a young man of the age of Geoffrey Warriner, a villager of Torksey and well known to the Warriners. Gerard Archer brushed dust from his shoulders, and the front of his tunic, and slapped his cloth hat on the side of his leg before placing it back atop his head.

'Mr Warriner, Mrs Warriner,' tipping his hat deferentially, an almost nod to some of his boyhood friends standing there, inquisitive as to Gerard's visit following the quake, and curious for news.

'Gerard,' Gamel acknowledged, an arm akimbo, the log leaning against him.

'Ah, Master Warriner. Thar's ben qouit' a catastrophe, sir, a' Lincoln. Almost whole a' cathedral's fall'n, from the shakin'.' The attention of Gamel and Alice Warriner there in that small yard heightened, and their eyes waited on the messenger.

'I's a soight to see, sir. Most of it rubble. An' more 'n a handful a' folks under i' all. An' there's more's collapsed in village an' all. I's hard t'see, Mr Warriner, 'tis.'

'I's a tragedy to be sure, young Gerard. I thank ye for comin' to tell uz this. What other news then?'

'I's all a tangle, sir. Is family missin' from most and no knowin' how some'll get by. Some wells is cracked jus' t'add t'troubles. Mos' men are ou' cuttin' wood an' stone already, t'fix wha's broke. Lot a' work t'be comin' t'all of us. Lot a' families needin' help. 'Ard times my mam's sayin', 'ard times.'

'Yer've come far t'tell uz this, young Gerard,' Gamel said.

'Aye. 'N 'fraid I di'n jus' come to tell ye this, sir. There's more I've been sent t'tell ya, sir. There be a call for builders 'n' masons, 'n' Father Taylor's sendin' me all o'er t'ask fer 'elp, fer some a' yer boys, sir. 'Specially Gree 'e's said, t'be goin' t'city t' be rebuildin' i'. There's call fer 'undreds from roundabout.'

Gamel was silent, watching the bearer of this news. Young Gerard, anxious at the big man's response, avoided looking into his face now that his news and mission was told. Alice had stood from her shady position a short distance away and walked nearer. There hadn't been much thought of the effects elsewhere of the quake, and she was shocked now to hear of such destruction and sadness. Registering an order to send some of her own away was puzzling her now, and she wondered if perhaps she'd properly heard what their visitor had declared.

Dem Warriner, working a soil row at a garden to one side, stopped his hoeing and looked from his father to his friend to his mother and back again, unsure of the announcements that he'd heard. Was there to be more that would upset the day-to-day of his existence?

Husband and wife felt a burden slowly descend from this request; increasing in itself the longer they stared at its bearer. Men spent lifetimes engaged in such construction and a son that went to aid this undertaking could just as likely be killed in a fall from some great height or else anyway never return at all, and the loss of any workers from a household, especially strong grown sons, meant an increase in others' work. Gamel was lucky to have so many strong sons, and although not afraid of hard work, he nonetheless could foresee a struggle ahead with the absence of any of them. To say nothing of the distance to Lincoln, a journey he himself had only ever made twice in his whole life. Any inkling of a daydream he might have remaining from his own youth that saw for his sons a different life from this drudgery was an absurdity he did not consider. But to commit one to never return, to be tied the rest of his days to an existence completely unknown to himself and others like him, for this he was afraid. For this there was not a ready answer or reaction.

'Father Taylor y'say?'

'Aye, sir.'

'An' y'been goin' all o'er tellin' this?'

'Aye, sir.'

'An' i's for buildin' and carvin', y'say?' Monotone responses from a man taking his time to ponder something bigger than himself.

'Aye, sir.'

Not another boy knew to speak for the moment, nor even move, such was the energy pending in their father.

A long wait among all. ''Ow many a' my boys wanted then?'

'Well, i's Gree, as everyone knows is carver, Mr Warriner. But i's muscle as much thar wantin' I 'spect too, sir.'

''E's no' carver. Jus' a bit a' whittlin' e's good fer. I's nuthin'.'

'Aye', avoiding the gaze still. 'Jus' same, sir, i's Gree 'as been mention boi Father, an' i' be that you go' seven boys as everyone knows, Master.'

'Six boys I go', young Gerard Archer. Six.'

'Aye, sir. Six. Course.' Gerard glanced to the strange creature most everyone looked away from and saw that he was smiling for no reason and apparently at nothing. It gave Gerard an eerie feeling and he looked away, hoping none detected this in him.

Thomas sat cross-legged on the ground at his mother's feet, closely examining a small collection of pebbles, which he then lined up very precisely in a straight line, each pebble just touching on its neighbour. This was something he did much of the time. Occasionally, he halted to stare at nothing and no one.

Efforts advanced from within the Nothingness about him, to apply another sort of pressure to the little boy, and it drew his attention, after a fashion.

'So, 'ow many's want'd by Friar then? Is thar' a number y'been bound t'give t' me, Gerard?'

'Aye, 'i's three, sir.'

'Ow' many?!'

'Three 'tis, Master Warriner, sorry.'

Gamel knew there was no recoiling from this demand, the Church standing as it did at the pinnacle of law and order. Neither though could he have expected as exacting a bid as this. Each for their own reasons, Gamel and Alice fought against unfamiliar and hostile inclinations in that moment; Gamel to refuse, Alice to bid her husband refuse, both impossible.

'Three! Three!' An inability to accommodate his internal uproar and silent remonstrations with the Church rooted Gamel Warriner to the earth. He had no argument with the Church. His obligations were as plain as solid engraving on walls, rutted into his brain, and encompassing at once this small house, his wife and sons, and delineating his immediate duties. With this decree a wall was breached, and unable to defend his keep from the particular adversary Gamel felt beaten, and this did not sit well.

Alice's suffering from the loss of children, one after another, had never diminished, and she felt again an unbearable ache from one shoulder to the other and down to her belly. The weight in her chest pushed her down on to the earth just as she'd risen a moment earlier. She scanned her sons thereabouts, one older one and two younger, and Thomas, not even counted as a son to his father apparently, but of course she knew this at heart. It would be her eldest boys, of course, who would go to Lincoln, so far away. Already she prayed for their safe keeping. Simultaneously, she reproached herself for her selfish nature. There was nothing so great as service to the Lord, and to build a Church! My word, but that was a noble undertaking, surely.

Gerard stirred restlessly. 'Oi'll be on to next farm then, sir. Father's wantin' t'see lads off quick. Reckon 'e's feelin' obliged t'Bishop 'n' all. Oi'll be tellin' 'im then, will oi? Tha' Gree 'n' them'll be on way for 'im, t'Lincoln 'n' all?'

A chasm of inevitability filled a long pause. Gerard Archer stood in his own disquiet, wondering if he may endure a lion's roar or a bear's from the big man before him. Gerard knew that the division of a family in this way was no comfort to any father, although as a young man he thought it an adventure to go to the city and indeed hoped to go himself, although he was only one son in his family and thought his own father would most likely be allowed to object to such.

'Aye,' slowly, 'you be tellin' 'im then.' Gamel was stern, staring the young man back to his mount.

Gerard Archer thought better of showing the recognition he had of the despair across Gamel Warriner's face. He made a barely audible acknowledgement towards Gamel and Alice and strode quickly to his horse, leapt on, and gee'd the animal away as fast as he'd come. A cloud of yellowy brown dust inflamed the air, dissipating slowly as the Warriners looked in the direction of Gerard's trail.

Still no Warriner moved; parents weighted as they were. And the boys there, noting that anchor, knew it was not theirs to make the first movement or word, excepting to look cautiously towards each other and then away. Alice likewise waited for her husband to speak. Thomas cocked his head to one side and back again, as if he too was waiting for someone to say something, but this was simply coincidence.

'Dem!' Gamel called around gruffly to his second eldest boy. The small explosion of his name put the boy on alert. 'Go 'n' get yer brothers!'

Dem Warriner put aside the hoe he'd leant on the last few minutes and hurried away to the fields where he knew Gree and Thurston were repairing a stone wall shaken down in parts two days prior. Dem knew this injunction from the Friary implied some prospect of adventure, unheard of to him or his brothers, and he was scarcely able to control his eagerness as he bolted away.

When his eldest sons returned, Gamel knew Dem would have told them of their 'good fortune' as they would no doubt view the arrangement. But he didn't care for their adventure. He had shooed his younger boys away and stood just as he had when he'd listened a few minutes ago to the Friar's young emissary.

'Yer to go t'Lincoln, to cathedral, to work.' He told in a loud and dismissive tone. 'Friar's bid ya' go 'n' tha's as it'll be. So ya' can gor now,' looking round to challenge any alternative expectation, and seeing some of the elation subside. 'Nothin' for i'. You won' be needin' anythin', so bes' ya' star' out. So orf ya' gor then.' He didn't so much look at his sons now as his eyes lit on parts of them and the air around them.

The boys stared open-mouthed and unbelieving at their father, stupefied by this apparent urgency with which they were to take their leave of their family and their home. The news from Lincoln, of death and the Cathedral, had passed by them in their anticipation of an adventure, but now some more unrest returned with this abrupt announcement. They glanced to their mother who'd stood again, also manifestly taken unaware by the suddenness of her husband's dismissal of three sons from their home, desperate to seize hold of them now, desperate to wonder aloud to her husband. She had no reason to fear him but still she would not challenge him. No righteous woman would.

'Per'aps . .. ,' Gree braved, the excitement gone out of him. He was assuming he and his brothers would collect a few meagre things, some bread and water for their journey.

'Ye'll go now!' boomed Gamel, the ground threatening to shake anew.

And with this different kind of an earth-shattering announcement, time stopped for this one peasant family. It was not a comfortable moment in time, but oddly, it was the juncture of the Warriners' greatest unity, and even concord. The anguish they felt – all except Thomas – at their powerlessness, at their parting, at the boundary-slicing necessity of their father's temperament, inflated around each of them as a bubble, a blister of blackness, until each dark orb collided with the next and the family existed momentarily inside their own tiny, isolated planet of suffering. And with this, each one – father, mother, and sons – acknowledged what he owed the other, a sad litany of duty, loyalty, respect and love, and above all of unquestioned submission to providence. Momentarily they were whole, a unique and intimate grouping of humans who depended on each other. In that space, all the forces, pressures, potential and Energy of their lives, that pushed and pulled them, that dictated their direction, their orientation, and their bias, all these forces now dwelt momentarily and forcefully in the space they occupied together, and each of them felt its invisible density.

The material of them united with the emotional of them, and there was no gap between these, uniting all the forces of all the particles that moved their bodies and moved their spirits, creating a unity none understood.

As this act of Nature failed to be defined, so too were the Warriners' unable to keep alive their meagre nexus. As the grief of their attachment threatened one simple man beyond his endurance, he turned his back to his sons, rupturing the unified darkness that held them. He walked to his wife and the idiot child and bid the woman gather him up and go inside, and then he followed her and whipped a sack curtain across behind them. Not a look. Not a reassurance. They were riven, as the split of an axe, as an army breached in two and destined for a certainty of death.

Shock wave upon shock wave settled on each boy's being and registered on their faces, the more on young Thurston, just fourteen and only recently allowed to take the Monday cart ride to

Torksey's market with his elder brothers. A moment ago the three had come running from the fields whooping and yelling, bounding walls and stiles, full of questions for their elder brother who'd once already voyaged to the massive walled port at Lincoln. That frenzy stuck in their throats now like a delirium, confused and knocked over.

Geoffrey put his hand to his younger brother's shoulder and steered him away.

'Bu' we can't, Gree. Iz madness. Wo' 'bout Ma? We can't gor without a kiss. Gree? Gree?' he pleaded.

'This is the way 'tis with him. We have t'go now. It's what's needed,' pleading back at his brother, but commandingly.

Thurston's tortured face beseeched his eldest brother even though he allowed himself to be tugged gently away to the road.

How could they be going? How could they be going like *this*? How was it so?

Although Geoffrey's eyes were cast down to the ground, he kept his firm embrace about his young brother's shoulders. What they had come to rely on was no longer. In its place was a new reliance, on himself and his authority and power to keep intact and unassailed this small company of youths. This new exigency seared into him and he knew that some position as this had been ordained and fixed in his birthright, and he assumed it now as a load, with all the obligation and guilt that implied. He no longer had a father or mother. He eschewed their place in the narrow vista of his world view, erasing them as if from a sketch.

'C'mon, Dem. There's a long walk to take. There's hope I s'pose we'll sleep over friary tonight 'n' take to cathedral tomorra'.'

'We've no water anythin' to sup on way, Gree.' Dem's fear and surprise was still apparent in his voice and face.

'Nothin' for it, Dem, as to keep movin' now. We'll manage.' He could see his brothers already finding purchase for their souls with their eldest brother's reassurance.

'D'ya think this is doin' of dead swan, Gree? Is anybody'd say t'were, all earth rumblin's and what-no'. 'S'got be some't in i', don' ya think, Gree?' 'S'no' roight we're a-goin' off loi' this, is i'? 'S loik i's forever an' no way art'iv i'. Whoi, Gree, whoi?'

But Gree couldn't explain to his brother, even if he'd had words to do it. He felt that some shadowy force unknown had crashed into their lives and turned things on their end. He had only one training in his life, only one way to respond, which was to go as directed and without query, because query anyway did not draw much breath in their world.

As the boys traipsed on to the thin road, turning towards the town, Geoffrey took his arm from his brother's shoulder and trod on, walking between his brothers, ready to place a reassuring arm about them again if there was need. It was for certain there would be.

Inside their small house, Gamel Warriner had sat down in a large chair by his hearth and stayed there staring into the ashes. He had few choices with which he could assert control of his own life and had been forced to exercise one of those now, or so he thought best, to make clear quickly and definitively the way things were to be. If a direction and rule were to be set, then best he have a part in it and make it his own. That at least would secure him some place of certainty and strength in his own existence.

Alice sat Thomas inside a padded wooden enclosure, away from his father. She'd had her husband and sons build this to keep Thomas in when she didn't feel she could always watch him. He was happy here, as though the close walls of its surrounds gave him a particular warmth and security. Old cloth was knotted around wooden slats to prevent Thomas from harming himself when he came to bang his head repeatedly as he did some evenings. Was he tired at the end of the day to make him hurt himself, or was it the noise of so many that somehow provoked him? Alice didn't know, but she wouldn't have him bruised, nor would she tie him up to prevent it either, as some had told her she should.

She searched her small house, its divisions and its corners, for any menial task to which she could apply herself with force and dedication, if just to slow a pain capable of slicing her in pieces from overtaking her ability to act or speak, not least since to speak, to speak *up*, was not a right available to her. Spying a long brush, she began an earnest motion to and fro that may ultimately have promised to clear the floor clean away, and she remained at this activity till the dust and the day's heat forced her back out to the air outside, where only a short time since her reality had been less dark than she found it now.

When laughter came from a small way away to her ears, a slim and tenuous ray of light briefly showed itself in her soul before fluttering away as if a mirage all along. But her three younger boys appearing – Alard, David, and Michael – did though take her thoughts away from her eldest boys, all but dead to her as she knew they may soon be, as she meted out chores and left the telling of their brothers' going from them for at least a while longer, till she could bear it even just slightly more.

It was in this way that she survived the loss now of eight children. For it wasn't just the three boys just gone that anguished her want to live in joy, but the five infants long gone now redoubled their memories to her. And her living boys just departed all became babes again, and Alice wondered where these many wee darlings had gone. The pain in her chest caused her to hunch her shoulders a little to cope, but she paid her heartbreak little mind since there was no point to do so and cause it to be an obstacle in an already harsh life. It was a large burden, but then burdens were God's and life's way. She would bear it; she was strong enough to do so, and not let their faces sneak into her mind's eye or the memories of their laughter to her ears. If her heart broke ... well, it was her soul that mattered more. Without her thinking so much though, Alice's being began to focus more upon her youngest child.

Her husband's way was to rise up each day from the corner where he slept, work himself and his younger boys in the fields and garden – herding, hoeing, mending, and building, till these younger boys too knew that their position was changed and they were now men.

Thomas though, unaffected by the storm that had blown through his family, held even less attention from his parents or brothers than usual. There was no reason to notice whether he had suffered or changed in any way following the tempest, and so, ergo, no one did.

A little while later, Thomas sat with his mother outside as she sewed and repaired some much-worn garments. Alice put her attention to her finger work to keep all else from her mind. Thomas picked up his stones and held them in his hands, feeling their roughness or smoothness in his palms. He wondered what they would like to do this day. He thought he would prefer to do as they wished. A most insistent but narrow beam of light, barely a whisper, reached out a cobweb-delicate tendril into Thomas's tiny realm, and with this merest suggestion Thomas touched upon a message of hope. He recognised anew the reflection of another just like himself, and from this he understood how to become more like himself than he already was. It was like an equation of the light, multiplying itself to create a mirror image and then adding light upon light through different layers of being to create a new reality, which was always there anyway if one was able to see it, and Thomas was.

Alice looked down at her son on the ground by her feet and noticed that instead of his usual straight-as-an-arrow line, Thomas had arranged a group of pebbles in a nose-to-nose perfect circle. For just a moment this struck Alice as something a little bit magical, and a new hope wafted briefly through her heart.

And what is happening in your small piece of heaven and earth, my son?

Thomas looked up at the reflection he'd noticed – his new friend – and blinked in the sunlight. They were playing a game now, he and the light, and each would try to be the first, but helping each other to be first also. Thomas was very pleased with the new game.

Is there more that you know, my love, than we would think? Perhaps there is more that you can be, for your father and brothers.

'Thomas?' Alice cooed quietly to her son. 'Thomas?'

Thomas looked around to his mother and smiled, and it seemed to Alice that she was most fortunate to have such a sweet child and she thought she would pay more attention than usual to his soul.

What do you peer out at through that mop of curly hair, Thomas? Are there Angels about you? Caring for you? I do hope so, my lovely. I do hope so.

Alice sat down on the dusty ground beside her son, putting her arm around him. Thomas looked back at the space in the light just above him, and Alice stared with him, asking that if God were nearby, to watch over this one of her children. And some other presence warmed her, and a little thread weaved a small part of her broken heart together.

Thank you, Lord..

6

Those who have passed on through death,
have a sphere of their own. It is not removed from ours;
but it is sanctified from time and place.
'Abdu'l-Bahá (1844–1921)

Timothy Watson was not the child his parents imagined,
nor indeed anyone. He was really very different.

He was also lucky. He did not have to feel pain in his life,
and the love that was his particular birthright helped him connect
to the world of Light, and to a world of detailed imagery that other
people did not see. This was not so uncommon for children that
were born as Tim was, although Tim had particular assets and
friends that even others like him did not. Being able to see the light
and the space between things and the patterns in the spaces – these,
many could see. Tim's light spoke to him, and further, the rock in
his life, which was his father, unwittingly strengthened his
confidence in who Tim was and what he may be capable of.

Not only did Tim receive light but sometimes when he
became white enough with the light himself, he was able to reflect
it back at his surroundings, like a pure white wall that reflected light
but did not absorb it. Tim as yet had no comprehension of this
ability, but in this way he could change things in his surroundings –
little things that no one noticed, like making people happy. Tim
could do that in the same way the light made him happy. People
around him would think themselves delighted because he was a
joyful soul and something beautiful and innocent to watch and
even to feel blessed by. They would go away feeling they had made
a special connection with a poor wee boy who had not much life to
expect for himself, and they would condescend to imagine they had
provided some mature, charitable, and useful support to his poor

parents. They satisfied themselves they were not so cruel as others or ignorant, but knowing all the while – not so deep within themselves – that they could not have coped with a child such as this. Indeed, that they would have been embarrassed if people knew they had a child like Tim. And all the while they believed it was they who brought some light into the child's day, not the opposite.

They also thought that inside little Timmy's head there was nothing much at all.

'Jesus, Pete. You're here all bloody day! It's not that hard to fold the fucking washing, is it?! It's not like I can come through the door and not notice this bloody great mountain, y'know. Does it not bother you? Can you not see it?'

Pete was hammered into unavoidable silence.

'Oh, fuck it! I suppose I'll just do it my bloody self then!'

Searching hopelessly for an opportunity to redeem not himself but the situation – since he was of the view that the presence of a mountain of unfolded washing did not warrant a barrage of this proportion – Pete sought to create some opportunity for Alicia to retreat from her attack position and recreate some common ground between them.

At this point though they succeeded only in widening their no-man's-land as Alicia inwardly fumed at what she took as Pete's refusal to rise to any admission of accountability with regard to washing – or any fundamental of housework – and Pete remained silent, bereft in fact of possible solutions or ameliorative response.

Alicia had arrived home a minute before. Jillie had come out from the living room where she was playing with Tim, and hugged and greeted her mother before returning to her play. Proceeding into their large kitchen and family space at the rear of the house, Alicia found Pete studying the evening newspaper with both the radio and the television news going. Pete was pleased to see his wife. He'd felt a momentary joy even at the sound of the front door opening, but as he tracked Alicia's journey up the hallway, bit by bit he felt that sense recede, first with the rapid internal judgement of the quality of Alicia's response to Jillie, then the fact that she did not call out her arrival, which would have been usual. By the time the washing pile monologue was launched he found himself contemplating some murky descent that had been sailing into his consciousness increasingly regularly.

'Aargh!' cried Alicia, part-way into her mountain rescue. 'I'm having a bath,' and she stormed out.

Pete folded his paper, considered the most germane alternatives, and rose to set about preparing a meal. He retrieved fresh vegetables from the refrigerator and set a pot of rice to boil, taking also a cardboard wine cask from the fridge and pouring two glasses of Chateau something-or-other.

When Alicia returned shortly after to sit at a kitchen bar stool, Pete took this as the extent of any attempt she was going to make to reconnect, and simultaneously congratulated himself on his ability to let sleeping dogs lie.

'How was your day?' he asked.

Alicia looked down into her wine glass and twiddled the stem.

'Oh, I don't know. All right, I suppose. I'm fucking bored. The fun stuff's all happening elsewhere, without *me*.'

'Aha,' said Pete, continuing with dinner-making.

Alicia sipped more than a sip from her glass and returned it to the bench with a that-hit-the-spot sigh. She looked up at Pete.

'Sorry.'

'It's okay.' Pete smiled back briefly. 'So tell me more.'

'Well, the French experiments are exciting, but no one in the department could care less. Except Dryden that is. Maybe. He's probably only trying to be nice. Humouring me like a good H-O-D should I suppose.'

'Tell me about the experiments,' asked Pete.

'You wouldn't be interested,' said Alicia.

'I might be.'

Alice looked up from her glass for the first time and watched as Pete poured diced vegetables from a chopping board into a waiting fry pan.

'Rice and veges again?' She asked.

'You got a problem with that?'

Alicia took a deep breath. 'What the Paris group say they've found is that particle A can communicate with particle B, even if they're a million miles apart, but they have to have previously been in the same location at some point.'

'And this means ...?' Pete asked.

'The possibility of bending time,' Alicia responded.

'Bending time?' Pete repeated.

Alicia explained, 'It's always been held that you can't move faster than the speed of light, and if A can influence B across a million miles, then that theory is undermined.'

'And the implications are?'

'The implications', replied Alicia, 'are far too new-agey for most physicists to cope with, but for a believer – or a lunatic if you prefer – the implications are that you can influence the outcome of events on the other side of the world, or be influenced by them, with only so much as a thought. And secondly, which is even weirder, you can influence events in a different time period.'

Pete stopped stirring the vegetables to look up at Alicia..

'Really?'

'In theory,' Alicia replied.

'Cool!'

Alicia laughed a little. 'It's theory, okay. Just theory.'

'That's fun theory though. Anyway, what do *you* think? Do you think that's possible?' Pete asked.

'From the context of my particularly conservative work environment, I couldn't possibly say.'

'Coward.'

'Oh, come on. Be realistic,' Alicia fired back at Pete.

'About what,' Pete responded, 'the implications of the theory or your work environment?'

'Well, both. It's hard work being a natural born genius when you're surrounded by plonkers.'

It was Pete's turn to laugh. 'So what are you going to do? You could go and join them, y'know.'

'Don't be ridiculous.'

'I'm not.'

'Look, I don't have the right experience,' Alicia tried to explain.

'Well, get it then,' Pete replied simply.

'It's not so simple as that.'

'What would it take?'

'Another PhD maybe. Moving my research agenda, which is something I can't do as long as I'm here. It's a rock and a hard place.'

'All I'm saying is you should think about what you really want, what the path is to get there, and let's see what may or may not be possible. You can't spend the rest of your career being miserable.'

Alicia was silent and poured a mopey look into the bottom of her glass.

'Tired?' Pete asked.

'Exhausted,' Alicia replied sullenly. 'But I have no idea why though. I'm not sleeping so well.'

'I've noticed. Knowing you, you're probably thinking too much. I can practically hear the cogs turning some nights. You need to stop that.'

'I get paid to think, dummy.' Alicia managed a minute smile. 'And what do you mean you can *hear* me think, idiot?' Managed a bigger smile.

'It's palpable. Honestly, it keeps me awake sometimes. And you're not being paid at night when you're in bed with your husband. And you're not supposed to be thinking at that time anyway. You need to sleep, or at least give your intellect over to far more physical matters such as your husband's unfulfilled libido,' Pete teased.

'You complaining?'

'Yep.'

'Piss off.'

'Sigh.' Pete smiled woefully at his wife.

'How was your day then?' Alicia asked.

'Well, *I* have my own interesting story from the other side of the quantum actually,' Pete responded.

'What's that?'

'You know, when I went up to the Cathedral the other day and I met that deaconess, Rose, and we got chatting. She'd noticed something about Tim. Anyway, she invited me to this discussion group. It's this Thursday night. They talk about 'how do we know', or 'what can we know', that kind of thing. A sort of exploration into the mysteries of the universe is the impression I got.'

'Sounds a bit scary. Are you going?'

'Don't know. What do you think?' Pete asked.

'Sounds like you're dabbling again.'

Pete looked up. 'What's that mean?'

'Well, you know, you dabble. Fiddle with a car here. Write half an article for a newspaper there.'

'That's not fair,' Pete showed some sense of minor offence.

'Well, it's accurate at least. You don't have any direction. You never have had,' Alicia asserted.

'Oh, c'mon, I'm looking after our kids while you work. I don't get a lot of spare time – when I do, well, there's a few things I like doing – cars and newspaper articles being two of the few.'

'Well, you're not always going to stay home and look after the kids, are you? I mean, what about having some real work one day.'

'Bloody hell, Alicia. Where are you coming from? Looking after the kids *is* real work, and having Tim's not going to make it easy for both of us to work. Ever. I don't think.'

'I guess,' Alicia replied, looking prepared to swallow her words.

Pete threw unused food items back into the refrigerator, half slamming the door and set himself stirring vegetables on the stove.

'Well, it's just an evening out anyway,' he said.

'Hmm.' Alicia's focus was at the bottom of her wine glass again.

Pete noticed and lifted the carton over the glass, filling it.

'Cheers,' she said, and took a mouthful.

Silence held sway until Pete started to serve rice and vegetables on to plates. Alicia rallied herself to set a table.

'Jillie,' Pete called out. 'Can you wash your hands and bring Timmy into dinner, please?'

'I do forget the nature of the daily grind, I know,' Alicia said quietly in Pete's direction. 'Sorry.'

'You have adults to talk to during the day, even if you don't like most of them. It's a weird existence for me not to have any of that. Or very little anyway,' Pete said.

'Yep. I do get that.'

'Writing's a way for me to connect with Planet Grown-up.'

'And you write well. I know I should be more supportive. I'm sorry. And I do really hope you get something published that gets you the recognition you deserve. You must miss all the buzz of the newsroom,' Alicia proffered.

'Parts of it. Not the panic though, I can tell you that. It's nice that things operate at a different pace at home, that's for sure,' Pete said.

Just then the couple's children wandered in, taking their usual places at the dining table.

'I'm *starving*!' Jillie said.

'Well, I've got just the thing then,' responded her father, as he served up portions.

'Yummy! Rice and veges. *My favourite!*' Jillie exclaimed.

Pete smirked at his wife as if to say *well, at least someone appreciates my cooking.*

Alicia smirked back good-naturedly as they sat down with their children.

'Welcome, Pete! I'm so pleased you've come.' Rose Draper opened the door to her cottage in Lincoln's hill suburb, with what Pete assumed was probably her usual bouncy exuberance. Energetic chatter and stray laughter were leaking into the hallway from somewhere or other.

'Sorry, I'm late. Getting kids into bed and all that,' Pete said, proffering a dark bottle to his host as she gestured him inside. He wasn't quite sure if it would be the right choice, but he'd thought from Rose's personality that this red would probably be a goer.

'Oh no, I understand, that's fine. Lovely you're here. Come on in,' Rose responded.

Rose was no longer the cassocked chaplain from the weekend earlier, but a rotund and bright red be-smocked and hippy'ish ball of gracious and energetic hospitality. Vibrancy and good humour shone out of her beaming round face.

Rose's hallway was a delight in long-settled domesticity, sans child clutter, with curios, travel photos, some half-decent art, and a few expensive-looking pieces, lined up along dark red and wooded walls, an oak dresser with linen doilies, and an overflowing bookshelf. Pete felt instantly comfortable.

He walked through to the voices, and Rose came through behind, steering him to a spare chair near the corner of a large table.

'Everyone, this is Pete,' Rose announced.

Faces turned with acknowledgement, and Rose's firm hand briefly to his shoulder as he sat down, told Pete again that he could feel secure in this company. He nodded and smiled around the table. A dozen or so smiles and nods bounced back as Rose introduced a bevy of names and one or two side conversations resumed politely.

'Hello, Pete, I'm Loraine,' came a confident robust voice, and a large hand extended from beside him. 'I live here too.'

'Hello, nice to meet you.' Pete decided he liked Loraine at least as much as Rose. People would call them jolly, he expected. *Jolly smart too,* he thought. He watched their interactions with folk and observed their generous and comfortable hospitality. He was surprised at his level of ease within what was ostensibly a religious context. Perhaps he just hadn't met the right Christians before.

Rose was setting a glass in front of Pete and indicating a choice of red or white. 'You remember, dear, I told you about the little boy in St Hugh's Choir the other day.'

'Yes, I do. Well, very lovely that you've come, Pete. Maitland over here is about to regale us with the latest scientific proofs of the efficacy of prayer,' Loraine added, seemingly a little cynical of this forthcoming dissertation herself.

A very English-looking man, older than Pete, reached a hand across the table in his direction.

'How do you do, Pete? I'm Maitland,' he said, and they shook hands. 'How on earth did you get yourself mixed up with these two old chaps? You'll never get away now, you know.'

'Oh, well, I'm not sure I want to.' Pete smiled back. 'Seems jolly good so far.'

'Ah, the young,' Maitland signed in mock exasperation at Loraine. 'They'll learn, I suppose.'

'Very funny, Maitland. Get on with it now, will you?' Loraine responded in equally mock annoyance back at her guest.

Pete was buoyed by these ribald responses, especially from a member of the clergy. He sipped his red and eyed the new speaker.

'Well, as you all know,' began Maitland, clearly enjoying holding forth and bringing all eyes to himself, 'I don't hold much to this kind of nonsense. It's not at all scientific in my view, but after last week's conversation, I said I'd look all this up, so here is my discourse, for what it's worth. Don't shoot though, I'm only the messenger.'

Laughs all round.

Maitland was a sixty-something, balding, quite distinguished man, and his pronouncement brought, along with its chorus of chuckles, accepting looks from around the table. Maitland's attire mirrored some typical caricature of his age and breeding: grey flannels, tweed jacket, oval leather patches at the elbows, and checked brushed cotton shirt. He looked like a television character from *To the Manor Born*.

'Well, the jury is out,' he continued. 'That is the final word. There have been studies that have demonstrated prayer has worked and studies that have shown it doesn't. They are almost all flawed in their methodology. Probably the most thorough was conducted by researchers at Harvard and it involved nearly 2,000 patients, divided into three equal groups who were told either that they'd not be prayed for, or that they would be prayed for, or that they may or may not be prayed for.' Maitland half rolled his eyes at this last statement. 'The prayers were offered by groups of strangers who had just the patient's first name and a last initial, and prayers started and ended at a set time. This study in fact demonstrated worse results in the patients who *were* prayed for. So ergo I think we can agree, prayer either does not work or, in my view, it cannot be studied by a bunch of scientists in a laboratory and decreed effective or otherwise. So that's that. Rather a short summation but I assure you I have covered the gamut of published and/or remotely valid research. And the summation is that it's a poor showing for prayer. Sorry.'

'Oh come on. That's ludicrous. Why not have people praying for people they know? Surely that's the realistic situation. Surely that would show some positive results?' This was from a woman Pete's age he thought had been introduced as Sally.

'Just reporting on the facts,' Maitland responded smugly.

'I agree. That's not intuitively correct,' said another man. 'And what about praying for oneself? Plenty of physicians have commented anecdotally on cures in patients with a positive mental attitude haven't they?'

'Well just the same, the research is not looking good for God, is it?' Loraine chortled.

Pete noted appreciatively that Loraine's faith surmounted need of scientific proof and a surfeit of academic disproof made no impression.

'Well, I don't think that's it at all, dearest,' a slight air of sarcasm from Maitland, meant to be noticed. 'It's not looking good for *scientists* is the thing. God is surely above all this. We cannot be so reductionist as that. This is my strongly held opinion. We cannot put God into a test tube and expect replicable results. He or She does not, after all, *fit* in one, at the very least.'

Some 'hear! hear!' and a clap or two. Pete was enjoying this.

'But Maitland, surely the thing we can make an impact on is the thing we know, the thing we've been in contact with. Wouldn't that make for a better result?' Sally continued. 'The person we know well and love – for example, our own child or parent. One of my children often verbalises something that's in my mind also at that same moment. Those are common experiences for all of us, I'm sure.'

Pete's mind shot to the Paris experiments that had excited Alice, and he wondered what she would think of his evening out now. He thought about mentioning them, but he wasn't sure if he could explain the whole thing articulately enough.

'But you don't see my point, Sally. Yes, perhaps that would make some difference, but what about the faith of the person praying, which is to say, their skill at prayer. Even if you did decide to add this variable into the experiment, how on earth could it be quantified? It can't! And then, for heaven's sake, how are we going to quantify the greatest variable of all – God? I mean this assumes God is a consistent variable. Or is God not a variable? Is there just the prayer and the prayee – no God? Well, I'm sorry, that's not what it's about in my book.'

'You're right. Yes, I see what you're saying,' mused Sally. 'So, these experiments are poor experiments then – they can't control for other variables – at the very least the particular *power* of the prayer, the faith of the prayee, and *God*, the greatest variable of all. So, then, it can't be measured.'

'No, not at all. *In my view,*' Maitland added. 'But I'm not a scientist, of course.'

Pete thought he'd have a go.

'Ah, y'know, my wife is a physicist ...'

'Really?' Maitland told. 'How wonderful!' He was quite sincere.

'. . .. yes, yes. Ah, well, just harking to Sally's comment. The idea of influencing what we know, what we've been in contact with – well, I'm not sure how this fits in, but it just strikes me that it does somehow. Alicia – that's my wife – mentioned the other evening about some experiments done in France just recently. Apparently they prove that particle A can influence particle B across space – *and* time actually – where A and B have previously been in contact with each other.'

Pete looked around seeing what reaction this had; a little nervous that perhaps he'd just killed the conversation. There was a bit of a pause and he couldn't tell if everyone was taking in what he'd said or thinking he was potty.

'That *is* really interesting,' Loraine said.

'It is *indeed*,' Maitland agreed.

'I just knew you were going to be a worthy addition, Pete. I just knew it!' Rose interjected.

Phew.

'In fact it's brilliant. Is it too ridiculous then to expand that to say that person A can impact on person B – someone they know – in a positive, or indeed a negative, way? It follows. Of course it's a huge assumption. But if you assume a connection of sorts – emotional, spiritual, call it what you will – then this theory says there is a possibility of influence. I love it.'

'I may have to go and pay your wife a visit, Pete. Pieces of a puzzle, eh! Very interesting. You must bring your wife along some time, although I don't imagine a bunch of religious loons would be taken at all seriously by a scientist, especially a physicist, but we would take *her* seriously, my boy – yes, indeed.'

'Oh, well. I'll mention it. I'm not sure really.' Pete felt of two minds about bringing Alicia along to something she may actually enjoy with him, and on the other hand keeping his new-found friends to himself.

As the discussion pressed on, Pete observed the ease with which participants addressed various items of spiritual and intellectual concern and interest, and could see that some were firm believers, one or two atheists, one or two agnostics or undecideds, and many just wanting to find some nexus between the material and the spiritual world.

'I agree with Loraine though. There must be care not to belittle God,' Maitland had continued.

'But I don't think that's what it's doing at all,' another woman had said. 'I think it's raising the value of science. All that's in our material world – all that exists as *science* – God created. Surely we raise science to the spiritual, not take the spiritual 'down' to a level of scientific proof. Surely there *are* these proofs, for want of a better description. It's just a matter of science finding them and catching up, so to speak.'

Pete liked this thought immensely. 'Oh, I think so,' he agreed. 'Yes, we should get it round the right way. Indeed.'

'Ah, but which way round would your dear wife put it, I wonder?' Maitland added.

'Well, I couldn't be sure actually,' Pete said, wondering himself as to Alicia's place in all this. 'I'm not sure she'd use these words herself, but I think she has a view of the physical world that has a powerful underpinning that she herself would like to understand. I don't think she'd use the word *spiritual*, but I don't know what she'd use instead either. I don't think she knows herself.'

'Albert Einstein said that all religions, arts, and sciences are branches of the same tree,' Maitland continued.

'He also said he was a deeply religious non-believer,' added Loraine.

'Oh, I like that.' Maitland smiled. 'Now Pete, about your dear wife ...'

Maitland engaged Pete in a side conversation as others similarly rose about the table.

Their hosts, Rose and Loraine, had remained largely subdued, occasionally suggesting conversational direction or supplying some snippet of information from their own experience and in-between filling glasses, promoting the varying colour of the discussion. The idea that such an apparent free-for-all truly existed within the context of a Church-hosted evening seemed at least eccentric to Pete, if not entirely peculiar, but then these particular hosts were definitely unconventional, if not actually a little kooky – middle-aged, devoted to their Church, as well as apparently each other? Pete couldn't quite figure that one out. Anyway, it was unimportant. Their goal seemed sincerely to create a forum, not to direct its agenda – an absence of structure within a larger context of laws and precepts, tenets and commandments. It occurred to Pete that this required a particular awareness and set of skills to be able to engineer so dichotomous an activity. Despite all this though, he remained in himself circumspect and non-committal, albeit that the discussion and the company was stimulating and certainly unexpected.

Loraine, sitting between Pete and Maitland's conversation, asked, 'What are you searching for, Pete?'

'Ah, well, I'm not sure I'm searching for anything,' a little surprised, not for the first time, by the frankness of these two women.

'I suppose I mean, what are you curious about? You're here. I assume not simply because Rose invited you,' Loraine continued.

Whoa.

'Okay, fair enough. Well I guess I'm curious about my son.' This was news to Pete even as the words came out. 'He's autistic. It's been suggested to me by one or two of his therapists in particular that he's very spiritual. I've heard this said about other autistic children ...'

'Yes, so have I,' Rose interrupted.

'Well, it's somewhat of an empty statement to me. What does it mean? I can see that he's very sweet, that maybe − *maybe* − there's more going on in his head than we give him credit for, albeit that that's a bit of a mystery.'

'What do you think?' Rose asked.

'I don't know what to think.'

'Are there things he does that make you wonder about him?' Loraine asked.

'Yes definitely, of course.'

'Like what?'

'Like the way he seems to look at things that aren't there. Well, at least not that we can see. As though he's communicating.'

'I understand that autistic children ... Are they called autists?' Loraine started on a theme.

'Yes, I've heard that term used,' Pete responded.

'I've heard that they see a hundred times the detail in things that we do, and that simultaneously holds their fascination and then more or less spins them out from sensory overload.' Rose pointed out.

'Oh, that's it entirely,' Pete responded. 'And then the question is what is this thing 'a-hundred-times-the-detail'? Is he seeing ... I don't know ... wave forms? Sound? Light particles?'

'My goodness, what an interesting thought,' added Maitland.

'And then what does he make of whatever it is that he sees?' Pete asked rhetorically. 'I don't know how to think about that or what to *do* about that.'

'Well, probably you don't have to *do* anything. Anyway, you're here, you're open ...'

'Hmm, maybe.'

'You don't think so?'

'You know, we've been bombarded the last year with information about our son, what's wrong with him, what his prognosis is, what's the best way to teach him, to train him, to get him to speak, this new therapy here, that research there, and so on. I think we were very open, certainly to start with. But I think we're a bit bogged down with it all now to tell you the truth. There's too much to take in and process and decide on. And when what you really want is to get your kid to just talk and go to the toilet and sleep and eat with a spoon, then comments about his spirituality are frankly a little beyond our capacity to deal with.'

'But you're curious about that in some way, nonetheless.'

Pete thought *I don't want to say yes. I'm not saying no either. What am I saying?* He was momentarily exasperated. 'I'm saying I don't know where to start. And I'm saying I'm unconvinced of the value of any discussion around Tim's spirituality. And I suppose I'm saying ... don't push me.' Pete looked Loraine square in the eye. She smiled.

'Wouldn't dream of it, Pete,' she said with a bigger grin.

'Okay. Thanks. I do love my son, and I think there's a way into his head. I just don't know whether that's about psychosocial and speech therapy, or whether it's maybe about force of character – *my* character – and the feelings I have for him, and when I'm with him.'

'Here's a thought for you. How about keeping a journal about Tim? Note things down, anything at all. Perhaps it might help to make sense of things. I think journal writing can be quite a *zen* activity. Maybe it will help you get into the flow of what's happening – Tim's flow. Give it a try.'

'Okay,' Pete said slowly. 'Sure, why not. I like to write. That's a good idea.'

'And bring Tim to the cathedral again – perhaps that's a good place for him – who knows ...?'

Pete wasn't feeling at all sure whether he wanted to go within a mile of the Cathedral ever again, or not.

'Yes, I will.'

'Coffee?' asked Rose, rising from the table.

'Ah ...'

'Oh no you don't, you two,' called Maitland from the other end of the table. 'You're not getting your clutches into this poor man. Come on, Pete. *The Wig & Mitre* awaits our benefaction. My round.'

Pete wasn't sure a jaunt to the pub with Maitland was his best choice either, but it seemed a done deal.

'Ah, looks like I'm being dragged away,' he said.

'I can see you kicking and screaming.' Loraine laughed, not at all put out, which made Pete think perhaps he'd rather stay.

Pete laughed too. 'You know, you have made me think about a couple of things. And thanks for the suggestion about the journal. I'll probably do that.'

'Good. Well, I'll be interested in your observations. And I hope you'll come again, although I've no doubt Maitland is about to fill you with enormous doses of cynicism. Heaven knows why he comes here. Clearly, he's not right in the head,' Loraine finished off, to gales of laughter.

'I'll see you both out,' said Rose, as the two men donned jackets and nodded their goodbyes around the table, Maitland managing to look smug yet again.

'Hang on a minute,' Sally said. 'Maitland might think he's rescuing you from this lot, Pete, but who's going to rescue you from him? And it's *Thirstday* and I could seriously do a pint!' Sally stood, grabbed a coat and scarf, and did a round of goodbyes and a few cheek kisses. She followed Pete, Maitland, and Rose into the hallway.

'Bye, Loraine,' she called back.

'Here you are youngsters. Careful driving home,' Maitland cheekily lowered three pints to the table.

'Why on earth *do* you go to these evenings, Maitland?' Sally asked.

'Well, I do *believe*, you know.'

'In what, for heaven's sake?'

'In God, of course!'

'Well, why all the argy-bargy all the time? All the cynicism.'

'Well, I just don't believe there are proofs. I told you. I don't believe we can *know* God. It's a simple matter of Faith, pure and simple. And I choose to believe. But I'll argue to the bitter end anyone who wants to belittle an omnipresent, omnipotent God with their meagre proofs of divine existence.'

'So what about prayer then? Do you believe in it or not?'

'Of course I believe in it. But it's about Faith, nothing else.'

'Well, what's Faith then?' Sally persisted.

'The extent to which I believe.' Maitland's responses were curt, but not unkind or rude.

'That feels like cheating.'

'Why?'

'Science exists. God exists. Surely the two can coexist.'

'How do you know God exists?'

'I'm not talking about me right now – I'm trying to get to the heart of where you're at. *You* just said God exists ...'

'No, I didn't.'

'Yes, you did!'

'No. I said I *believe* in God.'

'So what in hell is the difference?'

'There's a world of difference. For example, I choose to believe in my wayward son's ability to secure a solid income for himself and stop sponging off his father, despite that there is absolutely no objective evidence of this likelihood at all. In other words, that he might create this future for himself does not exist, but I believe in it just the same.'

'All right then. Using that ridiculous example, *why* do you believe in it?'

'Because, my dear, I *choose* it.'

Silence.

Sally's eyes narrowed in mock evil at Maitland. 'You're toying with me.'

'Absolutely not. Wouldn't dream of it. How's your glass?'

'Another thank you. You semanticist, you.'

'I assure you I am not playing word games. Not my style. Pete, another?'

'Thank you. Let me get them.'

'No. Sit yourself down. Back in a jiffy.' Maitland headed for the bar, amid a reasonable bustle and the hum of a stereo mounted behind the bar.

Most patrons were locals but a good smattering of tourists as well, the one group quite distinguishable from the other. *The Wig* was a fairly typical old English pub, although it wasn't the business that had always been housed there, within the stone walls and low-beamed ceilings. Several hundred years old now, it was at least known to have housed a mortuary in one past life, and probably many more besides.

'What do you think, Pete? Do you think God exists, is provable, what ...?' Sally turned to Pete after losing herself for a few minutes in the hubbub about the bar.

'I don't think I've thought through it enough, Sally. It's never been a focus in my life, but I must say I enjoyed listening tonight to the different views. It's very interesting. And I like Maitland's contributions a lot. It's all making me think, that's for sure. What about you?'

'Oh, I'm a believer for sure, but I also believe science and religion must be able to be unified. What does give me pause is whether *I* need to have proofs to bolster my belief, and that's where I do really respect Maitland's stance. He *chooses* to believe, and he doesn't require proof. And the notion that scientific proof is an insult anyway to the idea of an omnipotent God, that's got some synergy for me – interesting, as you say. So you're not sure what to believe in?'

'I don't know. And I don't want anyone telling me either.'

'Well said, Pete!' Maitland returned, placing two pints onto their table with one hand and then giving a mock salute with the third.

'So why did you come tonight?' Sally resumed, lifting one of the pints in return salute to Maitland.

'Because I was invited and because I was curious.'

'So are you going to come back again?' Sally pressed on.

'Don't know,' Pete responded.

Sally rolled her eyes. 'You've caught his bug already! Look what you've done, you grumpy old sod – turned another innocent into a doubting Thomas.'

Maitland beamed.

'Oh no, truly I don't need Maitland's help for that.' Pete grinned. 'I have been committed to non-commitment my whole life. Or so my wife would have anyone believe, although I am appreciative of finding such a stalwart in Maitland. Thank you, old chap,' lifting his own beer to the mock salutes.

'Pleasure!' Maitland rejoined.

'Oh knock it off, Maitland,' Sally scolded, over the increasing noise of the pub.

'I do rather luxuriate in the idea of getting sozzled after going to Church, don't you, Pete? Something quite degenerate about it, wouldn't you say?'

'Except you haven't been at Church – you've been at Rose and Loraine's,' Sally interrupted.

'Even better. Post-Bible class pickling!'

'That was Bible class!' Pete was enjoying, keeping the mock impiety going. 'Goddamn!'

They all laughed.

The newly created trio wound its relaxed way through a fond evening, regaling each other with its odd recipe of cynical but respectful anecdote, tales of life and children and careers. When it was obvious it must come to a close, it was jointly anointed by its participants in typical understatement as a 'rather good night', by which stage all three were firm friends. They also, all three, could barely stand.

Arriving home after closing time, Pete found his way with some difficulty along the path to the front door of his house, momentarily wondering why Alicia had not left a light on for him. He was loosely cognisant of trying four or five different keys in the front door and then, having secured entry, gave up on trying to relock the door from the inside.

That his wife was awake and pretending otherwise was entirely apparent to him when he half stumbled into bed, but of little account to his furried consciousness then or later.

Alicia herself lay in a maelstrom of animosity, resentment and despair, jumbled with a general perplexity that all of these reactions were grinding their way round her head at all. Her release from the weight of all this angst, which seemed to sit somewhere behind her eyes, seemed via rage, and while she knew clearly the incompatibility of her anger with any kind of mature and settled life, she was completely without strength or faculty to do other than allow it its course. She had no coherent reason for the trajectory her bitterness took, which was clearly towards her husband and to a lesser extent her children, except logic offered guilt as a convenient understanding, and pragmatism gave her a basketful of both real and relatively made-up excuses with regard to her husband at least.

On the other hand, she knew none of that was rational either, albeit that bits of it suited her, at least as a means by which to avoid closer examination. She supported her family, and she and Pete shared responsibility for most aspects of household decision-making, especially as it concerned Tim's care.

What she ultimately could not abide was her inability to make everything in her life right and satisfactory, at least as much as she would like, which was a level she knew was unreasonable. She couldn't escape her want to make Tim normal, physics palatable – or a *career* in physics palatable, and Pete an attractive proposition again – Pete whose casual, indolent approach to daily life she could choose if she wished to brush aside in favour of once more being in love, or at least content, if she had a mind to..

No, she had realised she did not feel guilty. She felt incapable, impotent. She had relied in large part in her adult life on success founded on intellectual endowment – mental *grunt*. While she was not naive or foolish enough to think managing her marriage did not require something more than this, whatever talents she was without were not only not present, her ability to even *want* them, let alone develop them, was bizarrely concealed from her. And so from this position of weakness she fought, as though such flailing might eventually bring her into contact with some more advantageous or salutary temperament. And each night when this turmoil had whirled and rotated itself into more convolutions and revolutions than could be numbered or made sense of, it would finally dissipate briefly into sleep, to manifest on waking into a reluctance to emerge into the day or to engage with any part of it. Habit alone would pull her into routine and goad her to another daily round, through an obstacle course of emotions competing for ground in her over-engaged consciousness.

For now, Pete's late arrival and drunken noise, along with the reek of stale beer, gave her emotions a target and she eventually fumed and enraged herself to a sleep, but not before an infuriation of tears spilled silently to her pillow.

Friday, 3 April 1981

I've noticed Tim's generally more engaged with his surroundings lately, although I'm not sure what has brought about this change. It's undoubtedly a factor that Jillie spends so much time with him, and that she's always talking to him. It would seem entirely 'normal' if instead she went about as if he wasn't really there, or if she felt irritated by him, but she's completely devoted.

Tim's been quite 'disturbed' today though. There are times when he's quite scratchy, and perturbed by something – his surroundings, us, I don't know. It's puzzling. It's not behaviour that seems attributable, necessarily, to tiredness or to being a bit under the weather. It's as though some pressure is being applied to him – like a parent is insisting on a new standard of conduct in a child and the child is pushing, resisting. And then after a few days, the child surrenders and then all is peaceful again. There are times Tim does this with us, like when we had him change from sitting at his little child's table and chairs to eat, to sitting at the dining table with Alicia and Jillie and me. He absolutely was not going to play ball, and it took about four days to get him to make the switch. We were almost ready to give in and leave him at the little red table; it was such a battle. But then all of a sudden he just got up to the big table as if that's what he'd always done. But the rebelliousness associated with the table-changing episode was only evident just prior to mealtimes. This other kind of response – as though to some kind of pressure – is a general thing that's there all the time, usually for a few days. I imagine there are some 'connections' being made in his brain that act like a flickering light to his consciousness, eventually a new bulb goes in — a light goes on — and he settles again.

Friday, 10 April 1981

The big news of the day — all over the tele and radio: Bobby Sands won the Fermanagh and South Tyrone by-election today.

Events at The Maze are difficult to interpret. Are the hunger strikers really noble but oppressed men, left with no choice after hundreds of years trapped in the worst of Britain's shame? With decisions imposed on them by free men of a certain consciousness, who have not the willingness or ability to understand an Irishman's view of the world.

And then in my little world...

I'm not sure how to support Tim when he's having these unsettled periods. If it was Jillie, I'd just be creating some sense for her that I'm here when she needs me, but I don't know how to communicate that to Tim, except that I think it. And of course I say the same kinds of things to him that I would to Jillie, but it's hard to know what goes in. Maybe it all does the job well enough. It's not like there's any kind of acknowledgement though. Sometimes a look.

I took him to Brayford Pool again today while Jillie was at school. But the weather was crap and I decided against a stroll along the lake. I was sure he was thinking about the swans — I hope he wasn't disappointed. We went to the Cathedral instead. He made a beeline for Little Hugh's Shrine. He sat there looking along the horizontal line of the outer edge of the tomb. With one ear to the small black 'box', he looked rather comical. He seemed poised to knock on the 'lid'. He didn't of course.

We didn't see Rose.

The other big news, of course, is still the deconstruction of the attempt on Reagan's life the other day. Apparently the bullet that hit him wasn't a direct hit but had ricocheted off someone else — shades of JFK. The would-be assassin apparently had no beef against Reagan at all but was simply trying to impress Jodie Foster, having been virtually stalking the poor woman for months – only in America.

Saturday, 11 April 1981
Riots in Brixton. Watching it happening on the nine o'clock news right now. Scenes of petrol bombs being thrown. Is this Northern Ireland or London? Bloody hell. Would love to be reporting on the ground though. Kate Adie doing her usual great job – god love her!

Tuesday, 14 April 1981
Tim seems to have chilled out again after a few stroppy days. Jillie didn't seem to even notice his behaviour.
When he gets over these periods, he's quite glowing and bright.

Two slightly worn-looking gentlemen, one older, left the *Magna Carta* and strolled, carefully, down Steep Street.

Down's certainly easier than up.
What happened to your powers now?
Very funny.
The little boy's getting it, isn't he?
Yes. How exciting.
Do they know they're racing each other? Mind out for that loose stone there.
Thank you. Hmm, racing? I don't think that's quite what they're doing, but I suppose it's not entirely an unreasonable way to put it either. The older one needs more help, it's true. There is an onus here on the Bishop, to help him and to keep his own promises. We'll see.

117

Monday, 20 April 1981

Lissy's unhappy. Well, that's probably an understatement. She's looking for something she can't quite find. She's always good if she's got at least a couple of smart, imaginative postgrads, but she said they've been a boring lot this year, which I take to mean that they're 'tow-the-line' conservative types – born-again atheists all and not a one with an ounce of curiosity about the world. She'll have to try and convince a few naive undergrads to take on a Masters next year.

She lost it a bit with Jillie on Saturday, although Jillie coped well I thought. And then today I found a folded up piece of notepaper that came out of the dryer – must have gone through the washing machine and everything in one of Jillie's pockets. It was still readable. She must have gone off to her room and written it:

Do what Mummy says straight away.

Don't blame her.

Don't want anything.

Don't get into an argument.

Ask her if she wants anything every now and then.

Think everything is a great idea.

I laughed my head off!

Tim painted an amazing picture today. It was the first time the therapist had set him up with paints and brushes and an easel. She said most three- and four-year-olds would probably use just one colour, do a quick squiggle in the middle of the page and that would be it. Tim took nearly half an hour, used several colours and covered the whole page. Each brush stroke was accompanied by great concentration. You could really see the cogs turning in his head. I think I'll get it framed – it's really very attractive actually. We will have to do a lot more of this. I get the sense he has some great opportunity for expression through this, and maybe even communication. I've never seen him do that with anything before. Well, except for when he's focusing on those lines along the doors and the furniture, but even then that isn't for so long.

He's very proud of his picture. It's taped on the refrigerator for now, and he keeps coming by and staring at it, and putting his hand up to it. He watched Lissy very closely when she got home and was looking at it, as though he was interested in her reaction. Or maybe he was worried what she'd do with it. Anyway, there's some window opening here and it's fascinating..

7

The failure of human beings to independently investigate truth
is foremost among those ills that ravage society. Without impartial
investigation, civilisation cannot progress beyond the prejudices
that contribute to the disintegration of the social order.

Paul Lample

A large white Swan had taken to accompanying the Bishop
on his walks about Stowe. The sight baffled most, but Hugh found
a solace with the large silent bird. The stately-looking French
Bishop of Lincoln trod softly on the grass at his country home, his
big hands folded together behind his back. He wore a heavy black
cassock with a purple skullcap atop his head, a large pectoral cross
about his neck and hooked into a button at the front of his cassock.
A simple stole of exquisite green and purple embroidery was about
his shoulders, a gold cross sewn in one end and a gold rose at the
other, the latter a symbol of his English bishopric.

'Ah, good morning, my friend. And how are you? Hmm?
Now you will give me no trouble, will you? Or will you threaten me
with that great beak as His Majesty likes to threaten me with his
sword? Hmm? Ah, no, not you – my gentle friend. And what of
our cathedral, ahh – it is unbelievable. Some sign I must give pause
to – what do you think? Is God so vexed?'

The Bishop's companion cocked its head slightly, appearing
to listen, and perhaps, the Bishop thought, noting new lines and
worries upon its master's face.

It was the priest's habit to walk and think, pacing by the
stream running through his residence at Stowe, a small hamlet past
Torksey from Lincoln. Here he could be more at peace from the
great hammering and clamouring of voices and business in the city.
He loved the bustle of the ancient Cathedral town, but it was a

doing place, and a man of his status likewise needed a thoughtful place, and this was his.

Hugh of Avalon, who had become Bishop Hugh of Lincoln, was at once a fearsome and extremely kindly man. He had been at Lincoln for four years, arriving to take charge at the behest of Henry II. He had previously administered the monastery at Witham in Somerset, established by Henry as one of several acts of penance following the assassination of Thomas Becket on the steps of Canterbury Cathedral. *Will no one rid me of this meddlesome priest –* and four of his knights took him at his word.

Hugh had stood up to the overbearing King before – refusing to pay taxes to finance Henry's war in France – and he would do so again. The King's threats were of little concern to him. It was the King's soul that was of greater importance, and even more the example he could set to his own people. Not to mention, also, the other great kings of Europe, who would nonetheless continue to war with each other for many more centuries, shamefully often at the behest of clergy with a different view of their role in men's lives.

The Bishop was to meet with Henry in a few weeks and wanted to insist on holding Henry to an undertaking to lead a much-promised crusade to secure the Kingdom of Jerusalem, another penance prescribed by the now-dead Holy Father Alexander against the wayward King.

Hugh turned and continued his walking, head down and hands behind his back. The Swan waddled several steps behind him. Hugh had come to recognise his own Swan among the others that inhabited the gardens and waterways about Stowe, not only because it would emerge to follow him, but had a slightly twisted, possibly once broken foot, which endeared the bird to him even more. He would worry that the bird had enough food, or that perhaps its disability hindered it in some way, and he brought it morsels from his own plate.

Now, along with a self-indulgent King, Hugh felt the consequences of the recent disaster in Lincoln. A more self-serving man might have seen opportunity to build a monument to his own future glory. Hugh's concerns were for the symbol of the Church's strength, and for the many men, young and old, whose lives would now be sacrificed to this greater glory, knowing as he did that such an endeavour was years, generations even, in the reconstruction..

'You see, my winged companion, how things must be? And does the King give a whit? Nay, he resides in his beloved France still, with little care for England. And here I am, a Frenchman, caring for his flock.' Hugh felt his ire multiply. 'Aargh... there is no patience in me for the injustices of this world. You are lucky my friend that it passes you by, excepting that you must listen to my ranting about it, hmm? And what do you hear of that anyway? Oh I think you are just about keeping me company, are you not; no matter my mood or the circumstances?'

Hugh continued a quicker pace, attempting as he was to rid himself of his own sense of impatience and frustration with the demands of his office.

The swishing of a cassock alerted the Bishop and the swan that they were not just the two of them anymore. The swan backed away a little as a young priest scurried towards Hugh, the Bishop sighing as his reverie about to be disturbed by the world's intrusion.

'My Lord.' The priest bowed, mid-stride.

'Yes, Peter. What is it?'

'The architects and masons, Your Grace. There is a delegation come. They have some problems with the reconstruction.'

'I'll be there in a moment then, Peter, thank you.'

'Yes, My Lord.' The young priest bowed again, backing away a few steps and then turned and hurried back to the monastery buildings.

'You see my friend there is no rest. Now they shall tell me something in the new design is not possible or else they will want more men, or more money. And how shall I take more men and boys from their homes, or ask Henry for more money, or heaven forbid that I should have to ask Lucius, who can't even be found in Rome these days – he has so many arguments with the city fathers. Well, we shall see.'

Hugh had not yet been to the ruined Cathedral himself, but ordered the clearing of debris immediately though, and sending also for the Kingdom's finest in architects and masons. Until all the debris was cleared, the extent of damage would not be fully revealed, but in the meantime, there were new possibilities for design, and many new techniques in masonry and construction, and Hugh wanted to learn as much as he could to ensure the best of all possible outcomes – in design, function, expense, and in skills and labour needed, some of which might be in short supply..

As Hugh turned and followed the path young Peter had taken to the abbey, the swan resumed its own path behind him. The bird would wait patiently for Hugh in the monastery's courtyard and would be lucky perhaps for a few snippets from the monks' table, particularly from those that desired the Bishop's favour. And there were always those.

In Torksey, Father Taylor was seething.

Ungrateful! Ungrateful, that's what they are! They don't understand the pressures from Lincoln. That I must provide for those above as well as below.

The priest paced rapidly, stomping up and down his hallway. He'd had two groups of villagers come this morning already.

There's no reason they can't cope. These men do nothing anyway – sit around is what they do – make their wives and children work for them. One or two from each family had to go, that's all there was for it. The Church can't be without its centrepiece – that's the way it is. I am not to blame! And now these damned Jews around about, causing trouble, with their secret ways. I won't have it!

'Aargh!' He stormed to the door, heaving it open, and charged down a path to the church.

No man was probably less suited to the priesthood than this one. Ambitious but without much of any requisite talent, or at least not any great amount, nor the presence of mind to feign such, nor indeed the wiliness to secure some other route to advance his career, paying favour to the right men, manipulating others. The priest was too proud to humble himself to his betters and not crafty enough to wield the Church's power to create influence. Instead he was a dull weathervane, allowing himself to be blown east, west, north or south by whatever forces. He bowed to Lincoln, and he bowed to the Manor, although begrudgingly to both. He vociferated at his parishioners in turn and thus became an unwitting fuel to resentment and rivalry.

He did not care for Jews – they were usually cleverer than he – and as he saw it, their conniving dealings always upset someone who thought he'd been got the better of. And they kept themselves apart. It was hard to know what they were up to.

Their biggest crime, as far the priest was concerned, was just being Jewish. Their race had killed the Lord and was forever tarnished because of it. Although even Taylor knew no individual Jew could really be blamed for the greatest evil of all, but it did seem part of God's plan that this race should bear the stigma of that, and no matter what their lives now, wherever they lived, the Jews would always be trodden on and reviled. Father Taylor saw no test in that other than for the Jews themselves; it was clearly the nature of things and surely it was God's intention or otherwise why was it so. As a Christian he had no obligation to them and did not see that any man had particularly. That his 'parish' included all of its residents – at least in some wider moral sense – was beyond the man.

Right now, though, the priest had more than just the Jews on his mind. The sun was beating down hard on these parts and more than just the priest's own temper was flaring. The Thane had screeched at Father Taylor over what was assumed to be a failed poach and the death of the swan. *Keep your flock in order and I shall have mine secure!* The whisperings over the swan, the quake, the cathedral, and the Jews – anxieties were all around and the angry priest felt no control over events or people.

Father Taylor paused at the door to the small stone church, closed his eyes momentarily, and drew a deep breath. He knew enough to know that if ever he was to manage the peace, he must first manage his own.

He pulled open the door and went through, bowing deeply and with some considerable pause. Walking to the altar, he knelt and rested his head at the edge of it, one hand holding its rim to steady himself.

The priest had been angry as long as he'd known life, given easily to moods and self-doubt. He'd hoped he would rise further in the Church and while such proximity to the Cathedral provided one sense of proximity to greatness, it was not the one he wished for. He was not liked by his parishioners and he knew it. He knew that to love them would have brought some reward but he was unable to find this in himself, overwhelmed as he was by ambition. He prayed for an increase in virtue but even that, he knew, was insincere and would continue to elude him. So he prayed then for sincerity and on occasion he felt an inkling of God's grace. He searched for this now. Whatever else was waiting for him on this day would just have to wait. He would eventually emerge when some rare solace finally took root once again in his soul, however small, however fragile it may be.

Already though, more burdens were developing expressly for the tired priest's shoulders.

'I will have to go and see this great ruin myself then. I've put it off long enough. I cannot bear to see what is left, but I feel now I must.' Hugh sank into his large chair, in front of drawings and diagrams spread out on a long wooden table before him. 'Decisions have to be made and they must be the right ones or it will not do.' The Bishop's voice was authoritative, not the sort that many men would attempt to interrupt or dismiss, but it held a kindness as well. And with little sleep the past few days a tiredness was also present that was clear to all.

A dozen men were about the table. Some wore fine clothes denoting both their station and their success, for the one was rarely without the other in these days. Other men wore the finest they had, which was to say a much cruder dress and cloth than the notables among them. These though were master craftsmen who had earned their reputations through many years of toil, and in some cases even innovation, and had risen to a reputation – both esteemed and sustainable.

'Thank you, gentlemen, for travelling all this way. I know there is much to do and I am very grateful. I see you have an understanding of the problems we face. Please return to the city with these plans and carry on with the first stages of the work. I will arrive on your heels and we will see what more is to be done. It seems certain the debris will reveal unexpected concerns and many decisions are yet to be thrashed out among us. I'm grateful for your advice – very grateful indeed.'

Hugh dismissed the group of architects and masons from his room with all their *Thank you M'Lords.*

'Prepare things to leave, Peter,' he said to the young priest, and Peter took his leave also to ready for the Bishop's departure to Lincoln.

Hugh had been several hours in the stifling indoors with the group of men. He enjoyed their skill and their particular type of intelligence. They were the best in England and they had come in an instant from all over the country, with their plans and ideas, debating benefits, systems and designs with each other, mostly for the pleasure of achieving the best result, not simply their own aggrandisement in this future construction. Each knew it took more than just he to complete a project of this size, for it was indeed likely to be the biggest of any building ever in the history of the Kingdom. It had even been mentioned it may be the tallest building in the world.

Hugh knew little of what they discussed in their many technical details, although he intended to improve his education in this regard. Above all else, the things he must know were the cost and how long it would take. Beyond that he knew only to listen and observe the presentations of each of these men, to assess the validity of any particular recommendations of which there were already many competing ones. Hugh was confident of his rapid assessment of a man's character and worth by his tone and his demeanour in particular. And he could tell that however it was that such a band of craftsmen came to be in his house now, they were indeed the finest in the land and he felt reassured that he would at least be building a cathedral that would not likely fall again..

That said, their long discussions had tired him.

Lord, you are cruel with this heat to an old man in these thick robes.

Alone now, Hugh fell back into a large wooden chair, resting his head forward on one hand.

Aargh! Forgive me.

Hugh rose again quickly, aiming to resume his earlier ponderous walk about the gardens a little before leaving. He hoped also to locate some gentle zephyr thereabouts, although the latter seemed unlikely and he wasn't sure if the heat was more unbearable inside or out. He would leave today, stopping at Torksey to hear of the parish from its priest and from the King's Thane, both of whom complained interminably. He knew the scene of the crumbled cathedral would wrench at him, and he would put his sight of it off another day if he could. The rebuilding would be years and the principal focus of his Bishopric, he knew now, but he would not leave aside the progression and maturation of Christ's followers and their cultivation. But he *would* escape to find some communion with God whence he could and now was an opportunity for that, however brief.

His steady companion merged into step behind him as he came out again into the hot day. Hugh smiled. He'd thought to give the bird some name but none had come to him that seemed right. *This creature assumes responsibility for some part of me – my safety and comfort perhaps – why does it? How is it that I have attracted this follower? It follows no other, and it* always *follows me. I do nothing for it. And I talk to it in a language it knows not.*

'Aha!' he said gently to the great bird. 'I have it. You are an Angel come to watch over me. For if not, I shall do some terrible thing perhaps. But that is vainglorious and sacrilegious. I would not deserve such of the Lord's favour. Well, what shall you do, my friend, while I am not here? Perhaps you will join your brothers and sisters at the lake beneath our poor cathedral. And I will certainly be pleased to see you, although I'm not sure, I'm afraid to say, that I should be able to tell you apart from them upon that great lake. There are so many so you will have to come closer or give me a wink if it is you. Can you do that do you think?'

Man and bird contemplated each other again. Hugh smiled and turned into his walk, noting the bird stepping in behind him yet again, and feeling a great comfort from it, whatever it was that this strange spectacle meant.

Gamel Warriner's day had not gone well. Caution and thrift were the new drivers of commerce, and he had sold but a few vegetables at the market that day, and received only the smallest weight of grain for his wife's kneading hands. One solace, such as it was, was that it need feed fewer mouths, but this didn't sit so comfortably either.

Alard had come with him to Torksey today; and as usual Thomas. Alard was boastful that he had the eldest's responsibility now until his father cuffed him for the annoyance the boy's pride gave him.

Thomas did not notice any of these changes in his day or in his life, and he sat at the back of his father's cart now, legs dangling, grinning and gawping at people moving about the dusty square in front of him. He saw light was dancing all around him and he was enjoying its show. Most of those about were quite used to the strange little Warriner boy and most paid him no mind at all. Some older men and women, perhaps who'd seen others like Thomas in their time, would smile and make some comment or other to Thomas or to his father about him, generally not expecting much by way of reply from either. The boy never disturbed anyone and his parents were well respected and good people. And some even found some good humour in his odd laughter and funny ways, although they were careful how they'd express such in front of the boy's father.

As did others about them, so also did Gamel and his elder son load their baskets and pelts back onto their cart. Not many about spoke and the usual hubbub of market day seemed remote not for the first time in recent days. There was not much by way of profit to be had by any man lately, and most were as Gamel, with just a few of the necessities they were used to, to take home again, little to show for a day of work. It was not good for a man's soul any more than it was for his pocket, nor indeed his pride. It would upset the mood of all for a longer time yet, and the upset created no different an outcome in that regard from a poor harvest or a flood or a plague, which is to say that things went backward for most folk. This was a time when things were either the same or they were worse. Rarely if ever were they better and any such idiotic concept as progress was yet to be invented hundreds of years hence and would have been laughed at hereabouts.

Gamel spoke gruffly to his son as they loaded their cart, partly to keep the boy's head from swelling at his new status, but more from shortness of temper from the wasted day. Young Alard was not the only son kicked or boxed by a taciturn father this day. And the heat made the new hardships more acute still.

Gamel lifted Thomas aside with barely an effort, reaching past him to stow the last of their goods into the cart. Gamel had a great strength anyway but Thomas was so light as to almost warrant being tied down to the cart in even a small wind; he was easily moved about, content to be wherever he was put. He had his face raised to the sun, eyes closed and smiling, and Gamel was momentarily indignant at what would have been idleness in any other, but he quickly swallowed the thought, at once checking his temper, as he did often with the boy, and even on occasion the boy's mother.

Even though there was not much of the usual flurry about, there was still a stir of sorts, at once quite quiet, but pressing in on the minds and temperaments of those amid it. It carried a nervousness with it and the villagers' wariness of it caused them all to pack up a little quicker than usual.

Gamel lifted a final basket to the cart next to Thomas and as he did so the boy, with some power, lurched towards him suddenly propelled by some force from behind. Gamel was quick and caught the boy, toppling the basket and its contents in the back of the cart. Thereupon, the wailing of a half gutted pig, or the howling of some partly slaughtered cattle, rang at his ear, and he turned around about, the boy in his arms, expecting some wounded beast had escaped and was now about to hurdle his cart..

Although he could see no such thing, Gamel was all senses, spinning about and then back, confused, and for a moment unable to translate what he was hearing and seeing and sensing into any reality. Thomas was flailing in his arms like a wild dog, threatening to fall to the ground, and then suddenly it was his son's spasms made him realise that the horrendous sound beating at his ears was coming from the boy. Gamel had heard little or no sound ever from the strange child and this keening now unsettled him so as he had no thought for a moment of what to do and just stood with the boy half upright and thrashing about in his arms.

Villagers all around had halted their activities at the extraordinary sound, looking about likewise to see whence the sound came, and then to notice the large man they all knew so well stood helplessly with the idiot boy. Except now this small creature was very different from the harmless one they were used to, and the noise coming from him frightened them. Until now the boy was a defenceless innocent; in an instant he had become another unknown set to disturb their tenuous hold on anything solid in the world. What had got into the child? Was it suddenly mad? Was this a secret Gamel Warriner had kept from them? Perhaps they ought to think differently of this man they knew. They were already edgy from too many omens in recent days and the thought that this was some new devil thing was in more than a few minds.

Gamel understood none of this yet though, and with another second his alarm spiked. When he was almost beyond knowing what to do, a warm wetness seeped through his fingers, clasped as they were about the boy, and the sensation drew him back into himself and into his two strong legs on the ground, and he brought his focus to his own child in his arms and found enough composure to understand. He lowered Thomas to the dusty Earth, not quite letting him go. Long lines of blood percolated over Gamel's clothes and arms and into the hard clay ground. He was stilled momentarily, his arms beneath his son in the dust, finally making sense of all his brain was telling him as he knelt over the boy and stared at his wide open mouth and frightened eyes.

As Thomas's bellowing persisted, Alard stood dumbly by frightened by the sound coming from his brother, and now the sight of blood along with it. The warm earth raised such a forge of heat that it grabbed at them all. And it stunk. And the stink pasted their clothes to their skin, and the thick air relayed their fears even quicker among them.

Gamel yelled into the general milieu. 'Someone ge' Bennet, Bennet Williams – go on, won't ya. Someone go!'

There was a slow stirring, and a few youths stepped slowly out of the crowd, and then ran, to find the physician. For the most part, both the bystanders and the actors in the small drama they observed were held in some paralysing clutch, a vacuum where nothing seemed to exist about them, all eyes and Energy and focus hurtling in ultimately to the wounded boy's larynx and the sound coming from it.

Thomas's noise eased a little and Gamel found some instinct from somewhere to pull the boy to him and cradle him, with intense unease, and the wailing abated a little more. Gamel saw the whiteness of the boy's face and prayed the life not to go from him, and perplexed himself further with these actions on his own part, not to mention that he'd never felt any softness for the lad before. All about knew this was a man had lost a lot the last few days. Gamel looked up from his son and stared fiercely around him at the faces of people he knew.

'Who did this?' Gamel yelled into the surrounds, sounding a wounded animal himself now.

'Who did this?' he bellowed louder.

And people nearby appeared to back away from the sound of accusation, although in truth they could not move.

Returning his face to his son, he saw a bloodstained rock in the dusty clay at the rear of his cart, of such a size no child could have thrown it any distance or with any force. The mystery and shock this new offence brought was beyond the reach of his understanding. He could bring no judgement to it at all, save again an instinct to get his sons a way gone. Gamel stared at the spent missile near him, feeling anew the warmth of his son's blood stuck already to his fingers.

It could not be clarified in that moment – at least not with ease – as to what Thomas himself felt. He did not know he screamed; he had forgotten that a moment earlier he gazed at the bright sun, all radiant. He could not even be said to know himself that he was alive and living.

An Angel somewhere wept. And another focused a rain of golden Light that he bid find its way into the child's own Energy.

When a moment later Bennet Williams came running, he apprised the scene quickly. Gamel lifted himself and Thomas to the rear of the cart and bade Bennet take them at least away from the street where so many eyes held expressions he could not begin to speculate upon. He felt such an ill will towards some stranger of a sudden, and was not so frightened about what he knew he could do if he found out who that stranger be, but he knew his attention was best kept to his sons for now.

Bennet took control of the wagon and its lead, as Alard clambered up next to him, and they drove the curious panoply away from the assembled listeners and spectators. The crowd moved silently from their path and Gamel saw they dispersed quite quickly as they left that spot, no doubt to hurry away and tell their version of events to others. He studied them a few moments for some sign of a crime but no such thing showed itself to him, and he was pleased when the cart moved from their sight.

They bumped slowly through a few turns and along some pot-holed tracks till they arrived at the physician's own home. The two men lowered the boy and Bennet drew the patient and his father into his house, Alard behind them. He quickly brewed a draught that calmed Thomas further and then brought materials that cleaned the wound, less severe than the deluge of blood had suggested. The two men and the two boys stayed quiet in the small room, hot and stuffy as it was from the inevitable fire, set at a low flame, despite the heat of the day.

Bennet's wife took the father's and son's tunics from them and did her best with the splatters of blood on their clothes, setting them to dry over a stone wall in the sun. She didn't add any talk to the silence and neither man had yet explained the cause of the boy's accident. She could see their uncertainty though and kept her tongue in her head for now.

After a while, the boys and the men had all calmed more. The men agreed a story for Alice, and held Alard to it, that it was no missile that had harmed Thomas but some accident where he'd fallen. They knew the woman had concerns enough for her children and their safety at the moment without such news that one, her precious one, was now a target of thugs.

'Did yi' see what happened, Gamel?'

'No' a thing, Bennet. The boy suddenly flung 'imself a' me. Ah din' even hear i' with 'im makin' tha' din t' star' with. An' then all tha' blood. Ah saw a rock on ground, but ne'er seen 'oo threw i'.'

'What about you, Alard?'

'Wer' all a myst'ry t' me, sir. Ah ne'er seen nuthin'.'

'Did yi' see rock comin' at Thomas?'

'Naw, sir.'

'Well, what could possibly stir someone t' such a thing? The boy's ne'er hurt anyone. I tell yi', Gamel, there's a nasty air 'bout these last days.'

'Folk 'r' scared, Benne'. An' folk'll do all sorts when they're scared I reckon. Bu' this ain' right.'

'Folk'll just be lyin' low 'gain, as they've done last week or so. No one wants trouble, but it's their superstitions create the trouble.'

'Well, ah'll be lyin' low m'self, I'd say. We'll be get'n' away, Bennet. Thank yi' for yi' kindness. Yer a good man, Benne', an' a smart'r one than most.'

Their dried clothes were fetched and Gamel carried his now whimpering boy to their cart. Bennet drew his own horse to the back of Gamel's cart and rode with them to their home so that Gamel might comfort the boy in the back, and so Bennet might also then reassure the mother on the son. Their way was steady, thoughts of their poor day at the market returning to beleaguer Gamel anew. He would hand the child to its mother and dispense with his caregiver role. It was uncomfortable for him now and he discerned also that he would not – should not – take the boy with him to the town again. It was in Gamel's nature to go in the flow of things and never to rebel or fight or cause trouble with anyone. Even as he'd been wronged he would forget the event and his ordinary life would resume. If he took the boy to the town again he would be inviting trouble, since clearly it would not be in anyone's mind now to leave suspicion behind them. Gamel had no mind to remind people of such or make himself its object.

When later Bennet Williams rode back to the town, he felt yet again a pall over the town that was not the sort to hold any promise of cooling rain.

At the home of young Euan Draper, Euan's grandmother Berta, who kept his house and took care of his two young children since his wife had died a year earlier, sat in a rocking chair slowly and confidently apprising her grandson with the quandaries that seemed to her to have arisen to seize their small village's regard.

She had stood at the edge of the crowd that afternoon and just as a rock had struck the innocent boy so had Berta been struck with the recognition of events unfolded and unfolding. Had she not forewarned of catastrophe at the dying of the Swan a few days before? And so she beheld a line of events from the past to the present and into the future.

'It's not an easy thing this unfold'n' of time, the way 'as God weaves it all together, in a fine mesh. Folks think i's all one thing follows 'nother, but naw, i's all a complicat'd thing.'

It had never in all the history of the universe taken an educated person to be able to see, sense, hear things that were unseen, unseeable, and silent. Indeed, it was education and experience in the ways of the world that obstructed the senses of most to any likelihood of unseen, unheard messages. For those who could tell of it – which was few – some thought it was of God, some of the Angels, and some of the Devil. Others knew it was none of these things but a heightened sense of the finer Energies of the Universe, and an understanding of Nature and her ways of whispering and shining and bending events in history upon each other, laying a clear path heading into the past and the future that anyone may see if they knew how, and if they knew what to make of it.

Not being educated though made it always difficult for one such as Berta to give an explanation to others of what they knew, or more to the point, *how* they knew what they knew. And so generally, she didn't bother with trying to explain. She would pronounce what she knew, and if none saw anything in it then she didn't mind so much.

Being town dwellers, the small house didn't have the same smells of animals and the dirt of a peasant's hovel, but it was as small and dark and almost as bare. There was the same constant open fire which added more smoke to the place than was good for anyone, and the constant smell of a stew always simmering. Berta had made the place her own and now Euan often felt the guest. The rules for what was minded had become her rules and he kept to them rather than have the scratch of her tongue which once it set to was not short in stopping.

'There's a shakin',' Berta began, 'a dead great bird, and now an innocent attacked in a way as was very wrong. There's a reasonin' God has 'ere, but I can't say as I've reckoned what 'tis yet.'

'If you ask me i's the devil's work, seems lark i'.'

'Rubbish, boy. No such thing as devil. Just them churchmen made tha' up so as to keep you 'n' me in ther pockets. Naw, naw, i's a plan on high. 'N' there'll be more o' business as folks won' lark yet to be sure. Deaths there'll be. Folks get'n' killed.

In some ter'ble ways. Ther's a plan in i' tho'. Ther's a reason'n' fer i'.' Berta rocked in her chair, obviously pondering the meaning of events. That there was an explanation that bound everything together she knew as well as she knew the cracks and calluses in her own hands.

She put her head back, closing her eyes, seeing much of what was yet to pass. And even seeing what was still to pass that had already happened. Now how would one such as she explain that strangeness to anyone who would not think her mad or bedevilled. Berta knew well that one could see the future in the present and the past, and the past in the future, and all manner of orderings of time. She even knew that even as she'd seen the future come to be, that it was just as possible to change something already happened, if anyone understood too that each person had a power to do so.

Euan understood not a whit of her ramblings and paid no more heed except to acknowledge her with the occasional murmur. He cared nothing for her predictions and chose never to engage in any chat any villager would have with him about his grandmother. And to that end he preferred she limit her banter to the ears of those who also cared little, since he sought to protect his own and his children's future and her place in it. After all, he really did need the old woman, and she did seem to mind a good house.

At the home of Jared the Smith, young Peter, who had run from the scene of Thomas's accident earlier to fetch the physician, was acquainting his family with events. His mother, Thilda, looked to her husband as the boy spoke, and they both knew a disquiet that, although it had them not in any grip of fear as yet, had them considering the extent of the rules they imposed that usually bound their young children close to their house. The boy thought everything of late exciting and mystical. His parents knew better than to get carried away with notions of portents or omens, but times were unsettled. Folk heard things – more than just these few things of the last week. There was always religious talk or rumours of foreign kings and wars that stirred folk and easily led to a violence or greed or threat of some sort or another.

Thilda also thought she would see if she could find a way to send some small token to Alice Warriner, who she'd known since their childhood, and whose burden seemed at least as great as any woman's. Thilda herself had just the one son left living and it would be a sore day for even a nasty old priest to take an only one, even it was for the cathedral and the glory of God.

Jared Smith had sympathy likewise for Gamel Warriner as he knew the hardships of a family and poor trade. He thought he would have to soon press one or two of the villagers to settle their accounts with him as things were more than a little drowsy at his workshop the last week. It was a difficult business to take money on account from folk who had none. And harder still to take some small remaining animal or part of a crop, knowing some other child not his own would go hungry because of it..

When his parents weren't watching and seemed engaged in some other thing, Peter Smith slipped out through the smithies yard at the front of their small house. He was keen to meet his friends in the village and see what menacing pranks they may dream up. And he hoped one of them knew the identity of the afternoon's assailant, or at least they might guess at it and decide for themselves whether to make of the person a hero or a new victim for their boyish pleasure.

At the Thane's manor, Lord Abelard received Father Taylor.

Abelard was a tall powerfully built man who in different surroundings and clothes could have looked like one of his own peasants. He hunted, fought and went to war, and took part in any other kind of physical pursuit that guaranteed his strength and power over his peasants and any other Lord that posed a threat, which indeed most did if only for the King's favour. He did not tolerate fools and the local priest irritated him to distraction. Unlike the priest though, Abelard had always been successful in currying favour with those who could provide him some benefit, and the priest certainly did that, maintaining as he did the souls and religious zeal of the masses. He wasn't quite sure yet though whether recent events were something he should be particularly concerned about, and he eyed the priest for signs of weakness. He saw many and doubted the man's ability to manage the populace. He would have to keep an eye on things himself. Fortunately he had sufficient men to bully and cajole on his behalf if need be.

The Lord and the priest agreed on a hushed investigation into the origin of the afternoon's attack. Abelard, less moved by events in the village or with its occupants, was more roused to discuss the appropriate punishment for a poacher caught that afternoon on his estate and held now in his stables. He was, as was known, inclined to public flogging, although he liked to encourage the villagers' own self-righteousness by a turn in the stocks. He was disinclined to prison terms since it cost him in guard and keep, such as it was, and gave too much favour to idleness.

Father Taylor knew his presence irritated Abelard and never wont to stay in the Lord's company for more than was necessary, withdrew from the manor at the earliest moment. It did not seem to him that His Lordship would even notice, let alone care, should he find the agreed investigation waning. The stone-throwing was most likely a reaction of superstitious fools, hell-bent on finding another poor innocent to vent their fear upon. The idiot child seemed such a likely choice that it dawned on the priest how unusual it was that such a thing had not occurred before now. But then he supposed that it – the child – was surrounded always by its parents and brothers, well protected. And the father and mother were respected among the peasants.

No, he thought, perhaps he'd do better to put his energies into arranging the poacher's punishment for the Lord's amusement. He knew he really ought to pray for the poor sod, but that was largely a pastime he kept to himself and for his own benefit.

Later that day, when Hugh arrived at the small friary at the edge of the town, there were many tales to tell and concerns to digest. While much of what was told would lead simply to superstitious nonsense, there were new hardships to be borne and all combined among an ignorant mass to create trouble, or a good deal of concern for such. The attack on a child was evidence enough of such foolishness. Hugh's apprehension grew as he saw the local priest finding a situation beyond his capacity to shoulder, and he focused his attention that evening on settling the man's nerves and assuring him of his support, God's guidance, and the transience of life's trials. An unruly snake pit was brewing that the priest neither saw nor was capable of understanding, let alone managing. It was clear to Hugh that the man took a harsh view of most things and struggled with little heart to be truly pastoral in his outlook.

The Bishop listened through the evening to the troubled man, soothing and advising. As always, he knew that his presence did indeed provide encouragement and peace, and he was grateful for the Lord's gifts to him. He retired late and with a little too much wine under his belt for such an old man as himself. The next day would be trying enough. But even then he did not find sleep easily. Troubles gnawed at him. In these times, he knew more that were innocent, and even untarnished, would be victims. Even the priest had commented on the *annoying Jews* as though this was a flock of gulls come in from the sea instead of a law-abiding citizenry, and Hugh knew this opinion to be widely held. He urged the priest to consider all in his parish to be children of God, *especially* these, and that it would not be useful to peace to remark any further on any other such person or group in a similar manner.

'We are all equal in the Lord's eyes,' he'd encouraged the priest, although he wasn't convinced the man understood him. Indeed, the priest seemed surprised that the Bishop would defend the Jews.

'But it was they who killed Our Lord, Excellency,' Father Taylor had replied.

'Our Lord *was* a Jew, my son, and further it was the Romans of old who hunted and killed not only our Lord but his many followers for many years to come. The People of the Book are a good people, pious and obedient to the laws of our land. It does us well to protect and even honour them.'

Hugh knew he would need to return to this topic with the priest again, as well as with others in his flock, and further he knew he must need be unequivocal in protecting and defending those who would otherwise be considered unblemished and inculpable.

At the home of Jacob Yazd, a Jew, Jacob's wife Martha told what she'd overheard at the market after the events had occurred. At their mealtime, the family delivered up a prayer for the strange young boy. Jacob advised his wife and children not to gossip about this or any other event or villager and that God had his own reasons for the way things were. It was not for any of them to question. He charged each of them with kindness, neighbourliness, and respect towards their fellow man.

The slightly built man pushed a gnawing fear from his mind and put his trust in God. For generations, and probably centuries he didn't know of, his family had prevailed against many insults and repressions; he recognised them more and feared them less. He knew it to be the way of things for his people, but he had no wish to arouse concerns among his family, and he would have them become as invisible as possible in the busy little village.

8

Peace is not just the absence of war. Like a cathedral, peace must
be constructed patiently and with unshakable faith.

Pope John Paul II (1920–2005)

Monday, 27 April 1981

*World's an interesting place right now it seems: some amazing things
happening. One day we seem to be hanging in the balance, the next poised for
major change. The news is always very full these days.*

*Following a crash by an Air New Zealand plane into Mount Erebus
in Antarctica a couple of years ago, killing everyone on board, there was an
inquiry lead by Justice Peter Mahon. His report was released today. The airline
had concluded pilot error, but the flight paths were changed without the pilots
knowing and then there'd been an extraordinary cover-up. Fabulous quote from
Justice Mahon: '... an orchestrated litany of lies.' Imagine we'll be hearing that
one again. Love it.*

Tuesday, 5 May 1981

*Bobby Sands died today following his hunger strike in Her Majesty's
prison The Maze. He had a father and a son. Margaret Thatcher said he was
a convicted criminal who chose to take his own life. I wonder how many others
will die. I wonder how she sleeps at night. Must require copious medication or
else she really is made of iron.*

*I've been trying to take more time to sit and really study Tim. Really,
really look and see all the tiny nuances of his behaviour. Of course he has so
many different behaviours, many of which are really indistinguishable from any
other kid his age. It's his sitting and staring and laughing at nothing that
draws my attention most. Jillie can make him laugh too and he gets right into
that and can't stop giggling. But that's 'normal', and different from when he's
just laughing when there's no stimulus to the laughter.*

I had this idea that he was looking at some thing; *now I realise that's
not what he's doing. The thing he's 'looking' at is inside his head, and he*

focuses on it intently. Sometimes he angles his head up as though he's trying to get a better view of this thing inside him, a bit like if someone asks a question and you cock your head maybe, and look up, trying to find the ideal answer.

But still I feel like he's engaging with something other than just the ideas or thoughts or images in his own head, something that is 'beyond' him. Perhaps there is some connection to the 'real world', like a pathway he's trying to negotiate. I wonder how he sees us, how he processes what he sees and how he makes sense of things around him – does he make sense of them? In years to come, I'm sure – I hope – scientists will fathom the depths of these children's minds. Perhaps find ways to 'let them out'.

I don't think I can go any further with thinking about this. What can I know that I don't know already?

Wednesday, 13 May 1981

Alicia was in a shitty liver this evening. I don't get where she's at, and there doesn't seem to be any way into her head or her thoughts to find out.

She charged out of the house after dinner and came back an hour or so later saying she'd been for a walk, except she took the car, so whatever.

The Pope was shot in St Peter's Square today, by a Turk, Mehmet Ali Ağca, a member of the group Grey Wolves. *His Holiness is in a serious condition after his intestine was perforated multiple times. He underwent five hours of surgery, apparently losing nearly three quarters of his blood.*

Rumours are of Soviet conspiracy because of the Pontiff's support for the Polish labour movement Solidarity.

Friday, 22 May 1981

I spent much of the day in the workshop with the mustang. Tim seemed to enjoy pottering around in there too. He got into all sorts of things and got very dirty. Lined lots of things up he'd not lined up before – seemed to enjoy it: nuts and bolts and tools and bits of engine and pieces of wood. He had grease smeared everywhere. It was a pleasure to see. At one point, he handed me a pair of clippers which I took off him and rested on top of the battery. About ten seconds later, I found I needed them. Coincidence of course, but it was the only tool he handed me all day, and the synchronicity was delightful, if only momentary.

Heard on the radio that Peter Sutcliffe's been put away for the rest of his days. A lot of people creeped out by it even this far from Yorkshire. Don't like those 'outside the courtroom' reportings on radio and television – too sensational for my liking – but justice served and relief all round.

'What's this group of yours all about then?' Alicia asked. 'You didn't really say anything after you'd been, although I did of course note the hour at which you returned, not to mention the malodorous vapour you breathed on me the next morning.'

'Ah well, you see, there was this one somewhat lonely old codger who kind of twisted my arm a bit,' said Pete, thinking it best not to mention Sally's presence at the pub.

'Right.'

'It's true, he did.'

'Aha!'

'Well, anyway...'

'Well, anyway.'

'They're an interesting and I suppose quite sincere group of people – fairly diverse characters – and the format seems fairly loose. They talked about the effects of prayer. This fellow I went to the pub with – Maitland – he'd done a bit of research and said there wasn't really any evidence of any kind to prove the efficacy of prayer. It was quite interesting.'

Pete and Alicia had located a small tract of calm in their particular combat zone. Pete was enjoying the comradeship with his wife, and for her part Alicia noticed a respite from her usual fury. She'd got up early, evading Pete. Now a few hours later and a little guiltily she'd brought fresh coffee and eggs to the verandah where he was devouring the morning paper. She hoped her kindness, perhaps somewhat feigned, might allow her to further escape to her office in the afternoon.

'So what do you want from it?' Alicia asked.

'The group thing? No idea. Just curious. They seem mostly very smart. There's nothing happy-clappy about it at all. Didn't feel like I was being asked to swallow some line of doctrine or anything.'

'Yeah, well, that's how they get you though, isn't it ... creep up on you.'

'Don't be such a cynic.'

'Well, if I'm a cynic, you're gullible.'

'Not my style.' Pete was relaxed and didn't mind his wife's playful baiting.

'Aha!'

'Well, you're the family scientist. What do you think? Can prayer make a difference?'

'To what?'

'To someone's health, say.'

'Absolutely...,' Alicia replied.

'Really?'

'... and definitely not,' she finished off.

'Oh, well, that's precision for you. Which is it then?' Pete asked.

'Both.'

'You can't have your eggs and eat them too,' replied Pete, mopping up yolk with a slice of toast. 'Nice brekky by the way. Thanks.'

'You're welcome.'

'Did I do something to deserve it?'

'No, not a thing.'

'Very funny. So?'

'Okay look, the thing is I'm not a medical doctor and don't have any experience in that area, but I'm sure that prayer, or for that matter any kind of positive mental practice, can improve patient outcomes. There are always stories about people who've beaten the odds with, as they've said, their ability to laugh, or because they refuse to believe anything other than the best possible of all futures. But really that's not anything to do with prayer per se. Not in my view. I don't think prayer itself is necessarily going to make a blind bit of difference to anyone. I think there are too many other variables to consider.'

'So you don't believe in prayer?'

'Well, like I say, I do and I don't.'

'Helpful.'

'I'm not trying to be helpful ... '

'Obviously.'

'... I'm trying to add my thoughts. Take your plate?' Alicia thought there was no harm in carrying her good graces a little further.

'Sure.'

Alicia stacked their two plates and cutlery and wandered through the French doors to the kitchen.

'I mentioned those Paris experiments by the way,' Pete called out after her.

'What did you say?'

'Well I'm not sure I get them entirely of course. But it's just that idea of things having been in contact previously being able to influence each other.'

'And how was that relevant?' Alicia returned to the verandah.

'It just seemed like it was. The experiments in prayer were with anonymous people praying for anonymous patients and proved ineffective. So the comment was made, surely if one was praying for a patient one knew, that would be more effective.'

'Yep. That follows. But again there are so many variables.'

'But isn't this the kind of thing *you* want to prove yourself, to know and understand about yourself?'

Alicia stared at her husband. She sat back in her chair with a cup of coffee, blew on it, and sipped and stared into the cup.

'Dunno,' she said softly.

Not being quite sure why, Pete decided he'd leave her with that.

'Pete! Well, well, well. Thought that little drinking soirée of ours must have left you feeling out of sorts.'

Pete turned to see Maitland beaming along towards him on the footpath just as he was about to turn into Rose and Loraine's cottage.

'Oh good heavens, no. Just warming up!' Pete replied, pleased to have a familiar face before going in.

'That's the spirit! Oh dear, pardon the pun..' Maitland laughed. 'Good to see you again.'

The two men shook hands.

'Likewise! After you.' Pete flagged his arm towards the front door and then followed behind Maitland who let himself in, calling out a cheery *Hello* down the hallway.

Rose emerged into the other end of the hall, a jovial and welcoming host, and ushered the men through.

It was several weeks since Pete's last visit to the group and surprised as he was to find himself there again, he was equally content now to be in such easy company. A middle-aged man new to Pete was introduced as Arthur, Loraine's brother-in-law from Torksey, otherwise the participants were the same as his previous visit.

'Pete! Nice to see you, to see you ... ?' Pete couldn't bring himself to utter the expected *nice* in response to Loraine's blaring greeting, although he could see she was not really wedded to that particular vulgarity, and he grinned back at her with a jolly *nice to see you too..*

'Arthur's been embarrassing me with a few inaccuracies about my extremely intermittent ability to speculate on the future,' Loraine continued.

'Really? Can you do that? Maybe you can tell me if Maitland's going to compel me towards intemperance again this evening, because if he does my wife will be very unhappy about it,' said Pete, to general amusement.

'Ah nothing so precise I'm afraid. I have no control over it. Things just sort of pop into my head. But I'll let you know if visions of insobriety emerge,' she said with a chuckle.

'Like knowing old Ronald Reagan was going to get shot before it happened,' Arthur chipped in. 'That was her most recent prediction. Only the night before the event, it was. I couldn't believe when I heard it the next day on the car radio coming home.

'I didn't say it was Reagan, remember? I said a world leader.'

'And you said he wouldn't be killed though. I mean that's fairly precise, isn't it? She's done it the odd time before and no doubt it'll happen again sometime. I think you ought to train your skill somehow, Loraine. It could make you a lot of money.'

'Oh heavens; how awful! No, thank you very much.' Loraine laughed. 'That sounds terribly fraudulent to say the least.'

'Well, the world's full of frauds then, I'd say,' countered Arthur again.

'So how do you know this stuff?' Pete mused.

'I don't know. I don't know how it happens, Pete. It just does. It pops into my head, and I know it as though it's already happened. I know when it's really a real premonition. It has a very distinct feel. But there's no way of telling when it's going to happen, and I can't make it happen. It does it itself.'

'What is *it* exactly, that does it itself?' Pete sat down. 'Like a piece of information from the future presumes to set itself up in your consciousness?' Pete continued.

'Yes, as though that piece of information has a consciousness too?' Sally finished off the question.

Loraine looked at Pete with a cheeky smile. 'What do you think?'

'I knew you were about to say that!' Pete said.

Everyone laughed at the joke.

'I would think that such information would have had to have come from somewhere. It can't just have popped out of thin air. It can't have consciousness itself. It at least had to come from some*one* – the killer, say.'

'Yes, but John Hinckley intended to kill Reagan. Loraine's premonition was that he wouldn't be killed, and that was what happened,' said Arthur.

'Okay, you've got me. There is no reasonable, comprehensible answer.'

Pete took a seat round the large dining table, next to Sally, nodding and smiling to familiar faces.

'I remember, Pete, when I first saw you in the Cathedral,' Rose said, 'that you talked about Tim having an exchange with a swan at Brayford Pool. Now couldn't there be something similar in that? A bird and an autistic child appearing to have, what? A conversation?'

'Oh but really that was just childish fantasy – more the line my daughter touted about the whole thing. Anyway, how is that similar to predicting the future?'

'I was thinking about the exchange of an idea between two creatures, theoretically and indeed quite obviously, without the ability to exchange any real kind of meaning, real as we'd understand real anyway.'

'Well we don't know what they exchanged. It just *looked* like something, but it's pure conjecture. There was a comfort, an affinity, between a sweet child and an animal – that kind of thing must happen often. A lot of animals are sensitive to people's natures I suppose.'

'Yes of course, but at the time you'd felt there'd been something ...'

'Yes that's true,' replied Pete, resisting an urge to deny what he'd seen. 'It had felt like some kind of recognition, some mutual respect. It was uncanny. At least I felt that at the time, but now I'm not so sure. I don't want to get sentimental about my son and what he does. I want something more solid to work with. It's so easy to imagine these things. They're fantasy, a bit of sop.'

'Yes, but just the same, what do you think it was about?' Loraine persisted.

'I don't know, I don't know.' Pete tapped his temple lightly. 'I felt something at the time, I do remember. When I look at him, so often it seems like he's on a different plane. Well, he is. He's a wee boy trapped inside his own consciousness with little that enables him to find his way out of there. I certainly don't believe any more that there's nothing in there – in his head, I mean.'

'No, of course there's not, of course ...'

'And when I met you that day too,' Rose continued, 'some of the things you said did make me wonder about what Tim *knows*, and of course that whatever that is, is a difficult, maybe impossible thing for *us* to know.'

'Yes,' said Pete. 'But I don't have much in the way of explanation. I want to do the right thing – of course – all parents do. But what is that? The views on what is the right thing cover a huge gamut of possibilities – focusing on teaching him life skills – very practical and important of course. Pressure cooker play therapy ...' Pete wiggled fingers on two hands emphasising inverted commas and the notion of 'play therapy'. 'And then there's the almost inane response of a few – I'm sorry to put it that way – that Tim is very spiritual. Or even this idea that when he stares at nothing and laughs and smiles that he's communicating with some spiritual something-or-other that we can't see. With the *Angels*, some say. Well, that's not useful for me,' Pete continued with a little exasperation. 'There's certainly nothing in those kinds of comments that gives me, as his father, some kind of – any kind of – direction. I mean it creates huge hurdles to understanding, and I have no idea where the first hurdle even is.'

'You must have some view on religion, on things spiritual?' This was from Sally.

It hadn't passed Pete by that the discussion was focused on him, and he wasn't sure why. He couldn't fathom how his son provoked such interest from others.

'My personal spiritual – religious – experience is more or less nil. It's something I've neglected, deliberately I suppose. And I'm feeling bereft really, even more now that I find myself here.' Pete felt safely unjudged, despite the context, although a little uncomfortable at being the centre of attention, but intrigued by it also.

'What do you think the knowledge is that you want?' Sally asked again.

'I don't know. I guess I'm interested in people's experiences for starters.'

'You know, Pete,' Loraine spoke kindly and with sincerity, 'you can't just pick and choose, or take a wee peek – get your feet wet – just to see if you like it, or if it has something to offer you. You can't toy with God.'

Wow, how did we get here? Pete thought.

'That's the first rule if you like,' Loraine continued. 'It's not about you. It's about God, and God Power and God's Light and Universal Energy, and *it* decides what to give *you* – you don't decide what you might take. Your job is simply to be open, to listen, and to feel – not so much in fact to *understand*. You'll never understand God and Spirit in the same way you understand any other body of knowledge, or even in the same way you may intuit things about your children say, about their needs. You'll understand God because first and above all, you will feel the presence of God in your life, and you will submit to his, her, or its power.'

A long quiet set itself down in the room and Pete mulled over Loraine's words, as apparently were others. Maitland looked as though he may say something and then appeared to rethink the idea.

'Well, Loraine, despite that wee lecture,' grinning, 'I will say that I do have some trust in you, so I will go ahead and say what's on my mind right *now*, and that is ... what a load of bollocks!' He grinned widely at his host.

Maitland guffawed loudly, and Sally made an audible sound of relief.

Loraine hooted, 'Oh, good! I did feel reasonably certain I could make precisely that kind of challenge and you wouldn't get up and leave. But, nonetheless, I know you'll have another view as well.'

'I do. It is, in fact, all about me,' Pete smirked. 'Actually.'

There was more laughter.

'All right, you two, serious now,' said Rose.

'What on earth for?' Maitland chimed in.

'Because I was just getting interested, that's why. Shoosh you!' Rose grinned at him.

Pete continued, 'Okay, look. I get what you're saying. But I'm never going to be someone who starts from some point of ... what? ... submission to the will of God, or the laws of some particular Faith. I'm blessed with a mind and an intellect and I want to determine the truth for myself, not accept someone else's word for it.'

'Yes, but you've said yourself you have no experience, so how else can you start but with what others have to say? And before you remind me that you've said you *are* interested in what others have to say, what *I* mean by 'others' is the great prophets of the many great religions. Christ of course, but also Muhammad, Buddha, Krishna, Bahá'u'lláh. How could you presume that they have less to say than some ordinary individual from around this table, myself included?'

'Because the words of Christ and Muhammad and Buddha and so on all come to us via the interpretation of ordinary mortals like those around this table anyway. We don't have an unfettered version of their wisdom.'

'Okay, a reasonable comment, although not entirely true just the same. But even if it were – and I do take your point – of course there are many interpretations of, for example, the Bible's many meanings. You can't discount the greatness of the universal Faiths that have followed these men. And please don't be tempted to give me that worn out old argument about religion having been the cause of so much violence and bloodshed – I won't buy that, at least not in the way it's offered by the godless as an excuse for their godlessness.'

'Whoa, you really want an argument, don't you?' countered Pete, unthreatened and enthusiastic.

'Not at all. A debate maybe. And anyway you're clearly up for it,' replied Loraine.

Pete laughed again. Others seemed amused and bemused. Pete wondered at the vehemence, soft though it was, from someone exhibiting such restraint on his previous visit to the group. Was he the protagonist here or was his host? Either way he didn't mind being challenged on his beliefs, or lack thereof.

'You think I'm godless?'

'I think a lot of people make their spirituality about them personally and nothing greater. Or if they do concede something greater, then they certainly try to *un*invent God in favour of 'A Higher Being' or 'Nature', or some such – an approach I find juvenile and spoilt. I don't know yet whether you're in that category – you haven't told us what you do or don't believe especially. Do you believe there is a God?'

'I don't know.'

'Do you think you've ever *felt* God?' Another voice asked. A younger man – Pete recalled he was Jason. He had the look of someone a long time at university.

Pete took a breath and paused, taking in what he'd heard and wondering if there was some logical foothold in it somewhere.

'I think Tim brings God into my life,' he replied slowly.

'That makes sense to me,' added Sally. 'I think if anything's awakened me to the bigger universe, it's been the experience of having children and being a parent.'

'What does it feel like then, this God Tim brings into your life?' the young man carried on.

'It feels like ... some sort of ... happiness.' Pete looked at the young man. 'I could use words like peaceful but that's not really it.'

'And what does that happiness feel like?' Loraine continued.

'I don't know – what is happiness? – it comes and goes, doesn't it?'

'Happiness moves very fast.'

'What?'

'Happiness moves very fast,' Loraine repeated.

'I don't get that. What do you mean?'

'We don't own happiness. It's not part of us. It's owned by God. Sometimes we're fortunate to feel enthralled by it – maybe even quite often, those of us lucky enough – but mostly it's transitory.'

'I'm still not with you.'

'Well you don't feel happy all the time, do you?'

'No.'

'But all of us would like to.'

'I suppose.'

'Well then why don't we?'

'Why?'

'Because it moves ... happiness. It's a force. It's the animating force of all things *I* think. Some people might say it's love – it doesn't matter – same thing. And it moves. Everything moves. Whether you think in the direction of chaos – entropy – or in the direction of unity, it doesn't matter. The animating spirit of the universe is constantly moving and creating and recreating. We catch hold of it occasionally and we feel *in the flow*, or free, or in love, or joyful, or especially creative. But we can't hold on to it. Because it moves very fast.'

Quiet again.

'I like that, I think.' Pete seemed to chew his words. 'Are you saying you think Tim clicks into this happiness ...?' Pete paused, mouth open and ready to speak, but lost where he was headed.

'I think the world becoming happier is one part of our evolution – our spiritual evolution. I think it's about our ability to rise above our material circumstances and connect to a universal spirit. And I think a big part of that connection is that we become happier. But we have to connect to *it* – not it to us. And because it's evolving all the time, we have to keep up. That's what I mean when I say *happiness moves very fast*. The essence of happiness is freedom from the material – actually, I think it's freedom from time as well, but that's another story. So yes, that is what I'm saying. I think Tim, and many others in this world, probably have a greater ability to connect to that universal spirit of happiness than the rest of us.'

'So we are talking about Tim in spiritual terms ... ?'

'It's just a word.'

'What is?'

'Spiritual.'

'All right, religious then.'

'That's just a word too.'

'But you want us to believe in religion – isn't that what you said before?'

'I want people not to discount religion and the many possibilities it offers to learn about God from an infinite number of metaphors and parables, from the prophets and from poets, from any number of different angles and perspectives.'

'I think you're contradicting yourself.'

'I think you're not listening.' Loraine grinned and eyeballed Pete for the umpteenth time.

'You're part of an organised religion – Christianity. Isn't that the message you want people to get?'

'I think Christianity is a very coherent religion, through most of its denominations and manifestations. I don't think there's anything I've told you that *doesn't* fit within a Christian framework. And indeed, I do think there are other very highly developed frameworks, and I mentioned some – Buddhism, Islam, the Baha'i Faith – I just happen to belong to this one. Because I do think one must make some commitment at some point. At least that was my need. And Christianity was what I knew.'

Pete looked at Loraine, and again there was a discernible pondering going on around the table. No one seemed to want to be the first to speak, as if something of value may be dented if they did.

'Thank you my dear,' Maitland said in time, as pause for thought continued.

'Yes, indeed,' added another.

'There was a lot there to think about, my dear,' Rose complimented Loraine. 'You seem to have caught an essence that's likewise capturing our friends' hearts and minds.'

'And souls,' added Sally.

'Well, you're most welcome. I do get on my high horse occasionally, but there you are,' replied Loraine.

After another pause, Maitland declared, 'All right then, you lot. Where's that promise of intemperance – the *real* reason we come here?'

Some chuckling about the table broke the reverie.

'Coming right up, my dear.' Rose smiled and got up to bring in bottles and glasses.

'Well, I'm quite at my leisure,' Maitland leant back, folding his arms..

'Mr Bennet!' chimed Sally and Rose at the same time.

Maitland grinned, pleased with himself, and pleased his *Jane Eyre* mimicry had got the recognition he'd wanted.

As Rose circled the table, depositing glasses and pouring wines, smaller conversations began around the table, till a pleasant hum replaced the quiet of earlier.

'I've really got something from this. Thank you,' said Pete, turning to Loraine beside him. 'And I feel – perhaps a little arrogantly – that you have shown me a considerable respect by choosing to look me in the eye and poke me in the consciousness as you have.' Pete gave her a small nod.

'Well, I enjoy a good fish, Pete,' said Loraine.

'My God,' Maitland burst out. 'I've been outdone. Usurped! How did you, Pete, manage to get this woman to come out guns blazing? That has hitherto been my preserve alone. I salute you.'

There was laughter all around.

'My shout then?' Maitland proffered.

There was more laughter.

'Oh no, you don't, Maitland,' Rose said, starting to pour. 'You heard what Pete said before. Heaven knows what state you got him into last time he was here. If it's some imbibing you're after, there's plenty here. Just you stay there, Pete. And you, Maitland.'

'Well said, Rose,' Pete added. 'Well said. Be a dear and pass that red down here.'

Pete helped himself to a couple of glasses and poured for Loraine and himself..

'You've given me a great deal,' he offered to Loraine. 'Thank you. I need to figure out what that means in practise now. And for Tim.'

'Well, you must start with *you*, Pete, *I* think.'

'Yes.'

'Don't use your head too much. This isn't about working out what you believe. This is about opening yourself to possibilities. I don't believe we should sit down and make a list of what we believe any more than I think one should decide to believe just what someone else tells them. The greatest gift we give our children is that there is a big, wide world of people and cultures and beliefs, and they should explore all of that.'

'But you've also said we should make a commitment,' Pete replied.

'Yes, in due course. But first be open, and investigate the truth. You don't have to accept what I say. I'm simply making an offering from my experience,' Loraine stated.

'A particularly valid experience,' Pete added.

'Well I like to think so, yes – probably. I've spent a lifetime exploring these things, so I do think I can assist others, but by way of ideas not by reciting doctrine.'

'Well, thank you again.'

'Thank you, Pete.' Loraine smiled and raised her wine glass in mock salute.

Friday, 5 June 1981

Tim being very autistic today. Spent large parts of the day looking out the corner of his eye. Seems unsettled. Not my smiling, laughing boy. Guess he's got to work on catching up with happiness too sometimes.

They're reporting on a new disease affecting gay men; it's called AIDS – can't remember what it stands for. Churches already saying it's the wrath of God – spoil sports.

Still thinking about last trip to Rose and Loraine's. Complex and hard to put one's finger on it. Think I need to let go of all that for a while. Besides which there is enough to be dealing with here. I think I confuse my relationship with everyone around me by considering all of that. Tim's basic needs are the most important. Love and warmth. Food and survival. Maslow's hierarchy. Simple stuff. I'm barely up to more than that myself. Bit more warmth'd be a good thing.

Saturday, 13 June 1981

Timmy had a better week. Did another amazing painting the other day. Spent ages on it again. Lots of red. Not sure if that means anything. How would you know? He had other colours to use but did it mostly in red – few wee bits of black and yellow. It was very striking. The whole page was covered. Which in itself is interesting – most kids his age do a blob in the middle, but not him. And very concentrated about it too, he was.

Bloody Queen's been shot at 'n' all, at Trooping the Colour – blanks though – bet it freaked a few horses out – HM seemed rather cool about it. Good on her.

Marcus Serjeant was the idiot. Interestingly, he said he'd been inspired by the assassination of John Lennon last year, and the attempts made on the lives of Ronald Reagan and the Pope this year. He was apparently rather excited about the fame Mark David Chapman secured after killing John Lennon, and after John Hinckley's attempt on Reagan he said he fancied being the first one to take a pot shot at the Queen. He was just a teenager.

Sunday, 14 June 1981

Seven members of the Baha'i spiritual assembly in Hamadan in Iran were executed by firing squad today, following two years of persecution by the new Islamic regime there. When their bodies were later prepared for their funeral, it was apparent that six of them had been tortured as well. What's wrong with this World? How can a peaceful Faith such as this pose such a threat to Islam? I think so far the Baha'is represent the only major religion not to have killed others in God's name.

Thursday, 18 June 1981

Went to Rose and Loraine's again this evening. Someone back from some meditation retreat talking about meditation generally and what it feels like. Discussion about light and about connecting with God. Someone brought up this thing about Tim 'talking to the Angels'. Someone else launched into a monologue about the hierarchy of Angels. Didn't really get it. Loraine lent me a book on the way out.

Seems all the world's Holy Writings have a lot to say about Angels. In Islam, malaikah means 'belief in Angels' and the word is mentioned a hundred times in the Qur'an. There's a hierarchy of Angels, and the Islamic version of this is very similar to the Judaeo-Christian tradition. Angels as such are actually the lowest order in nine tiers, the next is Archangels, all the way up to Cherubim and Seraphim. They all have their different roles and responsibilities, having to do with maintaining order in Heaven, on Earth, and in the Universe generally. God's Energy is strongest in the higher levels of Angels – so strong that we mere mortals can't discern them. So it's up to the lower levels – the Archangels and Angels – to act as intermediaries between Heaven and Earth. These are the Angels that interact most frequently with humans and carry prayers towards God. Mystics in all the traditions believe it is our communion with these figures that brings us into the presence of God. Some of us would prefer to view this talk of Angels as imagery, symbol, and metaphor.

Anyway, my favourite bit in the book was this quote from Chesterton that I'd not read before: 'Angels can fly because they take themselves lightly'. How lovely is that?

Which reminded me of my favourite bit of Chesterton: 'The world is divided into Conservatives and Progressives. Progressives go on making mistakes and Conservatives prevent the mistakes from ever being corrected.' Well, I guess mistakes in the name of progress is at least something. Aren't we supposed to learn from them?

Wednesday, 29 July 1981

Royal bloody wedding – otherwise-thought-of-as-sane people going very gaga. Can't stand it. What is that obsession? It seems on the increase. Is it the fairytale? I guess so. Shame there's no such thing. As no doubt the poor royal sods will find out for themselves. Dear, oh dear. Who would choose such a thing?

As a juxtaposition, the Springboks are touring New Zealand and causing all sorts of mayhem. A match was cancelled in Hamilton the other day, in front of a full crowd, after several hundred protestors invaded the field. Apparently, there were rumours of a light plane being stolen and heading for the stadium. The Springboks beat Taranaki today, but the real tour action was outside Parliament. Kiwi police used batons on protestors. The news quoted Norman Kirk's (former prime minister) prediction ten years ago that a South African tour of New Zealand would cause 'the greatest eruption of violence this country has ever known'. Now there's a little prescience for you.

My life is disturbingly unromantic and uneventful. Disturbing? Perhaps too strong a word. Partly I like it that way. Partly I've chosen it, I suppose.

Sent off a cynical piece on the state of the English psyche but can't imagine any responsible editor wanting to print it – not what sells.

Life continues here along the usual furrows and fissures – Tim being Tim, Jillie growing up, Alicia obviously stuck (i.e. not growing up), me being a pain in the arse for her – apparently. One does try. Or maybe I don't. Maybe I'm as stuck in being as unresponsive as she is. I don't know any more what she wants from me, and I'm terrified to ask. It all seems a little pointless. What though is my responsibility in all this? What is my obligation to her? And to myself?

I wonder if she's thought about leaving. I suspect she has. Having Tim makes it harder of course. What man or woman would with conscience leave their spouse with an autistic child, or take one in tow on one's own?

I'm being very negative.

I wonder about the impact of the space she's in, on Tim and Jillie. She has no relationship to speak of with either of them at the moment. Do they feel that as a loss, some gap? Does her anger bear down on them in any way? Stop them from growing, from feeling free?

This is dumb.

Friday, 21 August 1981
Libyan fighter jets 'engaged' a couple of US ones in the Gulf of Sidra on Wednesday, and the US shot down one Libyan plane. All very tense. Sadat's mediation between East and West of crucial value. Not making him so many friends in his own region though. A shame. How is it that this thing that is Islam, at once so beautiful and accomplished, should be so riven?

'Do you think Timmy's got spiritual qualities?' Tim rang his wife at her office.

'What?'

'I've just been thinking about it. I wanted to know what you thought.'

'I'm at work!'

'I know, but I thought you might like a call.'

There was silence at the end of the phone.

'Right.'

'Sorry. Bad timing.'

'No. No, it's fine. Really. I'm bored anyway. Nothing unusual about that though, I s'pose.'

'I um ... just think sometimes there're things going on his head that we don't know about.'

'I think you've been going to too many of those meetings.'

'It's not about that.'

'Well, what's it about then?'

'Well, aren't you after some answers too? About your science. This is all part and parcel.'

'No, it's not. It's nothing like it. I don't confuse science with religion, Pete.'

'It's not about religion. It's about what we don't know and find hard to understand. It's about making sense of things. Isn't that what you want?'

'Sorry hun, but I don't think I'm with you on this one. Different planet for me.'

'Okay, well, I just wondered if you were curious about that. I guess not. See you later then, eh?'

'Sure.'

Friday, 21 August 1981 continued

Timmy having another 'disturbed' period. Unsettled. I don't know if I can ever make any really positive difference in his life. If he is 'spiritual' – if what he's all about is having some connection with the Universe that I don't and can't ever get, then I have no idea how I can ever support that in any way. Is it just enough that I love him and care for him and try each day to connect with him, and try to connect him to this world the rest of us live in? I feel some pressure to be something else for him. Is it possible that some instruction is being yelled in my ear but I can't hear it? Nonsense.

Have tried to broach this all with Lissy but there doesn't seem to be a way of discussing it that would be comprehensible to her.

Paradoxically she has written a paper in response to the Paris experiments which she asked me to read – it's way over my head. Nice that she asked though. She's spent hours, days and months pondering the implications of this. Is it that that draws her away from us, or does she pursue her work in order to escape us? Possibly she wouldn't know the answer to that question herself.

Monday, 24 August 1981
Lennon's killer sentenced to life in lieu of the non-effectiveness of his insanity plea. Odd it took so long for this trial and sentencing. Nearly a year. The year seems full of murder.

Tim lay down on the sofa. His mind was buzzing with information and shooting lights. He'd worked hard to decipher all of it and translate it all on to his painting paper at the easel. In the end, he was frustrated because he knew the message wasn't coming out right. He'd tried to tell this to those who came with the message, but they seemed intent on delivering *their* message and not hearing his. He was confused about some of the lines of things, which way the light travelled and when it was coming and when it was going. There was so much of it sometimes that it began to all spin round in his head and then it would lack clarity, and he didn't like it when everything was fuzzy. He wanted it all to be clear. When it got too fuzzy he would have to find a line to concentrate on, to try and make everything clear again.. Or else he'd have to lie down and close his eyes.

Even when it was fuzzy though it gave him lots of energy, so much sometimes he'd just jump up and down and up and down for such a long time. That helped make things clear too sometimes.

No one would have known that Timmy knew about other places and other times. No one really understood or believed either that if Tim jumped up and down enough then it would change the world, that his present affected the future. Some knew the idea in theory, but no one really believed that if a butterfly flapped its wings it could cause a thunder storm on the other side of the world. Nor indeed that in another dimension the future had already happened and that a particular flock of Angels were depending on the favours of small children to see and understand and create a different possibility.

Timmy stood at the crux of an idea between two worlds and many dimensions, and he had begun to gather the portent of his role in the universe. A great deal depended on his success.

9

Fulk was more animal than man – feral in nature, like the creatures he preyed upon. He'd known no person to make a difference to his life. His earliest memory was of straggling over a forest path alone, and later secreting through villages and peasantries in search of vague scratchings and rodents on which to survive. If he had another name other than Fulk, then it was lost to him, along with anyone who may have once known him, as well as from whence he came. It seemed an odd name to most ears, but Fulk knew he was Fulk and it seemed the right sort of name to him, although it wasn't much heard and he didn't much speak it himself, or anything particularly. He did not know his age since he didn't count much past his two hands; a few who noticed a little of such things might have said they'd seen Fulk around about since Berta Draper's husband passed on, or since Matthew Callim lost his leg to a foul creeping disease, or maybe even since Father Taylor arrived, a novice, to Lincoln, which meant around twenty-five years, and then there was the few years before that that Fulk had actually been on the earth at all. So he was not a young man. He had long hair like a mane, a beard which was really just a continuation of the mane, nothing for his feet to stand up in except the dirt that cased them, few teeth and quick-darting black eyes that held little thought behind them except an initiative to feed and avoid danger. His clothes were ragged and protected him from nothing. He smelt very bad, especially as it was hot these days, which at least meant he could be alive from the cold. Fulk didn't notice his own smell so much and not many others had ever come close enough for it to be a bother.

Fulk sat at a particular spot at the edge of the Thane's lands where he knew he was hidden from sight of the Thane's men who trailed the forest as a threat to poachers. Fulk was only a small bit worried that a man he knew and had seen taking a beast from the forest's keep had been caught and taken away screaming his innocence. Fulk didn't know what would happen to the man, nor did he care, although it was clear it was far from the man's liking, and Fulk thought to pay extra attention to his own movements. He knew better than others how to hide himself and was sure none of the groundsmen had ever laid their eyes on him.

Fulk had never acquired the traps other men used to catch animals. He was quiet and quick and he would catch small animals with his hands and rip their heads from their bodies or wring their necks. He could use his own teeth, such as he had, to bite into their fur and would skin the animals with his fingers. Commonly he caught birds, ducks, ferrets or rabbits, and he was not concerned to give a long wait to his trapping, and in this way he would surprise the most alert and quick of small creatures. He saw though that other men with their traps caught much larger animals and he found himself harbouring some small curiosity now about the taste of such beasts, in addition to some sense of the productivity gains of a trap in these stinking hot days. He knew where the man who had been taken had his traps hidden, and he knew also that the Thane's men had not found all of these. Already he had removed a hare from one such trap, dead from its bleeding. He didn't much like the hare – rabbit was more to his liking, but he didn't mind it so much as to discard eating it. He'd thought he would set the trap again somewhere new, somewhere only he would know to find it, and see what different beasts would come along. And so he sat here now with a full belly, hidden, watching the small clearing where he had reset the other poacher's trap and wondering what might come along to it. He hoped it would be some larger animal, and he laid down, still with an eye to the trap's spot and an ear to the movements and the sounds of the woods.

Bishop Hugh's carriage wound its way through wandering peasant folk and townspeople at the edge of Lincoln, those who recognised him doffing their hats or bowing a little as they scurried about their way. Hugh scanned the horizon of the city's walls and the structures rising up the hill of Lincoln. From this vantage point, he knew he should have seen the Cathedral, but as with the whole of his dusty journey across the vast flatness of Lincolnshire towards the hilltop town, there was no sight at all of its roof or towers.

The Cathedral had stood for much of the last hundred years and was the first cathedral ordered built by William the Conqueror. It had cost a fortune then, as well as a generation of labour, and would do more than that again now.

Still, Hugh looked out hopefully for some vestige of the great church and put thoughts of cost and sacrifice out of his head.

He wondered what the mood of the townsfolk might be. He couldn't tell, but he recalled the stories conveyed to him by the vicar of Torksey and the priest's fears about a rising tension. Things seemed usual within the city, albeit that there seemed more people about than was usual. But he wondered at the precariousness of it. For the most part the people were inherently superstitious and Hugh knew the collapse of a church would have tongues wagging. Few would have considered the likelihood of an engineering weakness or the age or height of the building, or just the sheer power of the earthquake. Hugh himself was determined to understand all he could in this respect, for he would have it that the new cathedral would not topple with such ease in the future, and he knew also he must maintain a calm and kindly exterior, one that would lead people away from superstition. He also knew what a challenge that path would be. For as long as people had believed anything at all, he knew they'd believed what they chose to, even in the face of stupendous evidence to the contrary. Subtlety and Faith would have to come together for the sake of peace.

The Bishop was settled back into his seat as he was conveyed through the city wall at the river gate and up the cobbled hill road to the crest. Once through the wall, he knew by now he certainly should have seen the cathedral rising proudly above all the surrounding structures, but he deigned instead not to look out and up. Already there were the signs of rebuilding as men carried all manner of tools and materials up the hill. Most seemed very young – boys even – and Hugh knew their labours were missed by their families already, all of whom would be poor. No family that was not peasant would feel cause to satisfy the Church's call for so many, and such others as these would contribute anyway, in materials or fine adornment for the new building or its deaconry, whether from obligation, or to assuage guilt, or to make evident their affluence or position. For some it would earn their own pew or burial within the Church; the poor would wait longer for their reward.

Nearing the top of the hill, Hugh's eyes followed a young boy, of thirteen years or so, who pushed a small flat-topped handcart along the side of the road. Hugh's own vehicle was slow as it wended its way up and through the streets of people and animals and carts, so he remained apace with the boy, who seemed singularly set on his task and apparently had no mind to the buggy beside him or the clergyman's attention to him.

The boy's clothes, although worn and old, were carefully stitched in many places, demonstrating some mother's proud attention to her own handiwork and thrift and possibly to some idea of what was decent or respectable. He was fair-haired and might one day be handsome. Hugh surmised the lad would have had little notion of God's intention for him or his kin, knowing nought but work and his place in the world..

He gazed at the boy as both wended their way across the square atop the hill. Something caught the boy's attention and he stopped and turned to a voice calling him from across the road. As he turned he caught the Bishop's face peering at him and puzzled at it momentarily before halting his small cart and remembering to drop his head deferentially and doff his non-existent cap. With the mass of workmen and equipment at the front of them the Bishop's carriage came to a halt and so the boy and the Bishop were left before each other, both briefly lost to the call of the wider scene and their role in it.

'Thurstan!' came a shout a way away. 'Ger'over 'ere, ya ijit!'

The boy raised his head to the shout.

'Arm comin', Dem,' he called back.

Hugh watched the boy veer his small cart away hurriedly to meet up with a bigger boy across the road, continuing then alongside the older boy.

Clearly his brother, judging from their likeness. Or perhaps cousins. Two boys from one family. They are some mother's sons.

The boys headed beneath the Exchequer Gate, disappearing from view amid the larger throng of workers, mostly young men like themselves.

Hugh alighted from his carriage and thanked his coachman. With the young priest Peter in step behind him, he weaved through the crowds of workmen and others, most of them clearing a way and kneeling briefly as he filed past.

Hugh noticed around the square a number of women begging, some with small children. There were always some of these, but today there were more, and most seemed afraid. Other folk about, who were not obviously workmen, sold bread and other provisions from baskets or the back of carts. Some were giving away some of their loaves to those begging.

On one side a queue of men lined up, and at the front of the line was another man wearing the leather apron of a master mason, vetting them as to their skill and experience. Most would be accepted he knew, for now. Hugh picked out the different occupations of the workers by their clothes, their tools, whether they worked alone or were consulting in small groups over drawings or samples of stone or metal. There was great industry afoot and far from feeling it as a sacrifice just yet, in fact Hugh could see from their faces that most of its participants were pleased to be engaged in a pursuit greater than themselves, and the youth among them on an adventure whose grand design mattered not. Not so much for God or Church did they labour, but because the edifice that would be this great new cathedral would stand for their labours for most likely hundreds of years, and indeed for a man to work in the creation of something so fine was a testimony to his prowess and skill, and this sat well with the good in many a man. Not to mention that the Cathedral was a symbol of the community's strength and resilience, and that also sat well.

Hugh felt his own dire mood lift as the buzz of the industry infected him and he found himself enthusiastic now for an ache in his shoulders that would prove a day's strong work, just as these many others about him would achieve. His mind was filled with facts of engineering and construction, of architecture and style, and he knew they would whirl in his head from the dawn of each day and again even as he tried to sleep at night. He would return each day to this scene for more of the consumption of hard work and its influence on his soul.

Hugh rejoiced in the ordered flurry of the scene. As people about him kneeled, greeted him, offered a blessing towards him, or even reached to touch the hem of his purple cassock as he walked past, Hugh prayed to God he would have the resolve to shepherd this great city and all that lay within and without its walls, in the direction of God's purpose.

Walking beneath the arch, Hugh saw beyond the throng, the sight that he'd briefly been distracted from and into which his eyes were now immersed.

One part of one front tower was the only substantially remaining part of the church, and it jutted obstinately up amid a great mass of rubble, around which circled an army of coordinated activity. The scene before him though did not shock or upset him. Whereas Hugh had experienced dread in anticipation of this scene, he now renewed a hope, alongside the tenacity and steadfastness of the Church propelling itself into the future, as this one remaining spire contrived to prove its own invincibility.

We will prevail.

As he neared the cathedral, one of the architects who had been at the Bishop's residence in Stowe a day earlier stepped up to him..

'Your Grace.' The man knelt and kissed the Bishop's ring.

'Master Goodman, my Lord,' Peter whispered into the Bishop's ear.

'Ah, Master Goodman. What a great hive of work you have afoot!'

'Aye, m'Lord. There's not a man here has taken his load lightly, sir. There's much to be done, as you know, sir.'

'Indeed. I am encouraged, Master Goodman. I want to know everything. Everything. How long until the rubble is cleared for a start?'

'I's not just a matter of clearing, m'Lord. There's a lot of sorting to be done.' The architect pointed to the largest pile of rubble and to men heaving stones aside. 'Much of the stone can be reused and each stone that's fallen is checked for how suitable it'd be and for what. Some look right, but they've cracks and can't be used as they were before. Some can be made into smaller stones. Th'rest is kept aside and poured into the new foundations. Nothing's wasted, sir. Not if we can help it – expensive business building a cathedral, sir.'

'Oh, my word, don't I know it. Then I'm very, very pleased, Master Goodman. For you understand one of our greatest trials in this regard.'

'Your Grace,' Peter sought a break in this exchange. 'May I suggest you seek some refreshment before your day takes you any further; it's been a long journey.'

'Oh, nonsense, Peter, but I will take something to aid my strength for this labour, if that is what you mean.'

'Of course, Your Grace.'

'Thank you, Mr Goodman.' Hugh looked about him again. 'I will return very soon, and I will want you to guide me through the cathedral.'

'Of course, Your Grace, although we will need to be most careful, sir, as there are still stones toppling sometimes.'

'Oh, I'm confident Our Lord will protect me.'

'Very good, sir. Then it will be my privilege, Your Grace.'

'It is all our privilege, Mr Goodman, to serve this great Cause.' Hugh looked up to the remaining spire.

'It is certainly that, sir,' the architect rejoined, following the Bishop's line of sight.

Hugh smiled and nodded at the man and his colleagues and allowed his young caretaker to lead him back through the arch to the temporary quarters that had been established for him at the Castle. Peter knew the Bishop would work himself literally to the bone should he be left to do so, and the young priest knew his own task, to ensure the well-being of his master, was as good as any mission in the cause of God and the Church..

The architects returned to their plans, and men around about who had seen the Bishop step into their enterprise, and others who knew who this man must be were able to tell those who had no clue to his identity, so that in a short time he was known to every man and boy awork at the site..

Geoffrey Warriner heard this news as he saw his brothers walking towards him.

''Ere, see tha' man in't purple thar – tha's Bishop, Bishop Hugh they say. Come t'see you two's doin' yer work roight, so be doin' it proper won' ya, eh?'

''E looked a' me, 'e did. Loik 'e knew me 'n'all,' said Thurstan.

'Ya fool. 'E don' know yer from a worm.'

'Well, 'e looked a' me jus' same.'

''E's a great man, 'e is. Go' no toim for loiks a you, ya' gi'.' Geoffrey Warriner laughed at his younger brother. 'Come on. Ge' this lo' loaded up. Go' plenty more 'a this lo' t'shift before we eat today.'

'Aye, y'worm!' Dem laughed at his younger brother.

'Ger' off!' Thurstan punched him back defiantly.

Alice Warriner was cleaning the soil from Thomas. He lay uncomplaining on his side, and she looked at the same time to the back of his head where she could see a scab forming already over the gash. She hadn't believed her husband's and son's and Bennet Williams's story about Thomas's injury, although she had no inkling to what really had caused it. She wondered perhaps her husband had become angry and done it himself, but she had never known him to such violence, and she thought he would not do so even now when he was roused to such a choler with the taking of his sons.

Thomas seemed now to pay his wound no mind, although did she see some particular quiet in him this last day? Was he simply hurt, or was he frightened, perhaps untrusting now in the limited understanding he had of the world he was in. Alice felt torn in keeping him to the inside of their home, and giving him air to breathe and different faces and activity to see, which she felt gave him some small abundance. There was hardly any need to think of such things amid the vast array of her work, but she still saw her very first duty to Thomas, a duty she knew no one else would ever adopt.

After she'd finished cleaning him she lifted him into his small pen and he sat quietly there, not watching her. Alice though watched him as she went about other tasks, from time to time drawing close to study how she thought he might be. Her husband and other sons had gone to the fields with some of the men from the hamlet to examine their flocks and had taken tools to shear and pick at animals in whatever ways they did. She would be alone most of the day, and now with so many fewer in their household this was an unimagined state of things, and Alice found the quiet an uncertain tranquillity. This made her tasks on the one hand easier for her; but on the other hand she found an unusual intrusion in her mind that let her feel the possibility of not completing one or two of her tasks, like an idleness had crept into her thoughts to suggest some new indulgence that her life could be other than a peasant farmer's wife and that there was something more she could have that would fill her up and make her a different person. She felt this as though it were something promising in the world – some new force of God's nature that she'd not known before, but it pulled against a lifetime of knowing her place and committing to the days' long labours. Into this seeming vacuum was sucked a vision of a light-filled destiny that found some form, and even words in her head, and Alice was happy to see her family leave each day so she had room to breathe in more of this picture. While she was careful not to yield to this intellectual extravagance too much, it became the case that there was a little more dust to her house, and a little less care to her food, and a little more grubbiness to the cloth of her family's vests and smocks, but she knew none other than an observant wife such as herself would ever spy such a difference, and so she worried less about this. Nor did she worry, in reality, that God had anything other than a peasant's drudgery and grief for her; and though she had long ago given up believing that beauty was of the devil, she still held to hard work as a reasonable path to His grace. She wondered though that God could put such thoughts in her head if they were not to be had, and she hoped He might offer some sign of his intention that she could perceive from her lowly vantage point.

As if she could possibly see this best in the open air, Alice stepped through the low door of her house and out on to the hard ground that was her front yard. As she did so, riding into her view was the perplexing sight of one whose arrival might otherwise herald more grief to her small family. She espied the pompous set and stride of Father Taylor upon his horse pulling up in front of her and she had enough thought to display the right deference to the priest as he clearly intended to dismount before her.

For Father Taylor's part, he had seen this woman he knew as the mother of the idiot boy who had only the day before been so unfortunately struck down in the village, but he saw her as no different from any other crude peasant, domiciled as she was in a tiny and squalid hut at the edge of the forest. He noted her proper courtesy to him and wondered what sense he would get from one of such limited capacity and reason, especially a woman.

'Good day, madam,' he called, dismounting and leading his horse to a tying post.

'Good day, Father,' Alice replied, waiting anxiously for whatever it was he'd arrived for.

Father Taylor stood and contemplated the woman.

'I've come to see how the young boy is. I was concerned at the incident yesterday and I feel it requires some investigation on my part. Do you understand?'

'My son is resting, sir. He seems mostly his usual self, I believe.'

Father Taylor realised he'd never heard this woman speak before and was surprised at some intelligence in her voice, although he thought perhaps it was just that she was not so rasping or crude as many. She would certainly be as ignorant as any other.

'Good. Good,' he continued slowly. 'There was some disquiet as to the manner of his injury. Apparently, there is no culprit to explain this unfortunate accident yet, but I will make it my business to find one. I don't wish to see these kinds of disturbances in the village. Things being as they are.'

'Yes, Father,' Alice wondered anew at the veracity of her husband's claims as to Thomas's accident.

'Did the boy himself speak of anything, madam?'

'He does not speak, sir.'

'No, of course. I'm sorry. I wasn't sure the extent of his ... affliction. Has he always been like this?'

'He seemed as usual a boy as any when he was born, sir. But he didn't grow up as the others did,' Alice replied. 'I had six before him, you see. All boys they were.'

'Were?'

'Three have gone to the Cathedral, Father.'

'Three? Oh yes. Of course. Well, with so many ... And it's a great task they commit for the Church of course.'

'Yes, Father.'

'And your husband?'

'He's gone to the fields today, sir, with the other boys.'

'Hmm.' Father Taylor nodded. 'These are difficult times, madam. You must pray for your sons. All of them.'

'I pray without cease, sir, for my sons and others, and for Thomas most of all.'

'Thomas?'

'The youngest, sir. The one injured in the village. He of all does not deserve such pain or suffering as that. I think of him as one of God's angels, put here to show us something of great meaning. I'm grateful for him really because of that. Blessed, I think God has made me, through him.'

The priest had far from expected more than a few words from the woman, and wondered how it was that she could articulate anything at all of God's will or indeed any other matter. The incongruity of this woman's lot with her good graces was one of life's unfortunate errors of birth, and he was grateful he'd not had the misfortune himself to wake each day to the filth of a peasant life.

'May I see the boy, please?'

'Yes of course, sir.' Alice turned and went back through the small cloth door, returning a moment later with an altogether normally appearing boy, albeit that he showed sleepiness and some inattention. Thomas squinted in the sun and rubbed his eyes, moving his head left and right and peering from the corner of his eyes. Although he looked to be searching for something out of the darkness, his eyes did not light upon the priest.

'This is Thomas, sir,' Alice said, her arm about Thomas's shoulder as she held her eyes lovingly to his great ruff of blonde hair which stood out every which way.

A great smile perched itself across Thomas's face and Father Taylor couldn't tell if he found this disarming or disquieting, and he studied the boy closely.

'He's a happy child then?'

'Yes, sir, he's happy, almost always, except yesterday of course. He seemed frightened when they brought him back.'

'Hmm,' the priest muttered again, still studying him. 'Can he do anything? Anything at all?'

'Not a thing, sir. He has no skill in anything.'

'Then it is an extra mouth for you.'

Alice looked up at the priest now. 'We don't mind him, sir.'

'No, indeed.' Father Taylor looked at the woman, wondering why he ought to feel chastened by this lowly creature. 'Well, be about your business, madam. I won't keep you.' And then he turned quickly without another look at Thomas, to mount his horse and turn it away from the small holding and back again down the dry clay road towards the town.

Thomas looked then to the departing horse and rider and the smile went from his face. Alice paid no more mind to the priest and his visit, not wondering as to its peculiarity in any way. There seemed no value in it for her. And if some misfortune her husband would not tell her had befallen the boy, then it had passed now and perhaps that would be the end of it. Perhaps she would keep him to their house a while though.

Fulk had been lying a good while in a new and hidden watching spot beneath the tree he'd previously occupied. There was nothing about hurry that Fulk needed to know of in his life. He was mainly about eating and sleeping and staying warm to the extent that he could. There was no trouble with that today though and the warm that there was had made him sleepy, and he'd dozed and not quite slept through the high sun hours.

He stretched now and sat up from his warm nest of leaves and other forest droppings. He needed to walk about now or he would be stiff later, even though it was warmer. Fulk got up slowly and quietly onto his big feet, crouching a moment and looking about, listening for any sounds that were not the usual ones always there. Sensing no risk or menace, he crept slowly, and a little stooped, to a large tree and stood quietly against its trunk, almost blending in entirely to the rough bark. He looked about once more and edged slowly away from this tree to another, again stopping a spell until moving on again, and in this way he manoeuvred slowly and quietly in the direction he wanted, without much insistence to get there in any more time than this method would take.

In a while, he got to the edge of the forest where a small lake rested ponderously in the warm day, and here Fulk sat back against another tree a while, thinking he might scoop a drink from the water since he found himself dry in his mouth. He was not too familiar with water, having never understood to wash himself, and only once having ventured a little way into a pond, to then have to suffer an unbearable itching for days from some mite that got under his clothes, which he'd had no thought to remove any part of before his wading.

Fulk liked the shining on the water. Things didn't shine in the forest much, at least not like this, not this much. This shine was so bright as to make him blink and close his eyes, and when he looked away, he couldn't see some things for a while; he thought this was not so useful, so he tried not to look at the water's surface where it was alight, but it was hard not to also because it caught his eye..

In between looking at the water and not looking at the water, a great white duck moved from behind some reeds and floated a small way towards him, coming side on to him and looking with a sharp dark red eye in his direction. Fulk hadn't seen these white ducks before. It was much, much larger than the usual ducks and had a very long white neck. In fact he suspected it wasn't a duck at all, but something else – just as a hare wasn't a rabbit but it was something else instead. He wondered whether the bird was dangerous with its big black beak, and he wondered whether he could catch one and what it might taste like. He'd seen ducks take off into flight from the water's surface, and he thought about what this giant bird would look like if it came up off the water and flapped its wings to fly. Possibly because it was very large it might be very slow to move, and this could give him some advantage to catching it. Perhaps it had claws instead of wading feet, but Fulk couldn't see through the water to tell this. Claws could be a problem. Not that the pain from bleeding or tearing was too much difficult for Fulk, for he'd had plenty of this, but he'd once become so ill that he'd known he'd lost several days, and he knew this had come from a sharp tear in his neck from a ferret he'd not quite handled in the best way. And he knew also that some animals' claws were bigger than others.

The bird floated across the water in front of Fulk, all the time looking at him, and he looked at the bird. It glided across the shiny patch of water, and for a few seconds Fulk couldn't see the bird at all, and then it swam across past the shine, and it was still looking at him. Fulk, the man, had only animal instincts and killing thoughts of the bird, but the bird itself had almost none of these.

10

Those who have ascended have different attributes
from those who are still on earth, yet there is no real separation.
When you do not know it they are able to make suggestions to you.
'Abdu'l-Bahá

The two men at the lake edge attracted no attention from
all those around attending to their own business, which was in large
part the loading and unloading of canal boats and barges of
different kinds and the transport of shipped contents to and fro. A
city such as this was notably full of those of some holy order or
other, as well. These two, one older and one younger, were less
conspicuous than many, dressed as they were in the coarse brown
robes of simple monks.

They walked slowly; anyone who spied them would say that
the older was stooped, and the younger walked slowly for his sake.
The truth was their thoughts, many and complex, slowed their pace
as they sought the essence of their discussion. It would also be
apparent to an observer that the younger was a novice of the older,
and this was more or less the case, although not in a way most
would understand. It was also true, as many would assume, that
their talk was not *of this world*, but that too was of another nature
entirely and may have been cause for alarm among some
contemporary quarters of the time, had any of it been heard. As it
was though, there was no one near enough to pick up the words
and their meanings, and the two strolled undisturbed bur for the
background of shouts and pulleys and rattling cartwheels and
horses.

It's not an easy life here.
No indeed.

So physical. And such poverty. Obstacles to spiritual development, surely.

Or a benefit. A bounty even.

Yes, perhaps. Tell me, why are they both boys?

No reason.

One is so disadvantaged.

By his poverty? No, as I said, not so much.

I was thinking more the lack of education, the lack of an aware environment.

Yes and no. There are some interesting and reverse correlations between the two communities.

I don't see the point.

Of what?

Of making it harder.

There's always hardship everywhere. You need to do better with this; you won't help them if you focus on the negative.

I don't connect with them well. I don't have your special powers.

Your problem is you think too much. You believe these children will succeed by learning to think?

No, of course not, much more by feeling.

No, not feeling either. Emotion is not much more useful than thinking and can get in the way even more. We've been through this before.

I'm struggling with how.

Explain to me then, when we meet with them ... how does that work? Do you 'see' them, do you 'feel' them, are you 'present' with them, what?

All and none of that.

Not good enough.

Why did you choose this task? It was never going to be easy. It's virtually impossible.

Nothing's impossible! I chose it because I believe it's possible. Because it presents an enormous opportunity. It's important to prove what's possible, to make a lie of supposed limitations – limits of time and space, obstacles of mind and body. We chose to help them. That's our role. To make the connection with them and get them to understand the possibility, the potential of making this huge difference in the world.

But no one will know. Even if you succeed. No one looks for a cause for something that didn't happen.

That doesn't matter. Remember the story of Odin, who walked among mortals; the poor but virtuous family whose cow died – such a tragedy, it seemed so unfair. But in fact nature had determined the wife otherwise would die. Until Odin stepped in and the cow was taken instead – who would have known that? Did it matter that they knew not? And then the wealthy and cruel family who built their mansion above a buried treasure and so never found it. It will be known simply because it will change what's possible, and the Energy of that in the Universe will influence more change. We are simply Scientists, my friend. That is the greater morality.

You mean it's more right?

Morality is not about right and wrong – that view is for simple, limited minds that can't see and refuse to understand.

What is it then?

It's whatever moves us more towards the light and enables us to make better use of our talents, our powers, and our faculties for the betterment of others' lives and the development of their talents and powers and faculties, and their ability to make that difference in others lives too, and so on. Ours is to have Faith, as is everyone's. Belief in what is possible. That is what will change the world – just Belief.

Well, that's simple enough.

Yes, of course it is. But it's made complicated by the minds of men. They want to put rules in place ostensibly to manage this development, but in reality few men are comfortable that those they support may exceed them in power, and especially not in piety and closeness to God. But there are some – some who can truly see.

So what is the morality in this situation then?

Which one?

Either. Both have a significant task.

Yes, their positions are handicapped in one way of course. But then they also have such direct connection too. They've set a task to go over and beyond their surrounding limitations; it's an enormously positive goal, with enormous power to advance the world.

But they have nothing to measure that by; no ability to paint even a picture in their own minds that would show them anything.

Your moral view is too one-dimensional. Think more broadly of the possibilities, of the abilities of their senses to interact with the Light in different ways. They chose this challenge, remember.

I'm not sure you could say they chose it.

By their actions, of course they did. They've always sought more and more, both of them. They were hungry for the challenge. And full of ego. Too much Self, both of them.

Well, there's no ego there now in these almost mindless boys.

Perhaps. Perhaps not. They're entirely in their own worlds. Isn't that ego?

Of a sort, I suppose.

This could be the ultimate ego struggle, locked in Self as they are, despite their innate affinity with the Light.

Their captivation with the Light often overpowers them.

Yes, in one way it keeps them from their task.

They simply play with it.

But still they receive substantial Energy in this way and this does feed their souls.

But with no one to lead them...

You must lead them. And there will be others. You'll see.

Me? This is your task foremost!

As you wish.

Most of their influences are the wrong ones.

No, no. Everything will unfold in the direction of good. You'll see.

I don't have quite your Faith. Well, that's obvious by now. I struggle even with knowing that Faith is all I need. I find myself needing to initiate or provide some skill. A physical skill virtually.

Then you must find your Faith. You are not a physical being so it is all you have, my friend. Otherwise your own thoughts will prevail and will shift Energy away from its right course.

I was never as strong as them anyway. I wouldn't have chosen their path.

You may yet. You're a novice. You could be stronger. Watch. The boys – their manifestations – will find their path. Stay with them. Don't focus on limitations, theirs or yours. Just keep sending out the message to them, their opportunity to make the difference.

But to change the future...?

To prevent a future that is not acceptable.

And the past? This past?

. . .. is where the future is rooted.

Footsteps brushing across the dusty path came near the two monks' sunny spot, and both turned to see a tall man in purple robes strolling slowly their way. The man's head was bowed in thought and then rose as he caught the movement of the two figures just in front of him.

'Excellency,' said the older monk, bowing low.

His companion followed suit.

'My sons,' responded the Bishop. 'I see you are seeking some silent reflection at the water, as do I.'

'There is a cool air comes off the water, Excellency,' the older monk replied.

'And that is certainly needed if one is to think clearly, or better, to find the voice of God. There is most certainly too much din atop the hill for a poor man of God to hear a thing.'

'I'm sure, Excellency, that God is never far from you,' spoke the older monk again.

'Oh, do not be defrauded by the Purple, Brother. It is no less difficult for me as any to hear and understand God's will.'

'I've no doubt, my Lord. What I mean is that, while you may not hear God, He is ever near to you. And in that, sir, I do think He *is* nearer you than most.'

'You are kind, Brother,' replied the Bishop, bowing a little to the monk. 'One's own limitations do distract one.'

'Of course. I will pray for you, Father. Yours is a great load to bear, and amid much expectation.' The monk bowed low again and motioned for his young companion to back away with him and leave the Bishop in peace.

'Thank you for ... your presence,' Hugh called, watching for a time as the two monks strolled comfortably away from him.

I felt that.

Yes, it's the field.

There really is a unified field?

Oh give it whichever name you like, but yes, of course. It's the same thing the family experienced for that brief moment as their sons left, but they didn't understand its value. It was not so long ago, a man made a system to mimic a magnetic field like that of the family in grief. It drew upon surrounding energy and sent a pulse, a signal of energy, a radio wave, across fifty *miles. Considering the times it was a long distance, so far indeed that it might as well have transmitted its signal to Heaven's own door. But our dearest Mr Tesla's oscillator was destroyed in a fire, and a year later, Master Marconi took the honour with a system some said ought not to have been able to send its message across a pond. So it is anyway, that spirit always meets science, for those willing to see and to find.*

It's the Holy Grail.

A facetious response; but in effect, yes. What a man such as that Bishop could find in conversation with a scientist of the modern world ...

There would be no telling ...

Unfortunately.

So the Bishop transmits a strong Energy?

Yes, which met our own, and there was a link between us, which no doubt he felt also.

What will he make of it? I wonder.

He has the power for great Good. And when that Light, that Power, mixes with its own kind, it grows far greater, more than the sum of its parts. This is what we are to do. So there, you see, you have had a real lesson in what it is that we are to do, what it is that can be created.

But I didn't do anything.

Exactly. You weren't thinking. You were happy to meet the Bishop and add your Energy, unknowingly, to his.

So I could create happiness?

You're getting the idea.

11

Reality leaves a lot to the imagination.

John Lennon (1940–1980)

Pete held Tim's hand as he locked the car door and dropped his keys into his jacket pocket. Tim bopped up and down and shook his other hand so that he looked like he was grooving to some beat or other and pretending to strum along. He walked along beside Pete like this – Pete didn't really notice because this was something Tim did a lot and anyway; he was mostly concerned to get speedily across the supermarket car park without getting backed into by a car or trolley-rushed by some unseeing shopper. He had a long written list of what was needed, and since he always managed to miss getting at least two or three things that were on the list and this always pissed Alicia off, he was intent on getting through the whole list in its entirety even if he had to circle the aisles a dozen times. He'd just let Jillie off at her school, which was a nightmare of bottleneck proportions at the school gate, with parents double-parking all along the school road, and others running the gauntlet between these and the school buses to cross the road. Pete always left Tim in the car and locked the car, but each part of this act was a detail he was afraid to neglect, and he was perpetually surprised that no parent or child had apparently yet been killed or at least maimed in this daily ambush..

Pete's schedule for the day was one child-focused task heaped on the next and barely a break in between any of these. After the supermarket, he had a psychologist's visit with Tim in Lincoln; then a play group that was entirely frequented by normal children with their mothers, making Pete feel doubly odd, despite his determination to make his presence as a father with an autistic child an acceptable exercise in parenting.

Inside the supermarket, Pete let Tim's hand go briefly as he pulled a trolley from a queue with the inevitable heave and jerk this required, narrowly avoiding sending the trolley singing into his son's head. He lifted Tim into the front of the trolley and veered around through the greengrocery. He knew he had about twenty minutes before Tim lost all ability to remain calmly in the trolley, which would not really be enough time, especially if the checkout queues were full and even more especially if he couldn't find something on the damned list. At that point Tim would start wailing and would want to get out of the trolley and Pete would assume everyone within a fifty-yard radius would both see and hear this and assume that he had either hit his son or was otherwise unfit to parent in some way, and this because to all the world Tim looked like any other child. Who was to know he wasn't? It was all very well to have the determination to parent his son regardless of the narrow confines of this English cultural context, but it wasn't easy just the same, and paranoia, or was it an accurate take on reality, frequently descended..

Fortunately there didn't seem to be too many shoppers and Pete worked through his list with reasonable efficiency. Tim looked around at the supermarket shelves, without actually really looking at them, and making toddler babble.

Because he was a sweet, good-looking child, like other such appealing children he attracted attention from adults who came into contact with him in some way – other shoppers and some store workers – all women. Most did not seem to notice that Tim wasn't the usual intellectual elevation of others his age; perhaps people thought he was just very tall for his age. '*What a lovely wee boy*', women would say over the sausages or the baked beans shelf or down the bathroom aisle, as Tim sing-songed to himself. Pete would always smile and say '*thank you*' or '*yes, he is*', and he wouldn't really think about whether Tim was doing anything odd or not at the time, or whether any of these people noticed anything unusual about him..

By the time Pete was at the biscuit and pet food aisle, he could see Tim's movements and sounds were starting to get subtly louder. Rounding the end of the aisle, he sank a bit to see several overstuffed trolleys waiting to go through the checkouts.

Bugger.

He walked the length of the checkout row and then missed one likely spot on the way back.

Shit.

He found the next most likely counter and waited, the second trolley back from the one now working its way through the exit. A lengthy standstill would further exacerbate Tim's impatience. Pete picked out a magazine from a rack near the counter and tried to block out Tim's movement and noise, which was in fact not possible, and his own impatience swelled slowly to irritation. The hum of the store was sufficient that Tim's crescendo had not yet risen to too noticeable a level, but Pete could see it threatened.

The front trolley was moving off, and the one in front of Pete had unloaded half its contents. Funny, he thought of the whole thing as a trolley, not a person and a trolley. The trolley unloaded its own contents – yeah, right.

God, is this what I'm reduced to? I'm a serious writer, and there's total garbage in my head. Think about something intelligent, you moron. Okay, car engines. Need to get some sparks for the car. Need to wash Alicia's car this Sunday and vacuum out the backseat where Tim's been stuffing leftover biscuits. Bloody hell – back to Tim again. How's he doing? Hang on, mate. Not long. Geez, this is a bit of crap writing in this magazine. Why don't they have the Guardian or something at the checkout – why's it all this rubbish? C'mon, lady. Move ya' bleedin' arse! Calm down, calm down. Everything's moving along, steady as she goes. Things take the time they take. Take a deep breath. Put that crap mag back!

'Hey, buddy. How's it going? Not long, okay?'

Tim was getting louder. A look from the woman in front. Sympathetic it seemed. So far.

C'mon, c'mon.

Tim was winding up to a major howl. Pete hated that people would think Tim was naughty or spoiled.

At last.

The woman in front had emptied her groceries onto the counter, and Pete could start unloading his. He'd got everything on the list – a minor miracle.

I wonder if a full grocery list shop entitles me to a shag. You're pathetic, Pete Watson, you know that.

Tim was at full throttle, and with only a few minutes to go now Pete felt he could ignore both the sound and any stares that came his way. He focused on unloading and piling, unloading and piling. The woman in front moved off, and the checkout operator started tallying Pete's items.

We're moving, we're moving. Yes!

'Ah, sir, d'you know which aisle this item came from?' He asked, holding up a curry sauce. 'It doesn't 'ave a price on it.'

Piss!

'Ah, not sure. It was some special stand somewhere over by the meat freezer, I think. Look, don't worry. Just skip it.'

'Oh, it's no trouble, sir. Le' me jus' call someone over.'

'Uh ...'

Too late, she'd rung the bell. Pete could see someone from the supervisors' desk coming over.

''Ave you go' a price on this, Hazel?'

'No worries, love. Back in a minute.' Hazel with the back end of a bus arse waddled off and the checkout girl carried on with Pete's other items.

Fuck, fuck, fuck.

Unload, pile. Unload, pile. Ignore the screaming. All Pete's items were through.

'Jus' be a sec on that curry, sir.'

'Look, really, I can skip it. It's fine.'

'Oh, here, she is.'

'Fify-six pence, Molly. Sorry to keep you waiting, sir.'

'Oh, it's fine. No problem. Thank you.'

Molly keyed in the last amount and gave Pete his total. Pete counted out twenty-pound notes.

'Your wee man's go' a set a' lungs, 'asn't e'?'

'Yes, indeed.' Pete feigned a smile.

'Here's yer change, sir. Thank you. You 'ave a nice day, won't you.'

'Thanks.'

Pete scarpered. The trolley's movement dropped Tim's screaming back to a whimper. They were ahead of time for the psychologist. If Pete drove round for half an hour, Tim would get a sleep and hopefully be okay again for their next appointment. He hoped to God there wouldn't be a wait when they got there.

Alicia left a message on the home phone and then tried Pete's car phone. Christ knows why he thought he needed the big honky thing, especially since he was hardly in the car – a remnant from journo days and needing to be on the spot, needing to be needed.

She was going to be late home. A faculty meeting. Visiting professor. Not quite boring, and anyway a reason not to have to deal with the pre-dinner scramble at home. She hoped at least for an intelligent discussion on the Paris experiments, or at least some that went beyond scathing or disinterested. She felt uneasy at holding her position among the rank and file of respectable physics citizenry in whose midst she was tolerated. Tolerated why? For her difference? Some eccentricity on her part or theirs? Some ironic middle class, academic gesture towards institutional fashion?

'You can have another appointment in October, Mr Watson. What's a good day for you?'

'Oh, any's fine. Just during school hours is good.'

Pete's morning with Tim had proceeded with more calm and the psychology meeting at the hospital in Lincoln had gone quite well. Pete wasn't sure they really had a handle on what to do with Tim any more than he did but they seemed engaged with Tim's learning, and they seemed to be indicating that Tim's progress was at the upper end of the scale and one had to be grateful for that.

Pete stood at the busy waiting room window. Tim, tired again, was standing loosely at his side, one arm about Pete's leg.

'Okay, we can do ten o'clock on the ninth. That's a Friday.'

'That's great. Thanks. Will you send out one of those reminder cards?'

'Yes, we will.'

'Great, thanks.'

'Just let me put this into the diary.'

A dozen or so people were seated about the waiting room. The hospital had the annoying practice of booking all their morning's outpatients into the same appointment time, so the wait was always frustrating, especially when children were involved. Pete had learnt to negotiate with the administration staff to arrive at a more precise time, although not without some consternation on their part, but he didn't much care about that and it had more or less worked to his advantage over time..

'Oh, Pete. Just before you go...' One of the psychology team had put her head round the waiting room door.

'Yep?'

'Can I just get you to sign this consent for the autism research project I mentioned? You don't have to do it now. You might want to take this information sheet away and talk it over with your wife. You could post the form back to us. The address is on the bottom of the page there.'

'Oh sure. I'm sure it's fine. My wife's an academic. She's always keen to support other people's research projects. I think she knows how difficult it can be to enrol participants in these things. But sure, I'll post the form back to you. Thanks.'

'And if you've got any questions just give me a ring any time. It's no problem. Or if your wife wants to call, that's fine too.'

'Okay.'

'Okay, thanks. See you later then.' The woman smiled and ducked back through the swing door.

Pete turned back to the appointments desk.

'That's all sorted for you then, Mr Watson. We'll see you in October.' The clerk handed Pete an appointment card.

'Thank you. Bye then.'

'Bye now.' And the clear window was slid across in front of Pete's face before he'd even turned away.

Typical.

Pete turned about. He had a very small and momentary instant of anxiety as he realised Tim was no longer attached to his leg nor standing nearby. He scanned the room, its participants reading over-read magazines or nursing or comforting small children or else sitting cross-armed in obvious annoyance at their wait.

Pete wandered a few steps, peering around and over seats and people.

Shit.

Tim wasn't in the room.

'Did anyone see where my son went?' he called out calmly into the room and was greeted by an array of empty faces.

He walked to the swing doors that went through to the clinic rooms and pushed one door open. There was no one on the other side. Going back to the appointment desk window, he knocked to get the attention of the clerk. She looked up surprised and slid the window open a few inches.

'Ah, my son didn't wander through there, did he?' Pete pointed imprecisely, trying to sound unperturbed.

'I don't think so, Mr Watson. I'll just have a look.' And she got up, walking out her office door to the corridor Pete had just peered down.

She took more time than Pete was content with, coming back to relay her findings that there was no sign of Tim and looking at him sharply as if to enquire how on earth he'd managed to lose a child in just a few seconds. Clearly she was not going to offer any other kind of assistance to the bewildered, anxious man, and he turned to look round the waiting room once more, as though he had most likely just overlooked him sitting contentedly in some corner a minute ago.

'I'll just...' Pete stammered slightly, more to himself. 'Okay...' and he walked towards the main hospital corridor.

Outside the clinic he looked up and down, not knowing which direction to go in, and headed towards the front entrance to the hospital. Passing an orderly coming towards him, he asked if the man had seen a small boy wandering along, but no.

'Look, I'll keep an eye out and ask down this way. If I find him, I'll take him to the desk at the front entrance,' said the man.

'Thanks.' Pete kept walking.

Jesus.

Pete fought a rising panic.

He'll be somewhere and any second now I'll see him. Someone will have found him and have him somewhere. Front desk.

Rounding hospital corridors, he came to the lobby. There were several small shops and kiosks, a florist, a snack bar, a gift shop, a travel agent.

What the hell is a travel agent doing here?

He peered into the different stores asking the salespeople if they'd seen a small boy, about this high, fair hair. No one had spotted him. He went to the desk in the centre of the foyer and spoke with the administrator, who'd not seen him either, but she said she'd keep an eye out and she'd send a message round to all the orderlies and let them know there was a child on the loose, yay high, etcetera.

'You would have seen him if he'd come right past here, wouldn't you? I mean if he'd headed out the door. I mean if he's gone outside...'

'I'm sure I would have, sir. Look, just go back the other way and keep looking. Come back here every few minutes. Don't worry. I know it's a big hospital, but people aren't going to let a small boy wander round on his own. Someone will have spotted him, for sure.'

'Okay. I'll go back the other way past the clinic then.'

And he went back the way he came.

C'mon, Timbo, where are you?

Pete shivered.

He went back into the psych clinic and tapped again on the glass window at the reception desk. The clerk looked at him as though she'd never seen him before.

'Look, I haven't found Tim yet. I've been down to the foyer, and, well, I'm just heading back the other way. I don't suppose...'

'We haven't seen him, Mr Watson.'

'Right ... okay then. Well, perhaps he'll turn up here again. Who knows?' Pete looked around, unsure of himself. A couple of people, who'd been in the waiting room before, now stared at him blankly.

What fucking planet is this?

'I'll keep looking then,' he said back to the clerk, who was already closing the window. He escaped back out into the main corridor and headed in the other direction.

He wandered along the corridor, not knowing really where he was going or where to look. He passed another clinic and went in – another waiting room and another glass window. This one's window was open, and he went over.

'Hi. Ah, I've just been at the clinic down the corridor with my son, and he's wandered off somewhere. You haven't seen him by any chance? He's four. Little guy. Sandy hair.'

'No, sorry,' said the younger, friendlier clerk. 'No one's come in here the last half an hour and I've been here all the time. Where have you looked?'

'I've been down to the front foyer, and I'm just coming back this way now. I guess he could be anywhere.'

'Okay. Look, I'll ring the orderlies...'

'Ah, the woman at the front desk already did that.'

'Right. Look, I'll come and help. Just a minute.' The woman got up and came out into the waiting room through a side door, walking back to the corridor with Pete.

They started to walk further up the corridor.

'You go up that way,' she said, 'and I'll go down here to the wards,' indicating where the corridor divided off to the left. 'Don't worry, we'll find him.'

'Thanks,' said Pete, refreshed by the woman's helpfulness, and he kept walking.

The corridor was longer here, and there were no doors or other corridors leading off anywhere till he got to a flight of stairs which apparently lead up to the staff cafeteria. He started up, and then heard an out-of-breath male voice calling up to him.

'Hey, mate, we've found your kid. He's back here.'

Pete looked back and recognised a large man who had been in the psych clinic.

'Oh God, thanks. Where is he? Is he all right?'

'Yeah, he's fine. Got himself into a bit of a cupboard and shut the door. He's a bit upset, I think. Back this way...'

Pete hurried back past the man.

'Which way?'

'Back to the clinic. Down there.'

Pete rushed back to the original clinic, bolting in to see Tim jiggling up and down, waving his arms, and crying out in a repetitive whine.

'Oh, there you are, Mr Watson.' It was the bitch clerk. 'Your son's soiled himself, I believe. Seems he got himself into the toy cupboard over there without anyone noticing,' indicating a low cupboard with a television and a fish bowl on top. 'He won't let anyone near him, I'm afraid.'

'Well, that's hardly bloody surprising, is it? It's okay, Tim-Tim.' Pete picked Tim up, and the boy latched on to him round his neck. 'It's okay. It's okay.'

'Really, Mr Watson. This has caused hospital staff quite some disturbance. I do hope...'

'Oh, really! And do you mind telling me how exactly it's caused you any disturbance? When exactly was it that you felt any need to be disturbed. To get up out of your bloody little glass cage over there and make yourself useful. Huh?'

'I really don't think...'

'You *don't* think, do you? You didn't think at all in fact! In fact, you don't really give a shit, and frankly you can go take a running bloody jump! C'mon, Tim, let's get out of here.'

The clerk was becoming red-faced. Pete launched his most full-on glare at her and sped round out of the clinic doors again, leaving the clerk standing there all huffed up with nowhere to go.

'Thanks,' he said hurriedly to the fat man just coming back in.

'No problems. Hope the wee fella's all right?'

Pete didn't answer and sped off down the hall to the front entrance. He stopped briefly at the front desk to inform the clerk there of his son's rescue and then bolted to his car. Tim had stopped his whining, and Pete laid him gently on the back seat to change his nappy and then secured Tim into his car seat, ultimately throwing the soiled disposable into a nearby rubbish bin, not caring in the least that this may have been an inappropriate gesture.

He climbed into the driver's seat, gripped the steering wheel, and took a deep breath, letting it out forcefully before starting the ignition.

Jesus, what next?

Another deep breath.

Oh dear. That was probably a bit over the top. 'Ay, Tim? Your da' just went a bit bonkers at that woman, I think. Probably won't have us back. Whaddya reckon? Take you everywhere twice, ay?' *My gorgeous boy.*

'Alicia, got a minute?' Dryden Cooper leant round Alicia's office door. 'Just want to introduce Gerry Bernstein.'

'Oh sure.' Alicia got up from her chair as Dryden stepped back and a man about her age came round behind Dryden and held his hand out to her.

'Hi, nice to meet you,' said Gerry Bernstein, tall, tanned, and fair-haired.

'Nice to meet you too. Welcome to Lincoln,' replied Alicia.

'Thanks, I'm enjoying being here.'

'Gerry's taking up the new appointment in the department, Alicia, and unfortunately, as Peter Dickerson can't make the lecture this evening after all, Gerry's graciously agreed to fill in. So we can look forward to some exciting new debate on holograms. Ought to rattle a few cages!'

'Yes, indeed! Great!' Alicia said.

'Well, I don't know about that. You know, I can speak to a lecture theatre of 500 students quite happily, but put a dozen of my colleagues and peers in a room with me, and I'm shaking in my shoes,' replied Bernstein.

'Oh, I know that feeling,' Alicia said. 'And they are wolves here, I should warn you!' She and Dryden smiled.

'Oh, thanks.' Bernstein laughed. 'I feel a whole lot better.'

'Oh, don't worry. Really. It'll be fine. We need a few fresh ideas round here, don't we, Dryden?'

'Absolutely. Someone to keep you company, Alicia!'

'Don't remind me.'

'Dryden's told me about your research, Alicia. I'm looking forward to talking with you about it. I guess you're pretty interested in the Paris experiments. I met with Alain Aspect and some of his team last month actually.'

'Really? Well, yes, I would love to talk about that with you.'

'Well, I guess you two have a date then,' said Dryden. 'We'll being seeing you this evening, Alicia?'

'Oh yes, for sure. I was planning on coming. Nice to meet you, Gerry. Look forward to talking to you more.'

'Indeed.'

The two men left.

Interesting...

Pete got to school early and got a good park. He carried Tim in his arms towards Jillie's classroom and Tim seemed happy to be held and didn't struggle to get down, to Pete's relief. He amused Tim in the school corridor, looking at the many brightly coloured paintings adorning the walls and reading the school notices that he usually didn't get round to giving any attention. Tim was calm. Other parents milled around waiting.

When the bell rang, a hail of classroom doors flew open on both sides of the corridor and several hundred children filled it in seconds. Tim buried his head in his father's shoulder, and Pete waited for Jillie to spot him, as she usually did.

'Dad!' Jillie yelled over the hubbub beside him.

'Hi, darling. Got your bag?'

'Dad. This is Louisa,' indicating a smiling girl of similar age beside her. 'She wants me to go to her house to play.'

'Oh, ah...'

'Hello. I'm Sally,' said a smartly dressed brunette coming up behind the two girls. 'Louisa's been asking if she can play with Jillie.'

'Oh, well, Louisa's welcome to come to our house if she likes. We live out at Nocton Fen.'

'Oh no, really. I'm sure it would be easier for you if Jillie came to us,' said Sally, apparently referring to Tim.

'Yes, yes,' said Jillie. 'Come to our house, Louisa. I've got a playhouse in my garden that Dad made for me. You'll really like it.'

'Can I, Mummy?'

'Well, really I think it would be better if Jillie came to our house.'

'But I want to go to Jillie's house. Pleeeease.'

'Um, actually, no, darling. If you want to play with Jillie, she'll have to come to our house,' said Sally, and then looking at Pete, 'I can easily drop Jillie home to you later on.'

And in an instant Pete could see all that was going on in the poor, misguided woman's head, and he didn't know whether to despair or be furious. Only he was exhausted from fury already, and so he stood there dumbly, staring at her, as she clearly pretended to project her enthusiastic hospitality for having his daughter visit them rather than her own daughter risk some unknown debacle that would surely ensue from contact with Jillie's brother. Pete would have liked to explain to his daughter that she was better off avoiding this kind of crap, but Louisa seemed a nice little girl and Jillie ought to have as many and whichever friends she wanted, or so Pete told himself.

'Well, whatever works I guess,' said Pete.

And amid the to-ing and fro-ing of the corridor, the two adults and two children considered this.

'I think I'll go with my dad,' said Jillie to Louisa. 'I'll come and play another time. Okay?'

'Oh well, we'll work that out for another day I'm sure,' said Sally, and she smiled at Pete and took her daughter by the hand and led her away, the two girls looking despondently and resignedly at each other.

'C'mon, Dad. Let's go.'

'Yeah, let's go.' And Pete turned and pushed his way through the crowded corridor holding on to his son who still had his head locked into his father's shoulder, and pleased to be with his daughter, who he decided in that moment was one ballsy wee chick and he was her biggest fan.

Pete lay on his back on the couch while Tim lay asleep face down on his chest and belly.

I love you, Tim. Everything's gonna be fine.

You just chill out, buddy. I've got the world all sorted for you. You don't have to worry about a thing.

I know you're in there, Timmy. And I'll find you. I'm looking. We'll do all this stuff we have to do to get Tim out of there. And to hell with... Well, we don't have to think about all that other shit. We'll make it happen for you. I'll help you, my wee boy. I'm here, and I'll always be here.

You just relax.

Me and whatever God in His Heaven have it sorted.

Okay? Everything's cool.

Everything's cool.

Wednesday, 9 September 1981

Tim did another amazing painting today – lots of reds and yellows and orange, with two thick black strokes down the middle and then some small black dots to the side. I watched him do it – huge concentration – like he was pouring everything he had into it. Looked like a couple of very tall buildings on fire. Don't know what the black dots were. He was exhausted the rest of the day after that.

12

'Pass us tha' chipper, Dem. Aye, tha' one.'

'Wha's i' gonna be, Gree. 'Nuvver one 'a them leafy things?'
said Denholm, passing a small adze to his older brother.

'Aye, bu' this one's special, Dem. S'gonna go in a special
wall wiv' blocks from all carvers 'n' masons. Carvers' library they're
callin' it – more loik jus' a practice wall t' me. So in 'undreds 'a
years, people'll walk through 'ere an' see as 'ow there were so many
of us built Cathedral back up again.'

''Oo's gonna want see tha'?'

'Ah, dunno, Dem, bu' tha's wha' they's sayin', an' I've gotta
make this me best tile ever, seein' as i's s'posed to last forever. 'Ere,
take this lotta chips away o'er there, willya? An' go find Thurstan.
'E's probly larrikin' abou' somewhere.'

'Orroight.'

The two brothers were in the far eastern end of the
Cathedral, in the southern choir aisle, surrounded in part by debris
still to be cleared away and in part by the detritus of rebuilding –
the two aspects somewhat indistinguishable unless one was closely
engaged in the restructuring of the great building.. The roof was
open here, and this brought either blessed relief when the
occasional wind blew through, or else the torture of the hot sun for
those workers engaged in some activity in its direct path, and worse
still if they were at the top of the wooden scaffolding slowly rising
further and further up the inside of the building.

Thurstan Warriner, the youngest of the three brothers sent
to the Cathedral site, had proved on occasion in particular need of
his eldest brother's authority as he had found in the grand
departure from his small home an explorer's spirit and a jester's
view of life, not the more restrained humour of the workers that
was inherent in his new surroundings. On the one hand this was

taken as a youthful exuberance within the large community of workers, but on the other hand Geoffrey Warriner knew his brother walked a fine line in a strict and punitive society. He protected and scolded his brother as he could and thought often of the reassurance and shelter of his mother's safe keeping. He had worried as much for her as for his own self and his two brothers in his charge, but mostly he remembered the sanctuary of his family. His own sense of the adventure to come had been curtailed quickly by the responsibility he bore for his brothers, along with his need now to be taken as an adult, a man among men, making his way in the world.

Gree had found a new opportunity to be accepted as such when the evidence of his carving meant he became one of many new apprentices to the guilded stonemasons at work now on the cathedral. It would be many years to become guilded himself and earn his own tools, but it was a better start than to be merely a labourer with a less certain future. His brothers had been taken on by the same mason, but theirs was just to fetch and carry, although Gree intended himself to give them some skill in hopes they may also find a greater destiny. His youngest brother seemed at times though little capable of any such promise.

'Where'd you see 'im last then, Gree?'

''E were 'ere a while ago. 'E could be anywhere now. Ask about. An' get 'im puttin' 'imself t'use somewhere. 'E ain't no good if 'e's foolin'.

'Aye.'

Denholm scooped up the chips from his brother's carving and deposited them in a barrow that was collecting rubble and wreckage to be taken away, or else sorted for foundations or other parts that needed filling. Dusting off his hands, he headed for the west end, mainly intact still and already covered to dizzying heights with rickety scaffolds, creeping away up its front and back.

Dem had no idea where his brother was but had discovered that due to his brother's clowning, just about everyone else now

knew his brother, so he judged it would not be difficult to find
him..

Fulk had nestled into a low branch again near the edge of
the pond, and had watched the swan watching him for some time.
He did not recognise the creature as beautiful since this was a virtue
– a morality – that was beyond his view of the world. He had
though considered the bird might have magical powers, and so he
thought to be very careful about it. He had grown to feel the bird
was now his, and he gave shrewd attention to the manner in which
he might capture it. He wondered if the other poachers had sought
the bird also and decided they must have since he could see its
breast was broad and held the promise of a considerable feast.

Fulk eyed the bird's long neck and knew his strength was
sufficient to snap it, but the real mastery would come in a necessary
speed and deception. He would wait. This was what he was used to
anyway. Except lately, and just the once so far, when he had used
the traps of the other men. Generally he used only his hands,
assured of his own swiftness and efficiency. He would wait for the
urgency to come upon him as it always did. When he waited and
watched long enough it always came. Everything was shut out from
his view, from all his senses, except himself and his prey, and he
would find himself suddenly moving from what had been a long
stillness, as though he were propelled by unseen forces, an instinct
that operated as a bond between hunter and hunted. He would feel
this bond such that he felt even the prey itself knew he was coming
for it, that it surrendered to its role as the hunted, just as he was
driven by the greater impulse to hunt. It was the way things were.

So he waited now. Sometimes he would wait days, watching
the way an animal moved, its habits, what frightened it, until he
knew everything about it, until he understood it and almost became
the animal himself. Because he studied his prey so closely, he could
mimic the movements and sounds of most animals he had caught.
And although he killed many animals, he considered most of them
his kin, his clan. This was not a view he had of people.

Fulk knew that some animals were greater than others, that they were more nimble, more resourceful, more discerning than other creatures. He could even see that some were more gentle, more imposing and impressive, more elevated than others. But this did not suggest to him that such animals were to be excluded as quarry. It meant instead that the hunt of them demanded a greater prowess on his part, and this was only fair and right, for no such animal should be duped by a mediocre huntsman.

It was a hot day and everyone knew that to be very careful on a hot day was always wise, or the heat took over men's rational minds and a lot of bad things could happen very fast that no one wanted to have happen, and afterwards they'd always be surprised that all hell was let loose when they'd never planned any such thing.

Father Taylor was not particularly of a mind to walk through the small, dusty lanes of Torksey, but he determined he would see for himself the state of commerce and community.

The priest fancied his presence may have some calming effect, though in fact the villagers viewed such a rare visit to their domain with some strangeness and not a little suspicion. Combined with the small priest's sharp demeanour, his brief sojourn beyond his own residence, calling as he did on individual families, served only to heighten the town's disquiet, not that the priest in his arrogance understood such.

The Father did not, in his visits, attend on Jacob Yazd, a Jew and a tailor. The priest held no ill t'ward the man but saw him simply as not part of his congregation and none of his responsibility, and it was not unfortunately, within his disposition or character to act with friendliness to all God's creatures.

Indeed, his singular lack of amiability was an extraordinary deficiency that may otherwise have changed the fate of so many. Berta Draper *saw* this lack in the man and the consequences of it when she spotted the Father emerging from the Smith's. She saw it as a picture of a disturbing unravelling future as he walked past the Jew's small home with what she perceived as a skewed sideways glance to the place. Perhaps there was a slight hesitation in his step also, that she would convey later, as she watched him proceed to visit the homes and workings that followed on along from the Jew's, and on down the lane.

Oddly, Berta was a villager neither afraid nor critical of the priest. She could see his fear as well as his stupidity and saw him as she saw any other man trying to make a certain way for himself, and like many without much of the necessary talent or opportunity to achieve his heart's desire. Such was the lot of most and Berta gave little mind to it. Nor was she concerned that the priest carried a suspicion as others did for the Jew. It was just that at the very moment she saw him walk past that place she saw also the connectedness between Jew and Church – Church as institution, Church as army, Church as politics, and Church as structure. And for sure the Jew did not come off well in any of what she saw in the future, near or long distant.

Father Taylor himself, despite his wanderings and his intention, was preoccupied. He had felt the strain of his discussions with Bishop Hugh. How could the Church lead the people away from their ignorance and fear? What did God have in store for them? Was God indeed to be feared? How was it that this agitation found targets in undue places – a bird, a small boy, the Jews? What could the Church bring to the life and soul of such as the Warriners? What would Hugh bring to a small village flock if it was he in the priest's shoes? Surely there was no future for them other than that prescribed by their current condition, or perhaps worse. But certainly not better.

The idiot boy himself the priest had found innocuous. The mother though bewildered him. He had seen her in his church for many years and he knew her to be a pious woman, one who had suffered much but acted always with charity and a quiet solicitude. He had felt in her presence an agitation – an agitation that was his

— that he could fathom only as a sure reflection of those very qualities he himself lacked, including a serenity that belied her lot. Among the general flotsam of his parish of rustics and boors, Alice Warriner posed a unique promise of the evolution of humankind, as well as a threat to this man, almost equally small-minded as those whose souls he deigned to guide.

'You must be the refuge in their storm, my son . . . ,' the Bishop had said to him, and he could see that the Bishop himself had all of the qualities and more that might carry the day, but for himself he felt more and more ill-suited to his purpose..

'. . .. and a balm to their suffering. This young boy needs your special care and attention, as do his family. That the rebuilding of the Cathedral has taken three of their sons is an enormous sacrifice, and indeed should not have occurred. The mother must suffer terribly. You must visit this family and provide the strength of the Church for their peace.'

And he had gone. But it was certain the woman had found no peace in him, and he had none to offer. He had left her repulsive hovel as quickly as he could.

But the Bishop's encouragement had meant a great deal to him, and he was determined to rise to the Bishop's notice and blessing, if only for the assuredness he might garner from one much greater than himself. Perhaps some of that beauty of spirit would rub off on him, if he could contrive to gain the Bishop's presence more often. Ah yes, he would find some excuse by which he might petition the Bishop's presence to this rotten town once more. And with this he thought he must not seek to bring so much of a lull to the townsfolk's ferment as he had earlier hoped. In this way, he knew he must walk a fine line, which being at least modestly calculating in his temperament was a project within his means, and one that would keep his thoughts much occupied, and certainly less so on the problems of his parish and the frailties in himself.

"E's off o'er there boy, yer brother is,' said a nearby stonemason to Dem..

Dem had climbed to the uppermost turret, still largely complete at the east end, but with some crumbled edges that a group of men now worked at. Thurston was among them, heaving cracked and broken tiles over the edge to an area below where they smashed even more, to be swept and carried away later by some other worker. Thurston yelped and hollered at the thrill of each toss, sometimes heaving large pieces of stone way out beyond the low turret wall, older men grinning and occasionally tut-tutting at the young boy's spirit.

'I 'ear Bishop's aground there, boy. You best not 'it 'im,' one man called out to the amusement of others.

Thurstan laughed and peered over the edge to check who or what was below.

'Na, is nuthin' there 't'all,' he replied, momentarily tottering at the edge for effect.

'Thurstan!' yelled Dem. 'Ya damn fool! Ger'on with yer work an' stop that larkin'.'

'Dem! Come 'n' look 'ere! Look! Ya' can see forever!'

Thurstan scrambled to the top of a pile of rubble at the edge of the wall, and spread his arms like a great bird looking to fly from the turret up into the clear sky and over the great city. The men about stopped their labours, enjoying again the young man's fun-loving energy.

'Yer an ijit and no one should give ya' time a' day,' Dem feigned indifference, nodding at the other workmen, who could all see he was doing his best to tame the younger boy.

''ere, lad.' A very large red-headed man nodded back at Dem. 'Give uz a hand wi' this lot then,' indicating a pallet of new stone that had been hoisted up at the outer wall.

Another man joined them, and they unloaded it to a stack closer in, and let the pallet back out over the edge, calling out to someone below to lower it back down..

'C'mon then,' Dem said to Thurston, 'we gotta ge' back down. Gree's go' things 'e wants doin'.'

'Just a bi' longer, Dem. I's a wonder 'ere. T'see so far. Look a' it, Dem..' Thurston stood on the pile of rubble still, his face shining in the sun as he stared out to the west of Lincoln and all round to the north and south.

'Aye. 'Tis a thing t'be way up here, fer sure.'

'Aye, lads,' enjoined the red-headed man, 'ther's no like it anywhere it's true.'

And the men hushed a moment and enjoyed the scene and their grand height, and the sun and a small breeze. Not one had ever stood higher, nor would they ever again.

'World's diff'rent from 'ere, eh? No' so troubled. No' so 'ard.'

'Aye,' said another. 'Crops look perfect an' all's broight int' sunshine. No' a care, eh?'

When their faces changed a moment later though, Dem would not be able to tell his older brother afterwards whether it was a look of surprise or a look of shock that overcame them, whether Thurston had really thought to fly from the turret, or whether the rubble had given way beneath his feet and he had fallen. One way or the other, in an instant Thurston was gone from sight with not a sound and no one remembered how his face had looked in that moment, except that an instant before it was of innocence and joy.

Had he really even been there at all, on that roof that day? Perhaps he'd been down below, working diligently away at the rock as he should have been. Perhaps he'd thought to take the dyke road back to their mother. Perhaps he'd been stopped by the Bishop himself; they said he was a kindly man, and perhaps Thurston's sweetness had moved the great man to give some attention to the boy.

Whatever it was had really occurred, Dem Warriner never remembered being atop the turret that day, and would refuse to go up it, or any other height, ever again.

The Bishop had left the Cathedral site a short while earlier and for now wandered the edge of the Brayford Pool at the foot of Lincoln hill. As he walked he considered the argument he expected to have with the King, confident in himself that he would prevail. After all, he must. There was a balance to things that Hugh believed now was askew, and that good works, indeed great works, must be a focus for the Church. And if it was a focus for the Church, then Henry and his nobles across England and Europe would need to make it their business also. They were, after all, the servants of the Church, not the other way around, despite that they all liked to throw the tantrums they did. In the end, they all unquestioningly believed.

It was imperative Henry go to Jerusalem. The Holy City was ever at risk from the increasingly dominant and marauding Muslims. Those who sought peace with this foe were to be admired, and Hugh supported every good will and intention brought to bear in this way, but the fear that the city would fall to Islam's power was real. And it was a bitter and tyrannical battle that threatened to ensue, since those that would ultimately gain power would have a vast control over the hearts of men, both Christian and Muslim.

Hugh knew a little of the Islamic Faith, and despite the suspicions of the age he had a respect for its tenets, not that he would ever voice such. Their armies were men of the desert, just as brutal as he knew soldiers of Christ could be, albeit that the Crusaders would always be painted the heroes in any tale, and their foe as wicked and ungodly. No, Hugh knew better than this. But what he also knew was the power of the image of an isolated Jerusalem.

A new crusade must keep the sanctity of the Holy City.

Henry had shown himself a fierce soldier, although not always an astute statesman. He had, it was true, undermined the power the Church had over society, but for the Bishop this was not to be minded, since he knew himself the tyranny and dogmatism with which the Church often manipulated the people, and he found the wranglings between those hungry for power within his own fold of great distaste and certainly far from God..

Hugh though did not fear Henry; he even enjoyed the exchanges he had with the King. He knew that Henry had connived to secure the assassination of the Archbishop of Canterbury, Thomas Becket, fifteen years earlier. He also knew of Henry's own deep remorse and the blackness that inflicted itself on the King's mind as he wrestled with his guilt, even submitting himself to a public flogging at the steps of Avranches in Normandy. It had been a barbaric display Hugh himself had witnessed, although he believed Henry had no knowledge that he, Hugh, even knew this had taken place, let alone that he had seen it occur.

Hugh was not one to read a multitude of possible meanings, or any sleight of hand, into his dealings with the King, or any other of the mighty and powerful with whom he engaged. He was aware that the King though saw, studied, and *imagined* he saw, many a slur against himself, and his soul had paid dearly with the excess of power at his disposal in condemning innocents and loyalists to many a horror. The entangled King was not to be trifled with, and Hugh determined to address him as always with the utmost sincerity and clarity, with due respect to the throne, but expecting at the same time the due of the Church..

Strolling the promenade, Hugh took in the view and sounds of industry along the port, noting the many canal boats arriving with wood and stone piled high and creating a need for great skill from their helmsmen as their loads threatened to overturn their boats and cargo into the river. There was a lot of calling out of orders and instructions, pointing and scurrying about for ropes and pulleys, and all the toolery of shipmen and dockworkers.

These men knew their task and it was not always simple. They would know, for instance, the way a boat angled and how best to steer it past the many obstacles clogging the waterways, altering their position according to their load. They understood the speed with which they may best affect a gentle landing of the equipment they delivered via pulleyed platforms to the shore. Their every task was a matter of astute calculation of the forces of the physical world, and they worked with intelligence as much as muscle. Hugh appreciated the depth of the appraisal and reckoning they brought to their efforts and knew there was many a skilful and resourceful wit among them. Indeed, he saw no greater skill or cunning in his own role and social status in this life, rather he knew these were merely an appearance of some greater distinction and class. The scheme of things though was that appearances, of class and rank, were to be preserved. While he may feel an impulse, as he did now, to throw of his holy tweeds and roll his sleeves with these men and dirty himself in their toil, and rub shoulders with the elements of the common folk, closer to God's inspiration than they knew, he would not act on this vision any more than any of these men would ever dream he might, and indeed they may consider him mad to do any such thing.

The complexity of the wharf's labours before him mirrored the complexity of events and needs that tossed like a juggler's batons in his head, each maintaining its proper orbit, all of them together trying to find their right pattern. Hugh's thoughts ran from the singular act of devotion of each individual workman at the rebuilding of the cathedral to the powerful image of that structure in the Universe of God's Church; from the ignorance of man towards the People of the Book to a great battle that must ensue with the People of the Prophet; and the rights and wrongs, and the balance of each one of these.

Hugh found his way beyond the hum of the port to a short and verdant walk at the far end of the pool, a calm spot, the flattened grass telling that is was frequented by others perhaps seeking some solitude as he did now. The water rippled to the edge of the pool, a small flutter from the rocking and manoeuvring of the boats behind him. The grass here was long and the dry path became obscured, although apparently leading through a small wood and further along the river. No one else was about, despite the industriousness not far from him, and although secure in himself, Hugh, vigilant nonetheless, thought to walk no further and stopped to look back to the top of the Lincoln Hill. He saw just a small crumbling spire of the Cathedral rising above its surroundings, perhaps a little less defiant than his impression a few days before upon arriving at the city. The import of his tasks had expanded in their weight upon him in that time.

Amid the reverie of his greyness, a movement to the corner of his eye lent his head around casually to a heart-lifting sight. A great swan emerged from long grass a little further around the pool, waddled slowly to the water and stepped gracefully in. Its red-brown eye apparently towards him, the giant bird waded silently towards Hugh, cutting a new ripple across the other that continued from the moorings at the wharf.

The bird seemed at ease and peaceful and as it reached the edge where the Bishop stood, it lifted its giant wings to propel itself to the bank, revealing its prodigious wingspan in all its majesty and beneath its large body its two orange webbed feet, one slightly twisted and bent in on itself.

The bird stood before him on his path, as though awaiting his instruction, an obedient servant. And Hugh stood in awe of the animal, standing as it did almost his own full height.

The bird cocked her head from side to side, perhaps waiting for his response, perhaps hearing other sounds beyond them, inaudible to Hugh. Then just as momentously as she had appeared, apparently to lift him from his thoughts, and as though her presence was merely a portent of something been or to come, the bird spread her great wings and turned back towards the pool, flapping a still wind beneath her as she rose across the water and into the trees. And then she was gone.

All thought of Kings, crusades and wars momentarily scattered as Hugh watched her leave and wondered at her departure and when he would see her again. He stood a while, and when he turned back along the path, his thoughts invaded again. Wishing still that he could stop awhile with the workmen at the dock, he knew undoubtedly there would be something needing his attention atop the hill, and he hurried on.

Fulk had sat long enough. He realised he was perhaps a little too excited by this prey and possibly not yet mindful enough of the bird's own instincts. But he decided that whatever may happen now was his moment, as the bird sat contentedly below his branch. He breathed deeply and sprang from his observation spot, leaping upon the bird's back. His hands instantly about the bird's neck, he was surprised in that moment how thick it was, thicker than his own wrist, thicker even than his forearm, and he struggled more than he'd anticipated, to put his large hands about it. He had not imagined the power in that length, and he could feel as well, just beneath the bird's down, two limbs of seeming brass.

The bird twisted and brought its powerful beak down on to Fulk's neck, but to Fulk, aroused as he was, this felt little, and he focused his mind and all his being on the white stem between his hands. The bird's wings came up and beat at his body and legs and threatened to topple him from his position astride the animal, but with a great force of his legs, he pushed the bird from its feet, and he lay atop it as it sought to right itself.

Despite a furore of leaves and forest floor beneath himself and the bird, Fulk differentiated a sound far off, and it alerted him to an even greater danger. Someone was approaching, and more than just one, as he heard a distant sound of voices nearing. With a great snap, his prey collapsed beneath him, but too late, Fulk knew, he must abandon his catch, and moved swiftly from astride the bird. He sprang silently away into the undergrowth, pausing quietly in a new hiding place, watching as two of the Thane's men came upon the site of his erstwhile wrestling match, stopping in horror at the sight of the swan's body amid strewn feathers and churned soil and leaves. Pallor whitened their countenance; Fulk watched and waited, his heartbeat slowly returning to a steady rhythm.

'Jesus Lord! What d' ya think?' one said to his companion.

'Le's get i' back to manor. Lord'll be fierce o'er this.'

'I's not me is gonna tell 'im.'

'Don' be coward, man. I's no' our doin'. Best we get bird to 'im. We'll scarper quick as we can after. C'mon then.'

'I reckon there's someone about still,' one of them said, drawing a knife.

'I'm no' gettin' caught in no scuffle. Been enough bloodshed round here a' late, and if's to be any more, t'won't be mine. Get a hold on this now.'

The men looked around briefly, knowing any attacker would most likely be alone and not so ready to take on two men of the manor.

'Anyway, may 'as not been a man done this. May 'as been some other beast. We don' know. Is no clue as to wha' a' all.'

They reached down slowly to heave the bird between them back to the manor.

''s heavy as hell!'

'We'll manage between us.'

With difficulty they grappled with the ungainly body and loped away awkwardly. They would stop often to re-handle their load and avoid notice from others who'd afford some gossip or telltale about the thing. The town and its surrounds were full already with enough tattle.

The housekeeper at the small manse next to the church in Torksey scurried into Father Taylor's library, afluster at the arrival of a visitor from Lincoln. The squat woman wrung her hands on her filthy apron, annoyed as much that her morning routine was about to be interrupted by who knows what impositions to courtesy that she knew the Father's own terseness and anxiety would render. It was not usual to receive visitors and certainly not those so unexpected as this. No doubt, she thought, the Father would delight in it and her own day would be disrupted with more orders than usual.

"E's 'ere, Father,' she said. 'An' I'm no' ready for 'im, but I'll do what I can. T'would be a help to know as 'e's comin'.'

'Who's here, woman?'

'Bishop, Father! Bishop's 'ere! 'E's waitin' in vestibule for ye, an' 'e's no' lookin' so 'appy, I can tell ye.'

Father Taylor's eyes widened, and he leapt up from his armchair, causing it to nearly topple..

'Lord, woman! I had no idea he was coming!' And he bolted from the room, leaving his housekeeper still wringing her hands and scurrying out behind him to attend to this new inconvenience.

'Your Grace,' beseeched the priest, rounding into the vestibule to the Bishop, who appeared near collapsed in a waiting but clearly uncomfortable wooden pew.

'Father. How kind of you,' replied Hugh, a little breathless. 'I'm wearying of the day and it's barely begun. Pray, do sit a moment with me here while I find my strength to move.'

Father Taylor, greatly relieved at this easy reception, took a seat next to the Bishop.

'How goes the Cathedral, Your Grace? What a burden this must be for you.'

'Ah, indeed it is. But I have great faith. The sight of the reconstruction is a wonder, Father. You must, if you can, travel to see it. We are watching a history being made there. A vast undertaking it is, a vast undertaking. It is a great thrill to see the workings of it all, the engineering, the tradesmen of all sorts, and their dedication and effort. It is quite something.'

Hugh put his head back and closed his eyes.

'But I have not come to tell of that, alas. I have a tragedy to report and felt some stirring need to bring this news to you myself directly. Ah, such a misfortune, it breaks my heart to reveal it.'

Father Taylor's anxiety rose anew.

'A mere boy, Father. A mere boy. Fell this morning from a steeple. To his death below. I can barely conceive such a tragedy further afflicts your small diocese, not to mention that it mars the unfolding of this great epoch surrounding our beautiful cathedral.'

Father Taylor had turned his head to wait the Bishop's further revelation, not fully understanding the import of Hugh's words – a death? Some young lad. Amongst so many workers, it was surely inevitable.

'And one of his brothers,' Hugh continued, 'witnessed his own brother's fall.'

And instantly Father Taylor knew of whom the Bishop spoke, and while he could not conceive of why, he feared the telling of this to the boy's family.

Perhaps reading the priest's thoughts, the Bishop continued, 'I would speak to this boy's family myself, Father. It is I that must bear some responsibility for this I feel. Such grief I cannot ask you to give news of yourself.'

Father Taylor felt a relief, although he wondered whether he was expected to protest from courtesy that such a task was surely his.

'I would ask you to convey me to this family, Father. Do you know perhaps of whom I speak? Warriner, I believe is the name.'

'Yes, Your Grace. I guessed when you said of the brother. It is the family of the young boy that was attacked recently in the marketplace. There were three older sons went to the Cathedral from this one family. There are seven sons altogether, and three could surely be spared for this great task. It is an honour for any family to assume such a commitment, Bishop.'

'Ah no, Father. It is surely not. What does this cathedral, my own great undertaking, do for these poor, really? Surely nothing. Such a loss, such a loss. Three sons gone, and now one never to return.'

The Bishop remained head back and eyes closed, and Father Taylor had no further word to add. He felt small and unworthy of this charitable figure before him, and wondered at how he continued always, despite his will, to think so poorly of the ragged and the peasantry where the Bishop seemed to understand their hearts and their lot.

The two men sat in silence, one in contemplation of the harshness of life, and the other, thinking of the harshness of his own.

After some minutes, Hugh asked, 'What do you believe, Father, is the role of our beloved Church in this world?'

The small priest wondered at the bewilderment in the Bishop's tone, and what appeared almost an intimacy from the Bishop in expressing some apparent lack of assuredness at his own role, and perhaps even confiding in himself, a far lesser churchman, a lack of confidence, even a fear. He saw an opportunity to impress the Bishop with some pert wisdom, some comforting selflessness that recognised a brief moment of equal burden, man to man, one man of God to another. Could he presume to share the Bishop's space in the world, presume to raise his smallness to some nobler, more humane level that could connect with Hugh's greatness?

'It frightens me sometimes, my Lord; that we presume to lead these many poor to some sense of purpose, of greatness, when their very survival day-by-day holds them to their small lives.' He paused. 'And we are just men ourselves.'

And he'd done it. He knew he had said something of reality, without harshness, and with heart and understanding for

225

their own daily trials as Churchmen, and for those of their parishioners.

'Ah, you see indeed, Father. Thank you, thank you. It is so difficult at times, and there are so few I can turn to. I am most grateful for your understanding.'

Father Taylor felt blessed. His star had risen. Momentarily, he understood the valueless character he had injected over so many years, into his world and how it daily turned back into his soul, halting his progress beyond himself and into the realm of a greater selflessness that he knew this man at his side occupied. He knew also how he would seek to reoccupy that position repeatedly, now that he felt its touch, and that in seeking it, it would elude him yet still. But something had cracked and opened in him, and he felt, oddly, his smallness, greater than ever before.

Is this what is demanded of us? Is this how one becomes great? By losing one's purchase to the realities of sadness and anger and hysteria?

The moment passed, and Hugh stirred from his collapse.

'You must take me now to this family, Father. I must unburden myself to this poor boy's mother. But if I may have a brief refreshment, might I prevail upon your housekeeper a moment?'

'Of course, Your Grace. Please, stay here and I will return,' said Father Taylor, and he rose from beside the Bishop and hurried away to find the harassed woman, feeling some new, albeit small and brief, sympathy for the poor hen.

'Tell me what you know of this family Warriner, Father.'

The two men rode Father Taylor's dusty trap, the day hot again already beyond belief.

'They are as like any other poor family, Your Grace, very hard-working. The youngest child, the boy that was attacked, is not right though – an idiot they say. He doesn't speak, and appears for all the world not to notice a thing, a burden to a poor family where he does not make any difference to their worldly goods. But the others are all strapping youths and as much like any other young men.'

'And the parents?'

'The father is a large and gruff character. The mother is unusual I feel. She has an insight that is almost perturbing. A certain grace, dare I say of one so lowly. She is as most mothers are just the same, a stalwart to her family and her village – capable and strong.'

'Then she will bear this grief like the many others she has undoubtedly had, with great heart and great sorrow. And the father will anguish and kick his sons more – this is the way of these things I see.'

Father Taylor drove on, searching for another piece of wisdom he may bring to the situation to endear himself further to the Bishop and bring himself within his orbit. But nothing came, and he rode the horse on in silence and discomfort. He had no particular wish to meet the Warriner woman again.

The once verdant village countryside was long browned as the unheard of heat of the summer drew to its peak. Bush and scrub were variously dead and dying, and even the largest of oak and willow appeared decidedly autumnal with browning leaves; water holes, and streams long dried up and clayed over. Dust from the hooves before them blew up and coated their black cassocks, their hair and hats and faces, and Father Taylor wished for a speedier, more comfortable travelling. Indeed, he wished for a better carriage although such was not the lot of a village priest.

The rattling trap passed over a deep rut in the road, tossing the two men about on their seat. The priest cursed himself that he had not kept his eye more to the road ahead so that he could slow at the sight of these many ruts, caused equally perhaps from the dry and heat as from the recent earthquake. He had no wish to cause any injury, or even discomfort, to the Bishop beside him. But the

Bishop seemed not to notice any inconvenience. Did these physical demands not afflict him?

Rounding a bend into a small copse, Father Taylor knew they would come upon the Warriner holding momentarily, and he remarked to the Bishop, 'Just ahead, Your Grace.'

The copse provided a brief respite from the burning sun, and the coolness gave a pause to the priest's heated angst, only to increase in its fervour again as the trap emerged along the final yards to their destination. Father Taylor could see the figure of the Warriner woman sitting at the outside of her small stone hut, and he noticed she looked up to their arrival, coming as it did with some clatter and much dust.

For her part, Alice Warriner could see straight away the figure of the priest and wondered why she was to be disturbed by his presence yet again. But then she noticed another figure atop the buggy next to the priest and wondered at this personage, seeming as he did – for she could see it was a man – to be someone with a gravitas more than that of the ungainly priest. Indeed, as they drew alongside the yard's stone wall, she knew it was this other man's due that she should raise herself to her feet, and so she did, moving a few steps towards this arrival. Thomas sat at her feet playing at his stones and circling them around and around like a snail shell, each neatly end to end as always. In between his careful placement of each stone, his arms flailed around him, as though to bat away an insect that bothered him. It did not seem he noticed any other thing in his periphery though.

'Good day, Mrs Warriner,' called Father Taylor, climbing from his seat and turning to be of assistance to the Bishop, although this was not the Bishop's requirement.

'Good day to you, Father,' replied Alice.

The priest felt himself momentarily ill at ease, not knowing quite how it was he should introduce the arrival of one such as a Bishop to such a woman as this. In his awkwardness though he failed to notice that no introduction seemed necessary since Alice

Warriner, with no real knowledge as to this stranger's identity, recognised nonetheless the heady position he represented and curtsied reverently and low.

'My dear woman. Please. This is not necessary,' spoke Hugh, moving towards the bowed woman before him. 'Please,' and he held out his hand to help her raise herself, and once she had done so, he still held her hand. Hugh drew a deep breath, anticipating his revelation to this woman, but then noticed the small boy on the ground beside where they stood.

Thomas babbled to himself, waved about, and focused still on his pebbles and the precision of their formation. He looked back to his mother.

'And who is this?'

'This is my youngest, Lordship. His head is not the same as the others, but he is a sweet boy just the same.'

'Yes, I see this,' said Hugh, and he let go the woman's hand and stepped towards the boy, kneeling down to him and putting the same hand, just as within the mother's, upon the boy's fair, dusty head.

Thomas Warriner had muck in his head. Forces not usually noticed by any other person moved rapidly in his brain, demanding his analysis, his contemplation, and his action. A hand upon his fair head he did not especially feel, but a glow that no one else would see emanating from that same source sent a tiny thrill of light behind his eyes, somewhere lost inside his complex brain, and he looked up into the stranger's eyes and noted a light behind them too, and being as that was a familiar energy to him, he smiled.

And the Angels wept.

Not for the first time of late, Alice Warriner noted something not usual in her son's behaviour – that he would look into another's eyes like this, so directly, and smile. She did not know that when Thomas saw a face – more than when he saw any other thing – he saw a thousand faces, and these many images would overload the workings of his brain so much that the energy of it made him feel he might explode, so although he knew a face to be a face, he preferred not to look at them.

But this face had clarity, and the thousand were synchronous and balanced, and this created a belonging, and Thomas did not feel he was a separate thing from this face, but a part of it and in it.

The stranger looked to the mother. 'There is more to this young man than we would know, I think.'

'I've always thought so, sir.' Alice was pleased to hear someone say such a thing about Thomas.

'Indeed,' stated the stranger, looking back to the boy and smiling at him again.

The stranger rose, seemingly reluctantly, and he turned back to Alice.

'I am a bearer of sad tidings to your house, good lady, and it pains me greatly that your burden should grow heavier.'

Alice could conceive of little that could add further weight to her life and thought the stranger, though clearly a comforting and noble sort, could not understand at all how she saw her life. But then she saw a sadness that seemed at odds with such a man.

'Mistress,' interrupted Father Taylor, 'this is His Grace, the Bishop – Bishop Hugh from Lincoln.'

Alice began another curtsy but was stopped by Hugh.

'My dear woman, that is not necessary, not at all.'

Alice contented herself with a head bow.

'You have a son gone to the cathedral at Lincoln, madam?'

'There are three gone, y'Grace.'

'Yes, yes. And it is my sad chore to say that a youth has fallen a day ago from the height of our great Lady, sadly to his death at the ground below. The youngest I think of your sons gone there.'

As this news crept slowly towards Alice, she wondered at it. She looked at the words as they came from the Bishop's mouth and floated to her ear, and she moved the words around, rearranging them as they floated there before her, and she could not be clear whether there was a pain attached to these words, whichever order it was that they fell into. And where she thought perhaps there was, oddly, no pain so attached, then she wondered instead at such an absence, and it was a perplexity that invaded her thoughts. She did not know what she should do with this information, and so she decided instead to walk her mind away from the words, and she smiled at the Bishop and said 'Thank you, sir.'

And because the painful words were said and were now left hanging in the ether between the Bishop and the woman, and because they must find a place to settle themselves and be heard, they floated back on the air to the Bishop, and he knew that the burden of this tragedy was once more his, and the imperative to the King for the safety of the Holy City was once more in his mind..

Something must put all this right.

Hugh turned and looked down again at the small boy who had continued to watch him, and once more he knelt, and once more his eyes locked with the child's, and in them he thought he saw the eternity of heaven and the suffering of humanity.

And how, sweet boy, do you understand this?

At which the boy's eyes averted to a *whoosh-whoosh* that flew across the small party, casting a shadow as if two dark dragons crossed them. Hugh followed the boy's eyes up to see two enormous white birds cross the sky, and then they flew into the sun's light and a sting came into his eyes, and when he looked back at the boy, he could no longer quite see him.

In the tiredness that was the evening, after Alice had told her husband of the Bishop's visit, the little time she had between work and sleep lay in watching her sleeping sons and stroking the heads of two. As she sat there and dozed off and then woke again, she tried to recall how many sons she had, and for a moment, the count eluded her. There were seven, once she knew, with some lost before and between those, and there were four with her now. Although their father only counted three, which seemed few, and she wondered at how this had come about, to lose one's children. She decided not to think too much on it, and instead offered up a prayer for those sleeping before her now.

When she settled on the mat next to her husband, she knew he lay awake staring above him, squinting as though he were trying to make out an insect on a rafter. She smelt him unwashed, saw his hands cut and gnarled and laid on his chest, and wondered how he would cut another wound from his soul, as he had before appeared to do in a heartbeat.

'They were already gone before anyway. But with still only three now... Not enough sons for a man,' he said, squinting less.

Not enough sons for a mother.

Alice closed her eyes. She wished for a prayer to come to her, but none was there, and she felt sleep descend on her, exhausted, a picture of Thomas and the Bishop in her mind.

There was a grunt next to her.

'We'll have more then,' came her husband's decided breath.

And Alice, sleepy, wondered again how many it was that she had altogether, and yesterday, and now.

As different numbers rolled groggily through her mind, her husband stirred. He rolled on to her, and she felt his hand pulling at his tunic and then at hers, lifting it out of the way of his huge legs which pushed between her own. Their strength moved hers apart and a haze she'd been thankful for a moment ago left with her husband's great weight full upon her. It would not have been her wont, but then neither was it something to deny.

She laid in her same place, less fearful as other times since she could scarcely breathe whenever he climbed on her and laid himself completely on her. It was never in his mind that he might bear his weight himself, and she would never tell him so. She thought that perhaps it would not take so long, although as he'd grown older he was slower. Sometimes he couldn't finish at all, and then he would always wake an hour or two later and get back on her.

An ache came into her shoulders and neck as he grunted and pushed at her harder, sweat falling from his head on to her face. She could tell he was becoming frustrated, and she pushed her hips up into him and back again, since this sometimes stirred him more to finish. He pushed at her harder awhile, not making any sound except that he breathed heavier.

When it seemed his business would not finish in this manner, he pulled out of her and back on to his knees, reaching under her hips and rolling her over in one strong movement on to her belly. He grabbed at her hips and pulled her up to him, entering her again, deeper now. She rested her head on the mat and bore his thrusts against her. She breathed easier now, until finally a roar and his weight came down on her again with his seizure. He laid a few moments longer on her and his breath was right at her ear. Then he groaned and heaved himself up and rolled off her. She knew he would sleep immediately.

Alice wished only for stillness now, but she stepped up quickly and deftly, thinking she would walk briefly, and if his spill seeped out of her, she would be pleased not to have another child and likely suffer its loss.

Hugh felt a weighing up in his head between the pressure he might ease from the plight of ordinary folk such as he had just met, and the great task of bringing Henry to a firmness of resolve in pursuing the security of the Holy City. He knew he must travel to France sooner to meet with Henry, for the King had forsaken his responsibility to his English kingdom, even in spite of the great need of his people here. Hugh was reluctant to leave even briefly the reconstruction of the cathedral though, the onus of which weighed even more heavily now with its recent casualty, so young.

The picture of the boy's mother and young brother stayed in Hugh's mind's eye and would not leave. He wanted to do something for this child, whose small soul shone so simply at him. There was a weaving together of the King's mission and this small boy's plight that reeled querulously about his brain, but its import eluded him. He felt at the turning point of an uncertain future, the unfolding of which lay just beyond his grasp, but nevertheless upon his shoulders.

Returning to the path along the Lincoln pool, he hoped his winged confidante might return to listen to his ramblings and accompany his mind's walk through these complex demands. He thought her loyal presence might provide him a mirror with the sum of his cogitations, an answer, a direction. But, alas, the pen did not find him there, if indeed she still looked for him.

At his return to Torksey the day before, he and the priest were greeted with more fearful tidings that another swan had been found slaughtered in the Thane's woods. No culprit had been found, although an earlier poacher's life now hung in the balance as it was thought he must inhabit a web of hunters who preyed upon the Thane's lands. Was this his own great bird, his own confidante? He felt sure it could not be. But the finding was some omen for him now, not any longer just for the gossips and doomsayers of around about.

Hugh turned back along the path again, back towards the dealings and industry of the wharf. He passed quickly by the dockworkers, acknowledging the customary courtesies offered him, as befitted both himself and those who noticed him. Any thought of revelling once more in their labours was past him now. And indeed the physical tasks before him, of rebuilding, were smaller. The moral tasks, to encourage a people and priesthood, were greater. But greatest of all was to understand God's will, and it seemed that this was to be found in the grace of a bird, the simplicity of a child and even the light glistening on the water, if one had just the right view to see and hear.

The dust and the clatter of the movement about him whispered to him the sincerity of the deed, and he slowed his pace and looked up to a workman ahead of him, intent on his task to carefully lower a pallet of goods to the wharf. Hugh watched the man's face, focused on his duty, observing and acknowledging others' shouts to him, mindful of other movement about him that may disturb him in his goal. He was an ordinary-looking man, no different from others about him. Most likely he had a wife and children. Most likely he feared God and mostly observed His laws. Perhaps he would get drunk at times or beat his wife. But for now, this man's purest thought focused on the job before him.

As Hugh came closer and was about to walk by, the man turned his head and nodded to the Bishop, without for a moment withdrawing his awareness of the undertaking at his hands.

Hugh understood there was no greater obligation then, than to complete whatever lay before him, great or small, with purity, with sincerity, and with an eye to perfection. To ease the plight of a stricken child was no lesser accomplishment for himself, for the world or for God, than it would be to secure Henry's promise to take up the call to crusade. To protect the innocent and support even the wayward and foolish to come to God; whatever his task, it would be accomplished with purity and thankfulness.

Hugh continued on past the boats and their workmen, the sun beating hard on them. A carriage stood a short distance away to convey him back up to the cathedral, a patient Brother Peter waiting at its door..

'No, Peter, I will walk. I have much to occupy my thoughts.'

'Yes, Your Grace.' Peter motioned the driver on and remained to walk with his Master.

'My dear young man, there is no need really.'

'I could not in conscience leave you to walk here alone, sir. It isn't safe.'

'There is no one about who would harm a Bishop I feel, Peter. More likely they would run away when they see me.'

'Then even so, Your Grace, I could certainly not ride when you walk. It would not be right.'

'It's entirely right, Peter, if you should get to the top of the hill and have not the breath to go fetch me some water.'

'I will have all the breath I need, my Bishop. I promise.'

Hugh looked in the young priest's eyes, which were instantly lowered in a bowed head.

'Then you will walk with me, Peter.'

Hugh set off. Peter fell into step behind him, as Hugh knew he would. Smiling, Hugh halted after a few yards, and Peter, looking down, walked to his side and stopped.

'*With* me, Peter.'

He set off again, with Peter almost by his side.

Some things are difficult to change.

A cart drew along near them, an old Jew and a younger man pulling a long handle each, their heads bowed and the long curls from their sideburns covering most of the view of their faces. The old man struggled and his companion, perhaps his son, looked with concern.

Hugh stopped. 'Peter, help that old man.'

Peter stopped and took a moment to take in the instruction. The Bishop clearly gazed on the old Jew nearby.

Hugh turned his head and smiled at Peter. 'Please.'

Peter bowed and walked briskly to the old man. The cart stopped, and with a small exchange and looks of both puzzlement and gratitude towards the Bishop, the exchange took place, and the cart moved away with the two younger men pulling more efficiently now. The old man looked around for a place to sit, and finding a low wall, propped himself upon it, hands on knees and concentrating on easing his own breathing. He looked up at the Bishop, nodding. Hugh smiled in acknowledgement and rejoined his own path to the top of the hill. Not a few passers-by had witnessed this small mercy.

The People of the Book who inhabited these parts were the topic of moanings and grumblings of many a villager and lowly priest. Laws were enacted at times by local priests and aldermen that had ignorance and prejudice at their base. Hugh would make himself an advocate for the plight and innocence of these peaceful and unassuming peoples and their families.

Hugh looked up the hill and towards the steeple towers that should have been in his view. Would he be remembered for some excess in their rebuilding? He railed against the weakness of such ego, seeking to replace its drive with an equal ambition to relinquish his own immortality for the creation of a greater strength of human heart. It all fit together.

13

Timothy Watson swam in light. More light than he'd ever been in. This day though, the light didn't come from outside of him, towards him. It came *from* him. It was Tim's light. He had been learning how to make it and to project it, and today was his best light day yet.

He had worked out how he could take a little bit of white gold and make it into a lot more white gold, an ancient alchemy. The Holy Grail. The Philosopher's Stone. Tim had calculated it out completely. Tim.

When one little bit of whiteness came, he could take it into his body, via his heart, up through a space behind his forehead and down into his belly, and then from there it fanned out all through him. And as it went through his cells, it multiplied. Because light prefers to grow, not diminish.

It was very important that the first bit of white that started off the propagation was a really good bit of white. Tim had had trouble with this bit sometimes. Some of the white he'd seen lately was faded or stained, and this white did not, as it turned out, produce a quality spawn. In fact, it wouldn't produce any spawn at all often, which was why it had taken Timmy a while to figure out that he could make light himself.

He had learnt that the best light came from light itself, from the light that so often spoke to him. But living things also had light, and there had been a few people and one animal that had given him good light. One person he spent most of his time with sometimes had good light and sometimes not, but lately it was consistently better, and this had helped. This came from Tim's father. Tim knew his father was his father because anyway he just understood more than his father thought he did. His sister had very pure golden light, but he wasn't supposed to borrow from her light because she had to use it herself, even though when you take from other people's light, it doesn't diminish how much they have left themselves. In fact, the opposite is the case, and the more people give their light away, the more light they have. This was a type of mathematics that Timmy understood very well. He had been experimenting with this mathematics and found he was quite good at it.

Today was Tuesday. Tim knew that too. He knew all the days of the week, and he knew today was Tuesday. He had not yet been able to tell anyone that he knew this, but that didn't matter to him. He hadn't noticed whether it mattered to anyone else and so that didn't matter either. Other things Tim knew were people's names, and what they looked like, and how they liked to live. Tim lived differently because he had to deal with all the things he saw that other people didn't see. They all thought he didn't really see anything, but he saw a thousand times what anyone else did, and sometimes he thought his brain was going to explode with all that information and then he'd jump up and down and wave his arms around because that would settle it all down quite a lot. He could throw all the data around in his body, and when he stopped moving, it was more inclined to settle down into some sense. Sometimes he'd have to move around like this for quite a long time before things calmed down in his head.

Tim had been working on his light experiments because he knew more light had to go out into the world, and if he knew how to do that, then he'd be able to help. Some of the light told him this. It didn't come in messages like words or sentences, but it was as though he could hear it and see it and so it might as well have come that way. He could understand it if he lined himself up just right and didn't look directly at the light. If he looked directly at it, then it would move just out of his sight, so he had to observe it out of the corner of his eye, in a kind of sneaky way that meant he was both looking at it and not looking at it. It was *very* scientific.

Tim had an idea that he'd missed a few opportunities to make a useful contribution in this way already. He had taken longer to learn what he needed to and that was a bit disappointing for him now. When he got disappointed he would lose sight of the little impressions the light would leave in the space around him, and he wouldn't be able to pick up the trail, and consequently, also, not the source. And then he'd get more disappointed. And then he'd do all sorts of weird stuff to try and pick up the whiff of it again: straight lines were his main strategy. Light travels in straight lines. So he'd look around for some straight lines. Or he'd make his own. You could make your own lines to the light; you didn't just have to find ones that were already there. He realised also that it was not useful to stay disappointed, or even to get disappointed at all. That got in the way. He'd figured out now pretty much all the things that got in the way, and getting angry was one of the worst. Tim never really got angry, but other people did and they'd block out his light if he let them. So he tried not to let them, but that was fairly hard to do too.

When the light was especially straight and wide, Tim could see how it changed things. He even knew he could change things for the future and maybe even for the past. He thought some light from the past had helped him make light for the future. Time had a hold on this experiment in his mind as well. Someone else more famous than Tim would write that experiment up into a scientific paper and become even more famous for that, and it would cause a lot of interested fuss in the world, and some not very interested fuss too. But Tim wasn't concerned about that. He was concerned about how to use his experiments to make other kinds of interesting things happen, other than scientific papers that could make you famous.

Tim's main experiment now involved him reflecting light. If he caught it at the right angle and reflected it back along the right trajectory in a certain way, then it would have a major impact. The new light, once transformed and reflected, grew so much bigger, and it could change the way people thought, and it could change their actions, and it could change the impact of their actions.

Tim didn't really see this power as the amazing thing that it was. He just knew he had to be really good at it, and he felt a very strong urge to get it right today. He did understand that the implications were enormous – he wasn't sure what, just that it was a very big deal – and he didn't want to let anyone down.

He had to get it just right. And he was focusing very hard on this; at the same time as he was *not* focusing because if he focused too hard, his head got filled up with stones and fuzzy darkness and then that stopped the light going anywhere at all, plus it gave him a headache.

14

Khalid had a dream. He would be a martyr, a son of Ibraham, a child of God. He would wake to Golden Light, the reward of infinite glory and the praise of his people forever. The angel Jibril,[1] stern and foreboding, held his arms open to Khalid Islambouli and beckoned him into his enfolding wings. Khalid Islambouli knew a supreme protection. He would become a modern Shahid.[2]

Khalid had become ashamed of the once-proud status of his beloved Egypt. Its ancient and noble history had been besmirched now for too many years by the actions of the country's biggest traitor. His Arab brothers and sisters were all betrayed. He, and others, would change it. They had heard the call of Abdel-Rahman to take the traitor's life.

Although he did not hear Jibril speak aloud, he knew in his heart and mind and soul the words of His bidding as they had been spoken by Abdel-Rahman, and he knew he would obey. There was a great fire in him now. He had been angry at the arrest of his young brother, Mohamed Ahmed, and he saw now how he might avenge him.

When he woke in his barracks each morning, he prepared his soul in prayer, as indeed he heard the call to prayer throughout every day. When he spoke with the men he knew would become his brothers, his eyes blazed and it lighted a fierce passion in them so that they made him their leader. Their brotherhood remained known only to them – not from any secret they harboured or any fear of exposure, but because the great love they shared for each other and for their mission was bounded and safeguarded by their

---

[1] (the Angel) Gabriel.
[2] Martyr.

strength alone, and any other's would surely desecrate and dishonour that strength.

He had not been chosen initially for the Parade, but his brothers had made sure another would not be able to attend and manoeuvred for Khalid's placement. When a few days later he was chosen, he knew Jibril was really with him, and he knew his destiny.

When 6 October came, a Tuesday, Lieutenant Islambouli rose to morning prayer, completed all the normal duties of his morning, and then set about preparing his unit for their part in the Parade. Their uniforms were perfect – clean and starched – although they all knew the sweat that would invade them as they waited in the hot sun. There was always waiting to be done in the military and always in uniform and always in formation, and with no leniency to the heat or an insect or an itch settling one one's face. None of this came within Khalid's orbit on this day though. His mind held only one thought, and he felt the strength of that focus bonding him with his brothers around him. They were one mind, and they acted with a single disciplined force.

The march past was long and slow – their Egyptian leaders showed off their force to the world, and this at least made Khalid proud. Eventually, the grandstand came into view and Khalid's heart raced, but he was not frightened. He knew he would probably be killed. He was aware of every part of his body and felt only that there was himself in the world, and his brothers sitting in the back of the truck with him – and their target. Every motion forward was made up of a million tiny movements, and Khalid registered every one. They went by him slowly, and he saw precisely the detail of them all unfold. He was patient with it, and he felt complete control over each millisecond, and each scene within that brief moment.

Their weapons were prepared, and more importantly their spirits and their resolve. They had rehearsed at the rear of a deserted barracks; each knew his part. Ammunition had been prohibited and their rifles had been checked before they got into the truck. But their planning was meticulous, and they had made sure to have what they needed about them.

Their truck eventually came alongside the President's platform, which sat in fact quite a long way back from the route of the cavalcade. There were four rows of guards surrounding the President and his platform, and the President himself was standing, with many other dignitaries about him. Khalid recognised some American military uniforms and an orthodox Christian clergyman of some sort. Come to pay homage to a false leader, a traitor to the Prophet. He was ashamed that the President wore a uniform; he had no right.

Khalid heard the sound of jets flying towards their location. The dignitaries and the crowds turned away from the oncoming parade just as the truck carrying Khalid and his brothers halted before the presidential stand.

'Now,' he said firmly.

Lieutenant Islambouli leapt down from the truck and marched in a straight line towards the platform. Three others followed behind him.

President Anwar Sadat turned to see the men.

The men halted.

Sadat waited on their salute.

Islambouli lobbed three grenades into the stand, the others with him emptying their assault rifles, while others still leapt from the truck and ran towards the rows of dignitaries as they fell, scurried, and hastened to protect the fallen President.

Khalid knew at any moment he would be stopped, perhaps with a bullet, perhaps by guards who might run right at him, but neither of these came quite so soon as he thought, and so he kept running forward.

Hours seemed to pass. Why was there no response? He could stand here forever and kill all the traitors. He could see Americans in the stand, and others who supported Sadat. They all deserved to die. The movement of every piece of the tableau was mapped out in front of him like a complex alignment of a zillion stars, and he had power over each movement. It was all so easy.

He was only metres from the President now. Sadat had been brought to the ground by those around him. When he was nearly on top of them and he smelt their blood and fear, he emptied his assault rifle into the bodies before him. The bounding of his heart and head rose louder in his ears almost than the sound of the rifle.

He threw his arms into the air, as a victor.

'I have killed the Pharoah! I have killed the Pharoah!'

White light shone and took over the view before Khalid. A weight crashed into him, and the heaviness of it surprised Khalid.

All praise be to Allah and to Muhammad his Prophet.

15

He who cannot change the fabric of his thought will never change
reality, and will never, therefore, make any progress.

Anwar Sadat, third president of Egypt (1918–1981)

Tuesday, 6 October 1981

*Another world leader being shot at and surviving, although only just it
seems. How any idiot thought they could actually get to someone as heavily
guarded as Anwar Sadat, I can't imagine. Seems others around him took the
bullets. With things the way they are in the Middle East it would have been all
downhill. I'm sure if someone of his stature was assassinated right now – one of
the few voices of reason...*

Eleven were *killed, and twenty-eight wounded. Two of the would-be
(actual?) assassins were shot and killed. Sadat was in surgery for eleven hours.
Amazingly close obviously; must have been touch-and-go.*

*There is some significance in all these near-misses; some forces for good
are at large in the world; that we are being saved from these particular losses.
Maybe. How doe we know what worse tragedy is averted from the grace of
saving one life. Perhaps even decades from now... I can't help but wonder at
this turn of events. It just seems a dead Sadat would mean a spiralling out of
balance and control Middle East. I don't know why I think that. He's not so
well liked, but there's a steady hand there just the same.*

Wednesday, 7 October 1981

Timmy seems especially tired today. Wonder if he's coming down with something. He is changing so much lately. I don't know that anyone else would notice, but I do. There are changes in his awareness I think. It's as though he is seeing and understanding more. There is some part of him that's very in touch. It's amazing to watch him sometimes, and especially to see him with Jillie. There's such a connection there. She said the other day 'When I play with Timmy, it's the happiest time ever'. What an amazing thing to say! And it seems so true. When she gets home from school, she goes straight away to play with him, and he brightens up when he sees her. I love it. I just love watching them. Sometimes I think Jillie teaches him more than any of the rest of us, simply because she always gets his complete attention. I feel privileged to have both of them in my life. And I'm sure Jillie came as a special gift for Tim. Lucky boy.

Right now he's just fallen asleep on the rug on the kitchen floor, curled up with a big soft Edward bear, with his mouth open and his nose squashed sideways. Exhausted, poor fella. I've noticed if he's a bit 'off', once he's over it, that is to say, these periods when he's a bit ill – then he's more aware – as though either the illness is a result of some internal struggle for awareness, or recovering from illness provokes a new awareness. Not sure which; bit of both maybe.

Friday, 9 October 1981

Well, whatever it was, Tim's fine now. More than fine. He called me 'Daddy'. You'd think he'd always called me that, he was so nonchalant. Followed by another couple of words – only about three times his record. 'Daddy forgot sugar.' I hadn't sprinkled sugar on his cornflakes. It seemed so natural that I was halfway to the pantry to get the sugar before I realised. He's a different boy.

He blew the therapists away at the psych meeting today. Must remember to tell Lissie. Tim's progress seems counterweighted by her withdrawal. I want her to see what's happening for him. I feel a little angry and disappointed that he's not in her view of the world right now.

Saturday, 10 October 1981

An IRA bomb exploded at Chelsea Barracks in London and killed a woman pensioner. The Maze hunger strike ended a week ago after ten deaths. Most of their demands – not to wear prison uniform, and so on – have finally been met. Several prisoners were eventually taken off the strike by their families. Most of them were in prison for 'possession of a firearm'.

Monday, 26 October 1981

Another IRA bomb exploded in a Wimpy bar in London and killed a bomb disposal 'expert'. In fact, correctly: 'Provisional' IRA. 'IRA' is really the turn-of-the-century force – the 'PIRA' emerged out of a 1969 ideological split. Not quite sure how it is that British newspapers are describing the end of the hunger strike as a victory for Thatcher – the IRA's membership and activity both seem to have been given quite a boost. Danny Morrison has described Thatcher as 'the biggest bastard we have ever known'.

Thursday, 12 November 1981

The Church of England General Synod has decided to admit women to holy orders. Celebrations tonight with Rose and Loraine – expect they will both be up for it.

Alicia had noticed some change in her son and felt compelled to acknowledge, if only to herself, that Pete's attentions, and those of Tim's many therapists, were bearing fruit. Correspondingly she also knew that any development in the behaviour of her disabled child was not particularly due to any effort of hers. She wondered when it was that she'd forgotten to love her children; when she'd last felt the depth of adoration, she knew she'd once had. She wasn't sure when she'd stopped being emotionally available to those that needed her most or why this had happened or how. It was manifestly not right, but to find it, to even look for it, seemed exhausting. And her response to exhaustion lay mainly in work, coffee, and a certain indulgent aloneness that she persuaded herself – and others – was the need of any professional, especially an academic.

It did seem a lie, but one Alicia was unprepared to challenge at the present, despite that she knew her current modus operandi was clearly going to make things worse. A deepening gulf between her and Pete only reinforced for her the selfish value of sinking further into her self-exile.

Sometime or other, Alicia knew she would have to deal with what she'd created.

For the time being at least, she felt some relief from the pressure to have to make a greater difference to Tim's existence. The essence of a certain esteem that she once felt from being a mother now sought its affirmation in the adoration of students and even the begrudging respect of a few of her colleagues. To have been at the centre of new science was preferable, but her position at its periphery still had enough hold on her.

A knock at her office door turned Alicia back to her current real world.

Gerry Bernstein opened the door slowly, putting his head around as he did so.

'Oh, hello. You *are* here.'

'Hi. Come in,' responded Alicia.

'You're awfully quiet in here, y'know.' He was mock serious.

'It is a university,' Alicia said.

'Oh, riiight.'

'Having trouble coping?' Alicia wondered if she was discovering a fellow rebel.

'Potentially. There's a lot of very stern, sober sorts around here I've noticed.'

'Ah, you've discovered the secret of our success then?'

Gerry grinned. 'Oh, dear. That bad?'

'Oh, not always.'

'I *was* wondering if you'd explain Paris to me,' he queried.

'With pleasure.'

'How about a drink this evening. Staff Club?'

'Sure. Love to,' responded Alicia.

'Splendid! As they say.' Gerry smiled and left with a wave.

Definitely a new accomplice!

Alicia returned her attention to the journals on her desk.

Later, as the floor emptied, Alicia knew from the cheery farewell that emanated from Gerry's office door a short way down the hall that probably there was only she and Gerry left. Would she saunter down to his office and casually say she was wandering over to the staff club now and she'd see him there, or would she wait and see if he came by?

Oh, for fuck's sake. Chill out.

'Hey!'

'Hey!' Turning, taking her mouse with her and trailing her keyboard half off her desk. 'Whoa!' Replacing things, and turning back to the door with a smile.

'You ready then?' Gerry stood in her doorway.

'Sure.' Alicia reached round under her desk for her purse. *Wow.* She decided her purse was unnecessary and grabbed her office keys.

'You comin' back later?'

'Probably. I've got a mountain of marking.'

'Same. Okay, let's go. Better make it a quick one.'

Whatever you say!

The staff club was an old homestead, once the residence of the Chancellor. It wasn't so busy, and they ordered beers and sat on the verandah. A pretty path wound past leading down to the river, and students and others passed by occasionally. It was a still evening with a warm sun, despite mid-autumn, lending a lazy feel to the evening.

'Paris then.'

'Huh? Oh yes. What takes your fancy?' *What a dumb fucking thing to say.*

'Well, it's on the edge of my interest, I have to say. But it's apparently your thing, so...'

He said thing 'thang', and she wasn't sure whether she detected a sense that her life's work was viewed as lacking in seriousness, as a play 'thang'. If it seemed arrogant, it seemed vaguely attractive at the same time.

Taking a different tack: 'Have you heard the local story about the Bishop of Lincoln?' *Not sure why I'm going here.*

'Which Bishop?'

He just checked out my tits.

'Well, there's one story in particular that's mildly famous among those in the know about these things. Bishop Hugh – he was French. He came here in 1181, a few years before the earthquake that destroyed the Cathedral. He was responsible for rebuilding it into substantially what it is today. He was canonised some years later and is still revered as a saint by many.' *He did it again.* 'There's a lot of stories about him actually, but a lesser known one is about a child who's buried in the Cathedral – it dates from Hugh's time – and they say that on the anniversary of the child's burial, you can hear weeping from Hugh's grave – well... apparently some people say they've heard it, and probably not for centuries, anyway... Ah...'

'Sorry, I'm listening. Go on.'

Not true.

'Actually, you know, it's dull. Tell me what brought you to Lincoln.'

'No, no. I'm interested. It's a good story. What's it got to do with Paris?'

'Potentially, Paris suggests the truth of such a story. Well, no, that's not really true. I'm making a giant leap into science fiction. But Paris tells us, put simply...'

'Because I'm simple.'

'Very funny. You're interrupting. Paris tells us that two particles may continue to have influence over each other from significant distance, and potentially across time, as long as they were previously, at some point, in the same place and time.'

'And that connects with the Cathedral...'

'Doesn't matter. Popular science. Not serious stuff. Don't go there.'

'Why?'

'Because you'll be isolated by the... what did you call them? The "stern, sober" sorts that inhabit this place.'

'That can't be so bad.'

'Yes, well, it's not so good either. You'll need their support some day. Heavens. Listen to me – the rebel – I'm getting soft!'

'Listen. I've been there. Just do your thing. No point doing work you're not happy in. Another drink?'

'Sure.' This would be her third and a known tipping point.

A hazy pink dusk was descending, but the air was still warm and quite quiet. There certainly didn't seem to be any reason to want to be anywhere else.

When Gerry set two more beers down and noticeably eyed her neckline for she didn't know how many times, she looked him back in the eye with a face that said *that's fine*.

'Thanks,' she said.

'I'm going to kiss you in a minute.'

Of course you are. Why wouldn't you?

She smiled slightly and sipped her beer, looking him in the eye. There was no nervousness now, no wondering what would happen next or wondering how to behave. Whether it was the beer or whether she was just swept up in someone's charm, or both, she didn't care. It seemed very easy.

They stayed quietly, sipping, the occasional glance, the odd not-so-coy smile. A couple trundled past, their feet crunching the fine gravel of the path. It seemed the right sound in the right place. They didn't seem to be in a hurry. Alicia took in Gerry's shape, the colours and texture of his casual linen shirt and trousers, an obvious tan, arms that belonged to a builder not an academic.

'Shall we walk back?' Gerry proffered.

'Of course.' *Of course.*

They stood up and wandered off the end of the verandah, on to the gravel path, headed back towards the science block. No hurry.

'I feel like a teenager.' Gerry grinned.

Good, that means I don't have to.

The main door was still unlocked. Gerry pulled one side door open for Alicia to pass, and they walked the few metres to the elevators. They didn't speak. Alicia wondered and didn't wonder.

Getting into the lift, Gerry placed his hand lightly on Alicia's lower back. It all seemed very normal. Alicia looked vaguely to the lights above the elevator door, watching the numbers climb. Alcohol disguised each moment as pleasure, a euphoric camouflage. The elevator announced their floor with a quiet *ping*, and the doors opened. As they rolled out, they instinctively listened for other signs of life, but no lights were left on. Even the cleaners had by now come and gone.

'Are you sure this is a good idea?' Gerry asked, clear that 'this' was understood to both of them.

'We're both adults.' Alicia was momentarily surprised at her lack of consideration of any other consideration, and then that consideration disappeared too.

How is this so easy? Never mind.

They turned the corner corridor that led to her office. Alicia unlocked it and stepped in, Gerry following and closing the door. She dropped her keys on her desk and turned.

Gerry leant against the door and for a moment they just looked at each other. In the same second they moved together. His arms were right around her and his lips instantly on hers. There was no space between them and no thought. Alicia felt another energy that was not her own free will controlling her actions – controlling both of them.

Gerry pushed her against the wall and the length of his body pressed on hers. She put her hands on his biceps, feeling the strength of his arms and up to his shoulders and neck. His hands grabbed her arse and then lower, up under her skirt, sliding the material up, handful by handful.

Jesus!

His kisses lowered to her neck, and she arched with pleasure. When a hand slid into the front of her knickers, she instinctively moved her legs apart, and he reached further in. Alicia reached down to Gerry's belt and fly and undid them, pushing him back from her briefly to slid his trousers down over his arse. She reached for his cock, which clearly knew where it was going. He bent his knees and, with both hands on her arse and hips, hoisted her off the floor and brought her down on him. She was pinioned to the wall now as he slid in and out of her, his face buried in her hair and neck. He moaned and let out enticing profanity.

'God, you've got a great arse.'

He came with a groan, and with only a second for her to wonder that that was a little early he grabbed her to him, still with her legs off the ground, squatted and turned and had her on her back on the floor. He was still in her.

Jesus!

'Bit of a sprinter. Sorry.'

He pushed up on to his hands and started to grind slowly into her again.

'You're kidding?'

'What?'

'You're going again?'

'You ain't seen nothin' yet, baby.'

He lowered to his elbows, smiling at her and moving still.

'Nice,' Alicia responded, smiling back.

'Just nice?'

'Very nice.'

His hand prised at her blouse, rescuing her breasts from beneath her bra. Instead of fondling them, as she expected, he watched them, and their gentle movement spurred on his until their bouncing released him again. Again he continued to move inside her slowly, and when his erection returned, he slid out of her, reached behind and grabbed a cushion from her sofa, scrunching it beneath her hips. With her hips high and kneeling between her legs, he entered her again, deftly massaging his fingers across her, sliding her own wetness up her clitoris. He was intent on his task, looking first to his fingers and then again to her gently rolling breasts. She felt her own surge start and unfold and explode, and she grabbed his hand away from her. He laid over her and finished again, staying still this time, breathing heavily into her shoulder. Alicia revelled in her moment, until he began again, hoisting himself to his elbows once more.

'No way.'

'Yes, way.'

'Wow!'

Alicia slid her hands under his shirt, holding his hips. This time he was longer, slower. His eyes roamed every part of her that faced him. They kissed, and she moved her hands across his back and arms and hips. When he finished again, he held his weight and her eyes a few moments longer and then rolled on to his back, sliding one arm beneath her neck and rolling her into him.

Alicia felt warm and wet, from sweat and saliva and semen, and her oblivion held only one other being, with an emotion in it shared only with him. There was only her office and the dark and the floor and strong, warm arms that held her.

'Well, ladies. Unaccustomed as I am ...'

'Oh, very funny,' said someone amid several titters, as Maitland rose from his seat at the familiar dining table setting.

The group was gathered as usual at Rose and Loraine's cosy house, the news of the Synod's decision having quickly circulated, and the assumption made by all that this was a moment of particular celebration for their hosts.

'Yes, yes, yes. Well, I do think this is quite exciting news. I don't know if you've ever considered ordination, either of you – apparently, it's not something we've discussed at this table (somewhat surprisingly). But it's long overdue, and I have to say, there's no two churchwomen would make finer members of the priesthood than you both. In fact, I clearly see a Bishopric looming in your futures somewhere.'

'Now, Maitland, the future's my party trick, and anyway that seems just too far-fetched,' Loraine responded.

'A toast, my dears.' Maitland raised his glass and others took to their feet also. 'To Rose and Loraine, the future of our beloved Faith, and what I'm sure will be a marvellous career for both of you.'

'Rose and Loraine.' Everyone chimed in.

When they had all sat down again, Rose said, 'It's probably going to be quite a while yet, you know. The Synod's said it's possible, but individual Bishops can make their own decisions about this.'

'Oh, Phipps'll be up for it, don't you worry,' said Maitland.

'I wouldn't be so sure. But we'll see... Anyway. Pete, I thought your lovely Alicia was going to come with you this evening. We've all been looking forward to hearing about her science.'

'You're changing the subject, my dear,' Maitland countered.

'Well, it's just that we're not here to talk about that, and I don't know that either of us has ever really got our own heads round the very real prospect now of ordination,' replied Rose.

'Really?'

'Yes, honestly.'

'Actually, I guess I always assumed too, that you'd be in favour of ordination if it came along,' Sally piped up.

'Really?' Loraine responded.

Murmurs and nods of agreement went round the table in the obvious expectation of more response from the two deaconesses.

Rose and Loraine both grinned and shrugged shoulders from opposite ends of the table.

'Well, of course, we support the idea of women in the Church, and indeed ordination,' said Rose. 'And, of course, we'll consider it. But I think we've been content for things to unfold as they will, and I guess we'll take that step in good time. Probably.'

'How can you be so relaxed about it?' said Sally.

'Why not?' Rose replied.

'I just assumed you'd be more, you know, radical about this.'

'We are.'

'Well, you don't seem very hot under the collar to me. That would be the collar you don't have of course,' added Maitland.

'Does one have to be angry and radical at the same time?' asked Loraine.

'Usually.'

'Hmm. Well, I choose not to be, if that's all right. Angry, that is. But still radical.'

Maitland regarded Loraine. Everyone regarded Loraine.

Loraine regarded everyone else and said, 'Oh, come on! Really! You want me to be radical *and* angry? No!' She grinned at her audience. 'Angry's just not useful.'

'This is the Christian Faith we're a part of,' Rose added. 'We're supposed to be loving, beyond all else.'

'Turn the other cheek then?' Maitland said.

'Absolutely.'

'Then how do you get what you want. I mean, I assume you've wanted to see this change. How do you advocate for it?' Sally asked.

'Simply that. We advocate. And we pray. And we do well at what we do. And we try to demonstrate that we as women have a part to play in the Church. And I think we do that well,' responded Rose.

'But don't you get angry? Frustrated? That you've been denied this particular opportunity?'

'Where would that get us exactly?'

'I don't know. More satisfied?'

'Absolutely not. It would get us precisely *more* frustrated!' Loraine replied.

'Well, perhaps.'

'Look,' said Loraine, 'things can change in the world without resorting to aggression – the serenity to accept what you cannot change, etcetera, whatever that saying is.'

'Yes, I know the one, and we all think it's wonderful, but no one actually does things that way. Not really,' Maitland said.

'Oh, Maitland, you're a cynic!'

'Absolutely! And proud of it!'

There were laughs and grins for Maitland's faux pride.

'If you add anger to a debate, you harm: first, yourself and secondly, the possibility of a positive resolution.'

There's always a place for good old righteous indignation, my dear,' responded Maitland.

'Of course, but you don't have to add anger. It's self-destructive. Leave anger out of it and you'll solve things much more quickly.'

'But,' Sally continued, 'it's normal to feel angry sometimes at what life's doled out to you.'

'Perhaps it is a *human* reaction, Sally, but it's our humanity also that allows us to manage our emotions and turn them to good use. And anyway, humanity, which does after all include the Church, develops in its own time, according to the exigencies of the age. We can't always make these things happen sooner than is possible.'

'Yes – and no. I can't agree that we can't push things along...,' Sally responded.

'Of course, we do what we can to push things along, as you say. But you do not quarrel with a rose tree because it cannot sing,' stated Loraine.

'Oh, now *that's* good. Can I use that?' asked Pete, smiling.

'Certainly, but it's not original,' replied Loraine.

'Will whoever said it mind?'

'I doubt it. He's dead. 'Abdu'l-Baha.'

'Who?'

'Baha'i faith.'

'Right. None the wiser.'

'Anyway, about your wife, and your son. I hope we'll get to see Alicia sometime. How's your son going? How are *you* going?' Loraine asked Pete.

'We're all great. Tim's making great progress. And I did rather think I might have had Alicia convinced about coming along, but she's had to get something finished at the University. Nearly didn't make it myself, but one of Tim's therapists stayed on. And as for Tim, I've decided I'm going to treat him as a fully functioning kid. *I* think, despite what the so-called experts say, he knows everything that's going on around him, but for whatever reason he can't express it – at least not as other kids would. In fact, I think he sees and understands things we don't.'

'Like what?'

'Don't know – doesn't matter. My job's to make sure he has every opportunity to explore his own unique world and participate in ours as a bright and endowed human being.'

'Well, that sounds like an enormous change. How do you think you'll go with that?'

'As I've been going, and hopefully with some intuition, and a measure of creativity.'

'Then that's wonderful. Just wonderful. What an extraordinary attitude towards it all! For certain your belief alone will have some effect.'

'Oh, so we're back on that then?' Maitland reiterated.

'But this is your field, isn't it, Maitland?' Loraine teased. 'Faith and belief?'

'Yes, actually. And you're absolutely right. And I agree with you too, Pete. Good luck to you, old man.'

Rose weighed in. 'I read the other day about a man in the United States that they're making a movie about – he's autistic, but he has a prodigious memory, can practically memorise whole telephone books. He can read a novel in a few minutes, a few seconds per page. *Even* this: his left eye will read the left page, and his right eye will read the right page.'

'That's bizarre!' Maitland. 'How is that possible?'

'Well, they don't know it seems. But he grew up "retarded", as they said then – awful word – and at some point his father discovered he had some extraordinary mathematical ability. And they're making a movie about him with Dustin Hoffman.'

'I've read about that,' commented Pete. 'It's called savantism – areas of brilliance in otherwise relatively poorly functioning individuals. Many of them are autistic, and they often have some other mental disability as well. And then there are *mega*-savants, like the fellow you're talking about. There's not so many of them.'

'Hmm.'

Pete had learnt to read momentary silences in the group as some sort of appreciation for the depth of a particular thought or discussion. Sometimes he thought he could just about see people's dots joining up. The group's openness to ideas was turning Rose and Loraine's house into a particular haven for him.

'Well then,' Maitland again, 'we'll be expecting something amazing from the young man one day. Mathematical ability you say this other chap has?'

'That's right.'

'Interesting. I wonder if most of their abilities centre on those *kinds* of areas of expertise. I mean to say, the more precise sciences. I wonder if there's extraordinary *artistic* ability, for example – things requiring higher levels of creativity and expression. You said it was expression that you think is the challenge for your boy, Pete?'

'I don't know for sure. I'm just guessing. Well, maybe not guessing entirely. It's my own conclusion, from knowing him and observing him. I think he understands more than we've thought up till now, and for whatever reason he can't express what he knows, but if he had the means to, then I think he would have one hell of a lot to say.'

'There must be research being done on this, Pete.'

'Undoubtedly. But, you know, it's not so easy to find these things out. But you're right. Every now and then one of his therapists mentions something, although mostly it's education and therapy focused. But I'll start paying more attention.'

Rose and Loraine's dining room was a familiar and comfortable space for those present. The content of the conversation varied enormously, and everyone went with the flow of it. It was almost always of interest, and the reasons for different individuals' attendance and contributions, known or unknown, were accepted. Had anyone ever suggested he would become a regular at a church group meeting, Pete and most people who knew him would have scoffed at the idea, but he'd been coming for some months now and had found it of increasing comfort, interest, and virtually his only source of friendship and socialisation. He – and he assumed others – hadn't really realised there existed a demographic that was both religious and open, as well as interesting. Was this the religious silent majority? Pete thought it a discovery well made.

Pete drew himself reluctantly from the good company around ten o'clock, resisting Maitland's gestures towards the pub as well, and heading home. Everyone else remained behind, and he was disappointed to be missing out.

When he got home, he was only partly surprised Alicia was not there yet; he paid the babysitter and stood by the front gate as she walked to her home a few doors up.

'Night, Mr Watson,' she called, turning into her own gate.

'Night, Carly.' Pete turned back into his own gate and up the verandah steps to the front door.

He peeked into each of his children's bedrooms, deciding to sit a moment by his sleeping son. Timmy's room was full of colour; there were posters of animals and a castle and a double-decker bus on his wall. Plastic bins of toys were stacked up, and a bookshelf was untidily filled with books, puzzles, and assorted bits and pieces. His bed was loaded up with cuddly toys, one of which, a faded, floppy, and ragged dog, he had his arm around as he slept.

Pete thought things were going to work out just fine.

Rose dried as Loraine washed up. Their guests had all left, and as usual they refused any cleaning up assistance. All part of the service they liked to offer was their thought.

'Shame Pete had to leave when he did,' Rose said, wine glass and tea towel in hand.

'Yes. I suppose it was quite late already. And he has rather got his hands full, I imagine, despite his assertions of his "normal" son.'

'Yes. Yes, indeed. He's quite different now from when he first started coming, don't you think?' Rose asked.

'He does seem more relaxed and more certain about himself; and about his son too. I'm sorry I haven't got to meet the young man myself,' replied Loraine.

'Oh, well, plenty of time.'

'Interesting discussion.'

'Mmm.'

'What *do* you think about ordination then?' Loraine asked.

'Why would we not?'

'Thought you'd say something like that. Have we got everything in off the dining table? No more glasses?'

'Yes, that's it,' Rose replied.

'Good.' Loraine pulled the plug from the sink. 'Do you have any idea what Phipps thinks?'

'No, perhaps we'd better find out.'

'Perhaps we'd better.'

'Do you feel you need to?' Rose asked.

'Become a priest? No, not necessarily. I don't need the recognition or the status. And I'm not of the view, in reality, that it puts me any closer to God.'

'So you wouldn't do it anyway?'

'Didn't say that. I'd need to be clear about my reasons,' replied Loraine..

'Career options?' Rose suggested.

'Rather simplified, don't you think? It's not about a career.'

'Of course it's about a career. You've chosen a career in the Church,' Rose stated.

'I've chosen a *life* in the Church, and I have that,' replied Loraine.

'Then how about simply *because we can*?'

'Now there's a good reason!' Loraine laughed.

Rose laughed too. 'Well, I'll make sure I bump into Phipps tomorrow then, shall I?'

'Good idea. Tea?'

'Lovely, thank you.'

Alicia turned out of the university on to Brayford Way, heading for the short drive along the A15, before she broke off on to the long Lincoln Road to Nocton. It was two or three in the morning – she wasn't sure precisely. After a surprising several more rounds with Gerry on the floor and the sofa in her office, he had ventured out to find an off-licence and come back with a bottle of Famous Grouse, a jar of pickles, a large wedge of Stilton, and a box of Carr's water crackers. She'd thought fish and chips would have gone a treat but hadn't said so. They'd tucked into their small feast and made a significant attempt at emptying the Grouse.

Alicia had wondered if after marathon sex they'd actually have anything at all to say to each other. They'd talked non-stop for hours, about their work, colleagues, England, America, students, and Lincoln pubs. There'd been no mention of spouses or families, nor any discussion about tomorrow or the next day. Alicia had figured, since she wore a wedding ring, her situation was obvious. Gerry's wasn't clear, and she hadn't asked. She'd assumed he was single. She didn't much care.

Eventually, she'd had some sense that it was well past any reasonable time at which she ought to be going home. Gerry had walked her down to her car, kissing her passionately in the darkness. It had seemed he would likely accept an invitation to the back seat if she'd let him, but she'd thought anymore and she might not be able to sit down in the car to drive home.

Now taking the on-ramp to the motorway she was leaning forward slightly and forcing her eyes wide open. There was no traffic and it was a clear night. Her mind whirled through the various excuses she'd been thinking she could give Pete depending on whether he woke up when she came in or not. She knew she'd have to have a shower as soon as she got in and that might wake him. If it didn't, then she figured she could fudge the whole thing more or less. Any other analysis of the evening would have to wait till tomorrow.

God, it is tomorrow!

Alicia wasn't sure what would happen next with Gerry and she didn't want to think about it now. She wanted to sleep more than anything else.

16

... there were Angels in the architecture, spinning in infinity ...
Paul Simon, 'You can call me Al', from the album 'Graceland' (1986)

Giles poured two more short glasses of Laphroaig. The chess players had unexpectedly changed their drink today; it appeared they were celebrating, and their chessboard was absent as well. Giles didn't mind a Scotch himself now and again, but he'd never stomached this strongest and smokiest of drops. He thought it tasted like floor polish, but these fellows clearly appreciated it; their first hadn't touched the sides, and they'd sent him off again straight away for another.

'May I ask what's your celebration then, gentlemen?' Giles placed their drams in front of them.

'We have saved the World, sir,' the older man declared, and both raised their glasses to Giles, although each just took a sip this time from his glass.

'Well, *that's* good news. Congratulations!'

'And what better way to celebrate than with *your* national drink, young man?'

'Oh aye, it's no' so much *my* national drink, sir. I'm more for a glass a' milk most often myself.' Giles's big frame shook with his jocular laugh. 'But I'll be happy to keep those poison swords coming your way though.'

'You are too kind.'

Giles smiled, tucked his tray under his arm, and turned back to the bar.

So he did it then?

The younger one. Yes. Well, he had set himself a challenge. And he's had some help of course. But quite remarkable, just the same.

And the father has understood something too.

Yes.

And the future is altered inexorably.

Hopefully.

And the mother?

That's up to her.

What about the older one? He doesn't have the same support.

*Yes, I know you think that's what it's about, but it's not so simple.
We still have a job to do, but those were difficult times.*

The Bishop sees.

Perhaps.

And the Mother.

Yes.

Although she's powerless.

Haven't you learnt anything?

What can she do?

*She can move the world. The same as any other being. Pope or pauper.
It doesn't matter.*

*But she doesn't understand the need. The Bishop at least sees some
connection.*

She sees her son. That is enough.

But...

She loves him. That is enough.

To change the world.

To change the world.

17

... thought passes back and forth between people
in a process by which thought evolved from ancient times.
David Bohm, physicist (1917–1992)

Hugh had made Peter ready his carriage from Lincoln and travel with him. It was a long journey and Hugh, feeling less charitable on an unbearably hot day, could not hold to the usual protocol of having the local priest accompany him. It was not that Hugh found him offensive, but on this day, Father Taylor's particular sycophancy was not best suited to Hugh's designs. Hugh's vision to serve even those he led was of greater difficult than normal with one so lacking in any active virtue, and the priest's habit of constantly ennobling his Bishop did not aid the imperatives of humility and emptiness needed for the task Hugh set himself this day..

Peter on the other hand went about his servitude to the Bishop more invisibly, without ambition certainly, but nor was he too begrudging of his status, so Hugh did not have to function within any immediate context of some other's sourness. Indeed Peter lacked much outward show of emotion and not having this to swarm about in his thoughts made Hugh's travelling reverie tolerable, and gave his mind and body a decent pause to rest from the litany of his own duties.

A warm southerly wind teased the hot dusty travellers with an idea of coolness that had no such reality and only made for shorter tempers than usual, particularly whipping up the road's grit and earth as it did, which got into the folds and creases of a horse's eyes and mouth and nose, and every part of a person. Hugh knew his drivers would curse even him, alongside their animals and carriage, each other, and anyone really that they came across. He imagined he would need to reward them with a little ale at their destination and a lot of ale upon their return. There was a demon to ale that Hugh had seen on occasion bring a hell to men, and a great misery to their women and children. The pleasures of common folk though were few, and he was keen to reward those who served him with that which might reasonably bring their continuing support to his household needs. It gave him respite from the consideration of such, albeit that that reality seemed nefarious.

Hugh puzzled still along their thirsty route. And as his discomfort grew with the heat, so too did his doubt and his sense of his own foolishness. And then he'd equally scold himself for a lack of Faith. And then the combination of his swaying thoughts, undulating beliefs, and the blistering day escalated the effects of all three further, until eventually Hugh tried to ignore every element and stare blankly at the passing countryside, which availed him of some brief peace from his own restlessness. As the carriage neared its destination, Hugh wondered what on earth he intended to do and say when he got there.

Thomas heard a voice inside him that he knew he must follow. The sound of the voice was golden light, and Thomas had seen this same light before and remembered snow-white wings and kind red-brown eyes.

There were not many things that sent light to him, one person mainly. But now he had seen another with good light that came firmly to him, and it felt like a very beautiful and good thing. He saw a web of connectedness between a white-clothed creature and a black-clothed man and some task to make clear for the world.

He sat with his mother, placing his pebbles carefully in an ever-widening spiral. When his pebbles were used up, he took the ones from the centre, one by one, and continued to place them end to end. His circle grew larger and larger. When it was bigger than any circle he had made before, he stopped taking the pebbles from the inside and moving them to the outer circle. He looked at the pattern on the ground. It pointed away, in a direction, and Thomas looked away towards the woods where the pebbles pointed. He tilted his head and puzzled.

Alice sat at her usual seat, peelings fallen to her lap and the ground about her feet. The stranger's visit the day before had not unnerved her, as perhaps it ought, and even the news of Thurstan's death left her unchanged from the day before she'd heard this. She'd known her boys were gone and had already rent her dusty smock from that parting. She fathomed at her own absence of feeling for a lost child, for he was just a child to her still. Had she reached the boundaries of what was bearable to her soul? Even more peculiar to her, she felt some queer thrill in her heart that could only be happiness, and this both troubled her and it didn't. She looked down at Thomas. He looked to any as a normal child, happy and babbling even to himself. There were changes in him of late that pleased her. Had the Lord answered her prayers for her youngest? There was no mistaking the touch of God on their small lives; at least Alice herself never mistook this.

She stood, letting scraps in her lap fall to the dust, and went inside. Depositing the roots and vegetables into a pot of boiling water over the fire, she brushed some grime from her apron and set to finding a brush to sweep the day's dust, already thick, from her door.

Thomas clambered awkwardly to his feet, bare and dirt-stained and warm on the clay ground. He stared briefly towards the sun and then looked away to the woods where his stones pointed on the ground, fine glowing spots before his eyes from the sun. Following a silent message to his light head, he sauntered off in a straight line to a special destination. He knew the straight line was important to follow, and he clambered over a small stone wall not far from where he'd sat. He felt the coolness reach out from the edge of the woods and that seemed a pleasant treasure to find on a dry and burning day. The coolness was also a darkness, but there was some light somewhere among the trees and he would find it. Thomas knew he was very good at finding light, and he was also enjoying having a job to do.

When the Thane's men dumped the swan in the centre of the village, they looked threateningly as they could, which was not difficult for them, to as many as they saw.

It was the Thane himself who had instructed them to do so and to place some fear in the villagers; since he had no care for them anyway, he had no knowledge particularly of the fear already there, and even what threat that may be to him.

As it was, already fearful, most that saw this were simply confused. Their world was turning on its head and for some this meant they should keep low and invisible; for others, there was much to occupy their loose tongues; and for others, who felt the need of some certainty in uncertain times, it gave the spur and a hunger towards violence, and it would be the tattle of others would give that tendency direction..

Father Taylor joined the Thane's men to question the villagers, not since he supported him, but rather since he was concerned the Thane's bullies would cause more trouble. He knew also that his actions would place him within the esteem of the people, and this he preferred.

And so he took to the dusty street again, calling not to accuse or bully but to measure the temperament of his faithful and gain a trust in the status quo and the Church's protection and the day-to-day goings-on of village life. Once again when he reached the Jew's house he intended, as before, to bypass it, but a thought flew past his mind that a visit might show his mercy and an inclusiveness that certainly would do no harm, and so he rounded into the Jew's yard.

Jacob Yazd himself felt his position had become precarious. Already word had reached him from cousins in Lincoln that fights were being picked, goods stolen, and accidents that were not accidents were occurring, always to other Jews, young and old, and men and women. There had been suggestions even that the King would turn a blind eye to such abuses, that harming Jews would not be punished under the law, and that perhaps even the King himself plotted against them. Or that his Lords did so. Jacob worked to protect his family every day. He would not allow his children to go further from his yard than he could see them, and his wife he begged to always stay in. He kept a satchel of coins, some knives, a small menorah and candles, and other small items to trade, always ready but hidden from sight. His family slept in their clothes and sandals, and he had rigged his cart in such a way he could hitch it to his horse with speed.

Despite these preparations, designed in part to give his family comfort, Jacob did not think he would fare well if any rash young village youth took it into their head to find some nearby scapegoat.

So when the local priest came to his door, he first wondered whether this was fortuitous or whether it might bring with it an attention he shied from.

The priest, having made a short journey of large faith, stood now without a word in his head to say to the Jew.

'You're welcome here, sir,' offered Jacob, bowing.

'Thank you, my son.' The priest's bewilderment lay upon him still.

'May I offer you wine, sir?'

'No, no. Thank you. I thought only to see if you are well.'

'We are quite well.' Jacob bowed a little again. 'You are very kind, sir.'

Both men paused, both staring and smiling at each other, one as puzzled as the other, and Father Taylor looking around also at the interior of the Jew's house, not so much different from any other – cleaner, in fact – with some items unusual to one of peasant stock: rugs, items hanging about the walls, and fine candlesticks.

'And your business, Master . . .. ah . . ..'

'Yazd, sir.'

'Of course. Master Yazd. Your business – it goes well?'

'As well as may be expected, my Lord.'

'Yes, indeed. These are difficult times. I do worry.'

'As do I, sir.'

The men paused again, looking at each other.

'Well, that's all. I'll be on my way,' the priest said.

Jacob bowed again.

Father Taylor turned to the door and was halfway out when he turned again. 'There is a „,' He struggled for the words, looking down at the smooth threshold. '...a ... a madness ... that infects people. You mustn't mind it.'

'I understand. Thank you, sir,' Jacob replied, thoughtfully.

The priest paused in the doorway. Unsure of what he was saying, he knew just the same that this man was an unfair target for others' fears. Even the Church had taken aim before now. Even *he* had, God forgive him.

He looked once more at the Jew, turned and left the small house. Pondering the exchange, Father Taylor went on to the next house, the memory of this visit remaining all the while in his mind.

Jacob Yazd told his family that day at lunch that they were blessed with the protection of the Church in this town.

A feeling of sudden momentousness made Alice look up from her sweeping and she saw Thomas's stones in a small half circle on the ground. Looking about her, she thought it odd that he would go away from her sight. She leant her broom to the wall, unperturbed and peered back inside their hut, although of course he could not have passed her through the only door. She walked to one side of the stone wall and back to the other, looking to find the boy. She turned to the wall at the front of the yard and went to the gate, open upon its old hinge, threatening perhaps one day to fall. She bent a little across the wall, turning her head this way and that, but Thomas was not anywhere there. Perhaps he had wandered to the fields where his father and brothers worked at a wall. Perhaps he had heard some shouting or other from there and wandered off. She felt sure this must be and thought she may as well go back to her broom. She would check again properly when she was done.

The news of the second dead swan had not reached Berta Draper, and so no more of her predictions had as yet come to hand, although folk knew it was only time.

Berta herself dozed off in her rocking chair, a light breeze brushing through the door before her, taking away some of the fuzziness the hot day put in her head. She wasn't quite asleep, but she wasn't awake either. She did notice, in her soporific state, that there was no noise about, not a thing at all, which seemed unusual but a special blessing on such a hot day and when one was as old and weary as she.

Berta dreamt of men on horseback, tall and triumphant. There were children running in streets in her dream, shouting and playing. A town was at joyful prayer. Golden dust swept around a battalion of warriors and their king rode at the head of this throng, proud and chivalrous. There were churches and steeples, a massive white-pillared colossus, and a pious people at work. Other kings appeared to pay homage to the divine. There were gardens planted and tended, and a gold-domed shrine atop a mountain.

Berta saw all of her dream; aware of the beauty of all she saw, and for a time revelled in it. When she woke, it had all gone, except she was left knowing the future held both strife and joy, and that all seemed about usual. She thought perhaps she'd withdraw herself from the pronouncement of foresights and attend less the glowers that accompanied them. It made no difference to anyone that she prophesied a thing. Furthermore, she suspected that the nomenclature of *witch*, which they all used, was not one that would always keep one's soul attached well to one's body in this world.

Aye.

And she got out of her rocking chair with a view to some busy-ness that would put her head nearer the ground where her feet now were.

It was a familiar voice she heard calling a little tentatively from her door, but one out of place, so she had to turn to see the priest's face there to put the sound with the vision.

'Ah, Mrs Draper,' Father Taylor greeted her, bowing just a little.

'Father, Sir,' Berta replied with an obvious confusion.

'Things are a little unsettled about and I thought I'd visit some of our townspeople; perhaps offer some calm.'

'Now there's a wise thing,' Berta responded approvingly.

'I know you have a heart for the people of this village, Mrs Draper, and I know you have a gift of sight also, but I'm wondering if... perhaps... it would not be a bad thing to...'

'...t'keep me mouth shut, Father. Aye.'

'Well, yes... It's just, you see...'

'Oh it's alright, Father. You'll not be causing any offence to likes of me. And it's as I can see things at times, that I knows now is not a good time for it. I shall be keeping m'self to m'self, Father, you'll be pleased. An' you're doing well to take yourself out and around to folks; it'll give 'em some faith, and they could do wit' some, for sure.'

'Thank you, Mrs Draper. I was hoping you'd understand. These recent events... there is a lot of suspicion, and I do fear it will bring itself to some unfortunate actions on the part of some. Perhaps. We shall see.'

'Aye, we will, Father, we will. An' you're stronger than you know, Father; I can see it in ya'. It's all very well we have those big men in the city Church, but it's local people that trusts local people, and you're one of us, and I thank ye for what ye do.'

'Well, Mrs Draper, I, ah...'

'Oh, you know me and the Church we don't always see things the same way, but it don't matter any when people are good to each other just the same. I got some healing ways that maybe one day you'll come for, who will know; but you can keep people from fear, and fear is the most dangerous cause of the most dangerous things, Father; so you keep on wit' yer visitin' and we'll all be better for that.'

Expecting as he had been some cross and possibly even unintelligible words from the old woman – indeed he'd hoped she may not even be in her house this day – Father Taylor was, for the second time today, both delighted and a little baffled by this meeting.

'Thank you again. I'm... you're very kind, Mrs Draper,' he said.

'We all have our place in this world, Father; I won't begrudge anyone his path. I know yours is not an easy one. People need ya, Father; you can be sure of that. They needs all the he'p they can get in their miserable, small little lives. Not so many can see a little further than theyselves; don't matter whether they be peasants or bishops – some see, most don't. I figure you 'n' me we both see a few things, Father, so's it's our job to he'p those that can't – give 'em a bit more 'surance that things are safe and no need to be goin' and gettin' in any bother.

'Yes, indeed. You're quite right. And I thank you again, ma'am, and I'll be on my way. I'm very pleased to have seen you. We understand one another more than I had realised.'

'You can depend on me, Father,' and I'll tell my son you called, and he'll be pleased to know we've the Church watching over us, and he'll be sure an' tell others he meets too.'

Father Taylor smiled more than he thought he could at this strange woman and backed out of her small house, tipping his hat as he did so. And when another few villagers in the lane saw him emerge, they wondered too that their priest would be paying a call to another house they wouldn't expect to see him in, and they were only a little suspicious until they heard that most every house in the town had seen the priest that day, and then they felt a little comfort.

Thomas walked with a kind of joy that had to do with being somewhere that he hadn't been before. The forest didn't seem strange to him though. He was quite comfortable in it and it was cool and it smelt nice. He actually wondered why he had not been in the forest before, and it was unusual for Thomas to wonder such things. And then he wondered about that. But that hurt his head too much so he looked sideways very sharply and the feeling went away. He kept walking straight though and lost his footing down a small ditch, which had once been full of water but now had just a muddy trickle at the bottom. Thomas wasn't hurt but he rolled in some mud; enough that he thought it was quite good fun so he rolled in some more until he was fairly well muddy all over. He sat in the small ditch for a while, looking up at the treetops and all around and out of the corner of his eye. After a while he remembered he needed to go somewhere and he got up and out of the ditch and carried on. Mostly the ground in the forest was hard and dry, and a little bit soft every now and then where there were a lot of leaves or some moss on it. Either way it wasn't hard for Thomas to walk on. Thomas didn't have a discernible direction, not one he could have said or even indicated, but there was one. Direction wasn't a linear kind of thing for him; nor was time, or even light though that was supposed to travel in straight lines. In Thomas' world, direction was something that could be touched, and light was something that could be heard, and time mostly went in circles, and it could go both ways around a circle too. So what the forest felt like to him, and why he was there, wasn't something that could be explained or understood easily, but Thomas himself was as certain of it as day and night.

He glanced sharply to the other side of him, seeing if the light was where he was used to seeing it. He wasn't surprised to see another person standing there to his side, but he was surprised at the sort of person it was, because he looked very like a tree. Thomas stood still and continued to look at the figure that looked like a tree out of the corner of his eyes. This was easier than looking at the figure straight on – when he looked at most things straight on he got so much information about the thing he was looking at that it would confuse him and he would have no idea what he was looking at at all. He wasn't sure if the figure was a part of his direction, and so he considered that a while, and when he realised that wasn't any part of the reason he was here, he looked to the front of him again and took a step forward.

When that step ripped every ounce of certainty from him, his first thought, in that very split second, was that this wasn't supposed to happen; that some error in the fabric of time itself had undermined the enormous steps he'd taken to get this far, and that more than one tragedy hung on this unexpected turn of events.

In the next split second, when Thomas felt the jaws of a great beast grab at his leg, he fought at the power of the thing with the totality of his soul. This encumbrance, this obstacle, deterred him from his expedition. Pain was not foreign to him but these fierce teeth wrestled with him like none other. It was only a silent scream that escaped him but its force transformed itself into sound and the noise of a hundred creatures running from their branches and to their burrows masked the size of it.

Thomas fell to the ground and when he looked to what it was that locked him so tightly he saw a pair of great metal teeth dug deeply and inescapably into him. Blood spewed about the thing, making it shiny and less ugly, mixing with the rusting metal to make a picture of reds and greys that sat uncomfortably within the surrounding greens and browns of the forest.

Thomas writhed and could not reach the metal trap. And then nothing of him could move at all, as if to stay still it might go away of its own accord. Fear grew out of the pain and screams rang inside his head as bolts of light shot around in his brain behind his eyes, threatening to blind him. He drew his sight to a focus, at a single leaf at the end of a twig above him. He wished for the leaf to help him, and he cried out a sound that didn't manage to escape from his wide open mouth.

Thomas forgot why he was in the forest. He forgot his pointed stones. He forgot the light.

Fear and disappointment enveloped his being, and as they crawled up his arms and legs, up through his body, taking over his head, Thomas's last sense of anything in the world was that he would fail at something, at which he was supposed to have succeeded, and he reached out, with only a pinprick of light, to some other soul, perhaps a boy like him, to make the journey to the light in his stead.

Hugh's carriage bumped him from a dream. He blinked and shook his head. He knew that Henry would not go to Jerusalem, although he would no doubt promise again to do so, leaving the Holy City at risk of Saladin's overrun. Perhaps the brave son, called Lionheart already, may honour his one father and His Other.

'Peter!' he called to the young priest asleep opposite him. 'Peter!'

Peter jerked awake, looking around.

'Peter. We must turn around and go back.'

'My Lord?'

'There's no point, dear boy. None. Just the idle fancy of an old man. I'm tired. Have the coachman turn around.' Hugh slumped his head back and sighed. He'd been foolish, thinking that some young boy with a light in his eyes would be a missing part to his puzzle – an answer from the heavens above, perhaps even an

Angel. Or was it the mother he'd thought had something of great value. He couldn't even remember now.

I should have seen earlier at least.

'Tell him to go back to Stowe,' Hugh added. 'I'd like to walk in my garden. I need to plan once last time a confrontation with our sorry king.'

Put not your trust in princes...[3]

Fulk didn't mind waiting again, his earlier frustrations at a lost meal forgotten now. It wasn't in him to bother with anger for too long, since it didn't feed him.

He was patient and still, sitting low in a tree, and dozing. He was pleased to hear some animal approach, although when he looked up he couldn't tell what it was at all. He would get a clear view when it came right in front of him.

Why the creature stopped right in front of him though puzzled him. He knew he couldn't possibly be seen and he hadn't made a noise. And what it was wasn't like any animal Fulk knew.

He stared at it, unmoving, and it stood there. It only needed to take one more step.

And then it did.

Fulk jumped down knowing to put the pained creature away from its anguish as quickly as possible and he took a rock from the ground and brought the thing down on its head. No animal should be made to suffer; Fulk knew this to be right. But the creature was strange to him and his cleverness told him it would not be wise to eat it if he had no clue what it was. He would not leave its carcass to be feasted on by another though, and he'd seen enough of the soldiers who kept coming into the forest and disturbing things, so thought to bury it in some way.

He pulled apart the metal trap from the creature's leg and dragged it by its good leg. It was very light and bony. After a few

---

[3] Psalm 146:3

paces the creature's strange skin peeled off its body and up over its head and then Fulk, paying closer attention, was afraid at what the thing now could be.

Fear for Fulk leapt quickly into action. His survival required it, and standing about weighing up some situation was not of much use to him even if it was something he was capable of.

He knew instantly what to do with it and turned back to dragging the carcass along as he had been.

When he came upon the well near the edge of the Thane's manor, he hoisted the thing over the crumbling wall and dropped it. He was surprised at a small and distant splash heard beneath.

Jacob Yazd's son felt that extending the boundaries imposed on him by his father's fears was not such a problem. Taking a yard stick from the back of his father's shop, intent on knocking cones from the trees in the woods, he set off along a worn trail, his leather shoes kicking stones along the way. At the edge of the woods, he saw a dense flight of birds suddenly rise from the treetops and couldn't imagine that his own arrival caused such reaction. He thought perhaps he heard a scream, but then guessed it to be a bird or animal from far away.

He took to knocking cones at the edge of the wood. He didn't like to go far into the trees; there were tales he'd heard of things even a grown man might not want to discover hidden in there. Once he had a goodly pile, he took off his tunic and tied knots in the neck and sleeves and used it for a sack to carry his cones. He didn't keep all of them; there were some not opened and no use for anything, and so he used them to practise his throwing, hefting them at other cones higher up in the trees.

When he'd had enough of that, he heaved his makeshift sack over his back and took the same path back again to the town. The cones were sharp on his bare back through the shirt's cloth, and he stopped often to change the way he carried it.

Nearly back to the village, he recognised two of the Thane's men coming on an intersecting path towards him, one of them with a sack of something across his shoulder. The boy worried at the menacing look in their eyes when they spotted him, but he felt unfortunately compelled to stand stock-still and watch as they passed by just ahead of him. He thought he saw two bony arms and hands hanging out of the sack down the man's back.

The priest, in his buggy, met the two men along his way and had the contents of the sack laid down on the ground before him. It had been a very strange day. Not anything like any other. So another curious sight, albeit grotesque, hardly seemed to dent the priest's composure. He wondered anew at his own balance of mind that he could feel very little when he looked upon the figure before him in the grass. Then he quickly realised that wondering at himself was not of any meaningful use, and immediately he had the Thane's men bundle the awful load into the rear of his carriage. His thoughts dictated he should take the body to the Cathedral; a thought he questioned since surely he should head to the child's parents, but aside from finding this a barely tolerable option, he felt pulled towards the great town and its centrepiece, and he hoped also its spiritual leader, the Bishop. He himself could barely make head or tail of events and was resisting any new panic for the future of the wavering peace about him.

Finding yet another unusual voice in his head that day, he bade the Thane's men return to their lord and not bother the town.

'And tell your Master he must send word to the boy's mother,' he instructed.

Then seeing the first hint of defiance, he added, 'And be quick about it!' surprising even himself with his new-found authority.

He didn't begin to consider the nature of the child's demise, except that he knew others would invent every absurd possibility their imaginations and suspicions could invent, and he determined he would present some new firmness over those who would invent such nonsense, and those others who would take power from their weakness.

The men scurried away exchanging a range of looks that summed things up for them, including some new regard for the hitherto awkward cleric. The priest had a new layer of strength about him.

The priest thought better of wasting time indulging in any sense of accomplishment. He eyed the wrapped bundle behind his seat and gee'd his horse forward, with more than a little anger in his soul, and a path before him that he felt God alone had lit. His was to follow.

It was a few days later when Geoffrey and Denholm Warriner were called to a stop in their stonework, and followed the other men to the ground and through what had been the Nave of the cathedral. The purpose was not so clear, but theirs was not to question: it was something or other and they were to be there. As they followed behind others, they heard whisperings that some poor innocent was to be entombed in a new piece of wall, as some acknowledgement to the power of the Church and its mercy. Some other man spoke of what he'd heard, that it was some heathen act of the Jews. And yet, some other talked knowingly of Jewish legend and devil sacrifices and candles and had others about him intrigued and turning with the same knowing to their neighbour. An older man, standing near to the boys, was heard to say to himself – or whoever wished to hear it – that most of these pronouncements were rubbish and most likely another had lost his life to the Church's walls and scaffolds.

'Let's move t'front t'see wha's hapnin', Gree,' urged Dem and pushed his way anyway, and without much thought, forward through workmen lingering by..

Dem followed his brother, apologising to a few he thought had been shoved too much by his sibling.

'Dem!' Gree whispered loud. 'Take more care!' And he grasped his brother's shoulder firmly and halted him.

Dem reached nearly to the front though, where he saw a great man in purple dress, and priests about him.

'It's Bishop, Dem!' Gree whispered again. 'Lower your head!' To which Dem did as his brother bid, peering up through the hair hanging over his eyes.

The purple man looked momentarily at him and then to Gree over his shoulder, and for a second only both thought they were to be called out of the throng for some crime, such was the look of knowing from the Bishop..

'There's our Father there,' Dem spoke quietly back over his shoulder to his brother, indicating Father Taylor.

'Aye. Wonder what he's about here.'

They watched as the priest looked briefly at them also and then whispered something in the Bishop's ear, provoking a long stare from the taller man towards the priest and then around and about the workers standing there.

Meanwhile, another white-clothed cleric stepped forward and a reading began. And so followed a service, none of which many, or any, understood, for it was spoken in Latin, but most knew their own parts by heart and where to say them and when to kneel and when to cross themselves.

Then to everyone present it was apparent the Bishop would speak, either from the deep breath he took and exhaled slowly, or knowing that it was just that at this moment it was he who was suddenly at the centre of the great Nave's orbit. A silence stretched up from the stone floor and harnessed itself about every man's shoulders. It was a cold draught of death, and each present stooped a little and bowed his head and more than a few felt a shiver from it.

The Nave was open in parts to the sky, although the Bishop stood in a small shaded part, all the better the boys thought since he seemed to wear many layers of clothes.

'Let us pray ...,' he said in a quiet voice that carried to the back row.

No one among the working men seemed to know who was the dead, and the brothers could not see a body or its coffin from where they stood.

Dem said to Gree, 'Ought be our brother as gets put in the wall here, seen as 'e's given his life to the buildin' of 'em.'

And while he might have thought something similar to himself, mostly it pleased Gree that nobody appeared to have heard his brother's opinion.

When the thing they'd been called to was done, the workmen turned away to their work and soon after that the thing itself was forgotten, excepting that they tended to take a little more care each day where they trod and how they balanced.

Alice and Gamel Warriner, who stood to the side away from where their elder sons may have seen them, were each committed in their own way not to look about for Denholm or Geoffrey among the many workers who descended upon their unusual scene. Nor had either wondered particularly why another son was now to be buried in the Cathedral, except that it was the express wish of the Bishop himself who had some special care for the boy. Gamel thought better of even contemplating that. Alice understood that another besides herself had seen the glow of Thomas and the tragedy of that light having gone out. She would not really remember being in the Cathedral that day, but she would always remember the Bishop's face alongside that of her Thomas.

When Father Taylor's message reached Hugh en route to his country house, again he turned on the road, to head this time for the Cathedral and its town. He'd met there with a rather new Father Taylor who had taken charge in his absence and remarked to his Lord Bishop that he'd felt it best to quell opinion, to which the Bishop could only have agreed.

Hugh had found the man a new comfort to him, and together they had planned a Christian burial within the new Church walls, hoping to use the opportunity also to herald a new day of tolerance, and fear only of God. But in the days leading to the funeral, and beyond, the bravery they brought to their mutual defence and protection of the Jews of Lincoln seemed in vain. With this limited success, Hugh determined to further scold the King for the absence of his royal protection for a faithful community of subjects, and for refusing any punishment to wayward princes and lords who took the law and the King's name in their own hands, as seemed to be their wont..

Ultimately, though, he was perturbed that he could not balance in his mind the sure loss of Jerusalem he had seen in his dream, with the vicious backlash that eventually saw the hangings of nineteen Jews, with the loss of the boy, and then after a while longer with what he assumed as his own swan gone. Each was a tragedy for his soul: one the weight of responsibility to the world for a failure in Christendom, one his inability to curb a prejudice that he could see clearly threatening the truth and beauty he strived to keep alive albeit flimsily among the Christian faithful; the other his own sadness to lose his winged helpmeet who would no longer come to his side, alongside the violence and distortion and prejudice accompanying the passing of one of the most innocent of all, the young boy Thomas Warriner. Which of these was to be mourned the most? It was a tragic irony that his efforts to protect the Jews, through the plans he agreed with Father Taylor for the boy's interment, became instead an opportunity to blame the Jews for the tragedy of the boy's death. So many absurd stories surrounded the child in time that he could scarcely believe the shallow hearts and minds of his fellow Christians.

He ached to the core of his soul and his mind, and neither of these gave him any solution or any respite as they circled painfully about each other, dark and unrelenting..

It would be many weeks before he would let go these sorry occurrences from his mind and collect his strength and character to a resolution that would again support a true Christian community, with the knowledge forever that he had either misread or seen too late some indications with which he might have acted sooner.

After his impromptu dash to Lincoln, where he had sent urgent word to the Bishop and then simply waited for his arrival, Father Taylor realised he must next return to the boy's parents, who would not have been informed well by the Thane or his men. And he would visit again with the townsfolk and ensure their well-being.

The priest knew something had happened that changed his view of the world, and he was glad of God's mercy to him. His load was now a different one, to bring a balm to the suffering, and he determined he would seek the counsel of the Bishop more often.

The storm that broke though nearly consumed Father Taylor, and it required every speck of his new-found finesse to handling every intricate stage of what then unfolded. There was no telling what had brought the death of the boy really, and the priest had as much faith in the testimony of a Thane's man as any other thug. But in the end, there was no escaping the baying for blood, and the village and the town had sought their prey in the Jews. Out of nowhere the King, and then the Duke of Cornwall, joined the fray ostensibly to bring a swift and strong justice, but even Father Taylor knew this noble virtue eluded them as much as they cared not a jot for the boy, preferring any reason to support the further frailty of the Jews. In all, ninety-odd Jews were arrested from around about and held in the Tower of London no less. A clemency was sought by Hugh, and the priest knew that when only nineteen were hung that this had more to do with the power of the Bishop than any mercy on the part of the King.

As for the boy, the villagers' suspicions at this own idiot child's ways were quickly renounced in favour of martyrdom which had not been the Bishop's and priest's intentions either.

In time the hubbub waned, as much as did the priest's ambition. He would soon find entry into the hearts of these ignorants, offering a new wisdom, hard-won and inspiring.

Gamel Warriner had a great relief at the demise of his youngest son, at least following the business of his interment at the Cathedral, a somewhat overwhelming event for a peasant. He had fewer mouths to feed and no longer felt the weight of the view the world had of his awkward family. He sensed no loss in his wife, even though he knew he wasn't always able to see these things anyway. Of course, he knew that the passing of two young boys was a loss to the world and provided a reason for people about to make note of their going, but it didn't seep a lot further into him than that.

He expected his three sons to work their share and make their mother's life not too hard. He cared enough that there was some kind of respect paid her, and he knew that was odd enough among men too, but it was his way.

Alice sat with her hands inside a ferret's guts, the slurp and suck of it engaging her skilled fingers, and her cold-numbed feet absently brushed aside a collection of pebbles askew in the wet mud beneath her. She looked alike to any other peasant at work in the small circle of her dimmed livelihood. A man and three tattered boys squabbled behind the wall where she sat, and a yelp escaped through the open door so that she knew one had been kicked or lobbed at by another for some doing, who knows if in silliness or wrath.

The skies were darkening and heavy with rain and the potential for thunderclaps. The respite of coolness was not relished for long, as the ground turned dark with the onset of so much wet. There was never a good weather one way or the other, and now the cold demanded more food for all men and beasts.

Alice cared less for it all and kept her prayers briefer, and her soul was not so hungry. The darkness did not encase her though; she just was.

18

Ismat ad-Dīn Khātūn, known as Asimat, was a wife of kings. Her first husband, Nur ad-Din, had been king of all Syria, uniting its many domains into one great sultanate. He had died from a poisoning as he plotted the defeat of his own protégé, Saladin. Saladin was Ismat's second husband, and he had taken her as his wife after defeating Nur ad-Din's thirteen-year-old son and successor and uniting Egypt and Syria.

Asimat was not Saladin's only wife, and she would not bear him any children now, as indeed she had not for Nur ad-Din, despite the twenty-seven years she had been married to him. She was though Saladin's favourite. She was two years older than him, and at forty-nine she was no longer young, but she knew how to please him, and she could speak with him about his battle strategies as none of his generals could, and certainly none of his other wives. Asimat had travelled with her first husband through the second Crusade, and she had proved a valuable confidante to Saladin throughout his many military successes.

The night before, Saladin had talked again of his most fervent wish to free Jerusalem from its Christian King and to create a universal city of peace for Jews, Christians and Muslims. The Jerusalem kings had been many, with much infighting and intrigue, and had little concern for their station as rulers. The old King Baldwin had recently died, a crippled old leper, although a worthy opponent despite that on many occasions. But he'd left a five-year-old in charge of his kingdom with various notables squabbling for the regency.

Saladin and Asimat had talked about whether the city could be ruled by all three religions, segmented into thirds. A challenge though was the proximity of some of the different Faiths' holy sites to each other, so it would not be an easy truce. Saladin was determined though, as he talked of the beauty of Abraham's children, Christ's followers, and the Prophet, and his hopes that they could live together in peace.

Asimat believed Saladin to be the greatest of leaders, with a powerful vision for the world. The nine years she had been with him were the happiest of her life, and her fervent desire was to see his wish of a unified Holy City come true. But more and more now she was afraid she would not; the pain she felt in her abdomen was so great some days that she could hardly walk or even breathe. She had kept her illness hidden from her husband so as not to distract him from his mission, and she would send a messenger to him to encourage him to take another wife on the days and evenings that she was ill. She hated to do so, but he took this action on her part as a sign of her generous spirit, and it only served to make him think more highly of her. When Saladin came to her, she would use every ounce of her loving encouragement to support his plans, persuading him to discuss in ever closer detail how he would take the City. She had heard that the English–French king, Henry, was not enamoured of his duty to fortify the Crusaders' strength in the Holy Land, which could only serve Saladin's interests further; but that Henry's son, who they called the Lionhearted, was a worthy and, some said, greater opponent than his father.

Thoughts and plans of battle excited Saladin, and in turn Asimat, and their lovemaking was as explosive as their talk once they had finished picturing each victory in stupendous detail. Asimat knew Saladin's younger wives had firmer bodies than hers, and breasts that were full and pointed skyward, and that by comparison her own body had long since begun to soften and sag. But she knew also that it was she Saladin most wanted. Sometimes when he had had too much wine, he would indiscreetly tell her how they did not compare to her and that his liaisons with them had few of the pleasures Asimat herself offered. This pleased her and made it easier for her to tolerate their presence. She was pleased that most of them feared her.

It was Saladin's regard for Asimat that had led him to appoint her as patron of a new university and of many other religious and civil buildings in Damascus. Asimat knew she represented her husband with great honour and pride in such matters, and she would affect her most upright and noble bearing whenever she was in public on some engagement or other. She would give speeches in his honour, and for Syria, and she had come to be known as a woman of wisdom and courage.

And now this morning she had kissed Saladin as he left her bed and went to meet with his generals to lay out the plans they had conceived that night. He was energised and vital after a sound sleep and his lengthy morning prayers. Asimat prayed for him. She would accompany him into battle for yet another day.

'I'm not well, Nigel,' the prince moaned to his page behind his inner tent curtain. 'This damned heat ...'

'There is a man arrived from Saladin, Highness,' the servant replied in Richard's native French. 'The English translator says he claims he is Saladin's physician and he is sent to offer his assistance to you. But the English has said not to trust him, Sire.'

'It's that damned English I wouldn't trust as far as I could kick!' Although his father was the King of England, Richard had virtually never set foot in the Kingdom and spoke no English. 'Send this gift from my noble Saladin to me. Bring the bloody English to translate, but he's *only* to translate. He can keep his opinions to himself!'

'As you wish, Sire.'

'Yes, I damned well wish, sycophants and arse-lickers all of you. Christ,' Richard muttered to himself as Nigel backed out of the tent.

Richard, known as the Lionhearted, had taken up the Church's call where his father Henry would not. Richard loved to fight; he lived for it. And he'd had no nobler opponent than

Saladin. He'd heard much of the Sultan's prowess before reaching the Eastern Mediterranean and he had determined not to underestimate him, but he had to admit now that even despite this he had not reckoned on such a masterful general as Saladin. It would take all his resources and intellect to devise a plan that would succeed in defending the Holy City.

When they had battled, he had seen Saladin at a great distance, and he focused all his thoughts on the man's mind, attempting to know the secrets of his soul, just as he knew – indeed, he felt – Saladin was also doing. By God, he was brilliant. Not for the first time, he wished he could send all the generals and soldiers away and meet Saladin alone in the desert for an hour. He thought they would have a fine time. What a brilliant ally the man would make!

'Sire, here is the man.' Nigel returned with an older, bearded and turbaned man who bowed low to the prince lying on his sickbed before him.

'Let him in. Let him close here,' Richard beckoned to the Arab to come closer.

'His robes were checked for hidden weapons, Sire.'

'Oh, rubbish, Nigel. Get out. Saladin would not do such a thing. It would not be any kind of victory for him. Get out! You! Englander! Stay here in case we need your translation, but stay over there where I don't have to smell you.'

Richard fell back on to his bed, coughing, exhausted from his outburst. Saladin's physician stood by patiently until his fit had ended and then knelt before him.

'Your master is most kind,' Richard said wearily.

The Englishman translated quietly, and the physician smiled and nodded to his patient, replying with the strange guttural sounds Richard had come to recognise but knew none of.

'He says his master is a great man, and it is his pleasure to now serve two great kings in his life,' said the translator.

'Ha, another arse-licker. Don't translate that!'

The Arab put his ear down to Richard's chest and then rose and tapped on the back of his hand which sat spider-like upon his chest.

'What the devil ... ?' Richard rolled his eyes.

The Arab spoke again.

'He says the drumming on your chest makes different sounds where there is congestion, and so he can hear how severe your illness is.'

'Is that so?'

The Arab continued to speak.

'He says you'll live.'

Richard laughed out loud, and so brought on another coughing fit, which once contained gave him enough pause to laugh again and bring on yet another fit.

'Dammit,' he said, flopping on to his back again, smiling.

He looked up at the physician, who continued to kneel looking at the prince and smiling also.

'Hmm, not such an arse-licker then, eh? Ha ha. And what do you prescribe then?'

Richard looked into the man's eyes as he spoke, seeing a pride that was strange to the king in one who was a servant.

'Rest. A lot of water. Fruit, fresh or dried. Nuts. No wine and no bread. You will be better in three days,' came back the translation.

The Arab stood, bowed, and then stayed before the prince.

'Thank you,' said Richard, unused to thanking servants.

'Thank you,' said the physician in perfect English, with a nod of his head. 'My master sends his very best wishes for your recovery, Your Highness.'

'By God, you prickly old bastard!' Richard grinned. 'You've understood every word.'

'I apologise if I have offended you, my lord.'

'Not at all. Tell your master he has my greatest regards and my undying respect.'

'I will, Highness.' The Arab bowed again and reversed to the tent opening, whereupon he turned and walked away.

The translator stood open-mouthed at the departed physician.

'You see, you are a useless cunt after all. Get out!' Richard yelled.

'Tell me again, my love.'

Asimat sat at the edge of her sleeping mat. She was in pain but had not been able to refuse her husband's enthusiasm as he burst into her tent to regale her with the story of his own physician's visit to Prince Richard.

Saladin sat cross-legged and turbaned, dressed all in white with a short sword at his side and light sandals on his feet.

'Imad is a Sufi also, and most adept, very wise. I'm sure it's what makes him such an excellent physician. He can read his patients. He sees exactly what ails them.' Saladin stroked his chin, visualising the meeting with his great foe, and nodded.

'He said Richard has the finest humour and suffers no fool.' He looked up at his wife. 'But I would have imagined that to be so, wouldn't you, my love?'

'Of course.' Asimat felt she may not be able to hide her suffering much longer.

'He sent me his regards and his respect.' Saladin feigned a boastfulness and smiled.

Asimat made herself smile back at her husband.

'I will beat him though. He has one great weakness. He fights first and wishes for the esteem of his Faith second. Make no mistake he is the finest I've seen in battle, but it is to win that he fights, and for himself and for his England, and a little less for God.'

'And so to Tiberius then.'

'Yes, yes. Guy and Raymond can't decide how to fight me. They argue among themselves as to who is Lord and King. It will be their undoing, despite the Lionheart, and then we shall have our victory. I hear their whole army will be lined up for us, so it will be all the more pleasurable.'

'You must go and prepare then. There is much to do.'

'Yes, of course. I wanted to tell you of Imad's meeting with Richard. And his good humour. It will be a shame to defeat him. But I will not kill him. I refuse to, even should the opportunity come. I would let him escape, for assuredly I will then have the chance to face him again one day. He will want to return, I've no doubt.'

Saladin rose, kissed his wife, and departed.

Asimat fell back on her mat in a faint.

Eleanor of Aquitaine was a wife of kings. She had married her first husband, Louis VII of France, when she was fifteen. Louis was pious but weak, and at age thirty, Eleanor divorced him. Very soon after she married nineteen-year-old Henry, Duke of the Normans, who two years later became Henry II, King of England. Eleanor had borne six sons and five daughters; the two eldest daughters to Louis, the rest to Henry. Two sons died in infancy, and tragically the younger Henry had also died a few years since. Of the others her favourite was Richard, now nearly thirty and Henry's heir after the death of his elder brother. They called her son *Coeur de Lion*, the Lionhearted.

Eleanor had travelled to the Holy Land with her first husband, Louis, during the Second Crusade, and now her beloved Richard dwelt there in the desert with his opponent, the Muslim king, Saladin, not far away.

Eleanor adored Henry, her second husband. He was the great-grandson of William the Conqueror, fiercely intelligent, a brilliant leader, an unwearying sportsman and athlete, and the most generous of philanthropists. He was a match for Eleanor in every way, including, sadly, in temper. Once, their fighting had been a precursor to their ferocious passion; but this turbulence eventually established itself as such an enmity that, after more than twenty years of marriage, in return for supporting her sons' rebellion against their father, Henry had taken Eleanor to England and imprisoned her for ten years. She had been somewhat freed in recent years, more so as Henry could ensure Eleanor's wealth and lands were not denied her by some usurper or other. She travelled with him again now, overseeing his English estates and other affairs, although Henry ensured some protector, as he liked to call it, was always at her side. Henry had pressured Eleanor to annul their marriage for a time in part, as he hoped to marry his mistress, but more to secure Eleanor's lands. The mistress died, some say poisoned at Eleanor's hands, although such was court gossip, and Eleanor had never relented in her marriage to Henry. Now past sixty, she could still tempt her husband, and did so on occasion.

Through their many inheritances, intrigues and power, Eleanor and Henry had controlled or influenced much of the Western world, and while it remained the power and intrigue that inspired them still, both were still able to be persuaded by an appeal to righteousness and what was holy.

Such was Eleanor's consideration now for the most unusual of letters she had received. She knew of her correspondent of course, as she realised she herself was known. It would have been impossible for two queens in the extraordinary context of the Kingdom of Jerusalem and the crusades not to have known of each other, particularly these two who had vicariously entered battle against each other with their four kings. But they had never met.

Ma Chere Soeur the letter had begun, in a perfect script. Had she narrated this to someone with the capability of both languages? It was difficult to believe otherwise, although she had heard of the woman's learning and reputation.

Only now, as I face my last days, do I see the futility of what has engaged us all for so many years. It is the pursuit of power and territory, ostensibly for peace, that alone undermines the reality of any such outcome. Oddly, it is my second husband who has been both the greater in battle, and yet the greater also in his vision of a kingdom where all live according to their duty to Allah, to God; to, I believe, the One God who is both yours and mine.

My husband seeks this day to secure the Holy City of Jerusalem for all people, Muslim, Christian, and Jew, and I believe he will achieve this. I beg of you, Great Lady, as the temples and tombs of both our Prophets are put within reach of all, that you will incline your heart to this vision of unity and seek among the Kings of Europe no further overlordship of the Arab people and their world.

For nigh a hundred years of war, it is time surely for peace.
May Allah bless you all your days, beloved Queen.
Your Sister,
Asimat

The letter arrived with the news of the death of its author, and the fall of the Kingdom of Jerusalem to Saladin. Eleanor was surprised that it was the former who consumed her heart and mind the more.

In her life, battle was battle, very occasionally for its own sake, often by way of projecting one's lordship, but mostly in either the defense of one's land or the pursuit of another's. One's right of rule was mostly determined by one's birth and inheritance, but simultaneously by might. Little, if anything, affected any obligation *not* to rule, excepting as it may be in one's strategic interests. The idea that one might consider any values or faith of the ordinary people under one's rule was not only absurd, it was virtually without meaning. And yet Eleanor *did* consider it. Peace was, without doubt, of value; certainly the cost of war had depleted more than one king's reserves before now. And the deaths of too many left the countryside without sufficient labour, which only depleted resources further and could give way to unnecessary civil unrest.

Eleanor grieved the loss of an extraordinary counterpart, this sister queen, and felt it appropriate to her memory that she, her only equal, give a respectful regard to the views she had written from her deathbed. She determined she would discuss them further with her son when he returned from his defeat, since he would surely want to reclaim what was now lost.

19

We have inscribed a new memory ...
a memory of love that lays down its life for a friend,
even a friend whose name it never knew.
President George W. Bush, 11 December 2001

Tim knelt in front of Little St Hugh's shrine, his head resting atop it, staring along the horizontal line of the small black box. It felt soft and warm despite its stoniness. The stone was smooth and glowed a little from its hundreds of years of wear.

Behind him, his parents, hand in hand, looked at the mason's practise wall. Alicia touched a fleur-de-lis square with her other hand.

'Some are more worn than others, aren't they? See this one's quite defined, quite sharp. Do you think it's newer maybe?'

'I think it's different stone. I guess some wear better than others. Or maybe it's different styles, different tools they used.'

'I can see now why you like being here. It is amazing.' Alicia smiled at Pete.

'And now you want to leave it all behind.'

'Was that a question?'

'Not sure. It's quite a change of plans – a *major* change.'

A woman's voice was heard via a sound system in the background. *A warm welcome to our visitors to the Cathedral today* ...

'It's just an idea. But it's one that's seriously stuck in my head right now.'

'Explain it to me again.'

'I'm not sure I can. I just need to change. I want *us* to change, our life to change. It's not working for me here. And you know there's no challenge for me professionally.'

... we ask for God's blessings today for those who are sick, for those who may be alone ...

'Don't get me wrong. I'm not against it. In fact I really like the idea. I just think we need to be clear why.'

'It's a feeling, a strong feeling.'

'I'm good with that.'

... and if you would like to speak with someone today, then please feel free to approach me ...

They turned back to see their son still snuggled into the black stone box against the other wall.

'C'mon, Timmy.'

Let us pray, as our Lord has taught us ...

From a long time away, Tim heard metal on metal, and a light dimmed, but not in vain.

... thy kingdom come, they will be done ...

The couple and their child crossed the Transept to the Nave and paused.

Lead us not into temptation but deliver us from evil. For thine is the Kingdom, the Power and the Glory, for ever and ever, Amen.

The woman at the large pulpit turned and stepped carefully down the spiralling staircase to the floor, holding the wooden rail with one head and lifting her white cassock with the other, enough not to trip on its length. Looking up and around her she saw the couple, smiled and waved.

'Is that one of them?' Alicia asked.

'That's Loraine. Let me introduce you.'

The red-headed chaplain walked over. 'Pete. Hello! How lovely!'

'Loraine.' Pete hugged the chaplain briefly and gave her a kiss on the cheek. 'This is my wife, Alicia.'

Alicia stepped forward, arm extended. 'It's so nice to meet you, Loraine. I've heard a lot about you.'

'And I you, my dear. I've been looking forward to meeting you,' Loraine beamed. 'And this must be wee Tim,' she added looking down at the blond boy clinging lightly to his mother's leg. 'I can see you are just as lovely as your father's described.'

Alicia and Pete smiled at each other.

'Well, you two look gorgeous, I must say, quite the perfect eighties couple.'

Alicia smiled with surprise and felt slightly embarrassed.

'Best you both be up to the cottage this week, I think. If I tell Rose I've met you, Alicia, and you're not there, she'll blame me. Tell me I'm a bolshie cow and must've scared you off.' Loraine laughed. 'Well, that's bolshie in itself, isn't it?' She laughed some more.

Pete and Alicia joined in. Tim put his head back and looked up to the ceiling high above, smiling broadly, on the verge of laughter.

'I guess I'd better then,' replied Alicia, warming to Pete's friend. 'Should we be laughing in the Church, though?' She lowered her voice to a mock whisper.

'God loves laughter, my dear. That's what I always say.'

'Oh,' replied Alicia delightedly. 'Well then ...' She was aware of her own sense of warmth and goodwill to this woman and wondered how relaxed and skilled Loraine must be, to be able to put people at ease so rapidly.

'Pete mentioned you may join the priesthood soon.'

'Oh my, I think that's a way off yet. I think there's to be some more talk yet, but it's possible, it's possible.'

'It would be a shame not to exercise the option to crash through another glass ceiling, don't you think?' Alicia asked.

'I hadn't thought of it in that way, actually.' Loraine considered Alicia's remark.

'Oh, well, I'm sure there are many good reasons other than that one, but I do think when an opportunity comes along to advance society along some critical trajectory like the equality of men and women, then we should grab it with both hands,' said Alicia, enthusiastically.

'Oh my goodness, how right you are! We've tended to think this is about *us,* which for two people who do rather like to rock the boat just a little, is odd really. Thank you for that, Alicia. You've made me consider this from another perspective, one I ought to have given much more thought to.'

'You're quite welcome. And it *is* very nice to meet you, Loraine. And I *will* come along with Pete.'

'Wonderful! I must away. See you soon.' Loraine gave the couple a broad smile and headed towards the western front of the Cathedral.

'My goodness, so *that's* one of your new girlfriends then! How delicious!' Alicia teased her husband.

Pete smiled, enjoying once more what he'd come to expect from Loraine and Rose and their unique approach to people.

Sitting at lunch at the Wig & Mitre pub, Tim sat quietly, observing people about him, much to his parents' great pleasure.

'I've been so angry, Pete.'

Pete sat quietly, looking at Alicia. He put his hand on hers, resting on the table in front of them.

'I know.'

'Do you?'

'Yeah.'

'I don't even know what I'm angry *at.* You, work, myself, the children, everything.'

'It's okay, hun.'

'It's not.'

'It is.'

Their lunch arrived, and all three quietly ate. Tim lifted fries from a bowl and put a few down on the table in front of him, blowing on them gently. When they had cooled, he munched on them calmly and then put a few more chips in front of him, repeating the process.

'We'll get through this,' Pete affirmed.

'You're a good man, Pete.' Alicia looked him in the eye.

Pete smiled.

'Tim's doing well, isn't he?' Alicia asked.

'Yep. He's been smashing.'

'Thank you.' Alicia continued to look at Pete, who placed his hand on hers again. 'Thank you, thank you, thank you.'

Pete smiled a bigger smile. 'Any time, babe.'

'I've been a bitch, haven't I?'

'Yep.'

'Quick answer.'

'Ha ha.'

'I'm sorry. I know I've been a cow.'

'No need to apologise.'

'Yes, there is. I owe you more than that.'

'You owe Tim and Jillie more than that.'

'Ouch.'

Pete said nothing.

'Okay, you're right. Being angry isn't useful. I know that. I've just not had anywhere for it to go.'

'You can't quarrel with a rose tree just 'cos it can't sing.'

'Eh?'

'I dunno. Sounds good though, eh?'

'Yeah, I guess. Are you on something?' Alicia laughed, more so as not to cry.

'I'm on whatever works.'

'Then that sounds ... workable.'

Pete picked up Alicia's hand and kissed it.

'Wow, didn't know you had that in you still.'

'Me neither actually – just seemed the thing to do.'

They held hands and looked at each other.

'I can't guarantee I'm going to stop being a bitch any time soon.'

'Whatever. Shut up and eat.'

'Shut up yourself.'

Tim picked up a chip, blew on it and put it on his mother's plate, and then repeated the act for his father.

'Chip,' he said, looking at them in turn. 'Yum.'

Alicia's affair with Gerry Bernstein was short-lived. She knew before it even began that she only needed some respite from her duelling with Pete, as well as from her own self-doubt. It was all mixed together in her head and just needed a brief explosion, to let the pressure off, to go back to normal. She allowed herself a few brief fantasies about some life of endless sunsets and margaritas – all sex and no responsibility. It was all part of what she indulged herself with, but she knew that all of it would end and she would find some new momentum for the full life she had truly chosen, the one she'd chosen with her soul and not the one she imagined with a burnt-out heart and a twitch in her arse..

She knew before she began that it was a meaningless exertion for the sake of a personal rebellion, to say to herself that she had some freedom, that she was not trapped within the confines of musty colleagues, a science that showed little usefulness, a husband and children who needed her but with whom she could not, presently, feel a sense of herself..

It ended politely. A strange way to end an affair, but it was significantly courteous. University life proceeded as before, and no one was any the wiser; Alicia and Gerry were barely any the wiser, at least not yet. Alicia had decided not to do much thinking about it. She found some germ of understanding and commitment somewhere in her that she brought into her home and nurtured and was surprised to see how it became a steady force in her. She guarded it carefully, as possibly the only thing that could hold her to her own values, which although abused by her own actions, could remain clearly articulated still on her tongue and a newly resurrected heart. She created her life herself.

'The psychologist discussed the results from Tim's tests today, y'know, this research project he was enrolled in.'

'Vaguely. What was it again?'

'Partly to do with differentiating the nature of different kids' talents.'

'Tim's got talent?'

'Seems so.'

Pete and Alicia sat beside each other on their porch, each with newspaper and coffee in hand.

'So?'

'He appears to have mathematical ability.'

Alicia dropped her paper into her lap and looked sideways at Pete.

'Truly. Apparently, he connects numerical concepts in a way that kids his age can't, at least normally.'

'So what does that mean?'

'Possibly that he has a capability for savantism.'

'You're kidding.'

'Nope.'

'So ... what then? Is there some way of developing this?'

'His therapy should focus more on numerical exercises, and language. They've done some experiments getting autistic kids to use a keyboard to write about themselves. There are some kids who have managed to communicate in this way. Although they're kids older than Timmy, but the team wants to give all this stuff a go with him.'

'Right. Well, I guess that's good.'

'Yeah. And I'm going to pray for him too. I think that's one of the best things we could do.' Pete raised his paper and scanned the page in front of him.

'Right.' Alicia looked sideways at Pete again, and then she too raised her paper.

A moment later, she put it down again.

'You're serious.'

'Yep.'

'Right.'

They went back to sipping their coffee and reading.

'See those two over there with the chessboard? Don't you think they look like they've got an interesting story? I've seen them in before.' Rose sat at a table outside the *Magna Carta* with Maitland, with her second large coffee.

Maitland nursed a pot of tea. 'I'm far more interesting. Listen to this.'

Rose grinned. 'Yeeeuus ... ?'

Maitland glared at her momentarily over his glasses and returned to the papers in front of him. 'I've been in the archives, and I've found this. It's a letter from Hugh to the King ...'

'*Saint* Hugh? To Henry?'

'Yes, my dear. Now listen.'

'I'm all ears.'

'"*What hath befallen our Church art of graveth fear to Us.*" This was apparently after he'd got wind of Jews being hung after the incident surrounding *Little* St Hugh.'

'He wasn't Little St Hugh then. That happened later.'

'Yes, I know. But it was never the Jews that did it.'

'No, everyone knows that now.'

'Well, I think that's deserving of some recognition.'

'Like what?'

'An interfaith project between the Cathedral and the Jewish community of Lincoln, recognising the prejudice that occurred and the actions taken against the Jews at the time.'

'You're quite brilliant, Maitland, y'know that?'

'Of course, I am dear.'

'I still reckon those codgers over there are more interesting than you though.' Rose sipped her coffee and grinned smugly over her cup.

'We'll ask them then, shall we? See what they know about Bishops and Kings. Not a lot I expect.'

'Betcha ...'

'I'm not a betting man.'

'Yeah, you are. Pint a' Guinness?'

'You're on.'

Pete finished restoring his mustang. He had a brief moment of anxiety during the spray painting when he found Tim with both hands well into a pot of paint, large dollops of it through his hair, and clearly in his mouth; how much he'd ingested was anyone's guess. Pete had come to his rescue at the point where the taste of the paint had gone beyond the curious and obviously was attaining some level of dissatisfaction that provoked a loud bellowing from the small boy. He had all but thrown him in the back seat of their station wagon and sped into the hospital in Lincoln; despite Tim's obvious discomfort at the taste of the paint, Pete didn't think he was going to be in any particular danger. They got to the Emergency Room in time for Tim to volunteer a racing green, projectile vomit. He didn't like to vomit, and the experience brought on another hour of bellowing; Pete having to reassure the nurses that this was not a response to pain or illness but just that he was disturbed by the loss of control over his body.

It was a horrendous clean-up job, and Tim had shades of racing green in his hair for weeks after, not to mention that they were all over the interior of the car as well. His teeth and mouth were green for three or four days, and Pete thought better of taking him out anywhere.

I mean, let's face it, he's bloody odd our Tim; don't need any more bloody stares than we already get, eh?

For his maiden run in the mustang, Pete waited till Jillie was at school and he strapped Tim's car seat into the front passenger seat, plopped the roof back, and the two of them spun out of the driveway into the verdant Lincolnshire countryside: Tim laughing away and Pete praying for a cop-free blast.

20

The two monks stood side by side within the southern choir aisle of the Cathedral. The older dropped to his knees before the throne-like structure that had been erected over the small tomb.

It was hardly a whisper we blew his way, and it so swelled my heart that day he understood.

The younger monk stood still and wept.

We could not have foreseen ...
How is it that he failed, the older one?
Did he? I hoped perhaps the presence of the Bishop would come earlier into his life. This might have seemed to have created some order to his purpose, should that have occurred.
How would this have helped him, when his mother was so strong? Surely she had this influence.
Yes, but she was lost in her time and her context and could not rise above that.
But the Bishop ...
He was a powerful figure and knew his responsibility to us. Certainly the boy heard the call, but circumstances were against him. His task was far more difficult.
But the world was dire for the younger boy and far more complex. We cannot deny the challenge set him, in that time. And yet ultimately, he could prevent a disaster of far greater proportions.
His father rose out of his times.
Of course they will never know.
How can any of them ever know what influences they have had? This is the challenge to all the race – to go beyond, with no knowledge of the power they can wield, to change things.

Simply with their openness to our realm ...

Yes, indeed.

Will there be others, do you think?

There will always be those who will try, and many will fail – most, in
fact.

Let us see who else can go beyond themselves, as the great ones before
them ... The Son, The Prophet, The Glory ...

They will always be with us, and with them, and their Word is
emblazoned forever.

Morality is unclear to men. They twist and turn it to their own devices.

Yes, of course. They are men. They will always put their own
interpretations to it. But not all. Not all.

No, not all.

We must prepare a welcome for the older boy. Despite his immediate
failure, he left behind his own influence. He left a call to the younger boy. That
was not an easy thing to do. He found the connection across time – this is not
easily understood, and yet he found the key. This was a great courage on his
part. And there were nonetheless some great men of the time – sons of the
Prophet even – who were greater and more beneficent that others may have
thought, then or now.

Yes, the Bishop didn't see it in this light. Just the words, but not the
reality.

And this is the problem after all – words alone. But without
application they are worthless.

Perhaps, as you say, he did not really fail.

The monk stood from his kneeling, and the two turned
together and walked solemnly from the Cathedral, past the building
going on around them, and the noise, and the gaping holes still in
the side of the great Church.

All the religions are one.

If there be an ear to hear, or a heart to understand.

Lord Abelard sat by a large fireplace, his booted feet crossed and resting on the table before him.

'How many did you say?'

'Over a hundred, my Lord,' replied the Priest, sitting opposite, comfortable but not so much as his host.

'Well then, we'll round them up in the town and send some packing down to London.'

'I don't think that's necessary, my Lord.'

'Why the devil not? If the King wants Jews, I'll give them to him.'

'Because the Bishop *does not want* Jews, my Lord.'

'I see.' Abelard dropped his long legs to the ground and stood, wandering nearer the fire.

'So you're the Bishop's man then? Well, I'm the King's!'

'I would say you are both, sir, and it is perhaps not so simple to put a preference to such a thing. Nor indeed wise.'

'Who the devil do you think you are to tell me what's so wise, Priest?'

'Merely some advice for your Lordship's consideration. There's been enough to stir the folk about lately, and I think – and our Bishop agrees – that it would be best if we leave things to calm for a while. The King has enough to make his foolish example of.'

'That's a brave statement, to call our King foolish.'

'Just his action, sir. Just his action.'

'Hmm. Well then. Is there anything to suggest a crime then?'

'Not particularly. The boy had wandered and obviously been caught in a trap. It would have been easy enough for him to fall.'

'Bloody poachers! What happened to that last one? Best we at least make an example of him then.'

'I believe he was given a beating by your men and thrown out on a road with his arms broken. I expect he's been set upon by thieves or some such by now. Certainly, he's not been heard from since, as far as I'm aware.'

'Well, get back to your flock man and don't be bringing me any more of these problems. Keep them settled, for God's sake!'

'With your help, sir ...'

'Not with my bloody help! The next nonsense you bring me and I'll have someone's head.'

'Indeed.' Father Taylor stood and bowed his head just a little, waiting for the Thane to reciprocate.

An acknowledgement almost imperceptible came and the priest turned and left the room, hearing some piece of furniture kicked or thrown behind him as he closed the door. The Father smiled at the frustration exhibited from the other man.

I was such, once.

There was a balance to restore among the people of these parts, and he thought it would bring a fresh vision of the future for many simple but noble lives.

The Bishop walked the path from the wharf; his assistant, Peter, in tow. The days were cooling, much to everyone's relief, and tempers had burnt out likewise.

Thank God.

'How are you, Peter?'

'Eminence?'

'How are you?'

'I'm well, my Lord. Thank you.'

'There were two monks here recently, along this path – one older and one younger. Do you know them?'

'There are so many come to the city, my Lord. No, I'm sorry.'

'No matter.'

The two men, Bishop and priest, walked on together. There was no hurry today.

'I'm sorry about the bird, Eminence.' Peter braved a comment before being spoken to, which would not have been his usual way.

'Thank you, Peter. I'm sorry for it too.'

'Are *you* well, Eminence?'

Hugh stopped and looked at the young priest. He smiled.

'Thank you, Peter, for your concern. You have been a loyal servant in such trying times.'

'I've seen the weight of it on you, my Lord.'

'Yes, yes, it has been that.' Hugh resumed his walk, and the priest continued the pace alongside.

The Lord prevails.

'The Lord prevails, my Lord.'

Hugh smiled.

Jacob Yazd lit the seven candles on the table before him and bade his family bow their heads in their usual daily prayer, grateful for their safety, for a growing calm, and for Angels living and dead that some part in even the most meagre of fortunes. Although life could not be thought of as meagre.

Berta Draper nestled back in her chair, smothered in rugs, and closed her eyes.

The puzzle of many events linked together in a picture in her mind.

Well then. Sometimes I'm right. And sometimes I'm less right.

21

Walking along the lakefront beneath her office, Alicia's mind floated in a joyful melancholy of her present being. It was a state she enjoyed, and it gave her pause to reflect on what had been and what was, well beyond her own existence and those in her immediate surrounds. Alicia relished change at the same time that it also swept her into wallowing in her own history, followed by a wonder at how she had achieved this new intersection virtually without knowing it was to come upon her.

The excitement of change, the planning of it, the events and such that had occurred for herself and for her family, an enlightenment as to several new realities in their lives, the prospect of something better – all this rolled into a giant ball of light and energy in her consciousness that she revelled in. It seemed only perfect that the day was light, the colours of autumn were at their picturesque best, and the air was still. There was even the warmth that sat at the comfortable optimum between too warm and not quite warm enough.

Alicia smiled at those passing by her on the path, and noted as she did that these recipients of her blithesome charm were a fuller, more caring, more spirited humanity than she'd noticed in a while, and she made a mental note to reassert her intellectual views on the depths of human kindness and of humanity in general.

With a wrapped-up sandwich and a bottle of juice in her shoulder bag, Alicia settled on a wooden bench just off the path and closer to the lake and pulled out her light lunch. A pair of swans immediately paddled near.

'Don't even think about it, all right. You're not having any. Shoo!' she waved an arm at the two birds and they retreated a fraction. Alicia pretended to ignore them and hoped some other passer-by might attract them with the promise of more enticing snacks.

Munching her sandwich, Alicia's reverie extended to the history of the place she sat, the two-thousand-year-old town and its thousand-year-old cathedral, and she marvelled at how many had walked this path before her and for what purpose. She felt sorry to be leaving the town just as she was uncovering its inherent riches, not to mention that she had overlooked the pleasure her own family had taken in Lincoln's many stories and figures, and for that she resolved to take better notice of what the people in her life were thinking and doing and becoming..

Finishing off her crust and resisting the urge to throw it out to the swans – lord only knows they'd be back at her in a shot wanting more, and bringing all their friends with them – Alicia picked out her second sammie and smiled at an elderly gentleman who'd just that moment sat at the other end of her bench seat. He tipped his hat to her with a polite nod and a smile and wrapped his overcoat across him, apparently cold despite the day.

It was less than a minute had gone by when Alicia felt compelled to make a further acknowledgement.

'Cold?' she asked.

'Oh yes.' The man turned his head and smiled again, as though he were nonetheless about some purpose in sitting there.

Alicia knew she was going to be saying more although she could not have said why that was the case.

'It's a lovely day though, isn't it?'

'Oh yes. Yes, indeed,' the man responded similarly, turning briefly to her and then back to a purposeful stare across the lake. He spoke very well, and Alicia fancied he was probably well educated.

'I've been thinking what an incredible spot this is,' remarked Alicia, 'and how many must have walked this path over so many hundreds of years.'

The man smiled again, but this time without turning his head or saying a thing, as though he were enjoying a private joke. For Alicia's part she could see the thought entertained him and wondered why. She looked at him a moment further and then returned also to a concerted stare out to the lake, and the simple pleasure of an egg sandwich.

After a few more minutes the thought entered Alicia's head that the man had intended some purpose in sitting next to her, and as she was thinking what further enquiry she might make of him, he spoke instead to her.

'Even these swans have been here these many years as well. One even speaks with our Bishop, I hear.'

'Spoke,' said Alice.

'Beg pardon?' said the man a little absent-mindedly.

'A swan *spoke* to the Bishop,' she repeated.

'Oh yes, of course.' He was smiling again.

The two sat again quietly.

'What do you do?' Alicia asked after another minute or two.

'Oh, I'm retired now, my dear,' the man replied. 'But I keep active,' he went on enthusiastically. 'I like to impart my worldly wisdom where I can,' he dipped his head to her and smiled.

'Well, the world could certainly do with more of that. In fact, I've found *myself* in need of some lately,' said Alicia, 'and it's a hard thing to come by. Our lives are very complicated, aren't they? It's a challenge to balance it all and make sense of it all. Don't you think?'

'I think we *make* it complicated,' the man replied, 'when really it's very simple.'

Alice had the feeling the old man had a lot more to say but was only going to do so if she asked him, as though he had no wish to impose his views unbidden. In that case, she decided she ought to ask him.

'Why do you say that?'

'Well, what in your life is complicated, tell me, my dear,' he responded.

'Well, I ...' Alicia started, taken aback. 'Well, I'm a physicist. I have a complex set of workplace relationships, and I'm married with two children, one of whom is autistic. And we're going to move to America, we've decided. And ...'

'Well, that all seems most *un*complicated,' the man asserted.

'I suppose when it's all in one sentence, it does seem fairly simple,' responded Alicia.

'So the question is, of course, *why* have you made it complicated?'

Alicia laughed. 'So my life's not complicated. *I* just made it that way.'

'Oh, it's not something to be ashamed off, my dear. Everyone does it.'

Alicia laughed again. 'Do you do it?'

'I'm not everyone,' he replied, leaning in towards her in mock conspiracy and smiling. 'But I did have to practise for many years before I was as good at it as I am now.'

'As good at what?'

'Creating my life myself. Knowing that I'm responsible for it all.'

'And making it less complicated too, I suppose,' Alicia asked further.

'We don't make something less, nor do we make something more. We just make it.'

'*Now* you are making it complicated,' said Alicia, smiling.

'Do you have a bone in your body, my dear, called "complicated"?'

'No, of course not.'

'Do you own a *thing* called complicated?'

'No.'

'Well then, this thing you want to make less, where do you start with that process if you can't find it to make it less?'

'But it's a state – a state of being,' replied Alicia.

'Is it?'

'Well, isn't it?'

'Life *occurs* for you as being complicated, but that doesn't mean it *is*.'

'So life *occurs* for you as being cold, so you wrap your coat around you – you make yourself warmer. Am I right?'

'Yes! Perfectly.'

'It's not just that it *is* cold?'

'No. There are some in the world who would find this quite tropical, I'm sure,' replied the man.

Alicia looked at her companion and weighed up whether he was mad, plain old eccentric, quite intelligent in a quirky kind of way, or some combination. She thought he was at least harmless, definitely sweet, and certainly quite sincere.

'Well, I shall be off on the remainder of my walk.' The gentleman suddenly rose. 'Very nice to meet you,' he said, bowing a little and tipping his hat to Alicia.

'And you.'

Alicia watched him walk away and noticed he tipped his hat to others passing by, as though his personal code insisted he acknowledge every person he came within several metres of. She wished she'd spoken a little more with him; indeed, she felt he'd had yet more to say, as did she.

Oh, well.

Alicia thought it was the nicest conversation she'd had all day.

Satchel in hand, Alicia stopped by Dryden Cooper's office on her way out.

'You off?' Dryden asked, looking up from his desk.

'Yes, in a mo,' Alicia replied, stepping in and closing the office door.

'What's up?'

'Just wanted to let you know, I'm been shortlisted for a new position,' Alicia stated.

'You're joking!'

'Nope.'

'Where?' Dryden asked.

'Columbia,' Alicia replied.

'New York?'

'Uh-huh.'

Dryden remained stunned a moment while Alicia gave a hope-you'll-understand smile.

'That's a big change,' Dryden commented, settling into the idea.

'It's the right time for Pete and I, and we think we can probably get Tim into more advanced treatment in the United States,' Alicia responded.

'And your research ... ?'

'. . .. will be part of a broader programme there and across much of the East Coast,' said Alicia.

Dryden paused. 'Well, good for you,' he said, smiling back at her.

'Thanks.' Alicia took a deep breath. 'I'll ... let you know.'

'Good. Good,' said Dryden.

Alicia turned and left the office quietly.

'They're negotiating nuclear weapons reductions in Geneva today,' Pete mentioned, as he strolled across Lincoln Square with Alicia.

'Good, but I'm freezing – can we hurry up?' Alicia put her arm through Pete's and pulled in close.

'Aren't you interested?'

'No, I'm fucking cold!'

'Fancy a pash under the arch?'

'My lips are nearly frozen and my tongue's practically hanging out. No!'

'Worth a try.' Pete grinned as they quickened their pace through Exchequer Gate to the Cathedral close.

'You don't think I'm going to be too much of an outsider, do you?' Alicia asked.

'No more than everyone that goes is,' Pete replied.

'So you're a bunch of oddballs then?'

'As best as I could describe it: yes. C'mon, here we are.'

Pete steered Alicia through a small front gate and up the short path to a cottage front door. Just as Pete went to knock, the door opened anyway, as much to Loraine's surprise on the inside, as to Pete and Alicia's.

'Hello!' Loraine exclaimed. 'Do come in.' She stepped back, pulling the door wide open with her.

'Hello, Loraine.' Pete smiled, stepping in and kissing his host on the cheek.

'You lovely man, how wonderful to see you! And you, Alicia! Come in, come in! I was just shooting out to the gate with the milk bottles, head on in. I won't be a tick,' she said, scooting out the front door.

Pete took his coat off to hang in the hall, keeping a foot at the front door to stop it slamming shut in the wind. Loraine tottled back in from the gate just as quickly as she'd gone out, and Pete closed the door behind her.

'Brrr, it's cold out. Well, come on through then,' Loraine repeated, guiding Pete and Alicia down the corridor.

Alicia could hear the chatter coming through the door ajar at the other end, relieved at not having to walk into a quiet room where everyone would be bound to stare at the newcomer. She was surprised then when most faces in the room they entered did turn towards her, and more so that a few cheers, whoops, and handclaps greeted her as she walked in behind her husband. She looked at

Pete, raising her eyebrows questioningly, and then turned a grateful smile to the group in general.

A gentleman Alicia knew instantly from Pete's description must be Maitland, rose from his seat nearby, holding out both arms to her.

'Welcome, welcome, welcome, my dear Alicia. We were beginning to think you didn't exist!' Maitland took hold of her shoulders and kissed her on both cheeks. 'I had in fact decided your husband was so thick and so ugly, no one could possibly have wanted to marry him, so my dear, you are *quite* a surprise,' Maitland beamed at her. 'Do come and sit just here,' Maitland pulled a chair closer to his own. 'And you, old boy,' he addressed Pete, 'go down there and don't bother me.'

Everyone laughed at Maitland's games; obviously, this was par for the course Alicia thought, watching her husband squeeze his way around the other side of the large table and to the far end of the room.

As he did, he passed behind a familiar face that nodded and smiled her way. Alicia returned the smile, trying to position the older gentleman in her universe.

'And this is Nigel,' announced Rose, indicating the same man. 'Maitland and I met Nigel the other day, frequenting, as he does, a particular watering hole, which ... oh goodness me, I can't remember ...' She was chuckling herself at what she knew most of her guests would know was a reference to *The Magna Carta*.

'According to Rose, Nigel "looks interesting",' Maitland added. 'Personally, I think he looks rather ordinary, but he has extraordinary taste in Scotch. That is why I invited him.'

Rose, Loraine, and a few others rolled their eyes at Maitland's not-so-false attempts at arrogance, while their new guest simply smiled in such a way as to acknowledge what others already knew was Maitland's general approach to relaxing the atmosphere.

'And while we're congratulating Maitland ... ,' added Loraine, smirking, '... he also deserves some praise I think for his adventures into interfaith understanding and development.'

Alicia continued to ponder the new guest Nigel, as Loraine then Rose and then Maitland talked about the suggestion for a project with the Jewish community, to commemorate the death of Jews wrongly executed for the murder of the child now known as Little St Hugh..

Alicia had heard the story of the child from Pete and since visited his small shrine in the Cathedral. Her hosts were pleased with the project, and she thought it sounded both humanitarian and practical to create a historically unifying project such as this.

The discussion brought congratulatory comments from around the table, and Alicia noted the real humility evident in Maitland's demeanour; one who otherwise preferred to feign arrogance.

At a pause Nigel spoke, and it was then Alicia remembered him as her brief companion at the lakeside a few days earlier. She warmed to his presence immediately, almost as if he were her best and only friend, his voice instantly as comforting as it had seemed then.

'What divine poetry,' he said, in a voice so assured that everyone looked towards him.

'How so?' Loraine asked, instantly engaged.

'Oh, an old man's amusement mostly,' he replied with ease.

How was it, Alicia wondered, *that an old man such as this, might command an instant rapport?*

Nigel continued slowly and philosophically as if in answer to her question. 'I've been many places. I've served in wars and witnessed many more. I've seen innocents killed in peacetime through ignorance in the main – and fear, in this town and those nearby and afar. I've also seen miracles. Things you could not imagine. Things I could not explain in words but that I know in my soul. And at some points, in my long life, I have experienced a few moments, when what's going on around me comes together at some particular point, where I can *see* the Divine movement of time, and the spiritual *taste* of God's mercy. And I can tell you,' he continued slowly and softly, 'that those moments come, not in the face of some beautiful sunset, or the pounding of an ocean, or the touch of the most beautiful woman.' He raised an eyebrow in acknowledgement. 'Although, those can be moments one senses the Great Beauty ...' Nigel smiled. 'But that crispest coming together of the great and complex matrix of a universe, both Divine and Earthly, most often occurs at the simplest of all moments ... just as one sits at a table of strangers-become-friends..'

Not a hair's breadth of movement followed, as the old man continued his beaming smile. 'Please forgive an old man.' He nodded to his hosts.

'No such thing is necessary,' Loraine responded, surprised at her guest's charismatic monologue. 'I do believe you have quite honoured us, and I thank you.' A few murmurs made clear the group's agreement. 'And I think I can say ... I believe, I understand of what you speak. This ... coming together. Can I prevail on you, perhaps, to tell us, what those compass points are that have given you this brief moment of awareness?'

Alicia noted a half, unspoken conspiracy between host and guest, as the one sensed a worthwhile thread to pursue, and the other graciously obliged.

'Well, I shall be happy to try ...' Nigel bowed his head briefly to Loraine, before looking up at Alicia, smiling. 'You, my dear,' he said, looking directly at Alicia still. 'You are a compass point.'

Alicia raised her own eyebrows, while others turned to look at her, and then back to Nigel.

'I really cannot put into words the synchronicity that combines your presence ... Alicia ... , that you have a most extraordinary young son . . ..'

Now it was Pete's turn to look surprised, and he looked from Nigel to his wife and back.

'... that here we are, only yards from one of the greatest Cathedrals in the world, a scene of so much history, including the tragic death of a young boy so many hundreds of years ago, not to mention the many more besides . A place of worship for kings,' Nigel continued as though in disbelief at the convergence of events, 'kings who fought *against* other religions, in the name of a Christ who had no such wish for their battles. And here you are,' he looked to Loraine, Rose, and Maitland in turn, 'bringing together, by such a simple act, the members of two Faiths.' He paused. 'My words fail me.'

'I don't think so,' said Loraine softly.

'You can never know all of the impact of what you do,' Nigel restarted, seemingly into another story. 'I can guarantee that every one of you here has done something in this world, at some time or another that was so selfless that its impact changed the world. You *do not know* what good you do.'

Nigel paused, as though to acknowledge each one at the table, looking around them all.

'Paradoxically,' Rose spoke, 'our question in these get-togethers is really *what can we know.*'

'Oh yes, yes, indeed. Indeed. And a valuable thing it is to ask it. Most certainly,' Nigel responded. 'But you must also know there is much more you can never know.'

'Yes, of course,' Rose replied.

Alicia wondered where the conversation and Nigel were headed, although it was reassuring to her that those present seemed far more insightful to be dreamy, and certainly far less than dull.

'Do you understand the idea of the butterfly effect?' Nigel asked, looking around.

'When a butterfly flaps its wings on one side of the planet,' Sally responded, 'it causes an earthquake on the other side. Or something like that.'

'Yes, that's it perfectly. It's an idea of cause and effect, and it's really talking about what we *can't know.*' Nigel was quietly emphatic, and looked around again. 'You cannot know. You cannot know that your prayers have changed the course of the lives of the people at this table. You cannot know that your actions have changed the future of the world. You cannot know that your actions have even changed the past.'

Silence reigned. Nigel's words and presence had such gravitas that no one dared move.

'And I believe, my dear' – Nigel looked towards Alicia – 'that is where you come in.'

His smile gave Alicia a reassurance she'd not known previously; she knew exactly of what he spoke; and further too of the weightiness of her work, which Nigel's reassurance bred a new faith in.

'You know of my work?' She knew the answer.

'You're a physicist, you said.' Alice knew, that Nigel knew, that being a physicist alone was not in the least sufficient to respond to his statement about the past, but it seemed of no consequence any more that this man, ostensibly a stranger, somehow knew of her particular area of interest..

'You're ... more or less ... addressing Heisenberg's Uncertainty Principle,' Alicia began. 'At least as I see it. Richard Feynman said that nobody understands quantum physics. And I think he's right. The majority of our theory is just that: theoretical. Of course, there has also been much application, but ...'

Attention was now firmly transferred to Alicia.

'But, well, effectively that's precisely what the uncertainty principle addresses: that we can't know everything. It's saying that as soon as we bring our attention to something, then that thing changes.'

'Yes!' Nigel cried out enthusiastically, making a few people jump.

Alicia smiled good-naturedly; Nigel's joviality was infectious.

'And this applies, *in theory*, to the past as well,' she added.

'Of course it must!' Nigel exclaimed again, and then sat back on his chair a little, dropping his hands into his lap, as if to say, *There! You see!*

'But, that's not possible ...,' Maitland puzzled, looked questioningly at Nigel, and then at Alicia.

'It's only theory,' replied Alicia.

'No, no, no! You mustn't say *only*,' Nigel offered a correction to Alicia, leaving the room quiet once more.

'But if we cannot know ...' Maitland proffered cautiously.

'Exactly,' said Nigel.

'Then we're left simply with belief,' responded Maitland.

'With Faith, yes,' Nigel replied.

'Faith alone?' asked Pete.

'Yes, of course. What else is there?' Nigel stated.

'Well, it would be nice if science proved something like this,' Pete replied.

'If it was proved, you wouldn't require Faith though.'

'And, forgive me, but your point is ...?' Pete continued.

'It's not about what you *know*. You can't change things by what you *know*. You *know* you should exercise more. Do you? But when you *believe* that you can, when you have *Faith* in a different you, *then* you'll make a difference. Don't you see?' Nigel explained.

'But to exercise more – taking your example – I must take action. It's not sufficient to believe ... to only have faith,' Pete responded again.

'Oh, there you go with that *only* again.' Nigel chuckled and paused to look at Pete. 'Then you do not understand what I mean by Faith, my friend.' He smiled at Pete and then turned to Maitland.

'Well,' responded Maitland, eyebrows raised and taking a deep breath, 'there's no difference between real Faith and action. Your belief about something will change it.'

'If you *believe* enough ... ,' asserted Pete.

'There is no *enough*,' Nigel explained. 'There is belief, and there is no belief. Belief *exists*. If there is no belief, there is no belief. And what is more, you hardly know everything you believe. In fact, you know but a fraction of what you yourself believe. It's why your life is created as it is. Not entirely to your satisfaction probably. You're a walking, talking, and breathing sack of beliefs that shape everything in you and around you. You shape your own future. You shape the future of people in this room. You've shaped the future of everyone you've met, and indeed many you have not met. And you don't even know it. You don't know your own power. But then nor do you need to, in fact.'

'Is it possible ... ,' Sally piped in, ' could you ... summarise that?'

Nigel laughed.

'No,' he replied to her.

'But ... ,' Sally went on.

'Why? Because you need to *know* it? But I just told you that you can't *know* it. But still you persist. You don't need to know. There is no knowing.'

More quiet.

'Here it is for you.' Nigel stood up. 'The full lesson of everything I can give you. I will put it on the table here before you, in all its golden glory, a crown of the finest jewels, for all to see,' and he mimed an extraction and tugging of something from within his head, pretended to mould it into a large shape, feigning admiration for the invisible thing, and placed it delicately on the table. 'You see, there it is, the great unknown, the answer to everything. Now that you can see it, you can *know* it. Right? Does that make a difference?' He sat down again and paused. 'My dear,' he addressed Sally, slowly and without patronising, 'you will *understand* this whether I've explained it sufficiently for your mind or not. It is a spiritual foundation of the Universe and therefore your soul will give it life within you.'

Alicia noted that Rose and Loraine exchanged the briefest of looks, that all at once said *this is brilliant* and *where did you find him* and *let's just let this run its course.*

'But, Nigel ... ,' Maitland started, opening and closing his mouth twice, before he saying, 'I believe you,' and he smiled. 'But we are so inadequate to the task.'

'Oh good heavens, no. You just *think* you are. Indeed, you *believe* you are, so ...' Nigel pulled a face and gestured suggesting *on the other hand.* 'My boy, God hears all your prayers. And by the way, you think far too much.'

'But then what part does Faith play?' Maitland asked.

'Young man,' began Nigel to Maitland, raising a few smiles about the table, 'you are about to get yourself very confused, and that would *not* be good for you.' He paused. 'You want to understand whether it is your Faith in God that may move mountains, or Faith in your own belief that mountains may be moved. Or is it whether you have sufficient belief in your Faith, or sufficient Faith in God, or ... ?

Nigel waited again.

'Faith,' He continued. 'Simply what is Faith? Is it belief? Yes. In God? Yes. In yourself? Yes. Can you *know*? No. Do you *need* to know? No. Can you move mountains? Yes. What else? As I told this dear lady recently,' he glanced at Alicia, 'you make your lives so complicated. It's really not necessary.'

'Then why does life feel such a burden sometimes?' Alicia chimed in, raising a glance from her husband, but feeling herself quite a part of this group by now, and sensing some of the heaviness of Nigel's words upon all, herself included.

'Because you believe you're alone,' Nigel replied.

It was not the answer any expected, but the realisation of its truth showed on most of their faces.

'But we're never alone,' Rose asserted. 'Not for a moment are we alone? Not for a second are we left to ourselves?'

'Such is your belief,' said Nigel conclusively. 'You've lived within the Church for some years, and I can understand that you would not have chosen such a path had you not believed this to be so.'

Rose smiled in acknowledgement.

'So what's it all about then?' Pete asked, almost with impatience, and certainly with some frustration, and a pleading look towards Nigel.

Nigel's calm, pleasant manner took in Pete's concern with obvious kindness.

'Well, you know, I do think perhaps I should hog the floor a little less, and I'm quite sure our hosts have an answer to that,' he said, turning to Rose and Loraine.

'Oh, my friend, we are *most* comfortable with you holding the floor,' Loraine responded graciously. 'But since you ask ... what's it all about?' She looked to Pete. 'I agree with Nigel that we can make it much too complicated. So to make it very simple . Faith. Love. Unity. These three. With these three you will move mountains. There is nothing more. Of course our evenings here explore much more ... what we can and can't know principally. And in that exploration some will find frustration, some will find emptiness and disbelief, some will find Faith, and others ...' She shrugged. 'We have free will. We can choose these things. I choose these three and no more, although I must say, after so many years, I think they choose me as much as anything. I'm less able to *choose* in the same sense, as perhaps I could when I was younger.'

'I thought it was *faith, hope,* and *love,* my dear,' responded Maitland.

'Yes, indeed. Corinthians 13, *and the greatest of these is love.* Of course. But I have my own personal sense that has developed over time, and I have a great belief in the value of *unity.* And anyway, I've never quite got the idea of hope, if anyway we have faith. But!

We cannot do what we do, alone. And while there cannot be sameness, there can be better understanding of difference. And indeed that is where we started this evening, with Maitland's wonderful idea for a unity project with the Jewish community.'

'Well, in point of fact … ,' Maitland began, 'how we started this evening was with the hope that we would hear some wonderful discourse from our other guest this evening,' looking to Alicia. 'And now that we have something deliciously wonderful in a description of the unknown spirit world, I am just so wanting to know what the view of a scientist *is* on all of this. And I believe then, given also such a delightful litany from Nigel here, I shall then die entirely happy.'

Chortles and grins followed and broke the weightiness of the air.

'Masterful, Maitland,' sighed Rose, beaming, not quite sure who was directing the evening any more.

'Thank you, my dear,' Maitland replied, and looked again to Alicia.

In the space of the few seconds that it took Alicia to look from Maitland to Nigel to Pete and back, her uncertainty as to her own faith, and her doubt as to her science, melded into a single sense of the unified field of all things, that found a home for her beliefs, knowledge, and doubts, as well as those of the people present, and in all certainty those of many others; and she understood also that this had somehow been a gift from Nigel and that his timing seemed impeccable.

'The knowledge of all things *does* exist,' she said. 'As a scientist I believe that. That is not to say we can in fact *know* everything. Doubtless there will be much that will remain hidden for many years to come. Perhaps some things will never be known, but … we cannot disbelieve that the knowledge of them does exist somewhere.'

Alicia floated in a moment where everything made sense, and her own and others thoughts were all part of one great whole that contained all of humanity, the world, its knowledge, and the reality of everything seen and unseen. She had experienced this moment only once or twice before in her life, and she knew it for what it was; that unique instance when time stood still, the moment that sportsmen described everything had slowed, and they knew they had scored the goal before their foot even struck the ball; a moment when anything was possible. It may last seconds, or minutes, or perhaps even an hour, but then it would be gone, almost as if it had never been there at all. Except that it had been, and Alicia sat within it as long as it would last. For in this particular moment, she understood the truth as well as the power of Nigel's words, and of Loraine's, and others.

'For me,' she continued, 'I want to continue to find the unseen, to describe it, and to understand that meeting point of science with the spiritual. Because I do believe there is one. I'd probably go as far as saying that they're one and the same if it wasn't for the possibility that my colleagues would then believe I'm *completely* crazy.'

Alicia felt the moment receding and savoured its last touch. 'But it's a cause of great happiness for any scientist – any person at all I think – when they discover some part of the meaning for our existence. There's a euphoria comes from knowing. All scientists, whether or not they would admit it, are searching for some part of the equation that is *meaning*. It's what we all do. It's the thing that gives any one of us the greatest happiness – knowledge. Despite that, as you say, we can't *know* that much.'

'Ready to leave us now, Maitland?' Rose teased.

'Yes, indeed, that was perfect thank you. Should I do so, my sweet' – he turned to Rose – 'then I should surely enter heaven,' joked Maitland. 'Thank you so much,' he said to Alicia. 'You have given us so much this evening. I'm overjoyed. I cannot describe my elation at the confluence of both your contributions,' he acknowledged Nigel.

'Well, I'm very pleased to be here, thank you,' replied Alicia. 'And that's exactly it, Maitland, I agree – a confluence.'

'A unity even,' he added, turning to Loraine, beaming.

'It is,' Loraine responded, 'a unity of science and religion.'

'But this idea of time,' Pete returned to an earlier point, addressing Nigel, 'and to ...' Pete struggled with his thoughts, 'to ... influence the past. It's not possible.'

'Yes, it is,' replied Alicia, and the two, husband and wife, looked at each other..

'At least in theory,' Alicia continued. 'It's complicated.'

'And does it matter, Peter,' Nigel added, 'in which direction your influence spreads?'

'No, I suppose not,' replied Pete.

Pete sat back, unsure what he had gained from the evening, knowing there was some truth spinning around him that he'd not grasped hold of yet. He looked across to his wife and noted that she had definitely embedded herself among those present. *She shone just a little*, he thought.

Maitland reached across the table to shake Nigel's hand, as conversation split into twos and threes; Maitland pursued the nature of belief with Nigel, and Rose moved around to Alicia to talk. Pete smiled at Loraine, who gestured him to follow her; apparently it was time to bring in food and drink. Pete circled the table, brushing his hand across Alicia's shoulder as he passed her. She smiled, obviously content to be here after all her protestations, and resumed her chat with Rose.

Loraine pointed Pete at a collection of glasses and cups, along with various bottles to be unscrewed or corked, and disappeared through to the kitchen, returning with already made-up plates of lamingtons and sandwiches.

As he passed glasses and cups out, Pete felt oddly detached from the group, although that did not bother him and his head was spinning from the discussion and the uncertainties it held for him. He was thrilled that Alicia had apparently taken a lot of pleasure from the evening, and he looked forward to exploring some of the ideas with her more. She had changed in recent weeks, to so great an extent he felt almost at sea trying to understand her state of mind. She was paying more attention to him, as well as to their children, and less to her work. It was as though she'd woken up, realised there was a life she was a party to.

He looked over to Maitland, engaged in mirthful discussion. Pete saw a man deeply loyal to his Faith, with an unshakeable love for humanity, and a heart ready and waiting for a kind act to pursue.

Next to him another stranger-become-friend arriving from who-knows-where to provide a compelling reality for stretching the dimensions of thought and spirit.

Pete poured himself a cup of tea and sat down again, not yet participating, continuing his scan. Rose and Loraine's generosity and influence seemed unmatched. They had an uncanny knack for finding the intelligent and gracious, always welcomed and never judged. Their good humour, and acceptable level of – at least in Pete's mind – of irreverence, drew others to them and provided an unlikely opportunity for the growth of a small, caring community of enquiry.

Pete loved these people. Theirs was not a company that desired more of him than he had to give, nor anything other than his willing presence and his deepest thoughts: both of which it was his pleasure to give. On this night though, and for a while yet, he would keep his and his family's changing destiny to himself. He had come here to find meaning in the otherwise apparent emptiness of a small child's life, his son. Along the way he had found greater definition of his own life, and evidently now he witnessed Alicia's renewal as well.

Was it simply that he took pleasure in an ongoing debate of sorts, with people he liked, or had there become more to his engagement with this world, as indeed he believed? He had few or adequate words for what he now believed to be an unseen world inhabited by more than what his five senses told him. Nonetheless, his senses would on occasion remind him that potentially there was no meaning but that which his imagination alone conjured. These thoughts though gave him little pleasure; indeed, none at all. And that his scientist wife now weighed in on the deliberations gave him enormous satisfaction. The future held appeal, but it was the present that was the origin of that future, and by far the greatest investment he knew he could make in the *now* was the creation of happiness, and helping provide that for others was increasingly a key to his own contentment.

Alicia caught Pete's eye and tapped her watch. He was sorry to have to go, but he also wanted to spend time alone with Alicia. Saying goodbye could take a while as well when some farewells became the start of new conversations.

'I'm sorry I've just met you and now I'm leaving,' Nigel declared, standing to shake both their hands. 'I'm returning to Syria tomorrow,' he continued.

'Syria? My!' Alicia exclaimed.

'Oh, family business.' Nigel smiled. 'We will try to meet again,' he assured them. 'But really I don't think you need me now.'

There were smiles and gestures all around, with kisses on cheeks and pats on backs, and arrangements were made for other gatherings, as a real family would do at someone's departure. Alicia revealed her genuine pleasure at the evening, and Pete was reminded of a pride he'd once taken in having a wife of charm and beauty and intelligence. The memory descended into his present reality such that a period of several intervening years all but disappeared into a catch-all of distant remembrances that were no longer quite real.

Pete took Alicia's hand, eager to steer her out faster. Finding their way into the hall he took her coat and scarf from the stand by the door, holding the one for her and wrapping the other about her neck gently. He quickly wrapped his own coat around him, opening the door for Alicia. On the pavement he took her arm through his and hurried off towards the Exchequer Gate.

'What's the hurry?' Alicia whistled against the cold wind.

'Just keeping warm.' He grinned back.

Circling around and under the arch, Pete stopped and pulled Alicia to him, wrapping his arms around her and burying his nose into her neck. Rubbing his cheek against hers, he turned his face to his wife and kissed her.

There was no surprise for Alicia as she sunk into her husband's embrace and kiss. A dim light crackled inside the arch and Alicia drew back with a giggle.

'What's happening in your world?' She grinned at her husband.

'I don't know. But I like it.' He grinned back, and then kissed her again.

22

Wednesday, 12 September 2001, New York City

Tim begins his Masters programme at Columbia today. It's been difficult to find the right supervisor – Lissy would be ideal but it's not a good look, and anyway she is overrun with exciting graduates. America has been such a wonderful academic environment for her – so imaginative.

Tim is very focused – as only he can be – and his quirky ways have sat comfortably in this setting – it's New York after all.

A postcard from Jillie – she's arrived in the Sudan with Medicin sans Frontieres. *She misses us already.*

Email from Rose and Loraine – thinking of hanging up their cassocks and moving to warmer climes. Not sure they could be too far from their adored Cathedral though. Apparently Little St Hugh *has been cordoned off – too many children sitting on his tomb thinking it's a seat. How Tim loved that spot. I must ask him if he remembers it.*

Maitland passed on last week. So sad. He'd become a stalwart of the interfaith movement in Lincoln, and much loved. The girls would have given him a superb send-off I'm sure. Would have packed the Magna Carta, *no doubt.*

Sadat has won a second Nobel – unprecedented. The Middle East continues to avoid disaster – precarious nonetheless but a great care is given continuously from all the West's leaders. There are oddball crazies everywhere but some sanity prevails among a united world leadership. Perhaps this new millennium may bring a new peace after all.

A small note: a National Spiritual Assembly of the Baha'is of Iran was elected in Teheran, after a twenty-year ban. Maitland would have liked that. Who knows – maybe he had something to do with it!

It's been a stunning autumn day – leaves turning in the Park.

New York is very chilled out. Well, it is New York.

Fact or Fiction

- All characters are fictitious accepting obvious and real historical characters, and others, perhaps less well known, as noted below.
- Torksey and Nocton Fen are towns in Lincolnshire with roughly the geographic relationship to Lincoln as the story describes.
- The Foss Dyke is the oldest canal in England constructed by the Romans around AD 120 and still in use. It connects the Trent at Torksey to the Witham at Lincoln, and is about 18 km (11 mi) long.
- Brayford Pool in Lincoln is where the Foss Dyke meets the river Witham.
- The 1185 earthquake destroyed most of Lincoln Cathedral; it is not known what effect it had on the Foss Dyke. Most of the West Front of the cathedral was left standing, and rather than being pulled down and rebuilt, it was incorporated into the new building. Probably this was for financial reasons. At any rate there is a mismatch in parts of the Nave where the 'old' and 'new' were joined up, creating very noticeable, but interesting, irregularities and asymmetries, in the vaulting in particular. The Great Transept and the Nave were completed in 1240, although the central tower collapsed just prior to this, and its rebuilding was not completed until 1256.
- The Brayford Pool is known for its large population of Mute Swans (*Cygnus olor*). The swans made the news headlines in 2004 over concerns about the animals' diet and overall health.
- There is no Physics Department at Lincoln University..
- The *Bell Test experiments* were conducted by Alain Aspect in Paris in 1981. These showed that Albert Einstein, Boris

Podolsky, and Nathan Rosen's *reductio ad absurdum* of quantum mechanics appeared to be realised when two particles were separated by an arbitrarily large distance. A correlation between their wave functions remained, as they were once part of the same wave function that was not disturbed before one of the child particles was measured. Aspect's experiments were considered to provide support to the thesis that Bell's inequalities were violated. Bell's theorem states: *No physical theory of local hidden variables can ever reproduce all of the predictions of quantum mechanics.* In quantum mechanics, a *local hidden variable theory* is one in which distant events are assumed to have no *instantaneous* effect on local ones.

- A personal family friend, bearing little resemblance to the Loraine of this story, did in fact see a 'falling star', and did make the prediction about a world leader's attempted assassination, precisely the evening before the attempt made on Ronald Reagan's life by John Hinckley.

- All references to the inside of Lincoln Cathedral stem from fact.

- The *Shrine of Little Hugh* is real, but it in fact dates from 1255. It is indeed the shrine of a small boy supposedly killed and mutilated by the Jews in Lincoln. In the few years prior to this, anti-Semitic feeling in England had led to many murder charges being brought against Jews. The story goes that the young boy was ritually murdered and his body discovered at the bottom of a well. A local Jew was found who 'confessed' that the Jews did this annually as a ritual act; he was tried and executed. The boy's body was placed in the Cathedral, and he was venerated as a saint and martyr, although he was never canonised. Six months earlier, Henry III had sold his rights to tax the Jews to his brother, Richard, Earl of Cornwall. Having lost this source of income, he decided that he was eligible for the Jews' money if they were convicted of crimes. Ninety-two Jews were arrested and held in the Tower of London and were charged with involvement in the ritual murder. Eighteen of them were hanged, and Henry was able to take over their property. The remainder were pardoned and set free, most likely because Richard, who saw a potential threat to his own source of income, intervened on their behalf with his brother. Anti-Semitic feeling was also high during Bishop Hugh's time, and the Bishop was one of their noted defenders. When the tomb was opened in 1791, the child's body was found intact, bearing no evidence of the mutilation alleged to have taken place. In 2009, an interfaith project between the Lincolnshire Jewish Community and Lincoln Cathedral developed the wording for a sign that now rests on the wall above and to the right of the Shrine of Little Hugh. It tells the story of Little Hugh and concludes: *This libel against the Jews is a shameful example of religious and racial hatred which continuing down through the ages violently divides many people in the present day. Let us unite here in a prayer for an end to bigotry, prejudice and persecution. Peace be with you. Shalom.*

- Towards the south-east of the cathedral, more or less opposite the Shrine of *Little Hugh*, there is a fairly innocuous carved wall known as the Stonemason's practice wall. The blocks are those of apprentice stonemasons who carved these practice shapes to perfect their skills before embarking on more important carvings elsewhere in the Cathedral.

- The *Harvard* experiment in prayer, described by the character Maitland, was conducted in 2006 by Dr Herbert Benson of the *Harvard Medical School* and measured the therapeutic effect of intercessory prayer in cardiac bypass patients.

- *The Wig & Mitre* and *Magna Carta* are real pubs, the former on Steep Street at the top of Lincoln Hill, a short (steep) stroll from the Cathedral, the latter at the top of Steep Street, in the square.

- The Stowe parish church is commonly known as Stowe Minster and sometimes referred to as the Mother Church of Lincolnshire. Its full name is the Minster Church of St Mary, Stowe in Lindsey. It was built in 1040 on the ruins of a church predating the arrival of the Danes in 870. Bishop Remigius refounded it as an abbey in 1091 and brought monks there from Eynsham in Oxfordshire. However, these monks were well gone by the time of Bishop Hugh, having been returned to Eynsham about five years after they arrived, by Bishop Remigius' successor.

- Hugh of Avalon was Bishop of Lincoln. A Frenchman, and procurator of the monastery at Saint-Maximin, Hugh was appointed prior at Witham in Somerset at the request of Henry II in 1179. Hugh was not elected Bishop of Lincoln until 25 May 1186, being consecrated on 21 September that same year; That is to say, a year following the earthquake in 1185 that destroyed much of the cathedral. For the purpose of this fiction, Hugh is placed in the Diocese as Bishop prior to the earthquake. He died in November 1200 and was canonised by Pope Honorius III in 1220. He is the Patron Saint of sick children, sick people, and swans.

- Hugh's primary emblem is a white swan, in reference to the story of the swan of Stowe which had a deep and lasting friendship for the Saint, even guarding him while he slept. The swan would follow him about and was his constant companion.

- Hugh did stand up to King Henry over taxes, among other things.

- Henry II had either commissioned the assassination of Thomas Becket himself or else a handful of his loyal knights had taken it upon themselves; either way Henry suffered considerable penance, including having to establish the Witham monastery, and even, in 1172, being flogged in public, naked, before the door of the cathedral at Avranches, which was his capital city in Normandy. He did also promise to go on Crusade. There is no evidence to suggest that Hugh of Avalon witnessed Henry's public flogging at Avranches in 1172.

- Pope Lucius III was pope from 1181 until his death in November 1185. He spent most of his short pontificate in exile, at monasteries around Rome, and in Verona in northern Italy. History occasionally records that it was Lucius who began the Inquisition, but this in fact began in the reign of Gregory IX in 1234. Lucius began preparations for the Third Crusade to the Holy Land in 1185.

- Hugh is the namesake of St Hugh's College, Oxford, where a 1920s statue of the saint stands on the stairs of the Howard Piper Library. In his right hand, he holds an effigy of Lincoln Cathedral, and his left hand rests on the head of a swan. Notable former students of St Hugh's College have included Kate Adie, one of the BBC's most renowned news reporters, having covered on the ground from the London Iranian Embassy siege in 1980, the American bombing of Tripoli in 1986, the Lockerbie bombing in 1988, the Tiananmen Square protests in 1989, the first Gulf War, the war in Yugoslavia, and the Rwandan genocide. It is not known whether Kate Adie reported from the Brixton Riots. The Burmese Nobel laureate, Aung San Suu Kyi, is another notable graduate of St Hugh's College.

- News facts recorded in Pete's diary were all real occurrences, with the notable exception that Anwar Sadat did not survive the assassination on 6 October 1981, as is described in this novel; instead, he was definitively shot and killed. As such, of course, he did not receive a second

Nobel Peace Prize in September 2001. In addition, persecution of the Baha'is in Iran remains, as does the ban on election of their Spiritual Assemblies; as such there was no election of a new national assembly in Teheran in 1981.

- Khalid Ahmed Showky Al-Islambouli arranged and carried out the assassination of the Egyptian president, Anwar Sadat, during the annual *6 October 1973 victory parade* on 6 October 1981. Lieutenant Islambouli was not supposed to participate in the October parade but was chosen by chance to replace another officer. When his section of the parade neared the President's platform, Islambouli and three others leapt from their truck and ran towards the President, lobbing grenades. Islambouli entered the stands and emptied his assault rifle into Sadat, shouting 'I have killed the Pharaoh!' Seven others were killed and twenty-eight were wounded. Islambouli was immediately captured. Over 300 Islamic radicals were indicted in the trial of Islambouli and twenty-three co-conspirators. Islambouli stated that his primary motivation for the assassination was Sadat's signing of the Camp David Accords with Israel. He was found guilty and executed with five others on 15 April 1982. The Iranian government named a street in Tehran after Islambouli in 1981, renaming it to *Intifada Street* in 2001 in an effort to improve relations with Egypt. (*Bobby Sands Street* also appeared in Teheran in 1981, following his death in *The Maze*; it had been *Winston Churchill Street* and is the location of the British embassy.)

- Sheikh Omar Abdel-Rahman, also known as *The Blind Sheikh*, is an Egyptian Muslim leader now serving a life sentence at a US federal prison. Abdel-Rahman and nine others were convicted of seditious conspiracy, following the *1993* World Trade Center bombings. Abdel-Rahman had issued a fatwa – a scholarly religious opinion (and a term understood more commonly in the West to refer to a death sentence) – against Anwar Sadat, following the signing the Camp David peace accords with Israel.

- The Camp David Accords were signed by Egyptian President Anwar El Sadat and Israeli Prime Minister Menachem Begin on 17 September 1978, following twelve days of secret negotiations at Camp David. The two framework agreements were signed at the White House and were witnessed by US President Jimmy Carter. The second of these frameworks, *A Framework for the Conclusion of a Peace Treaty between Egypt and Israel*, led directly to the 1979 Israel–Egypt Peace Treaty and resulted in Sadat and Begin sharing the 1978 Nobel Peace Prize.

- Danny Morrison is an Irish author and Republican activist. He variously had roles in writing and publishing on behalf of the IRA and was famously quoted in 1981: *Who here really believes we can win the war through the ballot box? But will anyone here object if, with a ballot paper in one hand and an Armalite in this hand, we take power in Ireland?* from which came the term 'Armalite and ballot box strategy' to describe the dual strategy of the Provisional IRA and Sinn Féin in the cause of republicanism. Morrison acted as spokesman for Maze hunger striker Bobby Sands, and he is quoted here from Richard English's book *Armed Struggle: The History of the IRA* published in 2004 by Oxford University Press.

- The story that weeping can be heard from Hugh's tomb is fictitious.

- Simon Wilton Phipps was Bishop of Lincoln from 1974 to 1987. He had a successful military career in the Coldstream Guards and fought in World War II, during which he was wounded twice and was subsequently awarded the Military Cross. Following the war, he studied for the priesthood, was appointed Chaplain at Trinity College, Cambridge, and was later an industrial chaplain in Coventry, before being appointed Suffragan Bishop of Horsham in 1968. Phipps was known for his close friendship with Princess Margaret, whom he counselled during her separation from Lord Snowdon. He died in 2001; *The Times* recorded that Phipps had combined *gentleness, tranquility, and sweetness of character with deep psychological insight and considerable strength of purpose.*

- The character Loraine refers to in Chapter 12 to Kim Peek, the inspiration for the movie *Rain Man,* which was not in fact released until 1988. Kim was generally considered an *autistic savant* until a study in 2008 concluded he had *FG Syndrome,* a rare genetic disorder. It was also discovered Kim had no corpus callosum, the bundle of nerves connecting the two hemispheres of the brain.

- The Kingdom of Jerusalem was recaptured by Saladin on 2 October 1187; not 1185 as the story indirectly implies. Salāh ad-Dīn Yūsuf ibn Ayyūb (1138–1193), better known in the Western world as Saladin, was a Kurdish Muslim, who became the first Sultan of Egypt and Syria. He led the Muslim opposition to European Crusaders in the Eastern Mediterranean, eventually recapturing Palestine from the Crusader Kingdom of Jerusalem after his victory in the Battle of Hattin at Tiberius against Richard, son of Henry II. Saladin was a Sunni Muslim and a Sufi. His chivalrous behaviour was noted by many..

- Ismat ad-Dīn Khātūn, Saladin's wife, died in January 1186 and thus did not in fact live to see her husband retake Jerusalem in 1187. Her precise age is not known. She was married to Nur ad-Din in 1147; if she was the same age as Saladin, this would have made her nine years old. The nature of her death is also unknown.

- Richard I (1157–1199) was King of England from 1189 until his death. He also ruled over much of France. He was known as *Cœur de Lion,* or Richard the Lionheart, long before his accession, because of his reputation as a great military leader and warrior. Richard led the Third Crusade

(1189–1192) as King, following the loss of Jerusalem to Saladin in 1187, in which he fought prior to his accession. He remained unable to recapture Jerusalem. Richard only spoke French and spent very little time in England. Richard's relationship with Saladin was one of mutual respect as well as military rivalry. Saladin had indeed offered his own physician to Richard when he was ill. Saladin also sent him fresh fruit with snow to chill his drink.. The two men never met face to face.

- Eleanor of Aquitaine (1121–1204) was one of the wealthiest and most powerful women in Europe. There is no evidence of any communication with Saladin's wife, Asimat, although both women must have known of each other's existence. Eleanor literally took part in the Second Crusade, leading her own soldiers, alongside her husband Louis VII, Conrad III of Germany, and Baldwin III of Jerusalem.

- The Kingdom of Jerusalem equated more or less to the area presently occupied by Israel, along with a western part of what is now Jordan. Aligned Crusader states (the Byzantine Empire, Armenia, Edessa, Antioch, Tripoli, and the Fatimid Caliphate) occupied most of the eastern sea border of the Mediterranean, today forming parts of Turkey, Syria, Lebanon, and Egypt, as well as Cyprus.

- There were nine Crusades into the Middle East, over 200 years, from 1095 to 1291. They were religiously sanctioned military campaigns with the aim of securing Christian rule of the Holy Land. (Other Crusades into other parts continued into the fifteenth century.) The Third Crusade began following the fall of Jerusalem to Saladin in 1187 and lasted until 1192 without the taking of Jerusalem.

- Henry II died in 1189. He never carried out his promise to go on Crusade to the Holy Land.

- *Put not your trust in princes, nor in the son of man, in whom there is no help. His breath goeth forth, he returneth to his earth; in that very day his thoughts perish.* (Ps. 146: 3–4)
- There is no known record of a letter from Bishop Hugh to King Henry.

Autism

Autism is classified by the World Health Organization and American Psychological Association as a developmental disability that results from a disorder of the human central nervous system. It is diagnosed using specific criteria for impairments to social interaction, communication, interests, imagination, and activities.

The causes, symptoms, aetiology, treatment, and other issues are controversial. Autism generally manifests itself before the age of three years. From a physiological standpoint, autism is often less than obvious in that outward appearance may not indicate a disorder.

The incidence of diagnosed autism has increased since the 1990s. Reasons offered for this phenomenon include better diagnosis, wider public awareness of the condition, regional variations in diagnostic criteria, or simply an increase in the occurrence of autism spectrum disorders (ASD, including 'high-functioning' autism, also known as Asperger's Syndrome, named after Hans Asperger who first used the term in 1981).

In 2005, the (US) National Institute of Mental Health (NIMH) stated the best conservative estimate as 1 in 1000; in 2007, the NIMH amended their estimate to 2–6 in every 1000.

There are numerous theories as to the specific causes of autism, but they have yet to be fully supported by evidence. Proposed factors include genetic influence, anatomical variations, abnormal blood vessel function, oxidative stress, former drug abuse in parents, and vaccinations. Their significance, as well as implications for treatment, remains speculative..

Some autistic children and adults are opposed to attempts to cure autism. These people see autism as part of who they are, and in some cases, they perceive treatments and attempts of a cure to be unethical..

There is a broad array of autism therapies with various goals; for example, improving health and well-being, emotional problems, difficulties with communication and learning, and sensory problems for people with autism. The efficacy of each approach varies greatly from person to person. To date, Applied Behaviour Analysis (ABA) is the sole approach that has been scientifically verified as effective in the treatment of autism.

An autistic savant (historically described as idiot savant) is a person with both autism and Savant Syndrome. Savant Syndrome describes a person having both a severe developmental or mental handicap and extraordinary mental abilities not found in most people.

The Savant Syndrome skills involve striking feats of memory and often include arithmetic calculation and sometimes unusual abilities in art or music. There is some research that suggests that it can be induced, which might support the view that savant abilities are latent within all people but are obscured by the normal functioning intellect.

There are about 50–100 recognised *prodigious* savants in the world.

End Note

While this book may appear to ascribe some judgement to the actions of some of the more aggressive of protagonists of Islamism, or even to judge the great Faith of Islam itself, no such views are held by the author. The intention of this novel has been to consider the potential that may, if only fictionally, exist within the minds of the autistic person to make such spiritual connection as to alter the course of history, towards peace, and even to avert such significant tragedies as those of 11 September 2001.

The author has the highest regard for all the great Faiths of the world, including Christianity, Islam, Buddhism, Hinduism, Judaism, and the Baha'i Faith..

The *Surih of the Temple* is taken from *The Summons of the Lord of Hosts,* a collection of tablets from Bahá'u'lláh, the founder of the Baha'i Faith. The Baha'i Faith ascribes the principle of progressive revelation, which supports the notion that the great prophets – Abraham, Moses, Buddha, Krishna, Mohammed and Bahá'u'lláh – are all manifestations of God.

CPSIA information can be obtained at www.ICGtesting.com
Printed in the USA
LVOW10s1147141215

466570LV00032B/3016/P